A tiny arrow of unrest lodged in her belly

Jessamyn plunked her cup down on the desk so hard the coffee sloshed over the edge. Out of the corner of her eye she saw Ben Kearney amble down the street in his lazy, loose-jointed gait.

Something ballooned in her chest when she watched him move. He reminded her of a big cat, a tiger she'd seen photographed once in a magazine. She imagined its hunting prowess, the taut, coiled strength ready to be unleashed in an instant. Ben's movements had that same animal grace and economy of motion. It was frightening in some way.

Without a break in his slow, easy stride, the sheriff mounted the board walkway and disappeared into his office. Jessamyn stared after him. Something about Ben Kearney's languid, controlled body sent shivers sliding up her backbone....

Dear Reader,

Lynna Banning made her debut as an author in our 1996 March Madness promotion with *Western Rose*. This month she returns with *Wildwood*, her exciting new Western about a young woman who puts herself smack in the middle of the investigation of her father's murder, despite opposition from the local sheriff, who would rather she butt out and let him do his job. We hope you enjoy it.

In *Tempting Kate*, longtime Harlequin Historicals author Deborah Simmons returns to the Regency era for her heartwarming tale of a haughty marquis who falls in love with the penniless daughter of a local earl, after she shoots him by mistake. We are also delighted with the chance this month to introduce our readers to a new Western series from award-winning author Theresa Michaels. The trilogy opens with *The Merry Widows–Mary*, the tender story of a marriage-shy widow who opens her heart to a lonely widower and his little girl.

The Bride Thief by Susan Paul, writing as Susan Spencer Paul, is the third book of the author's medieval BRIDE TRILOGY, featuring the youngest Baldwin brother, Justin, a delightful rogue whom his brothers have decided needs a wife to save him from his wayward ways.

Whatever your tastes in reading, we hope you'll keep a lookout for all four books, wherever Harlequin Historicals are sold.

Sincerely,

Tracy Farrell
Senior Editor

Please address questions and book requests to:
Harlequin Reader Service
U.S.: 3010 Walden Ave., P.O. Box 1325, Buffalo, NY 14269
Canadian: P.O. Box 609, Fort Erie, Ont. L2A 5X3

WildWood

LYNNA BANNING

Harlequin Books

TORONTO • NEW YORK • LONDON
AMSTERDAM • PARIS • SYDNEY • HAMBURG
STOCKHOLM • ATHENS • TOKYO • MILAN
MADRID • WARSAW • BUDAPEST • AUCKLAND

ISBN 0-373-28974-X

WILDWOOD

Books by Lynna Banning

Harlequin Historicals

Western Rose #310
Wildwood #374

LYNNA BANNING

has combined a lifelong love of history and literature into a satisfying new career as a writer. Born in Oregon, she has lived in Northern California most of her life, graduating from Scripps College and embarking on her career as an editor and technical writer and later as a high school English teacher.

An amateur pianist and harpsichordist, Lynna performs on psaltery and recorders with two Renaissance ensembles and teaches music in her spare time. Currently she is learning to play the harp.

She enjoys hearing from her readers. You may write to her directly at P.O. Box 324, Felton, CA 95018.

For Mom

With special thanks to Jean Banning Strickland and to fellow writers Suzanne Barrett, Janice Bennett, Ginny Coleman, Dore Corder, Bonnie Hamre and Terrel Hoffman.

Chapter One

Wildwood Valley, Oregon
1868

Benning Kearney speared one bite of the inch-thick steak he ate every morning with three fried eggs and black coffee, raised a forkful of meat to his mouth and halted.

Through the restaurant's front window he watched the seven-o'clock stage rattle to a stop in front of the Dixon House hotel across the street. The coach door swung open, revealing a young woman in a black traveling dress and mourning bonnet. She extended one small black shoe toward the ground. At least, her foot looked young. Hard to tell her age under that ridiculous hat.

The shoe retreated to the coach step. The other foot descended, and then it, too, withdrew.

Benning chewed his steak thoughtfully and watched to see what would happen next. Both feet now primly touched each other on the iron stagecoach step. Then—

Suddenly she leaped onto the ground and jumped up and down twice, like a frisky colt. He swallowed a lumpy mouthful. Goddamn crazy woman. Benning gulped down a swig of hot coffee and laughed out loud. He'd seen few travelers that excited about the western frontier.

Eyeing her through the glass panes, he resumed his breakfast. She looked a bit skinny, her waist no thicker than a wasp's. Probably had a temper to match, from the display of unbridled enthusiasm he'd just witnessed. The stylishly cut dress was Eastern, but that hat—nobody wore swishy feathers like that out here except the fancy ladies at the Red Fox, and this was no fancy lady. Quite the contrary. She looked like a Bible-thumping Good Woman if ever he'd seen one. He grimaced and gulped another mouthful of coffee.

The stage moved away, and in its wake Benning counted three shiny black humpbacked trunks stacked along the board sidewalk. Looked as if this one had come to stay a while.

Ben forked an unbroken egg yolk onto a square of toast and leisurely loaded it into his mouth, his attention on the street outside.

The woman pivoted, putting her back to him. The movement was so sudden her dark skirt swirled about her ankles, revealing a ruffled white petticoat underneath. Dainty, laced-up shoes, slim ankles. And a bustle bouncing enticingly on her backside.

She tramped onto the sidewalk and bent to peer into the barbershop window, one hand shading her eyes against the hot June sunshine. The bustle rose to attention, then bobbed as she straightened and moved next door to Zed Marsh's undertaking service.

What in hell would she want with an undertaker? He watched the bustle twitch as he absently slid his fork under the egg white.

Or the barber, for that matter? The pile of dark hair beneath that hat looked unusually neat.

The bustle fluttered as she moved on to the newspaper office. This time she didn't bother to look in the window. She pulled something out of her bag and bent over the door.

Benning stopped chewing. She jiggled the key in the lock, withdrew it, then thrust it in again.

Now, just a darn minute, lady! Nobody tried to sashay into Thad Whittaker's office without so much as a by-your-leave, even if Thad was dead. Not as long as *he* was sheriff, anyway.

Benning gulped the last of his coffee and stood up. He'd just mosey on over and see what Miss Bounce-Bottom was up to. He dropped two coins on the table, retrieved his hat from the rack in the corner and ambled out onto the board walkway.

Out of habit he scanned one side of the street, then the other before he headed for the door of the *Wildwood Times* office. He took his time crossing the wide, wheel-rutted street. Moving so deliberately the metal rowels on his spurs made no sound, he approached the wooden boardwalk at an angle.

Her back was toward him as she dipped and again peered through the newspaper office window. Straightening, she dropped the key back into her reticule and scrubbed her gloved fist over the dust-smudged glass. Once more she peeked through the smeary circle. With a sigh, she spit on the dark material and rubbed the dampened glove into a lozenge-shaped clear space on the pane. Bending at the waist, she squinted again through the glass.

Ben watched the saucy bustle ride up and down on her backside. She danced from one foot to the other like a bumblebee sizing up a honeysuckle vine, then wiped her glove across the glass once more.

"Merciful heavens," she muttered just loud enough for Ben to overhear. "A veritable pigsty!"

She jerked open her black bag, withdrew the key and again jammed it in the door lock. The bustle bounced as she rattled the knob.

Fascinated, Ben stood stock-still, one boot poised over the walkway. She snatched the key out, stared at it for a long moment, then once more shoved it into the lock. The bustle danced gracefully on her hips, but the door refused to budge.

"Lord have mercy!" she swore under her breath. She drew back a tiny foot and gave the oak door two swift kicks.

The noise jolted Ben to life. Without a sound he stepped one boot onto the boards. When she whacked the door again, he brought up his other foot and started forward.

She was hunched over the lock, poking about with a hairpin, when he came up behind her.

"Best not pick it, ma'am. Unlawful entry."

She jerked upright as if branded with a hot poker. "Oh!"

"Yes, ma'am."

"Heavens, where did you come from?"

"Across the street. I saw you get off the morning stage."

She stared at him, her mouth rounded into an O. "And you sneaked right over here to spy on me." She propped her hands on her hips and stared up at him. "Men!" she huffed.

"Yes, ma'am," he said. "I'm the sheriff here."

Eyes the color of Spanish moss flared into his, then narrowed to a bone-penetrating look. "I'm Jessamyn Whittaker. I own the *Wildwood Times*."

"Ben Kearney. Like hell you do."

She blinked. "I beg your pardon? I most certainly—"

"Prove it," Ben drawled. "Thad Whittaker left no surviving family."

"The only time Thad Whittaker stuck to the truth was when he was setting type! The rest of the time, I assure you, my father's forte was stories so fantastical it would put Fenimore Cooper to shame."

"Yes, ma'am. Still, would Thad lie about his family?"

"Especially about his family," the young woman snapped. Her voice softened unexpectedly. "He didn't lie, exactly. He just…tended to forget about us."

Unconvinced, Ben nodded. It would be hard to forget someone like Jessamyn Whittaker. Of course, Thad had lived in Wildwood Valley for almost fifteen years, long before a daughter would have grown up enough to wear a bustle. Maybe old Thad never even knew he *had* a daughter.

Ben leaned against the hitching rail, crossing one long leg over the other. "Can you prove you're Thad's daughter?" he repeated.

Jessamyn blew her breath out so fast the ostrich feather in her hat swayed. "Look, Mr....Klooney, I haven't jounced my way across this godforsaken desert for the last six days to be put off by a busybody claiming to be a law officer. You have no badge. And where's your gun? If you're the sheriff, I'll eat my—"

Ben straightened. "Kearney," he corrected. "Badge is on the desk in my office. Never carry a rifle, just a revolver. That's back in my office, too. Next to," he added with quiet emphasis, "the jail. And from the looks of it, that fancy hat of yours is going to make mighty fuzzy eating."

Jessamyn bit her lip and studied his face. Abruptly she dived into her handbag and pulled out a crumpled letter. Standing on tiptoe, she thrust it under his nose.

Ben snagged the envelope with one thumb and forefinger. "Miss Jessamyn Whittaker," he read aloud. "Care of the *Boston Herald.*"

He scanned the contents, refolded the letter and handed it back. "Give me the key."

Her eyes widened. After a slight hesitation, she opened her handbag and plopped the key into his outstretched palm.

"Lock sticks," Ben offered. "Trick is to lift up on it." He inserted the metal implement into the lock, brought one knee up to the knob and pushed upward.

The door scraped open. Before he could draw breath, Jessamyn Whittaker brushed past him, her bustle dancing a quadrille.

Ben swallowed. Next to those soft gray-green eyes, that backside was the prettiest sight he'd seen since—

Instinctively, he squashed the thought. Those eyes of hers were unsettling. Something about them made him sick for home, hungry for the smell of plantation tobacco and jasmine vines in bloom over the arbor. Suddenly he ached for all the things he'd tried to forget for the past four years. Things he'd lost.

She had no right to be here nosing about Thad's office as if she owned it. Not only that, she'd come from Boston. She was a Northerner! A Yankee. No Yankee had a right to have eyes that color.

The woman moved about the room, blowing dust off the scarred oak desk, opening cabinets, even inspecting the plank floor beneath her feet. Her mouth made continuous tsk-tsking sounds.

What the hell was she looking for? The last newspaper Thad had printed was a month old now, run off just a few hours before he died. Did she know her father had been shot? Worse, had she come out to the valley to meddle in his investigation of Thad's death?

Probably. She looked like a real busybody.

Thad had never mentioned a daughter. Ben knew the older man's wife had died during the war—sometime between Shiloh and Vicksburg. After Ben's internment at Rock Island.

An involuntary shudder moved up his spine. Outside of Jeremiah, Thad was the only human being Ben had ever told about the horrors of the Union prison in Illinois. The older man had listened, nodding and sucking on his pipe, until Ben's voice had faded and only the crackle of their campfire remained. Then Thad had hoisted his stocky form off the log he'd been straddling, squeezed Ben's shoulder and trudged off into the woods.

"Sometimes a man's gotta talk" was all he'd said.

Now Ben watched Thad Whittaker's daughter move to the open doorway of the *Wildwood Times* office. Turning her back to him, she peered out at the street and propped her hands on her gently curving hips.

His breath caught.

And sometimes a man's got to keep his attention on the business at hand.

He'd have to find a way to get Miss Busy Bustle out of his hair and back to Boston where she belonged. He nodded to himself. Shouldn't be too difficult. She looked as out of place in this dusty town as a silk bow on a steer's tail.

Jessamyn positioned herself in the doorway of her father's newspaper office and studied the dirt trail that passed for Wildwood Valley's main street. *I'm here, Papa, just as you wanted.* Her heart swelled with a mixture of joy and regret.

Something told her Wildwood Valley wouldn't be as enthusiastic about her arrival as her father would have been. Her throat closed. But here she was, as he had asked, and here she intended to stay.

She gazed at the ramshackle buildings on either side of the street and her heart sank. A dilapidated hotel and restaurant, a saloon—no, two saloons, one across the street from the other—Frieder's Mercantile, Addie Rice, Seamstress, the sheriff's office and three other weathered structures with painted signs that were no longer legible.

That was all? No church? No library? Not even a doctor's office?

Her father had exaggerated. This wasn't a town, as she had pictured it—whitewashed buildings and neat picket fences. This was nothing but a motley collection of graying clapboard shacks plunked down in the middle of nowhere.

No, she amended. In the middle of Wildwood Valley. Oregon, she thought with a shudder. Rampaging Indians. Drunken cowboys. Worn-out women with sun-scorched, leathery skin. Lord help her, she'd left a position on a thriving newspaper in Boston for this?

Yes, she had. She hadn't lurched in stuffy railroad cars and bone-rattling stagecoaches all the way from Boston to quail at the last minute. She'd come because Papa had needed her, and she wouldn't retreat unless she failed to accomplish what she'd come out here to do.

"And that," she said aloud with a determined stomp of her small, leather-shod foot, "a Whittaker never did." She was her father's daughter. In her entire twenty-six years of life she'd never failed at anything she set her mind to.

She drew in a double-deep breath of the warm, dusty summer air and straightened her spine. Well, then, she'd better see what was in store for her before she grew one minute older. God had no love for sluggards.

Jessamyn turned to face the open front door of the *Wildwood Times* office and prepared to embrace her future.

Chapter Two

Jessamyn ran one gloved finger over the black iron printing press in the center of the room and breathed out a sigh of satisfaction.

After her meticulous inspection of the *Wildwood Times* office, her fingers fairly itched to dust off the Washington handpress, grab up a type stick, and start composing her first issue. But before she wrote one single word she had to sweep the cobwebs out of the corners and give the grimy plank floor a good scrubbing. Papa may have been a first-rate newspaper editor, but his housekeeping left much to be desired.

Ignoring the sheriff, who still lounged casually against the front wall, she cast a glance at the dirty windowpanes and groaned aloud. *Mama, you should have gone with Papa when he went out West!* Her mother would have been too frail to work the long hours putting an edition to bed, but she could have cooked and cleaned for him, at least until she died. Maybe Papa would have lived longer if he'd kept regular hours and eaten nourishing food.

Jessamyn understood how physically demanding it was to publish a weekly newspaper. Lord knows she'd seen her father gray with fatigue often enough when she was a child. But Papa had loved his work.

And he had loved Mama, too. But not enough. At least,

not enough to resist the lure of establishing his own newspaper in the West. "Got printer's ink in my veins," Thaddeus Whittaker had said each morning before breakfast. Mama had preferred the cobble streets of Boston over the dusty roads of Oregon.

She sighed. Papa's zeal had more than rubbed off on her. By the time she was ten, she could set type faster and more accurately than he could. When her father left for Oregon, Jessamyn decided she would also become a newspaper editor. Like Papa. He had encouraged her through all the years of learning and struggle; in some indefinable way she had felt close to him, following in his footsteps, even though he was thousands of miles away.

How Mama had scrimped to send her to Miss Bennett's Young Ladies' Academy and then to Hazelmount Women's College. After she graduated she took a job as the only woman reporter on the *Boston Herald.* Then, just a month ago, his last letter had arrived.

Come to Oregon, Jess, Papa had written. *I need you here.*

She hadn't known whether to laugh or cry. She'd waited a lifetime to hear those words. She was twenty-six years old and unmarried. A journalist, inspired and nurtured by her father. And an acknowledged spinster. What on earth did she have to lose? Besides, her papa needed her. A siren's call could not have pulled her more strongly.

The day after she'd purchased her train ticket, a second letter had come. This time it was from a Dr. Rufus Bartel. Her father was dead.

She glanced down to find her hands gripping the press lever. A thread of pain encircled her heart. *Oh, Papa. Papa! I'm here now. I'll run your newspaper. I'll make it the best newspaper in Oregon.* She shut her eyes tight.

A low cough behind her made her jump.

"Seems to me, Miss Whittaker, you ought to nail down some lodgings for tonight."

Jessamyn gasped. She'd forgotten all about Mr. Kearney.

"Nail...what? Oh, you mean register at the hotel. I will, after I'm finished here."

"The good hotel fills up fast on Saturday," Ben offered.

"Then I'll stay at the other one."

"I don't think so, ma'am," he said in a quiet voice.

Turning her full attention on the man at her elbow, she folded her arms across her midsection. "Why not?"

"The only women who frequent that place are fancy ladies."

"Fancy ladies?"

Ben hesitated. "That's what we call 'em out here. Calico queens. That or—" he hesitated a split second "—soiled doves."

Jessamyn blinked. "Doves? Oh, you mean wh—"

"Yes, ma'am," Ben said quickly. "So, you'd better hustle your bu...uh...baggage over to Dixon House, on the other side of the street." He gestured over his shoulder with his left thumb.

"Other side of the street," she echoed. Her voice trailed off as she studied the man who stood before her. Blue denim trousers outlined slim hips and the longest legs she'd ever seen. A fringed buckskin vest hung loose over a crisp dark blue canvas shirt with silvery buttons that marched up the expanse of his chest and ended at the closed collar.

Her gaze flicked down to the polished black boots and the jingly spurs, then moved back to his broad shoulders. Slowly her brain registered something she hadn't noticed before. A purple scar ran from beneath one ear across his throat and disappeared inside his shirt collar.

She caught her breath. "You were wounded in the war, weren't you?" she blurted without thinking. "The War of the Rebellion, I mean."

The question hung in the lengthening silence.

The fine mouth tightened. "We call it the War Between the States. Yes, ma'am. Now, about your baggage—"

"The War Between... Oh!" Of course. He must be a

Southerner! Her reporter's curiosity battled with Miss Bennett's lessons on propriety. Curiosity won.

"Mr. Kearney, would you tell me about your battle experiences? As a reporter, I mean?"

His entire body stiffened, then visibly relaxed, limb by limb, as if given orders to do so. "Won't be time between now and the morning stage, Miss Whittaker," he said, his voice low and rough.

"Morning stage?"

"Seven o'clock. I'll ask Tom at the hotel to load up your trunks for you. That way you can enjoy your breakfast before you—"

"Mr. Kearney, I most certainly did not come all the way out here just to pay a ten-minute call and go back to Boston in the morning. I came to Wildwood Valley because my father asked me to."

"Your father is dead, Miss Whittaker."

Jessamyn's heart squeezed. "I know. He left me sole owner of the—"

"Thad Whittaker was shot in the back."

"Wildwood Ti— What did you say?"

"Your father was shot to death. Doc Bartel said he'd write you."

Jessamyn felt the floor tilt under her buttoned shoes. "He did write. He just didn't tell me... Shot? You mean with a gun? Oh, my Lord!"

Ben swore under his breath.

Jessamyn clenched her jaw tight for a moment before she could trust herself to speak.

"Who would do such a thing?"

"Don't know yet. So you see, ma'am, you'd best—"

She drew herself up to her full height and fisted her hands on her hips. The top of her head came just to his chin. "Do you honestly think I could leave? Especially now that I know my father was... Are you *sure* he was shot?"

"I'm sure. Happened right in front of my office. So you see—"

Jessamyn bristled. "Oh, I see, all right, Mr. Kearney. You think I'm going to turn tail and run, is that it? Just because my father..."

Her voice broke. She struggled to take deep, even breaths. "Let me tell you something, Mr. Kearney. Papa...my father wanted me to come out here. I know he'd want me to run his newspaper. Surely you don't think for one minute I'm going to let him down?"

Ben sighed. "Give it up, ma'am. The living don't owe the dead a thing." He growled the words into an uneasy silence.

"Give up?" Jessamyn heard her voice rise to an unlady-like pitch. "Give up?" she repeated in a lower tone. "A Whittaker, Mr. Kearney, never gives up. Never!"

Shaking, she clenched and unclenched her hands, then wrapped both arms tightly across her chest.

"God almighty," Ben swore. "You sound just like him! Stubborn as a mule."

Jessamyn flinched. "Stubborn? Because I want to stay and finish something my father started? You haven't begun to see 'stubborn' yet, Mr. Kearney."

Ben raised one dark eyebrow. "Yep, just like him," he said softly.

Jessamyn flashed a look at him, opened her mouth to reply and stopped short. The sheriff's smoky blue eyes shone with tears.

"Thad was a good man, Miss Whittaker," Ben said in a quiet voice. "And a good friend. But he was so damned in love with Goliath there—" he gestured at the iron print-ing press "—he figured he was Moses on the mountain."

"You mean he was a good newspaper editor," Jessamyn translated. Good heavens, couldn't they speak the king's English out here? She had to interpret practically every-thing the man said.

"The best," Ben grumbled. "That's what got him killed."

Jessamyn gasped. "Oh! Do you really think that?"

"Wish I didn't," Ben muttered. "Sure as hell wish I didn't."

"Well, Mr. Kearney, if you are the sheriff, as you say, what are you doing about my father's murder?"

Ben sighed. "Everything I can think of, Miss Whittaker. Every damn thing I can think of. And I don't need some nosy newspaper lady in my way."

"I won't be," she snapped.

Ben sent her a steady look. "I don't want you thinking you have any say about my methods, either."

"I wasn't," she retorted.

"And," Ben continued, pronouncing each syllable with deliberate emphasis, "I'll brook no comments from you, or your newspaper, until my investigation's over."

"I wouldn't think of it!" she lied.

"May take months," Ben warned.

She met his hard-eyed gaze with one of her own. Sheriff Ben whatever his name was—Kearney—gave orders like an army officer. "You have my word as a Whittaker."

"That," Ben muttered, "is just what I'm afraid of."

The door marked Sheriff's Office banged open, and Ben strode past the cluttered desk to the inner door leading to his private quarters. He twisted the knob and pushed the door inward.

"Jeremiah?" Leaving the door ajar, Ben turned toward his desk. A stack of unopened mail sat on top of his logbook. Curled up beside it lounged a ball of marbled black-and-white fur. He scratched the cat's underchin, then reached past the animal to rescue the coffee cup teetering near the edge of the desktop.

"Jeremiah!"

A square, bearded face appeared in the doorway. "I'm right here, Colonel. What you need'n?"

"Whiskey," Ben growled.

"Doc Bartel says—"

Ben yanked open the top desk drawer and rummaged

through the contents. "Rufus Bartel is a fussy old coot with an excess of irrelevant medical training."

Jeremiah nodded, his soft brown eyes twinkling. "Yessir, Colonel, that he is. Irrelevant."

"Nosy old sawbones," Ben grumbled. His fingers closed over a small brown bottle.

"Yessir, he surely is." Jeremiah moved forward, his stocky frame quiet as a cat's. "That doesn't make the doctor wrong, though." He snatched the bottle from Ben's lips. "Truth is, Ben, you quit drinkin' heavy. Thing is, you gotta stay quit."

Ben snorted. "Jeremiah, I don't pay you to nurse-mammy me." He sucked in a lungful of air as Jeremiah slipped the bottle into his back pocket.

"No, Colonel. *You* don't pay me a-tall, and I reckon you remember why."

Ben remembered. Both in the field and when imprisoned at Rock Island, he and Jeremiah had saved each other's lives so many times the two men were like blood brothers. Half of Ben's salary was paid to his faithful friend, along with considerable admiration and respect.

Jeremiah was more than Ben's deputy. The solidly built man was the only surviving family Ben had left outside of his younger brother. In fact, he felt closer to Jeremiah than he did to Carleton. After the war, when he and Jeremiah had come West, the two had made a pact. Half of whatever one had belonged to the other—whether food, horseflesh, whiskey, or cash money. They drew the line only at women.

"I need a drink," Ben ventured.

Jeremiah grinned, revealing a mouthful of uneven white teeth. "Talked to her, didja?" He nodded his head knowingly. "Thought so. Beats me how a woman can do that to a man inside of ten minutes jes' by talkin', but happens all the time."

"Jeremiah?"

"Colonel?"

"Bring two glasses."

Jeremiah executed a quick about-face and moved toward the doorway. "Damn troublous creatures, women."

Ben leaned his forehead onto his hands. Yes, damned troublous.

He didn't want Jessamyn Whittaker out here, poking about just like Thaddeus had, interfering with his job. A Yankee lady from Boston? She probably hadn't the sense God gave a bird's nest. She'd hamstring his progress just as surely as if she hobbled his horse. Thaddeus had been a constant fly in the ointment for years, and nothing Ben had said could deter him. "I got a good nose for news" was all the editor would say.

That the crusty old man had had. Ben could see in a minute that his daughter was just like him. He leaned back in his chair and closed his eyes. He had to decide what to do about her, and fast. A starchy Yankee with soft green eyes was the last thing he needed right now.

Jessamyn plopped the boar-bristle scrub brush into the pail of soapy water and sat back on her heels. She'd scrubbed everything in sight, including the plank floor, until it was clean enough to squeak. The rough oak boards had been so caked with filth she'd scoured them twice with lye soap.

Next she planned to visit Frieder's Mercantile to purchase the kerosene she needed to clean the iron printing press and order some other supplies as well—printer's ink and more newsprint. She'd found her father's storage cabinets almost empty.

Tucking a wayward strand of hair into the loose bun coiled on top of her head, she scrambled to her feet and swatted the dust off her work apron. The hem of her blue poplin skirt and the two starched petticoats underneath were gray with cobwebby dirt. Jessamyn seized the garments in both hands and switched them vigorously from side to side.

Clouds of dust puffed up from the folds of material, making her eyes water and her nose itch. If Miss Bennett could see her now, she'd have apoplexy!

She studied her red, water-puckered hands. At this moment Boston and the refinements of civilization seemed as distant as the moon. Her bed at the Dixon House hotel the previous night had been uncomfortable, the mattress so thin the metal springs had pressed into her back. Sleepless, she'd tossed and turned, thinking of Papa, of all the years he'd praised her talent for writing, remembering how bereft she'd felt between his newsy, heartfelt letters.

She also thought about the *Wildwood Times*. She would do anything to please her father, especially now that he was gone. Running his newspaper would keep him close to her.

Jessamyn sighed. Her back and shoulders were as stiff as her whalebone corset stays, and her knees ached from hours spent kneeling on the floor. She would much rather set type than do housework, but the place simply had to be cleaned. She couldn't stand walking on a surface that crunched under her shoes. Grabbing her skirt, she gave it one last, vicious shake.

"Miss Whittaker?" A man's low voice spoke behind her.

Jessamyn gave a little gasp and spun toward the sound.

Ben Kearney leaned against the door frame, one shiny black boot crossed casually over the other. "Sorry to startle you."

With one finger he shoved his hat back on his head. "Opened my mail this morning. I received a letter from an attorney in Portland regarding your father's will. There's something you should know."

Unaccountably, Jessamyn's heart fluttered, whether because of his soft-spoken words or the steady blue-gray eyes that bored into hers, she didn't know. She did know Sheriff Ben Kearney was a most disturbing man! Even with jingly spurs on his boots, he moved as quietly as a shadow, and his speech was terse to the point of rudeness. No "Good morning" or other social pleasantry, just a few succinct words growled from under his dark mustache.

"Well, Mr. Kearney, what is it I should know? And don't tramp dirt in onto my clean floor, please. I spent all morning scrubbing fifteen years' worth of pipe dottle, tobacco juice and God knows what else off those boards."

The sheriff's dark eyebrows arched. His mouth tightened into a thin line, then he cracked his lips and slipped out a few words.

"Thad owned a house."

Jessamyn blinked. A house? Her father owned a house in Wildwood Valley?

"I thought my father lived here, at the shop?" She gestured toward the back of the office where she'd found a cot, the bedclothes still tumbled, and a washstand and basin next to the small wood stove.

Ben nodded. "He did. But he'd bought a house. Took the mortgage over from Mrs. Boult when her husband died. Let her live there as a kind of housekeeper so she wouldn't have to leave. The place is yours now. Big white two-story house. Quarter mile past the livery stable."

"Mine? But what about Mrs. Boult?"

"She's expecting you. She knows you can't live at the newspaper office, since you're a lady."

Jessamyn's stomach flipped over. A house! A house all her own! A house Papa had bought, that Papa had— Good heavens, she hoped it wasn't the same shambles as the *Wildwood Times* office! She couldn't face another scrub bucket for at least a month.

"I'll just sponge off my face and get my reticule."

Ben watched her disappear in a swish of skirt ruffles. Before he'd drawn three breaths, she was back. No bustle today, he noted. Just a long, dark blue skirt that flared over her hips, topped by a high-necked cream-colored waist, the sleeves rolled up to her elbows.

She removed her white work apron—once starched stiff enough to stand up by itself he could tell, but now crumpled and dirt streaked—and hurriedly rolled down one blouse sleeve. She had the other sleeve down and buttoned at her narrow wrist before the door clicked shut behind them.

Ben's gut tightened. He hadn't exactly planned to escort Jessamyn Whittaker to call on Widow Boult, but the longer he looked at the delicately feminine creature at his side, the better he liked the idea. Besides, keeping a close watch on the *Wildwood Times* editor was only prudent. If she was anything like Thad Whittaker, the minute he took his eyes off her, she'd be rooting around where she had no business to be.

Except for her figure and that ruffly parasol she'd snapped open against the hot afternoon sunshine, she was the spitting image of Thad—same dark hair, same mossy green eyes. Same chattery, back-talking tongue.

Troublous. Just as Jeremiah said.

He glanced at Jessamyn's face, shaded under the circle of black silk. Same...no, it wasn't. True, her chin was slightly pointed, like Thad's, but her mouth was rosy and full. God almighty, he groaned inwardly. Even if she was a Yankee, her lips looked soft enough to...

Ben stepped hard off the end of the boardwalk, his spurs ringing. Odd thing about parasols, he thought. He hadn't seen one for years. General Denton's wife had one, back in Dakota Territory. The sight of it always made him homesick. Now the picture Jessamyn Whittaker made under the shadow of her frilly sun umbrella drove the breath out of his lungs. A lump the size of a musket ball formed in his throat.

Damnation, but he was lonely.

But not for any Lincoln-loving Yankee!

"Miz Boult, Jessamyn Whittaker." Ben stepped aside as Jessamyn extended her hand toward the buxom woman who filled the doorway.

Mrs. Boult folded her two hands around the younger woman's fingers. "Howdy." She gripped Jessamyn's hand tight, her callused palms warm and strong. Then she peered over Jessamyn's shoulder at the sheriff, and the warm expression in the older woman's snapping blue eyes turned wary.

"You again!" she huffed.

"Sorry, ma'am."

Jessamyn thought his voice held a hint of laughter, but his tanned face showed no emotion.

"Get along with you, Ben," Mrs. Boult ordered. "Miz Whittaker and I have some visitin' to do."

Ben tipped his black Stetson, quirked one eyebrow at Jessamyn and strode off down the street, his spurs chinking with each footstep.

"Pesky man," Mrs. Boult huffed. "Can't draw a breath in peace lately with him around. Nice-lookin' man, just won't stop askin' questions. He's been like a hibernatin' grizzly bear ever since Thad Whittaker— Oh! Sorry, my dear. I plumb forgot that's why you're here. Come in, come in!" She drew Jessamyn over the threshold of the neat frame house.

"This here's the front parlor. Set a spell while I rustle up some coffee."

Jessamyn opened her mouth to offer help, but the elderly woman bustled out of the room. "Won't be a minute," she called from somewhere down the hallway.

A green velvet sofa beckoned under the lace-curtained front window. Jessamyn settled herself on the cushions and let her gaze wander over the room. A pair of wing-back chairs upholstered in a swirly forest green velvet flanked the sofa. A hand-knit, teal blue shawl had been tossed over the back of one. A Brussels carpet covered all but the outer edges of the polished hardwood floor.

Stretching her feet toward a low tapestry-covered otto-man in front of the sofa, Jessamyn breathed in the faint scent of lemon oil and baking bread. What a comfortable house, so quiet and blessedly cool after the pounding summer sun outside. She noticed the window shades had been drawn, evidently to keep out the midday heat.

This wondrous haven of peace actually belonged to her? She could hardly believe it. In all her life she'd never lived in anything other than the house where her mother took in lodgers or—after Mama died—a rented room in Mrs. Dennan's boardinghouse. And now...

She squeezed her eyes tight shut, then popped her lids open. No, it wasn't a dream. All this belonged to her? Not the furnishings, of course—those would be Mrs. Boult's—but the walls, the roof, the silence! Just think! Here, in Papa's house—*her* house—she would never again worry about paying for lodging. Jessamyn snuggled herself deeper into the sofa cushion. Boston it was certainly not, but they'd have to pry her loose with a crowbar to get her to leave now.

"Here we are, my dear." Mrs. Boult swept into the room and set an enamelware tray of coffee, fresh sliced bread and thick purple jam on the square oak side table. Jessamyn's stomach rumbled. She'd skipped breakfast at the hotel, then worked right through lunch. "Oh, Mrs. Boult, that smells simply wonderful! May I?"

She reached for a small plate, loaded it with two slices of the fragrant bread and added a generous dollop of jam. She settled the plate in her lap. Miss Bennett would not approve, she knew. But Miss Bennett had never scrubbed floors all morning.

Mrs. Boult handed Jessamyn a steaming mug of coffee. "Call me Cora, my dear. Ever since my Frank died, I've not felt comfortable about the 'Mrs.' tacked onto my name. My full name's Cordella, but just Cora will do fine."

Jessamyn took a swallow from the mug to wash down the first bite of bread and jam. "Then please, do call me Jessamyn."

Cora bobbed her silver-gray head in agreement. "Now, Miss Jessamyn, when were you wantin' to move in?"

Jessamyn choked on her coffee. "But where will you go?"

Cora chuckled. "I got a sister over in Deer Creek been wantin' me to keep house for her. Might do that. Then again, I might——"

"Would you stay and keep house for me?" Jessamyn heard herself ask. "As you did for my father?"

The older woman set her mug down on the table and folded her weathered hands in her lap. "Difference is, Miss Jessamyn, that I didn't exactly keep house for your pa. More like I kept his house in order, but he really lived down at the news office. Don't know how he managed, but he did. Truth is, Thad Whittaker paid off my mortgage, bless his heart, but he never took possession. Said he was content to buy the place so's his daughter would have it someday."

Jessamyn's heart gave an erratic thump. "Did he say that? Really? He did it for…for me?"

Cora nodded. "I figure you'll want to move in soon as you can."

"Yes," Jessamyn said quietly. "I do. I've never had a place of my own. But you see, Cora, I'm a working woman, a newspaper editor now." She shot a quick look at the older woman's face. "I won't have time to cook and clean and put up jam and beat the rugs in the spring."

"True, I can cook," Cora ventured.

"Oh, I can see that—your bread is delicious!" Jessamyn held her breath.

"Come summer," the older woman continued, "I usually can tomatoes and beans from the garden out back and make my jams and jellies—that's huckleberry you're eatin' right now. Then in the fall, when the apples and pears come on… Oh, I couldn't, Miss Jessamyn. You won't want a stranger in your house."

"Cora," Jessamyn said firmly, "you're not a stranger. You're my first friend here in Wildwood Valley. I want you to stay. I want to make a success of Papa's—I mean, of my newspaper."

Oh, heavens! The import of what she'd just said hit her square in the solar plexus. *She* was now the sole editor and publisher of the *Wildwood Times*. She alone was responsible for gathering, sifting, writing and disseminating all the Douglas County news to the Wildwood Valley readers. She would be the voice of their conscience, the voice of truth.

She quailed at the realization. This was much more responsibility than just setting type and cranking the press lever. Those things she could do with ease. She had worked alongside her father in his Boston print shop ever since she could remember, had first learned the alphabet by running her fingers over the raised letters in the type trays.

But this—operating the newspaper in Wildwood Valley, being the only other publisher in all of Douglas County besides the *Umpqua Ensign* in Scottsburg—this would take more than mechanical know-how and long hours of work. Taking on the job of editor of the *Wildwood Times* would require insight and courage, moral fortitude and stamina, and—

And Cora Boult. Jessamyn rose and clasped both of the older woman's work-worn hands in her own. "Please stay, Cora," she whispered. "I'm all alone out here, and I'm going to need help."

"Oh, child," Cora Boult said on a sigh. "I never could resist a young'un with a problem." She freed one hand and dabbed at her eyes with a corner of her apron. "Besides…" She sniffed in a quick breath. "I don't get along too good with my sister in Deer Creek."

Jessamyn laughed with relief. She could do it! With her father's training and Cora's help, the *Wildwood Times* could be the best newspaper in Douglas County.

"All them bedrooms upstairs are empty, Miss Jessamyn. Frank and me, we always planned on havin' a family, but…" Her voice faltered. The plump widow spun on her sensible, high-laced shoes and started for the doorway. "Why don't we go up and pick out the one you like best? The biggest one has yellow-striped wallpaper. The one next to it has blue and white flowers, and the one down at the end of the hall..."

Her voice faded from Jessamyn's consciousness as she followed the older woman up the steep, narrow stairs to the second floor. Her brain whirled with ideas. She'd spend her days at the newspaper office, running down stories and doing interviews. At night she'd sit at her father's battered oak desk and write her features and weekly editorials. And when she finished she'd come back here, to the home her father had bought for her.

Papa would be pleased. Somehow she knew this was what he would have wanted. It was what she had longed for all her young years—sharing her life with him. It hurt that he was gone. But if it was the last thing she did, she'd make him proud of her.

A shiver raced up her spine. Her first story, she decided, would be a feature on Sheriff Ben Kearney and his investigation of her father's death.

"Miss Jessamyn?" Cora's voice rang from somewhere ahead of her. "This here's what I call the Yellow Room."

The housekeeper's muffled summons jerked her to attention. "Coming, Cora," she called out.

Smoothing her skirt, Jessamyn moved toward the open bedroom door at the end of the hallway, her mind already composing her first headline.

Chapter Three

The door of Frieder's Mercantile swung open with a jingle. The bell mounted on the timber frame above Jessamyn's head hiccuped a second welcome as she closed the wood portal. She paused on the threshold to gaze at the welter of supplies—yard goods, laces, curry combs and bristle brushes, boxed cigars, tobacco canisters, denim shirts and trousers, axes, shovels, even a crosscut saw. The shelves of merchandise reached all the way to the ceiling. Surely they stocked kerosene?

She inhaled a lungful of the heady air. Sacks of flour and sugar and dried beans lined the walls. A pickle barrel sat next to two wooden chairs flanking the black iron stove. Behind it she glimpsed a glass case with brightly colored penny candies displayed in oversize jars. The store smelled of coffee and sassafras and tobacco.

A pinafore-clad child of five or six with worn, dusty shoes that looked two sizes too big stretched one hand toward the glass case. "Want a candy," she wailed as her mother tugged her toward the door.

"Hush, Alice. Not today. You had too many last week." The woman nodded at Jessamyn as she swept past.

"How do you do," Jessamyn called. "I'm Jessamyn Whittaker, the new editor of the *Wildwood Times*."

The woman turned. A sharp-nosed, tanned face looked

out from under a green checked sunbonnet. Jessamyn sent her warmest smile and waited.

"Hello, Miss Whittaker." The woman extended a thin, work-worn hand. "Ella Kearney's my name. This is my daughter, Alice. Come away from that case, Alice, and say hello to the lady."

"'Lo," the child whispered, still eyeing the fat glass jars in the candy display. "D'you like ginger drops?"

"Why, yes, I suppose I do."

"Mr. Frieder has lots and lots of—"

"Come along, Alice. I've got bread rising."

"Mrs. Kearney, wait! I don't mean to pry, but is your husband Ben Kearney, the sheriff?"

"No. Ben's a fine man, but I'm married to his brother, Carl. We live on the Double K, the Kearney brothers' spread, about four miles north of town. Cattle ranch. Some horses, but mostly beeves. Ben lives in town."

"I see." An irrepressible bubble of curiosity rose in Jessamyn's chest. Ben Kearney evidently preferred life as a lawman rather than a rancher. She wondered why. And, she wondered with an odd flicker of interest, was he not married? Her experience as a newspaper reporter told her to file this question away for later reference.

Ella Kearney yanked her daughter toward the door. "Good morning to you, Miss Whittaker."

The bell jangled as the pair stepped out onto the board sidewalk. Alice cast a wistful backward glance at the candy case just as the door swung shut.

A broad, smiling man appeared behind the counter, good will beaming from his shiny face. "What can I do for you, ma'am? Maybe like some ginger drops? Young Miss Alice is usually my best customer, but this afternoon her mama too busy."

"I'm Jessamyn Whittaker, and I need some kerosene to clean the printing press at the newspaper office."

"Ah! You are the Miss Whittaker who comes from the East? I am Otto Frieder. My wife, Anna-Marie, is in the back. You wait." He disappeared, then emerged from be-hind a curtained doorway with a plump, dimpled woman of about thirty in tow. "Anna-Marie," he said with obvious pride.

The woman extended both hands past her distended ab-domen and squeezed Jessamyn's fingers. "We are so happy you come to Wildwood Valley."

"I— Thank you, Mrs. Frieder."

"We are much sorry about your father."

"Thank you again."

Anna-Marie immediately curved her palms over her belly. "Baby comes in just a few weeks," she said with a shy smile. "Our first."

Jessamyn looked into the round blue eyes of the woman facing her. How happy she looked. How eager for life. In just a few years the storekeeper's wife would have three or four young ones hanging on to her skirts, and then she would look exhausted. Worn out, like Mama.

"About the kerosene, Mr. Frieder."

"Ah, yes." Otto turned toward the back of the store where oak barrels lined one wall. "Kerosene...kerosene," he muttered. "Cigars...cartridges...nails...no kerosene. We just run out. Shipment is again late."

"I will also need newsprint and ink for the paper."

Otto sighed. "That I must order from Chicago—will take two, maybe three weeks."

"Three weeks!"

"Maybe four, even. Come by train to Omaha, then by wagon over the mountains."

Four weeks! Jessamyn groaned. That was a whole month! How could she publish a newspaper without ink and newsprint? If she was frugal, her father's supply might last for one edition, but it would have to be a very short press run.

"I'm sorry, Miss Whittaker. Your papa, he was always running out of supplies. 'Otto,' he would say to me. 'I need more ink, more newsprint.' He kept on printing his paper, though. I never could figure how he did it.''

Anna-Marie made sympathetic clucking sounds.

Jessamyn's spirits plummeted. Getting out her first issue would be more of a challenge than she'd thought.

Otto patted her hand. "I will get your supplies for you. There is else you need?"

"What? Oh, no, thank you, Mr. Frieder." She tried to keep her disappointment from showing in her voice. No ink. No newsprint. No kerosene. How *had* her father managed?

Otto gestured to his wife. Anna-Marie made her way to the candy case, dug a tin scoop into a fat glass jar and poured the contents into a small brown paper sack. She handed it over the countertop. "No charge," the young woman whispered.

Jessamyn smiled her thanks at the couple. Her mind churning, she left the store, snapped opened her parasol and stepped out into the late-afternoon sun. Deep in thought, she popped a candy into her mouth.

What would she do now? Papa had managed some way, but how? Jessamyn sucked on the gingery-tasting sweet and racked her brain. She was a Whittaker, she reminded herself. Like Papa. She wasn't beaten yet. After all, a Whittaker never gave up.

But how *could* she clean the press? With her tongue she turned the gingery-tasting sweet over and over as she thought about the problem facing her.

First she'd need a substitute for kerosene. She rolled the candy drop around inside her mouth with the tip of her tongue. The sharp flavor surprised her, hot and sweet like spices and pepper mixed up together. It made her mouth burn. Her lips felt warm and sticky, as if she'd been sipping...

"Spirits!" she blurted aloud. She could clean the press with alcohol!

Where, she wondered as she marched along the board walkway, could she get alcohol?

Across the street the plunking of a tinny piano drifted out the open front door of Charlie's Red Fox Saloon. Jessamyn halted midstride.

A saloon served alcohol, didn't it?

She set her uplifted shoe down with a resounding thump and stepped off the walk into the street. With one hand she hitched her skirt up out of the dust and with the other tilted the parasol against the slanting sunlight. Head up, shoulders squared, she headed straight for the Red Fox.

The piano player's spirited rendition of "The Girl I Left Behind Me" broke off the instant Jessamyn stepped past the swinging doors.

"Goshamighty," a hushed male voice spoke into the silence. "A lady!"

Jessamyn lowered her parasol and gazed about the dim room. The place reeked of cigar smoke. The pungent scent of beer and strong spirits reminded her of the brewery a block from the *Boston Herald* office.

She moved with care among the rough wooden tables clustered with card players and cowhands with tanned faces and sweat-stained hats. Ignoring the hostile faces turning in her direction, she advanced to the polished oak bar.

The bartender, a pudgy, red-faced man with a soiled towel tucked in his belt, regarded her in silence for a full minute. Finally he signaled the piano player to resume and stepped toward her. He swiped the grimy cloth across the counter.

"Don't allow women in here, miss."

Jessamyn quailed at his tone. Summoning her courage, she straightened her back and spoke over the noise of the piano. "Oh, yes, you do. The sheriff told me about your fancy ladies—that is the term? They are women, are they not?"

The bartender coughed. "Well, ma'am," he began in a strangled voice, "women, maybe, but not—"

Jessamyn looked him straight in the eye. "Then just think of me as a customer. Not as a woman."

"Kinda hard to do, seein' as how you're all fit out with them ladyfied duds."

What did he say? Oh, he meant her clothes. Good heavens, didn't anyone out here speak understandable English? Working to keep her voice calm, she replied, "Then shall I remove them?"

The man's eyes popped. "No indeed, ma'am! I got enough trouble with Sheriff Kearney as it is. Now you just git along outta here. This ain't no place—"

"Hold up there, Charlie," a gentle, slightly raspy voice interrupted.

Jessamyn turned to face a stocky, muscular-looking man with limp, sun-lightened brown hair and skin tanned to the color of coffee diluted with a dollop of cream. Keen brown eyes looked steadily into hers from under the drooping brim of a shapeless brown felt hat.

"You refusin' service to the lady?"

"Shore am, Jeremiah. An' no deputy's gonna tell me differ'nt."

The deputy lifted the shotgun he carried. "Well, now," he said without raising his voice. "Law says it's illegal to steal horses." He clunked the gun down onto the bar top. "Also illegal to serve rotgut whiskey or—" he cast an eye about the room, glanced from the stairs to the bartender and back again "—run a sportin' house."

He leaned both arms on the bar and laced his blunt fingers together. Jessamyn watched the back of one hand graze his gun stock.

"Dammit to hell, Jeremiah. Why don't you mind yer own business." The bartender slapped down his rag and swore again under his breath.

"Law *is* my business, Charlie. Now, I suggest you give the lady what she asked for."

"Oh, hell's bells. First it's serve that Indian-loving sheriff, then it's serve his Johnny Reb of a deputy and now it's serve the lady. Dammit, back in Abilene—''

Jeremiah unlaced his fingers.

Charlie snatched up the bar rag. "Okay, Jeremiah. Okay." He glanced at Jessamyn. "Just tell me what you want, ma'am, and then git."

"I'd like a bottle of alcohol. Whiskey, I mean."

Charlie's thinning eyebrows rose. "Gawd, ma'am, a whole bottle?"

"Maybe two bottles. Big ones."

The bartender gave her an odd look, dipped behind the counter, then straightened with a single quart of Child's Whiskey in his meaty hand. "One bottle. Should last a little lady like you more'n a year. Mebbe two."

"She said two bottles," Jeremiah said quietly.

"Two! What in hell does she need two quarts of my best—''

"Isn't none of our business," Jeremiah interjected.

"It's for my press," Jessamyn blurted. She looked from Jeremiah's placid, square face to Charlie's round, florid one. "The printing press at the *Wildwood Times* office."

"Huh!" The bartender spat onto the floor behind him. "Last time I looked, printin' presses drank ink, not whiskey. Ain't that so, Jeremiah?"

Jeremiah turned his chocolaty gaze on Jessamyn. After a long moment's perusal, during which Jessamyn felt her cheeks flame and her nerve begin to fail, the man's face creased into a wide grin.

"Whatever she wants is all right by me. Wouldn't put nuthin' past a lady who can write them elegant newspaper words. Make it two bottles, Charlie."

Charlie clunked another quart of Child's onto the counter.

"Thank you," Jessamyn breathed. She sent the sheriff's deputy a look of gratitude.

Jeremiah nodded, grabbed both bottles by the necks and reached for his gun.

"Hold up! I ain't been paid yet."

Jessamyn turned toward the bar. "How much do I owe—"

"Put it on my tab, Charlie."

"Your tab! You nickel-nurser, since when do you have credit around here?"

"I guess maybe since right now. I kinda like the idea. 'Sides," the deputy breathed as he started toward the door, "the war's over now. Reb money's good as anybody else's."

He nodded a good-night and pushed through the swinging doors. Jessamyn had to skip across the floor to catch up with him.

"Thank you," she panted. "I'll repay you, of course. I'm Jessamyn Whittaker, Mr....?" She paused expectantly.

"Jeremiah, ma'am."

"Jeremiah *what?*"

"Hull. But jes' Jeremiah'll do. Never had much need for a last name."

Jessamyn pricked up her ears. "Why was that, Jeremiah?" Her reporter instincts told her his answer might be interesting, maybe even newsworthy.

Jeremiah shrugged. "Well, I kinda belonged to the plantation, you might say."

Jessamyn blinked. "Belonged? You mean you were—"

"Oh, no, ma'am. Not a slave. My daddy was the overseer for Mr. Kearney. All of us—my mother and my brother and my sisters—we grew up on the Kearney plantation. When the war broke out, Mr. Ben, the colonel, joined his regiment. I joined up with him. We rode out the gate together, and I never looked back on that dogtrot house I was raised in 'ceptin' once."

Jessamyn stared at him.

"Miss Whittaker, if you'll just tell me where you want this whiskey..."

"Oh, yes, the whiskey!" She tore her gaze from Jeremiah's no longer smiling face and stepped up onto the boardwalk in front of the newspaper office. "In here, please." She bent to insert the key.

The lock stuck. She jiggled it three or four times before Jeremiah leaned his shotgun against the wall and stepped forward. He gripped the knob with his square fingers.

"Gotta lift up, Miss Jessamyn. Sometimes that lock gets the crotchets." He gave a little nudge and the door swung inward.

Jessamyn set her parasol on the battered desk, turned and lifted the whiskey out of Jeremiah's hands.

"I am in your debt, Jeremiah."

"It's gettin' on toward suppertime. You gonna clean that press now?"

"I am. I live with Mrs. Boult. She'll keep my supper waiting."

"Mind if I stay and...help out? It'll be full dark before you finish. I'll just step over to the sheriff's office an' bring a coal lamp to see by."

Jessamyn regarded the sheriff's deputy with interest. Was he intrigued by the workings of the printing press? Or was he tactfully offering to stand guard over her?

Maybe both.

Part of her rebelled at the assumption that she needed protection. But another, larger part of her liked the fact that he was interested enough in the *Wildwood Times* to give up his evening and help her clean the press. Anyone who liked newspaper publishing was a potential friend. Jeremiah was a kindred spirit.

"Jeremiah, I'd be honored. Why don't you stop by Mrs. Boult's and ask her to pack up some supper and bring it over to the office? Tell her I said to include two plates. You will join me, won't you?"

Without waiting for his answer, Jessamyn donned her work apron and rolled up her sleeves.

Chapter Four

Ben reined in the gelding on a hilltop so green with lush spring vetch it glowed like an emerald in the afternoon light. Land out here in the West wasn't manicured as it had been in Carolina, at least the way he remembered it before Sheridan marched his marauding troops through. But this Oregon country was beautiful nonetheless. The late-day sun washed luminous fingers of light against the rolling green-gold hills. His throat swelled into an ache.

Land, and the crops that could be grown on it, was more precious than gold. And the price more costly. All through history, lives had been laid down for possession of bits of earth. Sometimes he wondered if land—if anything—was worth fighting for. A war took everything a man had, sucked his spirit dry.

He gazed down at the farms and ranches spread over the wide valley below. From his vantage point, Ben picked out the southernmost pasture of the seven-thousand-acre Kearney spread—the one he'd bought after the war. After he'd gone home to North Carolina and found what that Yankee bastard Sheridan had done to the plantation and the life he'd known before.

After that he'd had no stomach for the North's version of Reconstruction. There was nothing to do then but come out West and start over. He'd worked hard to build a new life.

When his brother, Carleton, later followed him to Oregon, Ben had turned the ranch over to him and his new bride and taken the position General Van Dyke at Fort Umpqua had offered—Indian agent for the Klamath River tribes.

Carleton had been just old enough to join the militia when the war ended. He was inexperienced as a cattleman, but he learned fast. And Carl had a good wife to help him. His brother, Ben reasoned, would make a success of the ranch. He nodded approvingly at the fenced field of rye below him. Instead of cutting it for hay, in late summer Carl would turn his herd into the enclosure.

As usual, his sister-in-law had invited him to supper this Sunday. Ben's gut wrenched. Suddenly the last thing he wanted to do was ride down off this hill and join his brother's family. One evening of watching Ella, her face flushed from the heat of the woodstove in the stifling kitchen as she fussed and puttered around Carl, left Ben restless all the next week. The woman adored his younger brother. And it was just as obvious Ella was the most important thing in Carl's life.

The most important thing in Ben's hardworking, solitary life was Wildwood Valley. He knew his presence as sheriff made a difference to the ranchers and townspeople. If nothing else, his reputation as a marksman served as a deterrent to the drifters and unsavory riffraff that occasionally rode into town.

He'd been a good Indian agent, too. But by damn, sometimes he wanted something else, something he couldn't even name. He wanted it so much it almost suffocated him.

He pulled on the gelding's reins and turned the horse back toward town. A cold pit of despair yawned in his belly. It was going to be, as Jeremiah often remarked, another two-glass night.

He got as far as Carl's south pasture on his way to the

road when he glimpsed a tiny figure in a blue pinafore skimming over the grass toward him.

"Uncle Ben!"

Ben reined in the dark horse alongside the fence.

"Uncle Ben! Please, can I open the gate for you? Daddy says I'm too little, but I'm not! I can reach way up high. Please?"

Ben shook his head. "Not this time, honey. Tell your mama I've got some business in town." He pulled a bag of penny candy out of his vest pocket and stretched his arm over the fence. "No need to tell her about these, though, is there?"

The child grinned and shook her head. Ben tipped his hat and headed toward the town road.

Jessamyn unbolted the press lever arm and lifted the platen cylinder away from the roller. "Well, would you just look at that," she murmured. "Clean as a new penny."

Except for a film of surface dust on the exterior of the black-painted casing, the press was immaculate, the joints and connections free of old grease and dirt. The moving parts had been polished to a shine.

She had to smile. Papa always insisted on keeping his press in perfect working order. Cleanliness, he joked, was right up there next to banner headlines. He wiped his equipment down after every press run.

Still, she wanted to run her hands over every inch of the imposing piece of machinery. The press belonged to her now. It was her responsibility to see to its maintenance. Resolutely she smoothed her starched white work apron and reached for the whiskey bottle and a clean rag.

Jeremiah kept her company while she worked over the huge machine, and then Cora arrived, their supper swinging in a wicker basket over one ample arm. "Here y'are, Miss Jessamyn. There's plenty here, and more at the house iffen you want it."

"Thank you, Cora. Will you stay and have some with us?"

The older woman shook her head. "I like my chicken hot, thanky. Mine's warming in the oven, waitin' for some pan gravy to go with it. Since you've got Jeremiah watchin' over you, I'll just go along to my supper."

She bobbed her gray bun and headed toward the door. "Front door's unlocked. Jes' walk on in when you finish—" her china blue eyes took in the disassembled press "—whatever it is you're doin'. Night, Jessamyn."

Jeremiah politely held the door for her, and Cora bustled off down the board sidewalk, her solid footsteps reverberating against the pine planking.

Jessamyn corked the half-empty bottle of Child's and wiped her hands on her apron. "Let's have supper. I'm starving!"

The deputy declined her offer of a chair at her father's desk. He ate his fried chicken and potato salad standing up, periodically checking up and down the street through the now-sparkling front window. "Mr. Ben's gone out to the ranch for supper. I got to keep my eye peeled for any trouble in town."

"Trouble?" Jessamyn spoke over a mouthful of flavorful potato salad. "What kind of trouble?"

"Just Saturday-night kinda trouble, Miss Jessamyn. Ranch hands in town for a little fun, maybe drink too much and bust up somebody's head. But this here's Sunday—won't likely be any shootin'. That's why the sheriff rides out Sundays to visit his kin."

"His younger brother and his wife, is that right?" Jessamyn said. "I met his wife at the mercantile this morning."

"Yes'm. Mr. Carleton and Miss Ella. An' Miss Alice. There's a fine-lookin' child, 'cept for her eyes."

Jessamyn glanced up. "What about her eyes? They looked perfectly normal to me."

Jeremiah hesitated. "Got her daddy's eyes. Kinda hard

and shifty-like sometimes. Got her momma's nose and mouth, though. Guess she'll be all right when she grows up some.''

Jessamyn laughed out loud. "Jeremiah, maybe you just don't like children?''

"Mr. Ben grew up fine, he did," Jeremiah countered. "Handsomest man I ever did see, even when we was young'uns. His eyes were different from Mr. Carleton's, even then. 'Course, they're sadder now, since the war an' all.''

Jessamyn came to instant attention. She needed some background on Ben Kearney for the newspaper article she planned to write. Here, standing before her, was a walking, talking firsthand source.

"What about the war, Jeremiah? Tell me about it—about you and the sheriff, I mean. About your experiences.'' She bit into her second drumstick and waited as Jeremiah cleared his throat.

The town lay dark and quiet by the time Ben rode in past the livery stable. Crickets sang, their strident voices carrying over the occasional cry of a coyote. Heat rose from the dusty roadbed, the rich smell of honeysuckle and to-bacco smoke drifting on the warm night air.

Ben slowed the horse to a walk. Nights like these made his groin ache. He wanted to yell or break something to ease the tension curling inside.

He needed a woman.

He'd settle for whiskey.

The Dixon House hotel and Charlie's Red Fox glowed like Mississippi paddle-wheelers. The sheriff's office was dark. Jeremiah must be out keeping an eye on things.

He dismounted, tossed the reins over the hitching rail and pushed open the door to his office. Touching a match to the lamp wick, he watched the pool of golden light settle over the cat lazing on his desk. "Move over, Shiloh." He lifted the boneless animal off the clutter of papers.

More mail. Maybe something that would provide a clue to Thad Whittaker's murder.

And maybe not. So far, he'd run into nothing but dead ends. It shouldn't be that difficult to figure out who wanted the outspoken editor of the *Wildwood Times* silenced, but with each batch of new communications, Ben's investigation turned into a bigger ball of snakes. A corrupt Bureau of Indian Affairs administrator, shady railroad investors trying to outmaneuver each other, cattle rustled from valley ranches, Indians mad enough to smoke a war pipe. Ben ran his fingers through his hair and sighed. The war's end hadn't brought peace to the West. Far from it.

He scratched the cat under its chin until a throaty purr rumbled, then turned his rangy frame toward the open doorway. Maybe he'd leave the mail until morning and drop by the hotel for a steak and some of Rita's baked beans.

Across the street, light glowed inside the newspaper office. He focused on the paned front window opposite him. Then again, maybe he'd just see what Miss Starched Petticoat was up to at this hour.

He lifted his Colt from the hook behind the door, strapped the revolver low on his hip and headed for the *Wildwood Times*.

Jeremiah drew in a long breath and blew it out through pursed lips. "Can't tell you all of it 'bout the war, Miss Jessamyn. 'Twouldn't be fittin'. But some of it I can." He cocked his head to one side. "Yes'm, some of it I surely can tell you."

Jessamyn stopped chewing and listened.

"Mr. Ben and me, we went to war together, like I said. I was his aide-de-camp. Mostly I just do for him like his manservant always done in Carolina—wash his shirts, shine up his boots, be sure he takes time to eat. He was awful busy in the war—had near two regiments to command after the other colonel got himself killed. Mr. Ben got his horse shot out from under him twice at Shiloh. Madder'n a hen caught in the creek, he was." Jeremiah grinned at the memory.

Jessamyn resisted the impulse to reach into the desk drawer for her pencil and writing pad. Rather than interrupt Jeremiah, she'd commit the important parts to memory.

"How did he get that scar on his neck?" she prompted.

The deputy's grin faded. "He doesn't like to talk about it much. He took a minié ball. Tore into his chest and mangled him pretty bad up to about here." He tapped his throat with a chicken bone.

"The surgeon didn't fix it quite right, and it festered. Woulda been all right cept'n he was captured at Vicksburg and sent to a Northern prison. They had to cut it open to drain it and then sew him up again."

Horrified, Jessamyn stared at the deputy. "You mean it was a Yankee doctor who—"

Jeremiah nodded. "Fought like a son of a— Oh, 'scuse me, Miss Jessamyn. Weren't any use, though. I saw it had to be done. Otherwise, it'd have the gangrene in it."

Jessamyn's appetite vanished. "Oh, how awful."

"Yes'm, it was."

"You were there, Jeremiah? But why? Surely you could have gone back to your home on the plantation?"

"I stayed," Jeremiah replied quietly. "The colonel, he tried to get me to leave him when he saw the Yankee boys comin' over the hill at Vicksburg. I wouldn't budge, though. So, in the end they took us both."

"Oh, Jeremiah! How courageous that was!"

The deputy flushed under his tan. "'Tweren't no such thing, Miss Jessamyn. Ben and me been friends from the cradle, you might say. We grew up together, fishin' and ridin'—even some schoolin' afore his pappy sent him off to the academy. Besides, I promised Miss Lorena I'd watch out for him. A body couldn't refuse Miss Lorena nothin', so I stuck with him."

"Miss Lorena?" The question slipped out before Jessamyn could stop herself.

"Good thing, too," Jeremiah continued, purposely ignoring her query. "After the surgeon cut Ben's chest open, he like to bled to death till I poulticed him like my momma taught me."

Jessamyn found her hand shaking so violently she couldn't hold her fork steady. She laid it down on the desk. "No wonder he's so brusque," she said half to herself. "He must hate all Northerners."

"Oh, no, ma'am," Jeremiah offered with a chuckle. "Not just Northerners. Part of him hates most everybody, 'cept your pappy—Mr. Whittaker—and me. And sometimes I think he even—"

Something in the man's raspy voice struck a nerve. Sometimes, she supposed, the sheriff acted as if he even hated his faithful companion, Jeremiah. A resonant chord of understanding tolled in her heart. She knew from her own experience how devastating it was to be abandoned. She also knew how healing it could be to find a friend.

She had nothing in common with Sheriff Ben Kearney. He was a rich Southern plantation owner, she a poor Northern working girl. Ben Kearney was a man of few words, a loner, unfathomable and unyielding as an iron strongbox. Jessamyn relished every waking moment of watching the fascinating parade of people that made up day-to-day life.

No, sir, she had nothing in common with Sheriff Ben Kearney. But she shared an unspoken bond with thoughtful, soft-spoken Jeremiah. Then and there she resolved she would be the deputy's friend.

"Come on, Jeremiah," Jessamyn announced. "Let's have some of Cora's applesauce cake, then get back to work!"

She unwrapped the square of cinnamon-scented cake, cut it in two pieces with the paring knife Cora had provided, and handed one to Jeremiah. Just as she opened her mouth to take a bite, the door banged open.

Sheriff Ben Kearney leaned his tall form against the door

frame, the rowels on his spurs chinging. With slow, deliberate motions he pushed his hat up off his forehead and crossed one black boot over the other.

"Evening," he said, his voice lazy.

The look in his hard gray-blue eyes sent Jessamyn's heart skittering into her throat.

"Smells like a Carolina stump whiskey still in here," the sheriff remarked, his voice ominously soft.

Jessamyn bristled. "We were—I was cleaning my printing press, Sheriff."

"With whiskey?"

"Yes, with whiskey. The mercantile had no kerosene. Your deputy here—" She glanced toward Jeremiah and gasped. The solidly built man had vanished out the back door.

"Jeremiah came to my aid at the Red Fox," she finished lamely.

Ben's dark eyebrows rose. "The Red Fox," he echoed. "A saloon is no place for a woman, Miss Whittaker. I thought I made that clear yesterday." Flinty blue eyes bored into hers as he waited, arms folded across his chest, for her response.

"You did. But, you see, without kerosene, I had no choice but—"

"You had a choice," the sheriff said, his voice barely more than a whisper. "A choice that didn't involve my deputy in your difficulties. No doubt Jeremiah 'came to your aid,' as you naively put it, because he's an intelligent man and he saw that your presence at the Red Fox spelled trouble. In the future—"

"Now, just one minute, Sheriff," Jessamyn interrupted. "You don't own this town. You've no right to come barging in here and tell me how to live my life!"

"I've got the right," Ben said. His tone hardened. "You're a damn menace traipsing into a saloon in your petticoats and lace. When you Yankees mess with things you know nothing about, mistakes come easy. It's a wonder you didn't start a hell-fired hullabaloo.''

A heated silence fell. Jessamyn felt her cheeks flame. She rose to her feet, twitched her apron into place with short, jerky movements and turned her back on the man lounging in her doorway.

"Excuse me, Sheriff. I have work to do." She snatched up her rag and the bottle of Child's.

A hand closed like an iron band about her upper arm. "Put that down and listen to me." He gave her a little shake and pulled her about to face him. The whiskey sloshed back and forth in the container.

Jessamyn sucked in a breath.

His mouth thinned into a fine, straight line with no hint of a smile. "Put that down," he repeated. "Now."

His voice, Jessamyn thought irrationally, became oddly quiet when he was angry. The timbre of it sent a current of unease dancing up her spine.

She lowered the bottle to the floor, dipping her knees to settle it with care on the plank surface. "Take your hands off me," she said evenly, keeping her eyes on his.

A flicker of pain surfaced in the smoky depths of his gaze, masked at once by a careful shuttering. Jessamyn cringed at the unfathomable expression in his eyes.

He lifted his hands, dropped them to his sides. For a long minute their gazes locked.

Across the street the piano plunked out a ragged snatch of "The Blue Tail Fly." A moth batted against the windowpane, and the slow *tick-tock-tick* of her father's clock on the wall contrasted with her heart's erratic beating beneath the starched white waist.

Ben breathed in, out, in again, the air pulling raggedly through his nostrils. Jessamyn blanched at the carefully expressionless face of the man before her. It was plain as day he was furious at her. She had challenged his professional judgment as sheriff.

When, she moaned inwardly, *will I ever learn to keep*

my mouth shut? What was he thinking? Worse, what was he going to do?

At last his low, quiet voice broke the stillness.

"Let me explain something about life out here in the West, Miss Whittaker." He held her attention riveted to his face by the sheer force of his steady blue eyes and menacing tone. He enunciated his words in quiet, deliberate syllables, with no outward rancor, yet Jessamyn sensed a volcano of fury just beneath the surface. His demeanor frightened her.

"We live by a code here in Wildwood Valley," he continued. "Any lady who *is* a lady stays at home in the evening. She doesn't come into town after dark unless it's to attend a dance or a social, and even then she doesn't go about alone."

His voice dropped even lower. "And she certainly does not work, alone, late at night, smelling of whiskey and—" he sniffed the air "—some flowery-smelling perfume, even if she owns the whole building! Now, go—"

"I wasn't alone!" Jessamyn blurted. "Jeremiah was here, helping—"

"Of course he was, you damn fool. Jeremiah's a good man. He wasn't going to leave you to your own devices here at night, all by yourself. He did what any deputy worth half his salt would do—he stood guard over a rattlepated woman who doesn't know which end of the horse to mount."

Stung, Jessamyn raised her chin and straightened her spine. "This 'rattlepated woman,' as you so quaintly put it, is now the owner and publisher of the *Wildwood Times*. As such, I expect to work late, and alone, many nights. That's what printing a newspaper requires—hard days gathering information and long nights writing stories and setting type. As a taxpaying citizen—" she bit her tongue at the exaggeration "—I expect support, not criticism. So, if you have nothing constructive to offer, Sheriff Kearney, I will bid you good-night."

Ben sighed. Arguing wasn't going to solve the problem. Someone as stubborn as Thad Whittaker's daughter would have to be shown. God almighty, he'd give his right arm if she'd just climb back on the morning stage and go back to Boston where she belonged.

Ben took a step forward and studied her. To think Jeremiah had wasted an entire evening with this prickly, over-starched Northerner. He must be ready to chew nails by now. His deputy had hit the truth for sure; women were definitely troublous creatures.

He shook his head. "Troublous" didn't half describe Jessamyn Whittaker. He'd have to find Jeremiah and buy him a drink at the Red Fox. Inflicting this bullheaded Yankee lady on anyone, even for a few hours, was sure to raise a thirst.

"Miss Whittaker, pack up your things," Ben ordered softly. "I'll see you home."

"Thank you, but I'd prefer—"

"Now," he added in a rough whisper. He snagged the Child's bottle off the floor, set it on the cabinet against the wall. Folding up the handles of the wicker picnic basket, he lifted it from the desk and bent to blow out the lamp.

"Best take off your apron and get your shawl." He puffed once, and the room was enveloped in inky blackness.

Oh, my, Jessamyn thought. She'd gone too far. She needed the sheriff's help, not just to operate the newspaper, but to find her father's murderer. Much as she disliked Ben Kearney, she couldn't afford to make an enemy of him. Not yet, anyway. Not until he'd arrested her father's killer.

In the dark she untied her apron with fumbling fingers, felt around on the desk chair for her blue paisley shawl.

Without a word, Ben moved to her side. He made no sound, but she sensed him draw near in the pitch-black room, felt the warmth radiate from his body. She breathed in his scent, heavy with horses and tobacco smoke. The faint smell of mint lingered on his breath.

Jessamyn choked back a nervous hiccup. She must smell of—what was it he'd said?—stump whiskey and flowery perfume? Without thinking, she reached out to steady herself. Her fingers closed over his bare forearm.

He swore under his breath. His voice was so raw Jessamyn jumped.

"I—I'm sorry," she blurted. "It's so dark in here I can't see."

"Wait a minute, then. Your eyes will adjust."

My eyes, Jessamyn thought, *will never adjust to the picture presented by an angry Ben Kearney.* How could a man be so fine-looking and so unnerving at the same time?

"Maybe you're thinking you'd be better off back in Boston," he said close to her ear.

"I was not!"

His hand touched her elbow. "The floorboards are uneven. Don't stumble."

"I won't," she breathed. Acutely aware of his warm fingers on her skin, she took a tentative step forward. Pulling her shawl tight about her shoulders, Jessamyn let him guide her to the doorway.

"And, Miss Whittaker," he murmured at the threshold, "I trust you won't come here alone at night again?"

"I wouldn't think of it," she lied.

The door opened on a street bathed in silvery moonlight. Jessamyn stalked out onto the boardwalk and gazed down the street at the painted sign above Charlie's Red Fox Saloon. Laughter drifted on the warm night air, punctuated by the metallic sounds of the piano and a man's clear tenor singing an Irish ballad. Ladies who weren't ladies—soiled doves, the sheriff called them—were probably drinking spirits and dancing with the ranch hands.

Jessamyn sighed. Ladies who *were* ladies weren't supposed to have that kind of fun.

She studied the spill of golden light through the saloon's swinging entrance door. She'd risked everything, coming out West. She'd left her position at the *Boston Herald*, abandoned her comfortable, refined life in the East.

Had it been worth it?

The answer came in an instant. Yes! Every single, frightening, fascinating moment of her first day—and night—in Wildwood Valley had been worth it. After what she had experienced so far, she thought with a little catch of excitement in her chest, just being alive in this rough, dusty town was going to be exhilarating. And fun.

Tomorrow she'd ignore the sheriff and his silly warnings and put her next plan into action. She could hardly wait.

Chapter Five

"Jes' like yer pa," Cora sniffed as she bustled out the news office door. "Rather fuss over that newspaper than eat proper."

Nodding her agreement, Jessamyn bit into the ham sandwich the housekeeper had brought over for her lunch. She massaged her stiff neck muscles and continued her study of the morgue of old *Wildwood Times* editions her father had meticulously collected. Just a few more issues to skim and she'd be caught up.

So far, she'd found nothing extraordinary. Ohio Ratifies 14th Constitutional Amendment. Nebraska Admitted to Union. Impeachment Resolution Again Introduced in Washington.

In Douglas County Frieder's Mercantile's shipment from Chicago was again delayed by a blizzard. Rancher Silas Appleby reported twenty head of cattle missing; Klamath River Indians were suspected. Lizzie Bartel, the doctor's wife, delivered her second set of twins in five years, on Valentine's Day. Coos Bay wagon road was surveyed as a possible railroad route to the coast.

Jessamyn shook her head. Still nothing out of the ordinary for an Oregon frontier town—except perhaps having two sets of twins in one family. Mrs. Bartel would be far too busy to receive callers now; Jessamyn would tender her congratulations to the doctor, whose office she'd finally discovered just three doors down the street. Next to the undertaker, she noted. How convenient.

As soon as she could, she intended to visit all the townspeople, introduce herself and solicit ads for the newspaper. Then she'd sell each of them a yearly subscription for a dollar.

She swallowed the last of her sandwich and closed the cabinet drawer. Now, to plan her first issue. She munched on a crisp Red June apple as she laid out the first page in her mind. This afternoon she'd make the rounds, gathering the local Wildwood Valley news. Tomorrow she'd hire a buggy and drive over to Little River where the express riders brought the mail and wire service bulletins up from Steamboat Landing. And then...

Then she would dip her pen into a fresh bottle of ink and start her feature story on Ben Kearney and her father's murder. Surely the sheriff wouldn't object to her choice of topic? After all, it *was* news. She drew in a deep breath and stretched her arms over her head.

She allowed a slow smile to settle across her mouth as an idea began to take shape. Inept the sheriff was certainly not, judging from the battlefield heroism described by his deputy. But his lackadaisical attitude seemed to fit right in to the town's don't-upset-the-ship philosophy. A mercantile with no kerosene, cracked and peeling paint on the undertaker's and barbershop storefronts, saloons that stayed open all night long and on Sundays. Wildwood Valley could surely use some improvement.

To get things started, she'd light a fire under Sheriff Kearney. Why hadn't he found her father's killer yet? What was he waiting for? Surely he should be busy gathering evidence or clues or *something?* She exhaled in satisfaction. She'd give the good sheriff a roasting he'd never forget.

Already composing the lead sentence in her mind, Jessamyn attacked a second sandwich. Good ideas made her ravenous! As she chewed, she glanced idly out the front window.

A sorrel horse stepped daintily into view, an Indian girl perched on top, her back straight, her buckskin dress encrusted with shells and feathers arranged in an intricate design. The pride in her carriage riveted Jessamyn's attention.

Townspeople stared, but the girl looked neither left nor right. Purposefully, she stepped the horse forward. As she drew closer, Jessamyn glimpsed a clear view of her face and gasped out loud.

The girl was beautiful! Straight black hair fell in a single shining braid down her back, and her slim, elegant body moved sinuously with the mare's gait, almost as if she were dancing atop the horse. Fascinated, Jessamyn watched her come to a halt in front of the sheriff's office.

The girl swung her leg over the horse's neck and slid to the ground, dropping the reins where the animal stood.

And then she took a single step. She positioned one small, moccasined foot and then, crablike, hauled her body forward, her hip twisting in an awkward, lurching rhythm.

Jessamyn's heart caught. She was crippled! And she looked so young—no more than eighteen or twenty, her skin an unblemished, warm bronze, her face serene. The girl took another step, and another, laboriously working her way past the horse toward the board walkway at the edge of the street.

Two women crossing the street pulled their skirts aside in apparent distaste. The Indian girl paid no attention. When she reached the bottom step of the sidewalk the sheriff's door opened, and Jeremiah emerged. Grasping her elbow with one giant hand, he half lifted her up the step onto the walkway.

Wide-eyed, Jessamyn watched the sheriff's office door swing shut. Hoping for another glimpse of her, she waited by the window, nibbling the remains of her sandwich crusts.

Fifteen minutes dragged by. Jessamyn stepped away to

refill her cup, then settled herself at the window again. She sipped the dark brew, her gaze swinging back and forth between the dingy office door across the street and her father's wall clock.

All at once Jeremiah surged out of the sheriff's office, followed by Ben Kearney with the Indian girl in his arms. Jessamyn lowered her cup. What in the world was he doing?

She peered out the window. Ben strode toward the sorrel as Jeremiah retrieved the reins and held the animal steady. She noticed that the deputy never took his eyes off the girl's face.

With no apparent effort, the sheriff swung her up and settled her on the saddle blanket, then lifted the reins from his deputy's hands and laid them across her palms. Removing his hat, he tipped his face up toward her. His lips moved.

The girl nodded, made a sign and nudged the horse forward. Ben raised his hand. She looked back, hesitated an instant and then smiled. She called out something, kicked the mare and stepped her horse on down the street. Jeremiah stared after her.

Who was she? Jessamyn burned to know. And what did she want with the sheriff? Or was it the other way around— one of them wanted something of her? From the way she smiled at them, Jessamyn would guess one of them could have just about anything he asked for. But which one?

A tiny arrow of unrest lodged in her belly. Was this girl the reason Ben Kearney seemed different from the other men in town? Could it be that the sheriff was courting an Indian girl? Worse, was he so preoccupied he'd forgotten about finding Thad Whittaker's killer?

Well! She'd just see about that! Jessamyn plunked her cup down on the desk so hard the coffee sloshed over the edge. Hurriedly, she blotted it up with one corner of her work apron. Out of the corner of her eye she saw Ben

Kearney amble down the street in his lazy, loose-jointed gait.

Something ballooned in her chest as she watched him move. He reminded her of a big cat, a tiger she'd seen photographed once in a scientific magazine. She imagined its hunting prowess, the taut coiled strength ready to be unleashed in an instant. Ben's movements had that same animal grace and economy of motion. It was frightening in some way.

Without a break in his slow, easy stride, the sheriff mounted the board walkway and disappeared into his office.

Jessamyn stared after him. Something about that languid, controlled body sent shivers sliding up her backbone.

Ben rubbed his hand over his eyes. His lids felt grainy, and a dull ache pounded at the base of his skull. All night he'd lain awake on the narrow bed in the back room, thinking about Thad Whittaker, trying to tie together the bits of information he'd uncovered. Nothing fit. It was like trying to work a puzzle with the key piece missing.

It hadn't been a random shooting, that much he knew for certain. It had been too deliberate, too obvious. If his hunch was right, Thad had known something. The editor's death was intended to not only silence the newspaper but serve as a warning of some sort. But a warning about what?

He'd have to search the *Wildwood Times* office again, sift through Thad's private papers—every edition of the newspaper, every letter, even his account ledger. Maybe this time he'd find something he'd overlooked before, something that would tie things together.

He'd start tonight, after Jessamyn retired to Mrs. Boult's for the evening. He'd let himself into the newspaper office and spend whatever time it took searching for that elusive nugget of information. At sunup tomorrow he'd do what Walks Dancing had asked—start for the mountains and Black Eagle's hidden camp.

He wondered what the old chief wanted that was so important he'd send his daughter into town alone. Black Eagle wouldn't risk sending one of his few remaining braves. The townspeople were convinced it was the Indians who were stealing cattle from valley ranchers, and feelings ran high. An Indian wouldn't last ten minutes in town before he or Jeremiah would have to break up a lynching party.

Ben propped his boots on the desk, tipped his chair back on two legs. He closed his eyes, drew in another lungful of the warm June air and thought again about Thad Whittaker.

And Thad Whittaker's daughter. Even without her bustle, her sleeves rolled up to her elbows and a smudge of grease on her nose, Jessamyn was still something to look at. Her backside rounded invitingly below the slim waist, and even when she held her spine straight as a Yankee ramrod, the curves of her top half filled out that ruffly blouse just right. He imagined the tips of her breasts brushing against the frothy white lace. He'd like to lay his hand there, feel her heart beating against his palm.

Sweat trickled under his hatband. He pushed it back with his forefinger just as the door burst open and Silas Appleby strode inside.

"Morning, Si."

"Goddammit, Ben, it's happened again! Twenty head just disappeared overnight."

Ben's chair thunked down on all four legs. "No trail?"

"Not a trace." The tall, sunburned rancher swatted his dusty felt hat against his thigh so hard the silver conchas around the crown jingled. "Gotta be Indians, Ben. They're holed up somewhere. Starving, I hear. I wouldn't care if they took one or even two beeves now and again. Hell's red feathers, I'd let 'em have 'em with my blessing. But twenty head? All told, I've lost more'n sixty cows in just the last two months."

"Ranches on the east side of the river have been hit, too, Si. My brother Carleton's lost over forty head. But I don't think it's Indians. At least, not Black Eagle's band."

"You don't," the rancher echoed, his tone indicating disbelief.

"I don't."

"Well, then, who the hell…"

Ben ground his boot heel into the plank floor. "Silas, when I find out, I'll let you know. Until then, I'd suggest your boys spend their free time doing more night riding around your spread than poker playing in town."

The tall man gave Ben an assessing look. "I've known you a long time, Ben. You never was one to sniff too long up the wrong tree, so I'll have to trust you on this one. But I'm tellin' you—"

"Save it, Si. We've been through it all before. Ranchers think Indians are responsible for everything that goes wrong. Indians think the same about the white man. You mind your herd and let me do my job. One of these days, whoever is stealing your cattle will make a mistake—leave a trail, a footprint, something I can go on. I'll get him in the end. I always do."

"Yeah," the tall man grumbled. "You do. But waitin' is costing me money!"

Ben raised his eyebrows. "And it's costing me sleep at night. There's an old Indian saying, Si. 'When in doubt, do nothing—the situation could get worse.' Come fall, I'll have this wound up and then you can get rich and I can get rested."

Silas chuckled. Clapping his hat on an unruly shock of sandy hair, he turned toward the door. "I'll buy you a drink if you pull it off by September, Ben. I'll even stake you to a round of poker."

Ben grinned. "Five-card stud and Child's Premium. New shipment should be in by September."

The door closed on Si Appleby's laughter.

Ben struck his desk with his fist. Damn! If he found evidence of just one fresh beef carcass at Black Eagle's camp, he'd skin the old fox alive. He swore again. The cat sleeping on top of his logbook cracked one eye open, stretched and offered an elaborate yawn. Before he knew it, the animal curled up in his lap.

The door bumped open a second time, and Jessamyn Whittaker marched into the room. A lacy white blouse that looked crisp enough to stand up by itself bloomed from the waistband of her swirling indigo blue skirt.

"Sheriff Kearney?" Her voice sounded as if it, too, had been starched.

"Miss Whittaker?"

She whipped open a notebook, pulled a pencil from behind one ear and leaned over his desk. "As the new editor of the *Wildwood Times,* Sheriff, I'd like to ask you a few questions, if I may?"

Ben narrowed his eyes. The last thing he needed this morning was a grilling by a nosy Yankee newspaper reporter.

Jessamyn poised her pencil over the pad. "Who was that Indian girl?"

Ben stroked the purring animal in his lap. "Her name is Walks Dancing."

She scribbled in her notebook. "What is the significance of her visit this afternoon?"

Ben frowned. "Depends. Significance to whom—you? Me? The town? Herself? Just what do you want to know?"

Jessamyn tightened her lips in exasperation. Couldn't the man answer a simple question? "I mean, where did she come from?"

Ben plopped his hat onto the clutter on his desk and ran his hand through his hair. "She's a Modoc. The Klamath chief adopted her as his daughter some years back. Black Eagle can't risk exposing his braves—they'd be captured and sent to the reservation with the others. So he sent Walks Dancing into town with a message."

"What message?" Jessamyn said, her words clipped.

"None of your business," Ben returned. "Now, if you'll excuse me—"

"How was she crippled?" Jessamyn interrupted. "From birth?"

Ben expelled a long breath. "She was crippled because she's a Modoc. The Klamath and the Modoc tribes have been enemies for generations. Walks Dancing made the mistake of falling in love with the wrong man—a Klamath brave. She left her tribe and went with him. Her people found them the next spring. They killed him. Then they broke both her legs by running their horses over her and left her to die. She didn't. Black Eagle adopted her."

Jessamyn felt the blood drain from her upper torso. Suddenly dizzy, she dropped the pad and grabbed for the edge of Ben's desk. "How horrible."

"Sorry you asked?"

"Yes," she murmured. "I mean, no! How else am I going to find out what's happening?"

"Know what my father used to tell me? 'Keep your eyes and ears open—'" He leaned toward her and lowered his voice "'—and your mouth shut.'" He looked as if he especially relished the last part.

Jessamyn winced. His barb hit home. Very well, she'd do things his way. "Just one more question, Sheriff." She mustered as steady a tone as she could manage. "What are you finding out about my father's murderer?"

Ben studied her for what seemed an endless minute. "Damn little that's for publication."

"But what are you *doing?*" she persisted.

Goaded by her tone, Ben answered without thinking. "I'm going to talk to Black Eagle."

Jessamyn gasped. "About my father?"

"Maybe. Don't know yet."

"Where does this Black Eagle live?"

Again Ben studied her. "In the mountains. Two days' ride." He stood, upending the cat, and scooped her notebook up from the floor. "Now, why don't you go on down and talk to Mrs. Frieder—find out when her baby's coming." He thrust the paper pad into her hand.

"The Frieder baby's due in July," Jessamyn retorted. "I'll go with you to see Black Eagle."

"Like hell you will."

"But you said... How can I keep my eyes and ears open if I'm not *there?* No good reporter relies on hearsay."

"Can you ride?" His voice rang with impatience.

"A horse, you mean? N-not really, but I'm sure I could learn."

Ben chuckled. "Not damn likely. Not by sunup tomorrow."

Jessamyn straightened to her full height and looked Ben Kearney straight in the eye. "Try me."

She'd never been on a horse before in her life, but she'd never admit that to Ben. She was a Whittaker. If she had to fly to the moon to get her story, she wouldn't give up until she felt the green cheese under her feet.

"I challenge you, Sheriff. I challenge you to try me! Today. This very minute."

Ben resisted the urge to laugh out loud at her naive suggestion. Learn to ride in one afternoon? Impossible. She was so green she didn't even know it *was* impossible.

"Mr. Kearney, did you hear me? I said—"

"I heard you," he said, his voice quiet. On the other hand, he reasoned, maybe it would shut her up for a while. If she tried it, found how difficult it would be for a greenhorn to master a horse, he'd be rid of her. For a few days, anyway.

The idea had definite appeal. The more he considered it, the more sense it made.

"Miss Whittaker, meet me at the livery stable in ten minutes. And better stop by the mercantile on your way. Get yourself a shirt and some denims and a pair of boots. Otherwise, you're gonna get corral dust all over those fancy starched petticoats of yours."

Without another word, he grabbed his hat and strolled out the door, leaving it open behind him. When he reached the planked sidewalk he began to whistle.

Bet my money on a bobtail nag...oh, doo dah day.

* * *

"Mr. Freider," Jessamyn said when she could catch her breath. "I need a shirt—one of those plaid ones on the shelf will do—a pair of denims and some boots. Small ones."

Otto Frieder's bushy eyebrows lifted. "For yourself?"

At her nod, the storekeeper's eyes popped. "Miss Jessamyn, what you going to do?"

Jessamyn took a deep breath and hoped her voice would sound reasonably steady. "Learn to ride a horse."

Otto stared at her. "Anna-Marie!" he shouted. "Come quick! Miss Jessamyn needs—"

Anna-Marie's rotund figure appeared beside her husband's. Obviously she'd been listening from behind the curtained doorway. Jessamyn gave her as much of a smile as she could manage.

"For you, I think maybe small-size shirt, like for older boy. Trousers..." Anna-Marie turned away and pulled a garment off the shelf. "These. And will need a belt. Men are not built so..." With her hands she traced a shape in the air. "So...in and out."

Jessamyn unfolded the blue denim jeans, fingered the metal buttons that closed the front. They looked complicated. How did men ever...?

Instantly she banished the thought. Heavens, whatever would Miss Bennett say about the direction in which her mind wandered?

"Come." Anna-Marie beckoned. "You try on. Otto," she called into the adjoining room, "find some boots for tiny feet. And, please, a belt."

The shirt—a man's size, since smaller, boys' sizes were not in stock—hung off Jessamyn's shoulders and drooped past her wrists. At least it buttoned decently over her chest.

Cinched up with the wide black leather belt Otto handed through the curtain, the jeans hugged her bottom and thighs. The boots he thrust after the belt scrunched her toes together, but the storekeeper insisted the leather would soften and stretch with use.

"Too loose, will make blisters," he admonished. "These just right."

Jessamyn took a tentative step and winced. Just right? Maybe for someone who was used to such contraptions. Had she gotten them reversed—the left boot on the right foot? She glanced down. Her boots looked like all the other boots she'd seen in town. She'd bet they didn't *feel* like all the others, though. Or did people in Wildwood Valley simply smile through their daily suffering?

Otto beamed at her. "I put on your account, Miss Jessamyn. And will send your other clothes over to your home."

"Thank you, Otto."

"What now you do?"

Jessamyn smiled at the concern in his eyes. "I—I guess I'll walk over to the livery stable."

The storekeeper bobbed his head and headed for the front of the store. Taking a last look at Jessamyn, he disappeared out the door, the bell over the entrance jangling as the sound of his steps receded down the board walkway.

Anna-Marie lumbered to the candy counter and emptied a scoop of ginger drops into Jessamyn's trembling hand. "For luck," she whispered.

Jessamyn slipped the candy into her shirt pocket. On impulse, she hugged the bulky young woman. With all her heart, she wished she could trade places with Anna-Marie at that moment. She would gladly waddle about the mercantile with a swollen belly, even endure the pain of labor and childbirth, if only she wouldn't have to climb up on a horse.

A cold sweat started between her shoulder blades. Horses terrified her. So frightened she could barely swallow, she spun on her heel and clumped out the door in boots that squeezed her toes like pincers.

After a half-block walk toward the stable, she knew why cowboys always rode horseback. They'd do almost anything to take the weight off their cramped feet! She worked at not limping.

The main street appeared to be deserted. Both the doctor's and the undertaker's offices had Closed signs in the front windows. Even the barbershop was empty, the door shut and bolted. How odd, she thought as she strode onward. It was Monday afternoon. Didn't men usually visit the barber for haircuts and shaves before a night in town?

Oh, Lord, you don't suppose…

A gangly boy of about ten raced past her. "Hey, mister," he yelled. "That tenderfoot lady from back East's gonna try to ride a horse! Everybody's gonna watch—come on! You're gonna miss it!"

Jessamyn groaned out loud. Word of mouth spread like wildfire in a town this size. How she longed for the anonymity of civilized, populated Boston.

A vision of the coming ordeal flashed into her mind. A crowd gathered—like the ancient Romans at the Colosseum—to watch a spectacle. Only this wasn't Rome, it was the livery corral in Wildwood Valley, Oregon, and *she* was the spectacle! She wondered if Ben Kearney had spread the word about town just to make the challenge harder for her. Would he stoop so low?

He would, she decided. She recalled the satisfied grin on his lips when he sauntered out of the sheriff's office in that maddening, unsettling walk of his. That snake! She'd lambaste him the first chance she got. She'd blister him with words he'd never forget. She'd—

She'd learn to ride a horse, that's what she'd do! That would show him. She wasn't going to let Ben Kearney have the last word. Even in jeans and torture-chamber boots, she was still a Whittaker.

And a Whittaker, she reminded herself with a little half sob of fear, never gave up.

Chapter Six

Ben eased his back against the split-rail fence around the stable corral and crossed one boot over the other. Satisfied with the private arrangement he'd made with liveryman and blacksmith Dan Gustafsen, he inhaled deeply.

He'd known Gus from his army days in Dakota Territory after the war. The big, quiet Norwegian had fought for the Union, but when hostilities had finally ceased, Gus had set politics aside. When Ben met him in Dakota, he found he could deal with him man-to-man. Both had been officers; both had been wounded. Gus wore a black patch over one eye.

"Pick a horse that's not mean," Ben had requested. "Just not too tired, if you take my meaning." From the looks of the skittish bay dancing at the end of Gus's rope, the stable owner had indeed taken Ben's meaning. The horse was a beauty—sixteen, maybe even seventeen hands, a gelding with intelligent eyes and a precise, proud gait.

And, Ben could see at a glance, definitely not tired. He watched Gus pull the cinch tight, then give him a surreptitious nod. Even though he trusted Gus's judgment, Ben's gut tightened into a hard knot.

Townspeople began to gather along the perimeter of the fence. Ben nodded to Doc Bartel and the short, nervous undertaker, Zed Marsh, the physician's constant companion. He tipped his hat to Addie Rice and, a few yards beyond the seamstress, acknowledged two of the girls from Charlie's Red Fox Saloon. Addie must have closed her dressmaker's shop to witness the fun. Ben surmised the girls from Charlie's were losing money, too.

Silas Appleby heaved his rangy form onto the fence next to Ben and hooked his boot heels over the lower rail. "I hear that newspaper lady's a looker," he remarked. "Since I'm in town, I thought I'd just as well check out the rumors."

"You're practically a married man, Si," Ben reminded him.

"Hell, Ben, can't hurt to look!" Appleby jammed a cigarette between his lips and flicked a match against his thumbnail.

Otto Frieder picked his way through a gaggle of young boys in various sizes and shapes and settled on Ben's other side. A frown worried his shiny forehead. "You think Miss Jessamyn be all right, Sheriff?"

Ben fought a momentary pang of guilt at Otto's question. He trusted Gus's horse savvy. Jessamyn wouldn't get hurt—not seriously, anyway. Just enough to bruise her backside a bit and open her eyes to the fact that she wasn't riding into the hills with him tomorrow. Or any other day, for that matter. From what he had observed, hearsay had always been plenty good for most newspaper editors. Why should she be any different?

Because she's Thad Whittaker's daughter, that's why. Hearsay was never good enough for Thad; that was probably what got him killed.

"She'll be all right, Otto," Ben assured the stocky storekeeper. "I'd worry more about the horse if I were you. Miss Whittaker finds it difficult to take *no* for an answer."

Silas chuckled. "Looks to me like that gelding might have the same trouble!"

Ben watched Gus turn away toward a commotion at the far end of the corral yard, then glance back to catch Ben's gaze. The skin around the wrangler's one good eye crinkled in amusement.

Jessamyn crawled through an opening in the fence and sidled stiff-legged toward Ben, her backside hugging the fence so closely he could have sworn she'd pick up splinters on her rear.

"Sheriff Kearney?" Her words came out in a throaty whisper. "Is—is that the horse?"

"It is. Ready to mount up?"

Jessamyn licked her lips. "Isn't it awfully big?" She kept her gaze riveted on the animal in the center of the corral yard.

Ben shrugged. "Some are, some aren't. This one's about normal." For some reason, an unexpected pang of sympathy stabbed into his chest. She looked terrified.

"I want you to know, Mr. Kearney," she said in that same breathy whisper, "that I am not f-frightened in the least." Again she ran her tongue over her lips. "Not even a little b-bit."

She poked her chin into the air and visibly straightened her spine. "But if I—or rather, *when* I live through this, you p-puffed-up, know-it-all snake in the grass, I'm going to make your life so m-miserable you'd wish you were back in that Union prison in Illinois!"

She stomped away toward Gus.

Silas guffawed. "Puffed up? Why, imagine that!" He slapped Ben on the shoulder. "Makes you sound like one of Ella's banty roosters. My, that little eastern lady has got some spit and vinegar!" Chuckling, he settled back to watch.

Spit and vinegar wasn't all she had, Ben noted, watching Jessamyn's jeans stretch tight over her derriere as she marched up to Gus. The wide black belt pulled the too-large waistband snug around her middle, and the long sleeves of the red plaid shirt were folded back twice at the cuffs. She looked like a kid masquerading as her big brother.

A scared kid. A twinge wrenched his gut. Her bravado didn't fool him for a second. He'd seen that same look on new recruits' faces before their first battle. They fought—and died—because they were ordered to. Jessamyn didn't have to do this, he told himself. She didn't have to, but she wasn't backing out. In fact, at this moment she was about as unflinching as any soldier he'd ever commanded in the field. Her courage touched him in some way, as if a finger had been laid upon his heart.

Jessamyn looked up at the tall man holding the towering horse. He tipped his hat with his free hand and smiled down at her. "Daniel Gustafsen, ma'am. Everybody calls me Gus."

"What's the horse's name?"

He hesitated. "Dancer Jack."

Jessamyn nodded. "Gus, are all those people along the fence here to…to watch me try to—watch me ride this horse?"

Gus's one blue eye softened. "Yes, ma'am, 'fraid so. They all come out like grasshoppers on an August morning whenever a tenderfoot like yourself climbs up on a horse the first time. It's kinda like entertainment for them. The Greenhorn Follies, they call it."

"Entertainment!" She shut her eyes. She could almost hear the imagined roar of bloodthirsty Romans in her ears.

"Sure am sorry, Miss Whittaker, but it's true. Things out here in the West aren't civilized like they are back in the colony states."

Or even in Rome, Jessamyn thought with a shudder. Still, she wasn't beaten yet. "Gus, I'm going to ride that horse if it's the last thing I do. I want you to tell me how."

The wrangler nodded. "Now, Miss Jessamyn, just keep in mind you're gonna get this horse to walk. He already knows how to run. First thing you do is talk to him, call him by name."

Jessamyn moved toward the animal. "H-hello, Dancer Jack," she breathed.

The horse tossed his head and moved a step away.

"Don't be afraid, now. I'm not going to hurt you." She edged forward. "What now, Gus?" she said softly.

"Now you touch him, all over. Let him smell you, get your scent."

Jessamyn reached one hand toward the gelding's moist black nose. "Dancer Jack," she murmured. "It's me, Jessamyn. Or maybe for you it'll just be Jess."

She ran her palm up the front of his face, then spread both hands along his jaw. "Good boy," she said. "Good horse." Under her fingers, the warm hide twitched.

The horse stood still. Jessamyn smiled at Gus, who gestured for her to continue.

She drew in a breath and laid her forehead against the gelding's dark head. *Please, please let this horse like me!* she prayed. When the animal didn't move away, she slowly smoothed her palm over the neck, then stepped to one side and rubbed its hard, warm shoulder and withers. Next she ran her hands down each leg. The horse's limbs trembled as violently as Jessamyn's did.

"You're doin' fine, ma'am. Just fine. Here's his lead now. You hold him while I adjust the stirrups and go get a mounting block for you."

Frozen, Jessamyn stood motionless as a statue until Gus returned with a portable wooden step. He took the rope from her, tossed the reins over the saddle horn. "Climb up on the step and put your left foot in the stirrup. Grab the saddle horn and swing your other leg up over his rump."

Jessamyn stood on top of the block, raised her left foot until she thought she'd twist her thigh right out of the hip socket, and jammed her toe into the high stirrup. She reached for the saddle horn and pulled herself up to a near-standing position. She clutched at the saddle for support and tried to swing her right leg over the horse.

She couldn't get her leg high enough to clear the gelding's backside. On her third attempt she slipped out of the stirrup, breathing hard. Behind her, she could hear the raucous laughter of the crowd.

"Try it again," Gus urged. "This time, you give a little spring and I'll boost you on up."

Jessamyn measured the distance from the mounting block to the saddle. It looked impossible unless you had legs as long as Ben Kearney's. At the thought of the sheriff, she stiffened her resolve. She was doing this for her newspaper, and nothing—not even a corralful of avid spectators—was going to stop her. In fact, she might turn the situation to her advantage.

"If I make it," she said through clenched teeth, "will you buy a subscription to the *Wildwood Times?*"

Gus blinked. "Why, sure, ma'am. Anything you say."

Jessamyn again stuck her boot in the stirrup. This time she flexed her knees and gave a little jump. The wrangler put his shoulder under her bottom and heaved, and she sailed up and into the saddle.

"Now, remember, hold the reins steady and don't move. When he's used to your weight, I'll let go of the bridle. Then you're on your own."

Too frightened to speak, Jessamyn nodded. She looked down. The ground seemed far, far beneath her. She didn't have a choice—either she held on, or she died on the spot. Motionless except for her shaking hands, she waited.

"Steady, Dancer," she murmured. "I don't like this any more than you do."

After a moment she grew conscious of the noise from the townspeople gathered along the fence. It sounded like bees buzzing in her head. A child's voice yelled something that sounded like "go-it."

Very slowly Jessamyn lifted her head and stared at the crowd. Instinctively she stiffened her spine.

At that instant Gus dropped the rope and stepped away from the horse.

Nothing happened. The horse gusted air out, then in, then out again. Perspiration moistened the reins where they crossed Jessamyn's palm. Lord in heaven, maybe she could do it! Maybe she could sit high up on this huge, powerful animal and not die in the process. The thought gave her courage. Realizing she was holding her breath, she opened her mouth to draw in life-sustaining air.

Suddenly the horse arched under her, then plunged forward. Jessamyn slid sideways. She glimpsed the ground rushing up to meet her and closed her eyes tight.

The impact knocked the air out of her lungs and drove her upper teeth into her tongue. Coppery-tasting blood filled her mouth, trickled down her chin.

Frightened, she tried to breathe, but found she couldn't. Her chest felt as if a steam engine had rolled over it. Flat on her back, she lay still, unable to move.

Two hazy faces appeared above her.

"Is she all right, Doc?"

Ben Kearney's voice. Jessamyn wondered if he was close enough for her to kick him.

"Dunno yet, Ben. Get out of my way!"

Hands prodded gently, helped her sit up. She spit out a mouthful of blood and blinked back tears.

"She's okay. Looks like she bit her tongue. Nothing broken, though."

Jessamyn caught at the man's shirtsleeve. "Dr. Bartel?" she managed to croak.

"Yes, my dear? I'm Rufus Bartel. Just rest easy now."

Jessamyn looked up into the freckled face under the thatch of red hair. A completely illogical thought popped into her head. "Congratulations on your twins. Would you—" She coughed out another blob of spit and blood. "Would you like a year's subscription to the *Wildwood Times?*"

"Hah, Ben! You hear that? She's down, but she's not out. A born businesswoman." He grinned down at her. "I sure would. Come on, young lady, let's get you on your feet."

"I heard it," Ben growled. "I just don't believe it."

He knelt on her other side and slid his arm under her shoulders. He hated to admit it, but he didn't want to put her through any more. "Let's call it a day, Miss Whittaker. I guess now you see my point, and—"

Jessamyn scooted out of his grasp. She saw his point, all right. He didn't think she could do it.

The truth was, she was beginning to wonder the same thing herself. But if she wanted to go with him to see Black Eagle, on horseback, she had to learn how to ride.

"Don't you dare touch me! I am not calling it a day."

She grabbed Rufus Bartel's arm and hoisted herself upright. Pain shot down her spine, settled in her tailbone. Dizzy, she held on to the doctor while she steadied her legs.

"Listen, Jessamyn," Ben began.

Hearing him speak her given name made her heart catch.

Ben stepped in close. "It's good to know when to stop," he said in a low voice. "It's better, of course, to know when not to start." He held her gaze for a moment. As the soft green of her eyes flared to viridian, he realized he'd gone too far.

"A challenge is a challenge, Mr. Kearney. I'm going to ride that horse, so please get out of my way."

"Come on, Ben," the doctor said, his voice quiet. "Save your breath. I know a fighter when I see one."

"Goddamn crazy woman," Ben breathed.

Inwardly, Jessamyn agreed. Maybe she'd made the wrong decision. She was crazy to do this, crazy not to give up gracefully and wait in town while Ben rode off to Black Eagle's camp. But she didn't *want* to sit back and wait! She wanted to see things for herself, wanted to be part of it.

And there was another thing, she acknowledged. She wanted to prove something to Ben Kearney. That in itself was a goal worth struggling for. She didn't know why it mattered so much, but it did. She wanted Ben to see her as someone who counted. As an equal. Miss Bennett would be horrified! Oh, what was the use of puzzling it out now?

She'd analyze it later. Now she had something else she had to do.

Resolutely, she limped toward the center of the corral where Gus stood holding the still-saddled gelding.

Shaking his head, Ben headed for his post at the livery-yard fence. He wished he'd never mentioned riding into the hills to meet with Black Eagle. Stubborn as Jessamyn Whittaker was, being every inch Thad's daughter, she'd likely get herself hurt before she gave up. He hoped Gus was giving her good advice about riding that gelding. He didn't want her to be badly injured—he only wanted her backside to be sore enough to keep her flat on her back in bed when the sun rose tomorrow morning.

A frowning Jeremiah strode out to meet him. "What'd you say to rile Miss Jessamyn enough to ride that horse again, Colonel?"

"Enough," Ben grunted.

"Huh!" Jeremiah gave a snort. "Whatever it was, you oughtn't to have said it. She'll be lucky if all she gets is a faceful of corral dust. Plain as flapjacks she don't know nuthin' about horses, 'specially not one like Dancer Jack. Hell, Ben, that gelding's—"

"I know," Ben snapped. He wished he didn't. He wondered if Jeremiah guessed he'd put Gus up to it. He'd been convinced Dancer Jack would make short work of Jessamyn's all-fired enthusiasm for investigating things first-hand. Now he wasn't so sure, especially with Jeremiah tut-tutting in his ear. The truth was, he was worried about her.

"Troublous," his deputy murmured as they reached the fence. "Downright pigheaded, the both of you!"

Ben closed his ears to Jeremiah's litany. Instead, he watched Gus reposition the mounting block for the slim young woman in dusty jeans. He strained to hear the wrangler's words. The only word he caught was "tight."

Jessamyn nodded. Ben could tell by the stiff set of her shoulders that she was even more frightened than before. The way she stomped up the final wood step and grabbed the saddle horn told him she was just as determined as ever. Damned little fool.

The crowd quieted as Jessamyn tugged herself clumsily atop the gelding, reached for the reins Gus held. Hell, she didn't even have gloves to protect those city-soft hands of hers. Tomorrow her palms would be blistered right along with her bottom.

The horse tossed his head and sidled off to one side. Jessamyn held on. The animal then began to canter in an irregular gait, bumping her up and down in a butt-crunching pattern. Ben groaned inwardly. Watching Jessamyn's rump slap against the hard leather, he winced.

Beside him, Jeremiah noisily sucked air in and out, his eyes glued on the young woman fighting to keep her balance on the still-green gelding. A spattering of applause ran through the spectators lined up along the fence.

Gus yelled something. Jessamyn started to answer, but her first word ended in a cry of distress when the horse twisted and she tumbled off again.

This time she landed on her side, breaking her fall with one arm. She curled into a ball and lay still as Gus caught the horse and brought it under control.

Jeremiah surged forward, then halted when Jessamyn picked herself up and shakily regained her footing. She brushed halfheartedly at the dust on her backside with little fluttery strokes.

Before he knew what he was doing, Ben moved past Jeremiah, signaling to Gus to keep the horse clear while he talked to her. He came up beside her and positioned himself between her and the gelding. "You don't have to do this, you know."

She turned to face him, green eyes blazing. "You'd like that, wouldn't you? You'd go off without me, and I'll look like a perfect fool. Besides that, I'd miss everything!"

Her hairpins had come loose. Tendrils of shiny chestnut hair curled about her chin and straggled down the back of her neck. Her lips looked pinched, but her cheeks flamed.

Sunburn. He'd forgotten to tell her to get a hat. The other thing he'd forgotten was a way to allow her a graceful exit. Such a diplomatic device came easily to him when dealing with the Indians; somehow with Jessamyn, he felt considerably less coolheaded. Nevertheless, he'd give it a try. Anything to get her off that horse.

"Give it up, Jessamyn. No one's judging your reputation based on whether or not you ride that damned horse."

"Maybe you're not," she snapped. "And maybe they're not." She gestured vaguely toward the fence, now crowded shoulder-to-shoulder with hushed onlookers. "But *I* am."

She bent both arms, propped her hands on her hips. A flicker of pain surfaced in her eyes. She'd hurt her elbow. "I don't intend to give up until I can ride that horse!"

She spun away from him. "I'm ready, Gus. Bring him over here."

"Goddamn stubborn Yankee," Ben muttered. The chafing from stiff, new jeans alone would cripple most men. He moved to confront her.

"Jessamyn, listen. You're hurting now. By tomorrow you'll be even more swollen and sore and nothing, no amount of willpower, will get you on a horse again until you've healed."

"Get out of my way, Ben," she said quietly. "I'm going to remount."

"One hell of a goddamned crazy female," he muttered again. But she had grit, he'd say that for her. Might be crazy, but she sure had a soldier's courage.

"Here, put this on." He removed his Stetson, set it atop the drooping mass of hair piled up on her head and snugged it down to shade her nose and cheeks. "You'll get freckles." He pulled the leather gloves from his back pocket and thrust them at her. "And blisters."

She tipped her head up to see past the brim of his too-large hat. For just an instant her eyes softened, then narrowed assessingly. Her hands disappeared into the gloves.

Before she could speak, Ben pivoted and headed for the

fence. Behind him, Gus's low voice rumbled. "Try to squeeze your knees together, Miss Jessamyn. Might help you keep your seat."

Ben risked a surreptitious backward glance. Over Jessamyn's head Gus shot him a curious look and kept on talking.

By the time he reached his place between Jeremiah and Silas Appleby, Jessamyn had remounted. The crowd cheered. Ben clenched his jaw at the accusing look in his deputy's chocolate brown eyes and leaned against the fence to watch.

The picture Jessamyn presented made mincemeat out of his emotions. She sat proud and straight atop the gelding, her head up, the dark Stetson drooping around her ears. His black leather gloves flopped crazily on her slim hands as she clutched the reins. She looked like an outlandishly garbed farmer's scarecrow.

Except that she wasn't grinning. Instead, from the set of her chin and the thin, tense line of her lips, he knew she was fighting back tears. The look of fierce concentration on her face, almost obscured beneath his wide-brimmed hat, made his throat ache.

Under his navy canvas shirt, Ben's heart faltered. She was a sight, all right. Iron-willed determination in a body so delicate it looked as if it would shatter any minute. God, he hoped this time she'd fall loose and roll.

Gus spoke some words, and the oversize hat flopped up and down. Then the wrangler released the bridle.

The gelding stood perfectly still for a full minute. Ben's mouth went dry as a cotton ball.

Without warning, the horse lowered its head and plunged. Jessamyn grabbed for her hat. Ben heard the snap of Jeremiah's jaw as the deputy ground his teeth together.

The horse jerked sideways, and Jessamyn changed her mind about the hat. Instead, she clung to the saddle horn with both hands. The gelding lunged forward, and the hat sailed off into the dirt. Strands of dark hair whipped about her white face as the horse danced and sidestepped about the dusty yard.

Her body tipped, threatened to tumble sideways out of the saddle. She dropped the reins, clamped both hands to the saddle horn again and struggled to right herself. She regained a more or less upright position, and then with a snort, the animal reared into the air.

Ben's breath squeezed to a stop. Jessamyn tilted backward, sliding toward the horse's rump. She threw both arms about the animal's neck. Grabbing handfuls of his mane, she buried her face alongside the gelding's heaving body and held on. Four or five spectators yelled advice.

Gus shouted something. Ben watched her toss away one glove, then the other, and twine her bare fingers deep into the animal's coarse black hair. His own hands clenched into fists so tight his knuckles ached.

The gelding dropped its two front feet onto the ground and raced halfway around the corral. Stopping with a neck-snapping jerk, the animal whinnied and reversed direction. Jessamyn held on. The next time the animal came to a halt, she pulled the toe of her boot free of the stirrup, hoisted her bottom out of the saddle and let herself slip off the horse's back end.

She landed on her feet.

His eyes burning, Ben let himself breathe again. Relief shot through him like hot brandy. Relief and something else—admiration. And pride. He was damned proud of her.

The horse pranced off. Jessamyn staggered two steps to retain her balance, then stood still.

Gus clapped her on the shoulder and offered her the hat and gloves he'd retrieved. She nodded once at the grinning Norwegian, then marched in unsteady steps toward the fence where Ben stood.

A cheer broke out from the spectators, but Jessamyn appeared not to hear.

"Well, I'll be a..." Jeremiah hurrahed, then coughed self-consciously.

Head up, her lips pressed into a determined line, Jessamyn squinted against the late-afternoon sun and headed in
a slightly irregular path toward Ben.

He pushed away from the fence and moved to meet her.

"Newspaper lady, huh?" Silas Appleby disengaged his
boot heels from the fence rail and stepped into the corral
beside Ben. "Mighty pretty. Think I'll just have to renew
my subscription."

Ben frowned at the sandy-haired rancher and stepped to
intercept Jessamyn. Outside of the telltale pink sunburn on
her nose, her face looked pasty white. One shirtsleeve had
come unrolled, and the sagging cuff obscured one hand. In
the other she held his Stetson, upside down, the dusty
leather gloves stuffed into the crown.

She looked straight at him. Her eyes glittered like molten
emeralds, but tears shone on the edges of the lids. A lead
cannonball thunked into Ben's belly.

She shoved the hat into his chest and stalked past him,
hissing a single word into the charged air between them.

"Sunup."

Sunup! God almighty, didn't she know when she was
licked? Hell, she could barely walk steadily! She'd never
make it out of bed tomorrow morning, let alone sit down
for the next week.

In the next instant Jeremiah materialized beside him.
"Never did see the like," he murmured. "C'mon, Colonel.
I'm buyin'."

With a final nod at Gus, now leading the gelding back
to the stable, Ben slapped his Stetson against his thigh and
jammed it on his head. The faint fragrance of roses clung
to the felt, teasing his senses.

"I'll get the second round, Jeremiah. It might be another
long night."

The deputy chuckled as the two men shouldered their
way out of the crowded yard and headed for Charlie's Red
Fox Saloon. "Yessir," Jeremiah said half to himself.

"Downright troublous. Damn magiclike the way they crawl under your skin, isn't it?"

Ben jerked to a stop. "Jeremiah?"

"Colonel?"

"Shut up," Ben said quietly.

A grin split Jeremiah's sun-browned face. "Sure, Ben. Anything for a friend."

Chapter Seven

"Land sakes, if you don't look a sight!" Cora Boult hustled Jessamyn into the warm kitchen. "Let's get you outa them men's duds and right into a tub of hot water!"

With a tired sigh, Jessamyn gave herself over to the fluttery ministrations of the housekeeper. She hurt all over. Her legs shook like unset jelly, and her elbow throbbed where she'd fallen on it. She removed her pinch-toed boots and bent to massage her feet.

"Oh, Cora," she moaned. "Now I know why I don't see many women on horseback out here. They surely must have better—and less painful—things to do!"

Cora clucked sympathetically. "Ridin's like life, Jessamyn. The more you pursue it, the more natural it feels."

Jessamyn rubbed her fingers over every one of her toes, wincing with each motion. Riding would never feel natural to her. She wondered how that Indian girl could look so at ease on a horse, moving as if she and the animal were one being. She knew now what skill that required. Her admiration for Walks Dancing increased.

Cora disappeared onto the back porch, returning in a moment with a metal washtub. "The water's already heatin'," she puffed. "I knowed something was up when Mrs. Frieder stopped by with your skirt and all them petticoats. She didn't say exactly what was goin' on, but I figured it had somethin' to do with horses. Said the whole town was gatherin' down at the livery yard.''

Jessamyn groaned aloud. "Cora, I made such a fool of myself in front of everybody."

Cora propped her hands on her ample hips and watched Jessamyn shed her dirt-streaked jeans and shirt. "Chances are 'twon't make a henfeather's difference. In two days the townsfolk'll have somethin' new to jaw about, and they'll forget all about you."

"Oh!" Jessamyn stopped as if stricken. "But I don't want them to forget it all—just the embarrassing parts. I want every single one of them to subscribe to the *Wildw*— ouch!" She flinched as she eased her sore arm out of the shirtsleeve.

"Come on, child," the housekeeper ordered, gesturing at the washtub. "Climb in."

Dropping her underclothes on the floor, Jessamyn stepped into the tub. The bare cold metal soothed her burning feet.

Cora turned toward the stove, lifted the hissing teakettle with one hand and with the other pumped cold water into a pitcher in the sink. Pouring first from one container, then the other, she gradually filled the tub halfway up the sides.

Jessamyn sat down in the deliciously warm water, bent her legs and rested her forehead on her bare knees. A breath of air at her back told her Cora had slipped out the kitchen door. When she returned, the older woman laid two towels on the floor beside the tub and pressed a rose-scented cake of Emperor Savon soap and a washcloth into her hand.

"Scrub good, honey. You'll be so sore for the next day or so you won't want to move, much less bend yourself into a bathtub!"

"Thank you, Cora," Jessamyn murmured. She let her eyelids drift shut as more hot water dribbled into the tub. She wouldn't think about tomorrow. Not yet, anyway. She'd wait until her back didn't hurt and her legs could function again before she contemplated anything beyond

this moment. Right now she couldn't face even the thought
of getting on a horse again.

The water level rose. "Can you really spare all this water?"

"'Course, child. Afterward, I dump it out on my roses,"
she explained as she poured in another half kettle of steaming liquid. "And," she panted as she clanged the vessel on
the back of the stove, "I got lots and lots of roses."

An hour later Jessamyn sat by the stove in the cozy
kitchen combing out her wet hair. Cora trudged back and
forth between the back porch and her rose garden beside
the house. On her final trip, the bulky housekeeper plopped
a jar down beside her.

"Liniment," she announced. "Gus down at the livery
stable brought it by. Said to rub it in good."

Jessamyn flinched. The thought of anyone—even gentle-
fingered Cora—touching her stiff, sore limbs set her teeth
on edge.

"First, though, soon as you get those tangles combed
out, you'd better have some supper. I stewed a chicken this
afternoon. Dumplings'll be done in a jiffy."

Jessamyn attacked the mass of unruly curls with renewed
vigor. Good Lord, her arms felt stiff and heavy as stove-
pipes.

"You've got beautiful hair, child," Cora said, turning to
inspect a steaming iron pot on the stove. She patted her
own iron gray bun. "So did I, once. Dark red it was. My
Frank used to say it was prettier than his favorite sorrel."

"My hair is just…hair."

"Maybe, but it's nice 'n shiny, and it curls up so pretty
all on its own. How come you pin it up like an old lady?
Hides all them pretty waves!"

"I'm a working woman, Cora. I haven't time for fuss
and feathers. I pin up my hair to keep it out of my eyes
when I'm writing stories for the paper and off my neck
when I'm setting type."

"Harrumph," Cora responded. "Nuthin' but business in

your life can't be much fun." She set plates and utensils out on the kitchen table.

"It is for me," Jessamyn protested softly. "It's all I ever wanted—my own newspaper." And, she added silently, her own house. Her own life. Cora didn't understand, because she'd been a ranch wife, had relished cooking and cleaning for a husband, had wanted to be a man's partner, even the mother of his children. At twenty-six, Jessamyn had no such aspirations. Back in Boston she had been an acknowledged old maid. The day she realized it, a kind of relief had settled into her bones.

Maybe she wasn't like other women. All her life she'd been told she was smarter than most, prettier than some. But looks faded over time. After her mother died, Jessamyn had decided to put all her eggs in the "smarter" basket. Now she was about to get exactly what she'd wanted ever since she was ten years old. And she was prepared to pay whatever it would cost.

Tomorrow morning she'd get her chance to ride into a real Indian camp and gather material firsthand for a feature story she planned to write for her—*her!*—newspaper.

Tomorrow morning? She groaned aloud. Tomorrow was just nine hours away!

Jessamyn flexed her knees and tentatively arched her back, suppressing the moan the movements brought to her lips. Would her body be capable of motion by sunrise?

With her good arm, she reached for the jar of liniment warming on the stove.

Ben stepped inside the *Wildwood Times* office and quickly pulled the heavy oak door shut behind him. After a moment his eyes adjusted to the dark interior. He pocketed the extra key Thad had entrusted to him, drew a candle from his vest pocket and touched the flaming tip of a match to the wick.

A pool of golden light illuminated the cabinet against the wall. Inside were Thad's files, old newspaper issues, correspondence, even the editor's financial records. No clues there. He'd sifted through all the material twice the day after Thad had been shot. Still, some niggling voice drew him back. Maybe he'd missed something.

He tipped the candle, dripped a dollar-sized circle of wax onto the top of the wooden cabinet and stood the flickering tallow shaft in the center. Sliding open the top drawer, he ran his fingers over Thad's black-bound account books.

Suddenly he stopped, staring at a volume he'd never seen before. He swore it had not been there when he'd searched the office after Thad's killing. How had he missed it?

Bound in burgundy leather, it looked like a journal of some sort. With purposeful motions, Ben lifted the volume, opened it flat on the cabinet top and thumbed through the first few pages.

It *was* a journal. Folded letters spilled out, the paper tissue-thin, the ink faded to gold-brown. A lock of silky dark hair tied with a narrow blue ribbon nestled between the pages, then a sepia-toned photograph of a child, a girl with large, serious eyes, dressed in a baggy pinafore, and another of a solemn-faced young woman with flowing dark hair and a rose caught in her waist sash.

Jessamyn. All Jessamyn. Clearly Thad had adored his daughter. No matter that he hadn't once laid eyes on her since he left the East, the crusty newspaper editor hadn't missed one single stage of her growing up. The letter Ben unfolded brimmed with news and anecdotes about Jessamyn, even included school essays written in a careful student hand, scribbled poems, some pen-and-ink drawings.

Jessamyn Whittaker was a most unusual young woman. And it was apparent she had been wrenchingly lonely most of her life. Ben's heart stirred in sympathy.

Ben scanned a second letter, then bundled up the others and slipped them back inside the thick book. They were too personal to pry into.

He turned over a few more leaves of the journal, then paused as one page in particular caught his eye. A column of numbers ran down one side, the figures ranging from eight to forty-two in no particular order. Dates had been scrawled opposite some entries—the most recent only two days before Thad died. On the bottom of the sheet, written in hurried pencil, stretched a series of letters.

Ranch brands, maybe? Or initials? Two had been lined out—D.G. and B.K. His own initials and those of liveryman Dan Gustafsen. Three other sets remained. Thad wasn't an idle doodler; he'd been keeping notes on something. But what? Whatever it was, had it been important enough to get him killed?

Ben riffled through the few remaining pages, then closed the journal and replaced it. After inspecting the remainder of Thad's business files, he slid the drawer closed. An idea began to take shape.

Thad must have discovered something, something that was connected to that column of numbers and dates. A quick scan of the past year's issues of the *Wildwood Times* quickened his pulse.

Exactly as he'd thought. He had to talk to Black Eagle. There was no time to lose. As the new editor of the *Wildwood Times,* Jessamyn might also be in danger.

He puffed out the guttering candle, scraped up the telltale circle of warm candle wax with his thumbnail. Moving noiselessly past the desk and the huge press dominating the room, he eased the door open and locked it behind him.

Pocketing the candle stub and already making his plans, Ben strode across the street to the spartan quarters he and Jeremiah shared in back of the sheriff's office. Tomorrow he'd move fast, ride north and then east toward Black Eagle's hidden camp. He had to make it to Wild Horse Canyon the first night. Riding hard, and alone, he could just do it.

Jessamyn awoke to the chatter of finches in the plum tree outside her second-story bedroom window. Silhouetted against the faint rose-gray light, the leafy branches swayed

and trembled with avian activity. It was not yet dawn, and
already the tiny creatures were gathering their breakfast.

And so must she, if she was to meet Ben Kearney at
sunup. She threw back the yellow patchwork quilt and
yelped with pain. Her back and shoulders felt **as if** they
had been scrubbed up and down on a washboard. It hurt to
move her arms, her hands, her neck. It even hurt to breathe.

God in heaven, the upper half of her body felt as stiff
and brittle as dry cornstalks. If she moved more than an
inch in any direction, her muscles screamed in protest.

Well, it simply couldn't be helped. Taking a deep breath,
Jessamyn clenched her fists and slid her legs toward the
edge of the bed. Agony laced through her buttocks, bit into
her hip sockets. She ground her teeth together and tried not
to groan.

What came out was an unsteady growl, punctuated by a
hissing sound as her breath sucked in past her teeth. She
eased her feet onto the floor, commanding them to support
her weight. Very deliberately, she maneuvered herself into
an upright position, then managed to stand erect on thighs
that quivered.

Standing was one thing. Walking was another. And
mounting a horse…

She blanched at the thought. She had to manage it some
way; otherwise, her ordeal of yesterday would be wasted.
She would do it, she resolved. She wasn't about to let that
smooth-talking sheriff outwit her.

If she could just ignore her aching muscles, force her
body to obey the dictates of her mind. All she had to do
was pull on her jeans and shirt and get down the stairs to
the kitchen, then out the back door to the privy to take care
of her private needs. That shouldn't total more than about
sixty steps.

After some of Cora's strong black coffee, she would
walk—very gingerly—over to the livery stable and talk to
Gus. She could do it! Once she was sitting up on a horse,

she wouldn't have to walk any farther; the horse would take care of that part. All she'd have to do was hold on.

When she'd buttoned her shirt and cinched up the leather belt of her jeans, she looked down at her bare feet. She'd forgotten about the boots. She shoved her feet into them. *Don't think about your toes,* she ordered herself as she stood upright. *Just think about getting to the horse. Think about the look on Ben Kearney's face when he sees you mounted and ready to ride.*

That thought alone stiffened her resolve. With a final tug at the wide leather belt at her waist, Jessamyn half shuffled, half hobbled through her bedroom door and down the stairs, one halting, pain-pulsing step at a time.

Whistling, Ben left the Dixon House hotel dining room and headed for the livery stable. His breakfast of fried eggs and steak had tasted unusually good this morning. The coffee was hot and black, the soft predawn air peaceful and scented with pine, his problem with Miss Jessamyn Whittaker solved.

He looked forward to riding into the hills, unencumbered by a determined newspaper editor with more guts than good sense. Ben relished the quiet of the mountains. He liked being alone. He always had. Sometimes even soft-spoken Jeremiah was too much company, especially when Ben's inner demons needed a bit of settling down.

Lately he'd been having the old nightmares. He knew it was because of the war, but it made no difference. He dreamed the same dream over and over, that his body was split in half from his Adam's apple right down to his crotch. One half was paralyzed. Try as he might, he could not move a single muscle. The other half could move, all right, but it was completely numb; he could feel nothing but the weight of his dead flesh. Only his head remained intact. In his dream he could see, and smell, and hear. And speak.

When he woke and lay sweating in the dark, he knew rationally that he was still a whole man. But inside he felt only half alive, maimed beyond repair in some indefinable way.

Getting away by himself helped. Being alone helped him wrestle his doubts and his memories to a standstill. In the past, riding to see his friend Black Eagle had always afforded solace. Now would be no exception, especially since he'd be traveling solo. Anxious to get started, he turned the corner into the livery yard and stopped short.

In the corral yard a white-faced Jessamyn Whittaker sat stiffly in the saddle of a dappled gray mare. Ben blinked. How in the hell...?

Jessamyn raised her chin a notch. "Good morning, Sheriff."

Scowling, Ben touched his hat brim. "Miss Whittaker." He moved to her side and spoke in a low voice. "Just where do you think you're going?"

"With you, of course. To see Black Eagle." Her green eyes bored into his.

Ben sighed. "I'd like to talk you out of this, Jessamyn. It's—"

"A bargain is a bargain, Ben. You can talk all you want. I'm still going with you."

Mercifully, she said nothing further. Ben studied her as he waited for Gus to bring his horse. Her slim body was engulfed by the man's sheepskin jacket she wore. The shoulders hung off her slight frame, the sleeves doubled back at her wrists. He recognized the hat—Frank Boult's battered dark gray felt with the fancy conchas and feather band around the crown. That hat had been Frank's only vanity. Ben wondered how Cora could bear to part with it, even for a few days.

Tied behind her cantle, a thick bedroll and a saddlebag drooped over the mare's broad back. The bedroll looked fat enough to have a feather pillow or two wrapped up inside.

Ben groaned aloud. The last thing he wanted was company. And the absolutely worst company he could think of was a nosy Yankee female, a soft, citified woman like Jessamyn Whittaker, who'd need nursemaiding every mile of the way. Dammit, a woman like that made him feel... paralyzed.

Gus brought his bay, already saddled. "That gray's nice and gentle," the Norwegian murmured as Ben caught the bridle.

"Should be," Ben breathed. "That's Widow Boult's mare, Lady. I broke her myself that summer Frank was laid up."

Gus nodded. "If someone asks, Ben, are you riding 'south,' like always?"

"South," Ben acknowledged. "Jeremiah knows where I'm really going." He grasped the saddle horn with his left hand and swung himself up into the saddle.

Gus grinned. "Good hunting, then." Ben moved the horse toward the corral gate. Over his shoulder he spoke to Jessamyn. "We've got forty miles to cover. If you can't keep up, better turn back."

Jessamyn straightened her back. Ben saw that it hurt her, but she just lifted her chin and pressed her lips together.

"I'll keep up." She sawed on the reins until Lady nosed after his bay. "I'll keep up with you, Ben Kearney, if it's the last thing I ever do in this life."

Ben threw a quick glance behind him as he walked his horse out the gate Gus held open. The last thing he saw before he turned north was the ever-widening grin on the liveryman's face.

Jessamyn kicked the dappled mare into a faster gait, suppressing a moan of anguish as her backside bounced against the hard leather saddle. Already Ben had pulled far ahead of her, despite his apparently casual pace. She clamped her jaw tight and shut her physical discomfort out of her mind.

Just concentrate on not losing sight of that horse ahead of you, she ordered herself. *Don't think beyond the next hour.* She was a Whittaker. She could stand anything for an hour.

Couldn't she? Up to this moment Jessamyn had believed—or at least tried to convince the outside world—that she was invincible. Miss Leather Drawers, her school friends at Miss Bennett's Academy had called her. She wondered what Miss Bennett would think about one of her "laces and graces" graduates jouncing off on a trip into the mountains with a man. Alone and unchaperoned.

She choked back another moan. Miss Bennett would say she was ruined. Well, maybe just compromised. But Miss Bennett had never been to Oregon. Things were certainly different out West. Gus hadn't raised an eyebrow when she'd asked him to saddle the mare for her and told him she was accompanying the sheriff.

Even Cora accepted the situation in her usual matter-of-fact manner. "Take Frank's winter jacket and keep wrapped up good at night." Then she'd bustled about gathering together some food and a bedroll, tucked in a pair of her own almost new leather riding gloves, a tiny bottle of brandy "for snakebite," and the jar of liniment.

Dust puffed into the still air behind the gelding's busy hooves. She could breathe in the choking stuff, or she could drop farther back. She didn't dare fall too far behind. Ben had left the main road out of town and now headed cross-country on a little-used trail that, to her eyes, was almost invisible.

Pulling a blue bandanna out of her pocket with one hand, she managed to fold it in half and hold it against her mouth and nose. Even though this horse seemed extraordinarily docile compared with Dancer Jack, she didn't dare let go of the saddle horn and the reins long enough to tie the kerchief around her face. If she slipped off, she knew she'd never get back on by herself.

Why, she wondered suddenly, had Dancer Jack been so feisty? Was Cora's mare just waiting for her to relax so she could toss her off onto the ground? A flood of misgiving surged through her. Was she really doing the right thing, riding off alone to some godforsaken place with a man she barely knew? Maybe she *was* a "goddamn crazy woman," as the sheriff had said.

But Papa wouldn't think so! She just knew he wouldn't. Ever since she'd accidentally discovered his private journal, hidden deep inside the mattress he'd slept on at the newspaper office, had read through the letters she and her mother had written to him over the years, studied the thumb-worn photographs of herself, she knew Papa had believed in her.

Even now she often felt him close to her, as if his spirit were hovering near, whispering soundlessly in her inner ear. Papa would be proud of her, persevering in her twofold quest to find his killer and launch her newspaper with a blockbuster news story.

Her eyes stung from the dust kicked up by Ben's horse. She'd had enough of the hot, chokingly thick air clogging her nostrils for the past three hours. Why couldn't she ride beside him?

Smiling for the first time all morning, Jessamyn nudged the mare's ribs with her boot heels, and the horse jerked forward.

Ben heard the hoofbeats, but he didn't alter his speed. He'd been listening to the steady clop-clop of Jessamyn's mare behind him, wondering how long before the newspaper editor admitted she couldn't keep up his pace and turned back to town. He was surprised she'd lasted this long, considering the dust drifting up behind the gelding. In fact, he was surprised she could sit a horse at all, even a refined mare like Lady, after what she'd been through yesterday.

He arched an eyebrow as Jessamyn sawed clumsily on the reins and fell in beside him. He didn't want her along, didn't want her anywhere near him, much less riding at his elbow. But he had to hand it to her, she was tougher than her delicate looks and ladylike manner hinted. A lot tougher. If he weren't so mad at her for managing to out-maneuver him, he'd admire her pluck.

Jessamyn Whittaker was certainly one of a kind, annoy-ing though she could be. Jessamyn was…different. In a way, he conceded, he rather liked her.

On the other hand, he reminded himself as his gut tight-ened, she frightened him. Jessamyn was a lady—one of those women who expected things from a man. She un-nerved him. She made him keenly aware that he *was* a man. When he was around her, he felt somehow weighed in the balance and found wanting.

"Sheriff Kearney?" Jessamyn panted when she could talk.

Ben tried not to react to the slight quaver in her voice. "Miss Whittaker?"

"Could…could I ride beside you?"

Something flopped inside Ben's belly. Part of him wanted to spur his horse forward, away from her, lose him-self in the mountains where he couldn't hear that soft, throaty voice. Another part of him wanted to keep her near just so he could inhale the flowery scent of her hair, sur-reptitiously watch her eyes change from sea to shamrock green the way they did when she was angry.

"Suit yourself," he heard himself say.

He clamped his lips together. Even turned out in men's jeans and a too-large shirt, she looked—and smelled—like a woman. A distinctive, unusual woman. He shut his eyes for a long moment. The pull she exerted on his senses got under his skin and stayed there. He didn't need this—not this morning or any other morning. But it looked as if he didn't have much of a choice. He groaned inwardly. Hell, it seemed, was now in session.

There lay the rub. He *did* need it. That was why he re-sisted it so fiercely. He wasn't sure he could explain this to anyone, even to Jeremiah, but he recognized the truth of his perception. It resonated within him as clearly as a re-verberating church bell.

He liked her.

Ben gritted his teeth. All the more reason for him to keep his distance. He wasn't about to get burned by a woman twice in his lifetime. Once, in Carolina after the war, was enough for any man.

Chapter Eight

Ben Kearney, Jessamyn decided, was fashioned of toughened leather with iron bolts where his joints should be. Far ahead of her, he moved easily on the dark gelding, maintaining a bone-crunching pace hour after hour with no letup.

She had given up trying to keep pace with him. "That man," she muttered, "rides for hours on end and never even looks rumpled!" She could hate him without much encouragement. Not once had she seen him even look back to check on her. She could topple head over boots into the river and drown for all he cared.

But she wouldn't. She'd stay on Cora's mare until the sheriff called a halt. Surely he had to rest *some*time? And he had to eat! She began to count the hours before lunch.

The trail wound on through the long, gold-green valley, following the tumbling Umpqua River. Her backside bounced against the animal moving beneath her, and at every step her thigh muscles quivered in protest. The sun climbed higher, a searing magenta ball in the sky, and the pepperminty scent of Gus's liniment rose from her heated skin.

Abruptly, Ben turned east, away from the river, and struck out toward the hills, now a luminous yellow-green where the sunlight washed the ridge. Jessamyn followed the path of flattened grass where his horse had trod, pulling down the brim of her hat to shade her eyes. She kept her gaze riveted on his erect back as he shed his jacket, showing a sweat-soaked shirt underneath.

He turned in the saddle, watching as she picked up the trail. He rolled up the sleeves of his navy blue shirt to his elbows, wiped his bandanna over his forehead. Aha! Ben Kearney was suffering from heat and thirst just as she was! Without thinking, she kicked the mare and surged forward. She didn't want to miss a minute of his discomfort.

The closer she got, the less uncomfortable the sheriff looked. His horse moved effortlessly up the path through the rock-strewn foothills while Jessamyn rocked back and forth in the saddle, trying desperately to keep up. As Gus had instructed her, she leaned forward while ascending the steep parts, tipped back on the descents to balance her weight on the horse. Never mind that Lady turned out to be surefooted and steady—she quelled a flutter in her chest every time the mare started up an incline.

In spite of her discomfort, she smiled in satisfaction. Her first week out on the Oregon frontier, and she was sitting a horse, ready to capture the unsuspecting sheriff with her writing skills and immortalize him in print. He didn't know it, but he was going to sell newspapers for her like hotcakes to hungry husbands.

Ben never slackened his pace. He even drank on the move, twisting in the saddle and signaling her to do the same. The water in her canteen was lukewarm and salty. She fought back the urge to retch when she tasted it, forced herself to gulp a mouthful. Her eyes ached from the harsh glare of the sun off the rocks. For minutes on end she rode with her lids closed.

If they didn't stop soon, she would expire with exhaustion. She surveyed the surrounding shrubs and twisted pine trees, stunted from the hot wind, then glanced back at the valley below.

She gripped Lady's reins tight, fighting dizziness as she

gazed down at the verdant valley floor far beneath her. Now she guessed Ben would not stop until he reached their first night's camp. They had to get there before dark—how many hours would that be? Two? Three? She tried to judge time by the position of the sun. Good Lord, she'd been stuck on this saddle for eight hours!

She couldn't make it, couldn't go on any longer. She peered ahead of him, searching for a visible break in the mountainside, a pass, an arched rock—anything that would indicate an end to the physical torture of this endless, sun-scorched day.

Nothing.

Just when she thought she could not stand one more jolting step, the trail made a sharp turn and slanted down into a narrow, green valley. A tiny jewel of a lake, the water a shimmering turquoise blue, spread twenty paces ahead of them. Ben raised his arm and reined his horse to a halt.

"Thank God," Jessamyn moaned aloud. Just a few seconds more and she could climb down off this horse and collapse. She drew up beside Ben's gelding.

"We'll camp here," he announced.

Jessamyn let the reins go slack and leaned forward, bowing her aching head until her chin almost grazed her chest. "Thank you, God," she murmured.

Ben's low, gravelly voice jarred her. "Can you dismount?"

She stiffened. "Dismount? Why, of course I can dismount. What an inane question! The hard part is getting *on* a horse, not getting off."

Ben studied her, a speculative look in his smoky blue eyes. "Wait a minute. I'll help you down."

Oh, no, he wouldn't! She kicked her right toe free of the stirrup and tried to hoist her leg up. It refused to budge one single inch. She tried again, grimacing with the effort. No amount of willpower made a difference—her body simply refused to obey.

Ben dismounted and moved toward her. He took one

look at Jessamyn's flushed, sweaty face, her eyes gray-green with fatigue, and a wash of guilt flooded him. He shouldn't have pressed her so hard. After the first three hours on the old Indian trail he'd followed, he knew she wasn't going to turn back, no matter what. Part of him resented her presence. Part of him admired her spirit.

There was no room for a woman on a journey like this. While he knew Black Eagle as well as he knew any man, and trusted him more than some, he wasn't so sure about the Klamath braves gathered about the venerable old chief. They'd fled to Black Eagle to escape the reservation. Any one of the young hotheads could shoot Ben in the back before he was recognized, could kidnap Jessamyn—or worse. That hair of hers alone would attract all kinds of unwanted interest.

Jessamyn sat motionless in the saddle. He noted the exhausted droop of her shoulders as he moved toward the placid gray mare, already nibbling shoots of tender grass. The woman's chin came up as he approached.

"I can dismount," she said, fierce pride in her voice. "I just can't move my right leg."

Ben reached up with both hands. "Lean toward me."

With slow, tired motions, she wound the reins about the saddle horn and tipped sideways in his direction. He caught her about the waist, hauled her out of the saddle and set her on the ground facing him.

The instant he loosened his grip, her legs gave way. She clutched at his arm for support. "Can't stand up," she muttered. "Merciful heaven, my legs have died!"

Ben choked back a chuckle. "They're not dead, Jessamyn. Just played out. You need to keep moving—walk around a bit. Maybe dunk 'em in the lake. The cold water will bring them back to life."

Her fingers tightened on his arm. "I can't move, much less make it to the water." Her head dropped so low the crown of her hat brushed his chin. Mixed with the smell of horse and sweat and liniment, the sweet fragrance of her hair rose to his nostrils. Ben closed his eyes and drew in a long, slow breath. Goddamn, but she smelled good.

She was trembling, her body shuddering just enough to tell him she was completely spent. She needed food and rest. And some easing of the muscle spasms in her legs. She didn't have the strength to walk even the short distance to the lake.

"Come on," he said more gruffly than he intended. "Got to get you moving." He slid one arm across the back of her red plaid shirt and hooked his thumb in the belt loop at her waist. Turning her, he urged her forward. "Walk," he ordered.

She clung to his left forearm. "I—"

"Walk!"

"Can't!"

"Try, dammit!"

"I *am* trying! My legs don't w-work." Her voice sounded close to breaking.

"All right," he said softly. He scooped her up into his arms and carried her to the water's edge. The tarn glittered blue-green in the late-afternoon sun. He tossed her out into the middle.

She screamed. In the next instant she sank, bottom-first, up to her neck. Sputtering, she thrashed upward, her arms flailing like windmill blades.

Ben heaved a sigh of relief. At least she could move her arms. Her legs would work, too, in a few moments. The cold water was just what she needed.

"You snake!" Jessamyn screamed. She fought her way to a wobbly upright position, water sluicing off her shoulders. In the next instant she tipped sideways and sat down again with a splash.

"I can't walk!" she wailed, her eyes widening in terror. "I can't even stand up!"

Ben hesitated, then waded into the water after her. Grasping her upper arms, he hoisted her to a standing position and gripped the wide belt around her waist to steady her.

With small, deliberate steps, he half walked, half dragged her to the gravelly shore, where she struggled for footing. At last she made an unsteady turn to face him.

Ben released her. She opened her mouth to speak, but instead clamped her jaws shut and drilled him with eyes that flashed emerald fire. Water dripped off her hat brim, coursed in rivulets off her shirt and jeans. Her lower lip trembled. She caught it between her teeth as moisture pooled in her eyes.

That did it. Ben spun on his heel and strode to the horses. He had no defense against a woman's tears.

Catching the mare's bridle, he unsaddled the animal and picketed it with his gelding. Lifting Jessamyn's saddlebag and bedroll from behind the cantle, he laid them at the thick base of a wind-sculpted fir tree.

The *squish-squish* of wet boots at his back told him she was moving. He grinned, keeping his head down so she wouldn't see him. The icy bath had done her stiff muscles good. Now she had to get out of those wet clothes and keep her limbs moving.

He rummaged behind his saddle for a blanket, unrolled it and held it out to her. "You'll need this around you."

"I won't—"

In one swift move Ben enveloped her shivering form in army-issue wool.

"I'm n-not c-cold," she snapped.

"Suit yourself," Ben replied. "But take off your wet things anyway. Toss them over that huckleberry bush near the horses. In this heat, they'll be dry in an hour. I'll get a fire going and fix supper."

"What about my boots? They're soaked through, and so are my stockings!"

"They'll dry, too. Pull them off."

"I...I...um...can't seem to bend over."

Ben laughed softly. He knew how much that remark had cost her. Just like Thad, he thought. Pride so big and shiny she'd rather die than admit she wasn't invincible. Thad sure as hell hadn't been invincible; the crusty old editor had died trying to prove it. But Jessamyn...

Oh, hell. Thad's stiff-necked daughter was tired and cold and hungry and needed her boots yanked off. Ben chuckled deep in his chest. She'd never admit it out loud, but she needed help. *His* help.

For some reason, he liked that. A grin tugged at his lips, then he sobered instantly. Goddammit, he didn't *want* to like it. He didn't want to like one thing about Jessamyn Whittaker.

"Sit down on that flat rock behind you and stick your foot out," he ordered.

With a groan, Jessamyn gingerly settled her bottom on the granite seat Ben indicated and tried to raise her leg. She hadn't the strength. After her third attempt, she shook her head at him. Tears gathered in the corners of her eyes, and she bit her lip, hard.

Ben dropped the handful of sticks and small branches he'd gathered for kindling and strode to her side. Turning his back to her, he dropped to one knee, grasped the slick leather boot in both hands and tugged it off. Her stocking came with it, leaving her bare foot exposed.

He stared down at the delicate-looking appendage, the high, curved arch, five dainty toes and a slender ankle. Her feet were exquisite!

Jessamyn moaned in relief as the boot pulled free, and the hair on Ben's forearms prickled. He wanted to hear it again. He wondered suddenly if she would make a sound like that if he kissed her.

He covered her icy feet with both hands, rubbed his palms slowly over the soft skin to stimulate the circulation. She murmured something, her voice drowsy, and Ben sucked in his breath. Blood pounded into his groin. He gritted his teeth in exasperation as his body throbbed to life.

He dropped her foot as if it were a hot coal and quickly removed the other boot, taking care not to touch the white, smooth skin. Jessamyn made a low noise in her throat. On the back of her heel rose an angry red patch. Tomorrow she'd have a blister the size of a two-bit piece.

Ben snagged her boots, fished out the wet stockings and tossed the tiny garments into her lap. "Add these to the laundry bush along with your jeans and shirt and—"

"Yes," she interrupted. "I will."

Shaken, Ben stalked toward the rock-ringed fire pit. Reaching into his pocket for a match, he squatted to arrange the tinder and get the fire going. On purpose, he kept his back to her.

After a few moments he heard the unmistakable sound of wet clothing plopping onto the ground. He listened intently, counting the garments. Four. Two large—jeans and her shirt. And two small—her drawers and some kind of camisole, he guessed. Probably lace.

The picture he conjured in his mind took his breath away. He groaned and tried to concentrate on the fire.

Flames licked at the kindling. He laid on some small fir branches and dry bark, then lifted Jessamyn's boots and stuffed dry grass into the toes, ramming it tight with a stone. He set them a short distance from the fire.

"Move them closer," Jessamyn's voice called from behind the huckleberry bush.

Ben ignored her. Closer to the fire would dry them too fast and they'd stiffen up and crack. The woman knew absolutely nothing about survival on the trail. She'd been sheltered all her life like a Boston houseplant. He shook his head. A person had to be a little bit touched to make a trip like this with as little preparation as she had. No newspaper was worth risking your skin for.

At the thought of her skin, his breath caught. He'd bet money her thighs were chafed all the way to her...

"Cora send any supplies with you?" he blurted to stop the direction of his thoughts.

"She did," Jessamyn responded.

Ben started. Her voice was startlingly close.

"Some coffee and bacon, I think."

"Anything for sore muscles or..." His voice died. He couldn't bring himself to utter the word *thighs*. Best not think about any part of her body. He was painfully aware she was not five feet from him and completely naked under the tan wool blanket.

"Gus sent over some liniment last night. In my saddlebag. I'll get it."

"*I'll* get it," Ben countered. "You won't be able to bend over for a week."

Jessamyn gasped. "A week! What about my newspaper? I have an issue to get out in six days! Running the press takes..." She paused, gnawing her lower lip. "Bending."

Ben studied the stubborn tilt to her chin. "Hire somebody." He turned away, knelt by her saddlebag.

"Your deputy, Jeremiah, could help me."

Ben reached inside the leather pouch. A silk-soft garment caressed his hand as he felt for the jar of liniment. "Jeremiah has better things to do."

"But he's interested in the newspaper! Truly he is. He told me all about his schooling with you when he was young. Jeremiah's so proud that he can read and write—he greatly admires the written word."

Jeremiah, Ben thought, talked too damn much.

"*Could* Jeremiah help?" Jessamyn pursued.

Good Lord, what a single-minded woman. She was Thad's daughter, all right—bone stubborn clear through.

A welcome anger flooded his brain, a relief after the hot tongue of desire that had flamed a few moments earlier. And the searing, dangerous flicker of vulnerability that licked at him.

He couldn't afford to be vulnerable. His heart was split in two, lifeless as a cracked church bell. And his soul... God almighty, his soul was black with bitterness at the Northerners who had destroyed everything he'd ever loved in life.

He jerked upright and slapped the liniment into Jessa-

myn's outstretched hand. "Rub it in good," he growled.
He grimaced at the picture that floated into his mind's eye.
He saw his own hand, fingers splayed, moving slowly back
and forth on Jessamyn's pale skin.

Swearing under his breath, he grabbed the graniteware
coffeepot and tramped off to the lake for water.

How could he stand being around her twenty-four hours
a day for the next three days? And nights, he reminded
himself. She was maddening. Stubborn. Naive. Annoying.

And—did he say stubborn? He knelt over the coffeepot,
dumped in a handful of ground beans, then glanced back
at her, seated on a flat, sunny rock swathed in army wool,
finger-combing the tumbled mass of dark, wet hair.

She was beautiful. She made him ache she was so beautiful. If only she'd keep her mouth shut.

On second thought, he amended, let her talk! When she
talked, sooner or later he got angry. When he got angry, it
was easy to hate her. After all, she was a Yankee. A
damned know-it-all, winner-take-all Yankee.

Yes, let her talk.

Jessamyn watched the sheriff settle the coffeepot on the
flat rocks edging the campfire, then shake the smoke-
blackened pan in which four slices of Cora's bacon sizzled.
She closed her eyes and inhaled the tantalizing smell. She
hadn't eaten since breakfast—no wonder she was hungry!
Her stomach grumbled in anticipation.

She tightened her belly. She would not whine for supper
like a child. However long it took, she would wait it out
in refined silence.

She averted her eyes, watched instead the mare grazing
nearby, inspected her sore toes and finally forced her gaze
to her clothes spread on the huckleberry bush to dry. With
slow, painful motions, she rose, gathered up all the garments and stepped behind the spreading shrub to put them
on. She managed to get both her stiff legs into her jeans
just as Ben announced supper was ready.

"Bacon and hardtack," he said. "Coffee's in the pot."

Jessamyn settled herself on the flat rock beside the fire and took the tin plate and bent metal fork he proffered. "Hardtack?"

A frown creased the sheriff's tanned forehead. "You complaining?"

"Goodness, no! I—I've just never eaten hardtack before." She eyed the square cracker on her plate. Right now she was so hungry she didn't care what it tasted like. She poked it with her fork. When it neither bent nor broke apart, she picked it up in her fingers and took a bite.

She chewed a long, long time before she could swallow the gummy mess. It felt like a thick layer of leather in her mouth, and it tasted like toasted newspapers. Awful. But the bacon was savory enough for a king. A starving one, anyway.

She gobbled it down, then stretched her bare toes toward the fire and sighed with satisfaction. Deprivation enhanced simple things like food and warmth. Pleasure, she was learning out here in the wilds of the Oregon frontier, was relative.

She stared past the sheriff's rangy form to the narrow valley just beyond his shoulder. The tall trees were still visible in the tawny light of approaching dusk.

"Do—do Indians ever come here?"

Balancing the tin plate on his folded legs, Ben grunted. "Sometimes."

"What do they do?"

"Do?" He looked up from his supper. In the firelight his skin was bronzy gold. "Hunt. Pray. Hide out. Make love, maybe."

Jessamyn jerked upright. "I beg your pardon?"

Ben leveled a steady look at her across the flickering fire. "Sometimes an Indian girl being courted will invite the brave to meet her somewhere away from the camp. This is a good spot for a tryst. They come here in the fall, before the snow."

"Oh. Are there any here now?"

"Probably."

Jessamyn gasped. "Where? Do they know we're here?"

Ben scraped his plate leavings into the fire. "They do. They've been watching us all day."

"Watching us?" Her scalp prickled. Instinctively she hitched her body closer to the fire.

Ben gave a low laugh. "Indians don't miss much that goes on in these hills. But don't worry—most of them know me."

"What about the ones who don't?" she blurted. Oh, how she hated it when her voice shook. It was so…undignified. Miss Bennett always advised taking three deep breaths before speaking under duress.

Miss Bennett! Jessamyn choked back an unladylike whoop of laughter. Miss Bennett would faint dead away at the sight of her pupil hunched on the ground in men's clothes with her feet—her *naked* feet—in full view of a strange man, gobbling bacon with her bare hands!

"What about the Indians who *don't* know you?" she repeated.

Ben set his plate aside and reached for the steaming coffeepot. "Unless they were babes in cradle boards when I last visited, any Indian in these parts who doesn't recognize me has at least heard of me."

"What about me? They wouldn't know me! They'll think I'm a stranger. A man!"

Ben chuckled. "No Indian is that nearsighted."

Nevertheless, she wished she had four sturdy walls and a roof about her. Or a tent! Even a thin canvas wall would shut out the specter of unidentifiable night shadows.

She watched in silence as Ben poured himself a tin mug of coffee, then filled another and passed it to her. He gulped his in mouthfuls while she took ladylike sips. She drank in silence until she could see the grounds in the bottom of the mug.

"Time for bed," Ben announced.

Bed! Jessamyn eyed him over the edge of her cup. Where would she sleep? Where would *he* sleep?

Ben retrieved both bedrolls and spread his blankets out by the fire, then stretched out full-length, propping his head on his saddle. Jessamyn unrolled her bedroll on the opposite side of the fire. Pointing her feet toward the glowing coals, as Ben had done, she pulled on clean wool stockings and curled up on the makeshift pallet.

The night air was warm and soft, scented with woodsmoke and pine. This *would* be a good trysting place, she acknowledged. In the ebbing light the peaceful lake shone like a blue-black sapphire.

If *she* were an Indian maiden...

A hot flush washed through her chest, and she instantly squelched the thought.

A night bird shrilled in the tree branches. Jessamyn slid into a resting position, laying her head in the curve of her saddle. If she were an Indian maiden, alone with her chosen lover in a place as lovely as this, high above the civilized world, she would...

She would what? What on earth was the matter with her?

She stared up at the handful of stars glittering like jewels against the darkening sky. Never in her life had such a thought entered her mind. She closed her eyes. But then, never in her life had she experienced anything like the past twenty-four hours! Up until now, she had had a safe, protected life. Predictable. Insulated.

Her eyelids popped open. She gazed at the campfire, the blackened graniteware coffeepot, the body of the man sprawled on his side not two feet away, watching her with thoughtful dusky blue eyes.

This was real life. Dust and heat, hunger and sweat, unbearable pain and simple, exquisite pleasures like a cup of hot coffee on a full belly, or the look on Ben's ordinarily stern face when he was amused. She caught her breath. Or the feel of Ben's strong, knowing hands about her waist.

This—and not Boston—was real. This was what she'd

come out West to experience, to share with Papa. To write about.

But dear God in heaven, now that she'd tasted a big pungent mouthful of life as it really was, she wasn't sure she liked it!

She muffled a groan, closed her eyes and tried to recite a prayer.

The next thing she knew, someone was shaking her shoulder.

"Wake up, Jessamyn. It'll be light soon."

She moaned and cracked one eyelid. It couldn't possibly be morning already. Stars still shone overhead. She shivered under the scratchy blanket, brought her knees up to her chest. Her legs were so stiff and sore she could barely move them.

"Time to get moving," Ben's low, resonant voice reminded her. She snuggled deeper into her cocoon. The last thing she wanted to do was face another day like yesterday.

A metallic clunk close to her ear brought her head out from under the blanket. On the ground beside her sat a brimming tin cup. Coffee! He must have risen early to build up the fire and make it—or maybe the brew was reheated from the night before.

She pulled the blanket around her and sat up, reaching one hand for the steaming cup. The campfire crackled. She shifted her back toward the heat. Oh, if she could only stay in this one position for the rest of the day. Moving even one muscle of her battered body was a painful ordeal. And climbing on a horse…

Two long, denim-clad legs planted themselves before her. "You want me to roll you up inside the blanket and tie you on behind your saddle?" Ben's deep, gravelly voice carried a hint of humor.

"It's so early! It's not even light yet."

"Time's wasting. Want to beat as much of the midday

sun as possible, unless you like being fried on both sides like a sausage on a spit.''

Sausage! Her mouth watered at the thought. ''May we eat breakfast first?''

''Nope. We'll eat jerky and dry biscuits on the trail.'' He strode off toward the gelding, grazing a few yards beyond the fire. On the way, he scooped up her boots, dumped out the rocks and grass he'd stuffed into the toes, and placed them near her. ''You need help putting them on?''

''Certainly not!'' She'd manage somehow. She had experienced the oddest feeling yesterday when he'd pulled off her boots and stockings—her breath damming in her chest, the man scent of him making her senses reel.

She had felt off balance, as if at any moment she might be swept off a secure rock by a rambunctious river. She liked the smell of him, but the sensations it evoked puzzled her. She'd put on her own boots, thank you. Nothing could be worse than riding for hours. She had lived through yesterday; she could live through today.

She gulped another mouthful of the coffee, gritted her teeth, tossed back the blanket, and stood up. Every muscle in her body rebelled. Her back and shoulders tightened in protest, her calves and thighs quivered with the effort. The smallest motion of either leg made her derriere feel as if a giant hand had gripped one cheek and wrenched it. She felt the pull all the way up to her rib cage.

Tears rose in her eyes as she took her first step forward. She smothered a groan and took another step. By the time she reached her boots, she knew she was in trouble. She calculated the additional distance to the mare.

Ben loaded the saddlebags. When his back was toward her, she bent her knee and raised her leg. Biting her lower lip, she stuffed her foot into the boot top, then stepped down hard.

Overnight, the boots seemed to have shrunk one size. Balancing precariously on one foot, she lifted her other leg, aimed her toe into the leather hole and plunged it downward. She'd have to bend down to pull the boots up tight.

She took a deep breath and tried it. Her spine felt as if it would snap. She wasn't a horsewoman and never would be. But she was still a crack reporter. She wanted her first edition to be one Papa would be proud of—chock-full of timely hard news items and thoughtful, uplifting editorials. She'd won many Boston readers for the *Herald* with her eyewitness accounts of events. The day she rode a bicycle around the Commons in bloomers instead of a long skirt, ninety-seven new subscriptions had poured in—all from women!

She could do that out here. She *had* to do it here. She needed good story material and a siren's tongue. This piffling matter of getting her boots on and climbing back on the mare was merely a temporary difficulty.

Ben's lanky frame appeared in her path, the collar of his navy shirt open to reveal his throat and the narrow purple scar that disappeared into the sprinkling of black hair on his chest. Hands on his hips, he studied her as she shuffled toward him.

"Good God, you're all but crippled!"

"Am not," she managed despite the throbbing of her calf muscles. "Just can't get my boots all the way on."

Without a word, Ben moved to her side and knelt on one knee. Reaching his arms around her leg, he grasped the boot top in both hands and gave a short, hard tug. She cried out as her heel slipped into place.

Wobbling, she laid one hand on Ben's hard shoulder to steady herself, felt the taut muscles play under her splayed fingers as he jerked the other boot upward. Another jolt of pain. Jessamyn bit her lip to keep from crying.

His low chuckle set her teeth on edge. Did he enjoy watching her suffer hour after hour in the merciless sun?

"Can you mount?"

Jessamyn quailed at the thought. "Certainly," she snapped.

"Suit yourself," Ben said amiably. He stalked off, whistling a tune she couldn't help recognize—"Bonnie Blue Flag."

That's it! Jessamyn said to herself. *It's because of that damned war. He's a Rebel, and I'm a Northerner. He hates me!*

Anger flooded her with new resolve. Well, then. This Northerner would just show him why the Yankees won the war: backbone! Clenching her fists at her sides, she stomped toward the horse with deliberate, pain-ravaged steps.

Ben positioned himself at the mare's head, the bridle held casually in his hand. He waited for her, singing a new tune under his breath in a soft baritone.

"I'll sell my horse, and I'll sell my cattle,
    You can go to hell in your boots and saddle."

Jessamyn moved toward him with murder in her heart.

Chapter Nine

If it was the last thing she ever did, Jessamyn swore under her breath, she would mount that mare with no help from Ben Kearney. The sheriff surveyed her calmly, a grin creasing his bronzed skin. Snatching the reins out of his hand, she reached up and gripped the saddle horn. Now all she had to do was get her foot into the stirrup.

On her third attempt, Ben caught her boot heel in his palm and lifted her foot into the iron crescent. Jessamyn sucked in her breath as her muscles rebelled. Without a word, the sheriff dipped at the knees and put one hand and his shoulder under her backside. His palm scorched the skin under her denims like a red-hot brand. Miss Bennett would have fainted dead away!

The instant he touched her he stopped whistling, but he did not remove his hand. Heat surged through the lower half of her body, searing her backside into reluctant awareness.

He pushed, and she flew upward. Stunned, she swung her leg over the horse's rump and settled into the saddle.

Ben mounted his gelding and with a click of his tongue moved off ahead of her. Jessamyn sat motionless for a full minute before she urged the mare forward, pulling her hat brim low against the blinding sunlight bathing the trail.

She didn't belong out here in the middle of nowhere on

a horse she could barely ride. No matter how much she wanted to gather material for her newspaper, she wasn't equipped for this kind of life. If it weren't for Ben Kearney, she would be cold, hungry and lost.

At the thought, she tossed her head in defiance. If it weren't for Ben Kearney, she'd be home in her own blissfully soft bed with Cora downstairs banging the breakfast frying pan onto the iron cookstove and the scent of roses floating on the still morning air.

She resented her dependence on the sheriff. She'd been self-sufficient all her adult years, and dependence frightened her. The minute you relied on a person, they deserted you. Papa had left to come out West; Mama had died and left her alone.

What if something happened to Ben out here in the wilderness? Without him, she would be completely helpless.

Besides that, she had this odd fluttering in her belly when he so much as helped her onto her horse. Damn the man!

Jessamyn ground her teeth in frustration and kicked the mare into a faster pace. All the discomfort and unease would be worth it in the end, she supposed, when she published her first edition. She'd think about that, not her chafed inner thighs. And not Ben Kearney.

Jolting over the narrow, twisting trail, choking on the dust kicked up by Ben's horse ahead of her, she began to compose in her head the first paragraph of her lead story.

Late in the afternoon the trail disappeared. The horses clattered over rocks for a quarter of an hour, and then halted at the entrance to a deep, narrow canyon. Jessamyn craned her neck to see the sun.

Three hours until dark, she judged. As far as she could tell, they weren't anywhere near Black Eagle's camp.

She peered beyond Ben. A steep rock face rose on both sides of them, cutting out sunlight and dissipating the hot wind that had blown all morning. The mare's hooves rang against the stones as they descended into the cool shade, fragrant with pine and spruce. Sheer rock walls faced her on all sides, and at the far end a waterfall tumbled. There was no way out.

Ben twisted in the saddle, motioning toward the spill of water. Was he going to give her another drenching in an icy bath? He moved forward, and she hesitated. Then, with a shudder, she kicked the mare. She had no choice but to follow him.

They walked their mounts beside a narrow, gurgling stream that flowed to the end of the canyon and disappeared into a gaping rock cave. As they drew near the falls, Ben shouted something and pointed. The roar of the water drowned out his words. Mist swirled around her, and the mare whinnied nervously.

Ben stopped the gelding close to the water's edge, then turned in the saddle. Satisfied that she was still following him, he plunged into the blue-green pool and ducked under the falls. Jessamyn gasped. The sheriff simply vanished, horse and all.

Impossible, she reasoned. He had merely ridden smack-dab under the waterfall. Lord in heaven, he expected her to do the same! Following this man was an adventure in itself.

With care she stepped her mare into the water. Drawing a deep breath, she clapped her hat on tight, closed her eyes and nudged the animal under the falls.

The water hit her like an avalanche of rocks pounding down onto her head and shoulders. For an agonizing moment she couldn't breathe, and then suddenly the roaring ceased. The horse plodded into an echoey cavern hidden behind the falls. Jessamyn opened her eyes.

The trail slanted almost straight up, winding between shoulder-high gray-green lichen-covered rocks. After another twenty yards she emerged into warm afternoon sunshine. Beyond, a high, green valley opened before her. Surely she must be dreaming—the vista seemed to rise from nowhere!

Wisps of smoke curled from numerous tiny campfires, drifting into the blazing blue sky like ghostly wraiths. Cone-shaped tents dotted the valley floor, surrounded by thick stands of sugar pines and cedars. From the top pole of the largest structure hung a flowing horse's tail. Jessamyn caught her breath.

Black Eagle's camp.

Ben headed his gelding down the steep incline. Steam rose from his clothing as the sun hit his sodden garments. Shrouded in mist, he looked like some otherworldly creature from a myth or a fairy tale. Lancelot, perhaps. Or— God help her—the devil himself. Without a backward glance, she snapped the reins and followed the unearthly figure down the mountainside.

Nearing the encampment, Ben slackened his pace and reined the gelding to fall in step beside her. "Stay close," he cautioned. "These Indians don't see many white women."

Jessamyn started. She was riding into the camp of fearsome savages with a moody, enigmatic man she barely knew. She shuddered. Under the damp plaid shirt, her heart pounded at twice its normal rate.

Ben wanted her to stay close to him? He'd laugh if he guessed how desperate she suddenly felt not to let him out of her sight!

Buckskin-clad children tumbled out of the tipis, pointing and chattering as she and the sheriff rode into camp. A young woman, her back bent under a load of firewood, watched them with hard black eyes. An older woman, dressed in baggy buckskin pants and a tattered canvas shirt, spoke brusquely and the girl resumed her work, dumping the wood near a central fire pit. Jessamyn saw the girl sneak a surreptitious peek at her, and she tried to smile. Her lips seemed frozen. She realized her jaws were clamped tightly shut.

Ben raised his hand and said something to the old woman in a strange-sounding language. The woman's rheumy eyes widened. She dropped her load of sticks and brush and disappeared into the largest tipi.

The sheriff brought the gelding to a halt. Indians poured out of the tents, half-clothed braves with yellow and black designs painted on their bare chests, young girls with curious dark eyes and shy smiles, another old woman, her face creased with wrinkles like a dried prune. All gathered in a circle around them, whispering and pointing.

One of the old women edged forward. With a quick, furtive gesture, she fingered Jessamyn's denim pant leg.

"Don't be frightened," Ben intoned.

"Won't be," she lied over the thumping of her heart. *Frightened?* She was terrified! She almost screamed at the slight tug on her trouser hem.

"Don't let your horse drift."

"Wouldn't," she managed. She'd stick to the sheriff's side like ink on a dry roller.

"And," Ben breathed, giving her a quick sidelong look, his gray-blue eyes serious, "no matter what, don't open your mouth!"

Jessamyn sucked in a lungful of woodsmoke-scented air. "I wouldn't think of it."

This time it wasn't a lie. She'd never felt so frightened in all her life. Fifty pairs of dark, wary eyes stared at her so intently the hair on the back of her neck prickled.

Then a small spotted dog wriggled out of the arms of a solemn-faced, black-haired boy and danced around the mare's forelegs, yapping in high, exuberant tones. The mare sidled, and Ben reached down and grabbed her bridle.

The dog—an overgrown puppy, Jessamyn realized— leaped and barked. Finally an old woman—the same one Ben had spoken to—scooped it up and plopped it onto Jessamyn's lap. Shivering with joy, the pup slathered its tongue over her chin, and everyone laughed.

Ben shot her the briefest of smiles. Jessamyn held tight to the dog, her first friend in this alien place. It was fat and warm and squirmy, and she laughed out loud. The sound was echoed by the growing circle of sun-bronzed faces.

She scratched its muzzle, and the animal settled into her lap, laid its head on two floppy front paws and closed its eyes.

Again the crowd murmured. Jessamyn began to breathe normally again. Maybe this wouldn't be so bad after all.

The flap of the largest tipi suddenly snapped open and a tall, imposing man appeared. A headdress of feathers cascaded down the back of his fringed buckskin overshirt, and around his neck hung a necklace of shells and bits of fur. Or hair, Jessamyn thought with a start. Lord in heaven, maybe they were scalps!

Her hand stilled on the puppy's warm head as the olive-skinned figure stalked toward them, his stance erect. Jessamyn noted his buckskin breeches were worn through at the knees, but that did not lessen the aura of command that emanated from him. It had to be Black Eagle.

Five braves formed a phalanx around him, and behind them appeared the exquisite Indian girl Jessamyn had seen in town—Ben had called her Walks Dancing.

Black Eagle raised one arm. "It has been a long time, Iron Hand. You are welcome at my camp."

Iron Hand? Ben was called Iron Hand? Jessamyn made a mental note to remember the name for her news story. She resisted the impulse to dig her pencil and notebook out of the saddlebag; she didn't want to disturb the lump of fur snoozing on her lap.

Ben inclined his head. "My thanks, Black Eagle."

Black Eagle's eyes snapped with interest. "That is your woman?"

Ben hesitated a fraction of a second. "That is my woman," he acknowledged. "She is called Jessamyn."

"Jessamyn," the chief repeated. His black eyes studied her at length. "Has she good teeth? And a strong back?"

Jessamyn gasped. She opened her mouth to speak, then

caught Ben's warning look. She closed her lips and waited to hear what the sheriff would say.

"Her back is strong, my friend. Her teeth—" he shot her a devilish grin "—I have not yet tested."

Jessamyn firmed her mouth into a thin line. She felt like a piece of horseflesh being assessed for its age.

Black Eagle grunted. "You have not been long together, I see. Take my advice, old friend. Give her something to chew—many deer hides."

Ben's chuckle sent a bolt of fury into Jessamyn's brain. She didn't dare look at him. If he laughed at her, she knew she'd never be able to keep her mouth shut. Teeth, indeed!

Black Eagle pointed to the tent just behind his. "You and your woman will sleep there, Iron Hand."

Ben nodded.

Jessamyn blinked. In the same tent? Just the two of them?

"In the morning," the chief continued, "we will talk. Tonight we will smoke together and tell stories."

"I am honored, Black Eagle."

The old man nodded. "Go now and rest. My daughter, Walks Dancing, will bring food."

The chief turned away. The circle of braves closed around him as he moved with regal steps toward the large centrally positioned tipi and stepped through the entrance.

Walks Dancing crept forward, addressed some words to Ben in the strange, lilting language, and lifted the puppy from Jessamyn's lap. Ben released the mare's bridle and dismounted, then positioned himself beside Jessamyn's horse and reached up for her. In a single motion, he lifted her out of the saddle and set her on her feet before him.

He kept his hands at her waist. "Jessamyn," he said in a low voice, "can you stand up?"

"I—I think so."

"When I release you, I'm going to walk to that tipi behind Black Eagle's. If you can walk, follow me. If you think you can't, let me know now."

Jessamyn nodded her understanding. "I can, Ben," she whispered. "Just...don't walk too fast."

Chuckling, Ben pivoted and moved off ahead of her. Jessamyn inhaled a slow breath and took a tentative step forward. Her legs shook, but they both moved. She gauged the number of steps to the tipi entrance. Twelve, maybe. Surely she could manage twelve steps?

To her left, Walks Dancing advanced in her odd, lurching gait, grasped the bridles of both mounts, one in each hand, and led them away to be picketed. Jessamyn took another unsteady step and gazed after the slim figure in complete and heartfelt understanding. How terrible to be crippled for life. For Walks Dancing, no bath in an icy mountain pool would return the use of her twisted limbs.

Five steps to go. Moving as deliberately as he could, Ben had already reached the tipi. He pulled aside the flap, hesitated, then disappeared inside. With a final glance at Walks Dancing's laborious progress toward the edge of camp, Jessamyn followed him into the stretched skin enclosure.

Inside the tipi, the dusky light of early evening glowed against the smooth hide walls. Cool air met her, laced with the pungent scent of warm earth and sassafras. A single pallet, as wide as it was long and covered with dark furs, lay in the center; the rest of the floor area was carpeted with a thick layer of pine boughs.

Ben took her arm and lowered her to a sitting position on the soft pelts, then knelt before her on one knee. "Black Eagle honors us as his guests. After we've eaten, I'll go parley with him and his warriors."

"What about me?"

"You'll stay here," Ben responded. "White women are not allowed at Black Eagle's council fire."

"But—"

Ben looked into her face. "Please, Jessamyn. I need to dig some information out of Black Eagle. He's a tough old man, canny as they come, and the matter is delicate. Ranchers have been losing cattle. They're convinced the Indians are stealing them."

"Are they?"

Ben shook his head. "That's what I came to find out. Your presence isn't going to help me do my job."

"But what about *my* job?" Jessamyn persisted. "Cattle theft is reportable news."

"I know. Your father aired the problem in every issue he printed last year. Might have been what got him killed."

Jessamyn flinched. "You mean it was Indians..."

Ben sighed. "Maybe. More likely not. Just sit tight for a while, can you? I'll bring your saddlebag and you can scribble in that notebook of yours. If I find out anything, I'll let you know."

He rose and sent her a lopsided smile, but Jessamyn saw his mouth tighten before he turned toward the tipi exit.

The tent flap fluttered into place, and for the first time in two days she was alone. She wrapped her arms about her throbbing calves and rested her forehead against her knees. Exhaustion clouded her mind. And she was so hungry! She tensed her stomach muscles to quell the hunger pangs and closed her eyes.

When she opened them again, it was dark inside the tipi. Ben sat with his back against the tent wall, watching her.

She jerked herself awake. How long had he been there? Light from the central fire pit outside licked the thin hide walls in flickering shadow patterns. Her notebook lay beside her, along with her saddlebag and bedroll. She inhaled the mouthwatering smell of roasting meat, and her stomach convulsed. Eyeing the stubby pencil stuck between the notebook pages, she considered jotting some ideas, then shook her head. She was too hungry to concentrate on anything except that tantalizing scent.

Ben blew out a lazy breath. "Food's coming."

She was too tired to muster a smile. "I can hardly wait. It smells heavenly!"

The sheriff sent her an unfathomable look.

"Will it be soon, do you think? I'm so' hungry I could—"

"Soon enough."

Jessamyn flicked a glance at him. For some reason his face was as impassive as his voice, and she suppressed a groan of frustration. The man was impossible to comprehend. Not even the prospect of supper improved his disposition.

Or was something amiss? She studied the sheriff's tanned, angular face, the smoky blue eyes that avoided meeting hers. The slow, deliberate way he folded and refolded the bandanna he'd worn at his neck all day told her his mind was elsewhere.

"What's wrong?" she blurted. She caught her breath at the look that crossed his face. He knew something—something he wasn't telling her. Was it about her father?

"Tell me," she demanded.

Ben dragged the fingers of one hand through his dark hair and blew out a long breath. Recrossing his long legs, he met Jessamyn's gaze. "These people are poor," he began, his voice low and careful. "Most of the time they're close to starving. And they're proud."

"They're the ones stealing the ranchers' cattle?"

Ben shook his head.

"Then why are you telling me this?" Hunger hardened her tone. Exasperated, she hunched her body forward, trying to divine the odd expression in the sheriff's eyes. "You found out something, didn't you? Was it about my father? About who—"

"Jessamyn, shut up a minute. I'm trying to tell you something—"

"About who shot him?" she interrupted. "Well, tell me, then! Who did?"

Ben's eyes hardened. "I told you before, I don't know yet. That's not what—"

"Well, why don't you know?" she snapped. "You've had time to—"

She stopped short at the glint of fury in his gaze. His eyes blazed into hers for a split second, then instantly shuttered.

Before she could continue, the tipi flap parted and a slim brown arm thrust two steaming tin plates through the opening. Supper! Her stomach gurgled in anticipation.

Ben spoke some words in the strange language, and a soft reply came from outside the tent. After a slight hesitation, he handed one of the plates to her.

Jessamyn sniffed the aromatic dish of meat, still smoking from the fire. Gingerly she picked up a strip with her fingers, blew on it and popped it into her mouth. It tasted delicious—rich and slightly sweet. She gobbled another morsel and felt her spirits begin to lift. She might be sweaty and so tired she could sleep for a week, her thighs raw from the saddle, her skin and hair gritty with trail dust, but at least she was no longer hungry! God in His infinite mercy had taken pity on her stomach.

"This is delicious! What kind of meat is it?"

Ben chewed slowly, keeping his gaze on her. After a moment the movement of his jaw stopped, and he swallowed.

"Like I said, Jessamyn, Black Eagle's people are proud. They don't have much, but they honor their guests with the best they can provide."

Jessamyn ate another mouthful. "Yes, it's quite good. But what *is* it?"

The sheriff kept his gaze on his plate. "Don't talk, Jess. Just eat."

"But I want to know! Any good newspaper reporter would want to know."

Ben set his plate down. "You know, with very little effort, you could turn out to be the most wearying woman a man ever had the misfortune to travel with. Now, keep your mind on your supper and thank the Lord you're not shoveling in what Jeremiah used to call Klamath custard—fresh deer's blood mixed with ground acorns.''

Jessamyn made a face. "How disgusting. But this..." She held up a sliver of juicy meat. "This is wonderful. I just want to know what—"

"No, you don't."

Her head came up. "Of course I do! Don't tell me what I want or don't want as if I were a child. Just tell me what this is!" She jammed the tidbit into her mouth and glared at him while she chewed it up. "I might want to ask Cora to cook some."

Ben picked up his plate. "It's an Indian specialty."

"So I gather," she retorted. "I insist you tell me *what* Indian specialty."

Ben sighed. After a long pause, he told her what she wanted to know. "Roasted dog meat."

Jessamyn gasped. "Dog meat! You—you mean like that precious little spotted..."

At once she knew what he'd been trying to avoid telling her.. To honor her presence, and that of Ben, whom the Indians called Iron Hand, these starving people had killed the only live animal they had left in camp—the friendly little puppy she had held on her lap not two hours ago.

She clapped her hand over her mouth. The tin plate slid off her lap as she began to rock her body back and forth. She was going to be sick. She squeezed her eyelids tight shut and concentrated on controlling the convulsions rising from her belly.

In an instant Ben was beside her. "Jessamyn, you damn little fool, I didn't want to tell you. I tried not to, but you just wouldn't let it alone."

Jessamyn turned her face away, afraid she would vomit. Why, *why* had she been so set on digging the information out of him? She wouldn't have been able to eat one bite if he'd told her sooner. She knew she had to eat to keep up her strength, but now she couldn't bear the thought. Hungry as she was, she'd rather starve. Oh, the poor little...

She could not finish the thought. Choking back sobs, she clenched her fists in her lap and concentrated on keeping her lips clamped shut.

Ben's large warm hands grasped her shoulders. "Jessamyn." He pulled her around to face him. "It's all right. I'm just sorry you had to find out like this."

"It's not all right!" she said, her voice shaking. "Nothing's all right."

"What I mean is," Ben began, looking into her face, "you don't have to eat any more. It would be an insult to Black Eagle to send the plate back untouched, but— Oh, hell, I'll eat the rest."

Jessamyn groaned. After all she'd been through, the pain and humiliation of learning to ride in front of a corralful of entertainment-hungry rowdies, jouncing in the hard leather saddle for the past two days, eating nothing but dry biscuits and unchewable jerky all day long—this was the last straw. Turning her head into his chest, she let the tears come.

She knew she'd failed. She was too city-bred to ever adjust to the raw kind of life people lived out here in the West. She wasn't as tough as she needed to be to carry on in Papa's footsteps. She wanted desperately to succeed so he would have been proud of her, so she could build a life for herself in this wild, untamed land he had loved. But she wasn't made of iron bolts and whang leather. She was made of flesh and blood. And she was tired and hungry and she hurt all over, even inside. She'd never make it through another day.

Ben sat very still, holding her trembling body as she cried the hurt out of herself. After a very long time she quieted, but still he held her, his chin pressed against the top of her head.

When she could breathe normally, she spoke in a dull, tired voice. "I'm sorry, Ben. It wasn't your fault."

His heart flopped crazily and then stood still. "Jess, I've got some hardtack and jerky in my saddlebag."

"No, thanks." She gave a little hiccup that ended in a sob. "I'm not hungry anymore. I may never be hungry again."

Ben said nothing. He lifted his head, and his gut wrenched at the sight of her sun-parched, tear-streaked face. She'd been through a lot in the past two days. No woman he'd ever known could have managed what Jessamyn had.

And, he acknowledged with a niggling apprehension, no woman he'd ever known made his mouth go dry just from her scent. Even now, after two days on the trail, her hair smelled sweet as fresh clover.

He gazed around the tipi, wondering how she'd smell after a night on those bearskins. The question burned deep in his brain.

Goddammit all to hell, why had he told Black Eagle Jessamyn was his woman? Now the chief had put the two of them together in the same tipi, sharing the same pallet.

The thought of the old chief brought Ben up short. Black Eagle was no fool. Soon the council would assemble in the big tipi. Ben would smoke the pipe with his old friend and trade stories until the night was half gone, and then...

He glanced down at Jessamyn, still curled in his arms, her long lashes a dark fringe against her skin. Oh, God. With any luck she'd be asleep when he returned.

But if she isn't? a voice queried. Well, then, he'd roll himself into a blanket on the pine boughs and try not to think about her. Try not to listen to her gentle breathing and the little moans she made when she changed position during the night.

He'd try, but he knew he would fail. Jessamyn Whittaker was something he had never encountered before—a spunky fighting spirit caught in a woman's soft body. She was infuriating and admirable all at the same time. Worst of all, he was beginning to like being around her.

Dammit, he didn't *want* to like her! And he sure as hell didn't want to need her.

But, God help him, he did.

Chapter Ten

Ben stepped into the circle of light cast from the fire pit in the center of the Indian camp. Using the Yurok tongue, one of the three Klamath tribe languages Ben knew well enough to speak, he sought permission to join Black Eagle and his few braves sitting cross-legged around the licking flames. The chief motioned him to join them, indicating the place of honor at his left.

"Hi ye." Ben thanked the old man, then folded his long legs beneath him and seated himself in the circle.

"Many months have passed since you visit us," Black Eagle observed. "Now that I have set my eyes upon Iron Hand's woman, I begin to understand." The chief's black eyes danced.

Iron Hand's woman. Ben almost choked. If Black Eagle only knew what a handful Jessamyn had turned out to be. His gut twisted. He wouldn't think about her just now. Later, when no offense would be taken by eating other than the Indian meat offered in their honor, he'd get her some jerky from his saddlebag. Damn little fool—she'd cost him more than one night's sleep already, and the journey was only half over.

Black Eagle produced a long-stemmed pipe carved out of yew. Deliberately he packed the soapstone bowl with kinnikinnik from the pouch at his waist, then slowly raised it to salute the sky, the earth and the four quadrants before lighting it with a twisted wisp of dry grass.

"Your woman—" the chief paused to suck air through the stem "—weeps. It is good that you train her with a strong hand, old friend. Then, between the hour that the dove calls to its young and the moon rises, she will be sweet tempered."

Ben grunted. "That is not our way, Black Eagle."

Black Eagle drew on the glowing pipe bowl, exhaling with satisfaction. "If a man does not lay his hand on his woman, she grows uncooperative, like an unbroken pony. You must beat her often." He passed the pipe to Ben.

"I did not come to talk of women, Black Eagle." Ben clamped his teeth down on the pipe stem and inhaled the rich pipe mixture, puffing the heavy smoke out his nose in the Yurok fashion. The sharp scent of the pungent Indian tobacco made his eyes water.

Black Eagle's lined face wrinkled into a grin. "Men talk always of women." He swept his gaze over the small circle of braves gathered about the fire. "Especially when they are scarce, as they are now. Only my daughter, Walks Dancing, and my own woman, Dawn Star, and four others—one very old—have escaped the reservation."

"You are fortunate, old friend. Many on the reservation die of smallpox."

Black Eagle inclined his head in a brief nod. "I am fortunate indeed. Each night my woman brings comfort to my tipi. Soon perhaps I will have a son to follow me."

A son! Ben kept his face unchanged. Black Eagle must be nearly sixty, and he was still capable... He wrenched his thoughts from the picture that rose in his mind. He himself was not yet forty, but he felt incapable of such a feat. Fathering a child was something a man did when he was whole, inside and out. Ben hadn't felt whole since the war. Since Lorena.

"My woman is young," Black Eagle said as if reading

Ben's thoughts. "Yours, also. Perhaps you will get a son on her before this night is over." The chief's eyes twinkled.

Ben jerked as if touched with a hot iron. To cover his discomfort at the direction the conversation was taking, he puffed on the pipe and passed it to his left. A young black-haired man with a gray foxtail around his neck accepted it with a grunt.

Black Eagle was playing cat and mouse with him. Despite the fact that the chief had sent for him, the canny old man always enjoyed a verbal skirmish before getting down to business. Ben needed to turn the talk to the matter of concern.

"If women are scarce, your braves do not need many horses to offer for them," Ben observed, keeping his tone noncommittal.

Black Eagle snorted. "Braves always need many horses, even if they do not take wives. Besides, there are other things a man can offer for a woman."

"Cattle?" Ben held his breath.

Black Eagle shot him a quizzical look. "Cows are valued only for meat. We have very few of these."

"How many, my friend?" Ben asked the question softly in English.

The chief also spoke in English. "Why do you ask?"

Ben watched the pipe travel from one brave's hand to the next, and chose his next words with care.

"My brother and others in the valley below do not understand how the Indian can claim to be hungry."

The chief's eyes hardened into two black stones. "Your brother and the others are not hunted like dogs and imprisoned behind the white man's walls."

"This is true." Ben lapsed into the Yurok tongue. "My brother and my friend offer food to the Indian. Two fat beeves each rising of the new moon. Would you have more?"

The old chief nodded. "One more. In the winter, maybe two. We are a proud people. We do not like to beg."

Ben hesitated, then said in English, "Neither would you take what is not yours without payment."

Black Eagle stared at him. "Someone is stealing your cattle?"

Holding the old man's gaze, Ben nodded.

Black Eagle uttered an oath. Suddenly he shouted a guttural query at the braves gathered around the fire.

Blank looks passed among the assembled warriors. One, a tall man with gray-streaked dark hair, scowled and replied to the question in a querulous tone. "Why does Iron Hand ask this? Does he believe we are without honor?"

Black Eagle turned steady eyes on Ben. "Why, Ben?" he said in English.

"A man has been killed," Ben replied softly. "This man spoke of stolen cattle. He was shot."

"How many have been taken?" Black Eagle asked in English.

"Twenty, sometimes thirty head at a time. Been going on about a year now."

"Twenty cows would fill our bellies for seasons to come. Yet the bellies of our children are far from full."

Ben eyed the old man. "This is true, my friend. In my heart I have known it is not the Indian who raids our herds. But in the minds of others..."

Something flickered in the chief's black eyes. "My people are already hated by the white man. What would you have me do?"

"Why did you want to see me?" Ben countered. The two questions were connected, he was sure of it. Black Eagle knew something that put his ragged band of renegades in even greater danger than they now suffered. He wanted Ben's counsel, but he knew the chief would not reveal a thing unless it was absolutely necessary.

Inside, Ben had to chuckle. Black Eagle was as wily and cautious as any general, Confederate or Yankee, he'd ever known. And proud. His task now was either to outsmart the old man or gain his complete confidence.

Black Eagle gave him a penetrating look, then turned away to accept the pipe, which had now made a complete circle around the campfire. He drew on it, exhaled and handed it, stem pointing to the left, to Ben. The chief gestured for Ben to keep it.

It was a rare honor. Usually the chief retained the privilege of emptying the ashes and retiring the pipe for the night. Black Eagle's action spoke volumes.

Tomorrow Ben would speak privately with the chief. Tonight he would plan how to approach the slippery old fox. Tonight he'd—

Black Eagle rose and clapped Ben's shoulder with one sinewy hand. "Sleep well, my friend." His eyes shone in the firelight. "I wish you much joy in your woman."

Ben started. *Joy in his woman?* He ran his hand absently over his chin. Never again would he know joy in a woman. It was too easy to have his heart cut out with one brutal slash. He had long since come to a truth about himself. Lorena's betrayal, her callous rejection of him after the war, had maimed his spirit, undermined his belief in the goodness of life and his place in it. It had eroded his value as a man. If he ever opened himself to such hurt again, he knew he would never recover.

But a battle raged within him. He was hungry for the sight of Jessamyn's mossy green eyes and that stubborn little chin, aching to breathe in the fresh, sweet scent of her hair. He wanted to be near her, hear her voice.

He dreaded the coming night hours stretching before him. What in the hell was he going to do with himself with her not two feet away? He couldn't sleep with the horses— Black Eagle would surely know, and tomorrow the wily old chief would use that as another clever ploy to pull Ben off the track.

He gritted his teeth. Escape was not an option. Neither was avoidance of the tipi where he knew Jessamyn waited. He was trapped.

Ben moved toward the tipi like a man in a nightmare,

caught between two primal forces warring within himself—
desire and self-preservation.

He slipped one hand under the supple skin covering of
the tipi flap and unknotted the leather thong. Quietly lifting
the barrier, he stepped over the threshold.

He waited a few moments to adjust to the darkness inside, then muffled the jinglebobs on his spurs with his fingers and removed his boots. In silence, he set them by the
entrance.

He turned toward the sound of soft breathing. Jessamyn
lay curled up on the fur pallet, a blanket half-covering her
still-clothed body. One booted foot stuck out from under
the edge of the blanket. The other boot he discovered by
stumbling over it.

Ben stared down at the still form at his feet. She was
exhausted, so tired she'd managed to get only one boot off
before she'd dragged the tan wool blanket over herself and
fallen asleep.

The problem was, she'd used his bedroll for her pillow.
Well, let her have it. The balmy night air caressed his skin
like warm silk. Besides, he'd slept blanketless plenty of
times on nights colder than this.

He made a half turn away from her. The second problem
was that her motionless form was jackknifed in the exact
center of the single pallet, leaving no room for him. Ben
sighed. Just as well, he thought. He didn't dare get too close
to her.

He stretched his long legs out on the pine boughs car-
peting the tipi floor, stuffed the jerky strip he'd brought for
her into his shirt pocket and folded one arm under his head.
Staring up at the smoke hole at the top of the tipi, he let
his thoughts drift.

Huge, brilliant stars sparkled against the tiny patch of
blue-black sky visible through the opening. He gazed at
them so long his eyes began to sting.

A man was a small thing compared to the vastness of
the universe. As the sky wheeled and the seasons turned

throughout the eons, what would it matter that he had been a friend to the Indian, had kept the peace in an unruly Oregon county peopled with orating politicians, anxious railroad investors, weary, single-minded ranchers, and desperate Indians no one cared about now that the territory had gained statehood? Could what one man accomplished in his short lifetime be of much significance?

In another hundred years maybe it wouldn't make any difference, he reasoned. But it made a difference now. At least, it did to him. A man had to hold on to something in life—something of enduring value. As a frontier lawman, he figured he was doing what any honorable person would do when faced with chaos—try to keep order. But God almighty, he was sick to death of the never-ending strife. Sometimes he longed to go back to Carolina, pretend everything was the same as it was before the war—peaceful and orderly.

But he knew he couldn't. There was nothing left for him in Carolina—not land or family or the girl he had once loved.

In the end, maybe it was better that Lorena hadn't wanted him. At least this way she'd gotten what she did want—more land than any one plantation owner would know what to do with. But it had hurt. It still hurt. He'd wanted her, and she'd wanted something else—money, social position in the crumbling world of the South. But not him. Not after the war had torn up his body, disfigured him and spit out his soul.

Black Eagle had once told him suffering revealed a man's strength. It also defined a man's weakness with a merciless truth. Lorena had ceased to love him because the war had changed him. She no longer knew who he was.

God knew, he didn't, either.

Ben let his eyelids drift shut. He didn't want to think about it any longer. He just wanted to—

A sound brought him to attention. A muffled groan,

somewhere outside the tipi. Then another, and a man's low laugh.

Ben swore under his breath. Black Eagle and his wife, making a son inside their tipi. He shook his head, then had to smile. That fox of a chief was as randy as any young brave half his age.

A long moan rose, throaty and soft in the stillness. He cast a quick look at Jessamyn. Still asleep, thank God. The moaning increased, rose in pitch, and now a man's pleasure-filled grunting accompanied it. Ben swore again. *Come on, old man, get it done so we can both get some sleep.*

No luck. Black Eagle evidently relished physical play as much as jousting with words. The noises continued, along with suggestive thumps that mounted in volume until Ben was certain the whole camp lay awake, listening.

His own imagination flickered to life. Instead of Black Eagle, he saw himself, rousing a woman to slow, heated passion with his lips and hands, a woman with skin like thistledown under his fingers, a mouth hot and wet, opening to his. A woman with a sweetly rounded bottom, slim arms that reached up for him...a sunburned nose...

He groaned aloud. Jessamyn. Goddammit. Jessamyn.

Black Eagle's woman began to croon in jerky, breath-interrupted expressions of fevered arousal. Ben's chest tightened. Blood pounded into his groin. He laid one hand on his pants fly and tried to press his member into quiescence.

Jessamyn stirred. "Ben," she whispered. She rose up on one elbow, facing him. "What's that noise?"

"Nothing," he managed. "A coyote, maybe. Go back to sleep." He rolled onto his stomach, hoping to ease the swelling of his manhood.

"It can't be a coyote," she murmured. "Coyotes don't cry that way. And anyway, it's too close."

"Jess," Ben ordered, his voice hoarse. "Go back to sleep."

From Black Eagle's tipi now came a rhythmic thrashing sound, punctuated by high, strangled cries of pleasure.

"Ben!" Jessamyn gasped. "It's coming from—"

"I know damn well where it's coming from. Now shut up and go to—"

"Oh, merciful heavens," she cried. "It's a woman! And a— And a— Oh!" She broke off as awareness dawned. Her mouth dropped open in shock.

That did it. He pushed her back down onto the soft fur. "Don't listen," he growled. He rolled her away from him, stretched out beside her close enough to reach her if he extended his arms but not close enough to touch her with any part of his body.

"I can't help but hear them," she whispered. "They're...that's...incredible," she finished on a ragged breath. "Do people really..."

"Yes, people *really*," Ben said through gritted teeth. "Now shut up and lie still." He snaked one arm out and slid his hand under the side of her head. With his other hand he covered her exposed ear.

"Don't listen, understand?" he breathed near her temple. Under his fingers he felt her head move up and down in a nod. He pressed both palms tight against her ears.

And don't talk, he added to himself. *For God's sake, don't say anything even remotely suggestive.* Even if an emotional tie was the last thing on earth he wished for, he was only a man, and he sure as hell had a man's needs. Right now he wasn't so sure that his scruples about taking virgins hadn't been left back in Wildwood Valley.

Then Jessamyn did the one thing he'd never expected. She inched backward until her spine pressed against his chest. Her jean-clad buttocks teased his aching groin.

His body flamed into desire. If she so much as moved, he'd—

She didn't. She lay still against him, letting his hands cover her ears against the guttural, panting sounds of love-making just a few feet away. Ben tried not to think about what was going on in the adjacent tipi, tried instead to keep his trembling body from exploding with pent-up need.

It seemed like hours before the noises finally trailed off. When he could hear the usual night sounds again—an owl's soft call from a nearby thicket, the sigh of the wind through the sugar pines—he lifted his palms from her ears.

Without a word, Jessamyn turned toward him. Tears sheened her cheeks. She swiped at them with fingers that shook, then buried her face in her hands.

"Jessamyn?" Ben found it difficult to speak her name. "What's wrong?"

"I don't know," she sobbed. "Those sounds. Hearing them made me feel funny inside."

Ben winced. "I'm sorry, Jess. That's something no lady should ever have to hear."

Jessamyn raised her head. "Oh, no, Ben," she breathed. "You're wrong. I thought it was…" She hesitated, searching for a word. "Beautiful."

Ben jerked upright. What in the hell? This prim, overstarched Yankee lady with refined manners and too many petticoats thought the act of love between a man and a woman was…beautiful? He wondered if her empty belly was causing her to hallucinate.

He scrabbled in his pocket for the bit of dried venison and his pocketknife. "Here," he managed. "Have some jerky."

Jessamyn shook her head. "No, thanks. I'm not hungry now. Save it for breakfast."

She stifled a yawn, turned away from him and curled up on the thick fur. "Go to sleep, Ben," she said over her shoulder. "Tomorrow I'll make some notes about what I learned today."

After a moment she gave a soft laugh. "And what I learned tonight," she added in a drowsy voice. "It ought to sell newspapers like sarsaparilla on the Fourth of July!"

A soft scratching on the outside of the tipi roused Jessamyn from a fitful sleep. She opened her eyes to daylight and the sight of Ben's bare forearm draped across her midriff. His hand, palm down, the fingers loosely curled, lay on the fur pallet near her breast. She was trapped inside the curve of his arm.

Afraid to waken him, she lay perfectly still. Oh, if Miss Bennett saw her now, lying next to a sleeping man, whatever would she think? She was fully clothed, but even so, her entire being, right down to her toes, felt the heat of Ben's body. She pondered the delicious new sensation.

The scratching resumed. She raised her head a fraction of an inch. "Who's there?" she whispered.

The flap lifted, and Walks Dancing poked her head inside. The Indian girl beckoned, then her small, solemn face broke into a smile as she perceived Jessamyn's dilemma. She couldn't move a muscle without waking Ben.

Her smile broadening, Walks Dancing pantomimed a solution. Jessamyn shook her head, but at the girl's repeated unspoken urging, she decided she had to try it. It was either that or lie imprisoned and hungry until Ben awoke.

Very slowly, she slid her own small hand under the sheriff's larger one, lifted it and gently resettled it on his thigh. Her fingers brushed his jeans as she slipped her hand free. Ben mumbled something in his sleep but did not stir.

Silent as a cat, Jessamyn rolled free. When Walks Dancing motioned her outside, she rose to a standing position. Making as little noise as possible, she pulled off her remaining boot. Before she took a step, she gazed down at the figure sleeping at her feet. It was the first time she had allowed herself to really look at this remote, mysterious man.

Tousled black hair, laced with silver and long enough to touch the top of his ear, framed a lean, angular face bronzed by years of exposure to the sun. She bent closer, studying him. Awake, he reminded her of a tiger—quiet and purposeful. Asleep, he looked quite human.

Long dark lashes fanned the high cheekbones. She stud-

ied his mouth, the lips firm and nicely curved, watched his
nostrils flare as he drew air in, breathed it out in a slow,
even rhythm. She fought an inexplicable urge to smooth
her fingertip across his lips, coax them apart. She blushed
at her audacity.

A softly spoken phrase in the mellifluous Indian language jerked her to attention. She tore her gaze away from
Ben and crept in silence through the tipi entrance and out
into the hot morning sunshine.

Walks Dancing pivoted and headed for the wind-stunted
pine grove at the edge of camp. Barefooted, Jessamyn followed, grateful that this morning she could move with relatively little pain. She caught up with the Indian girl within
three strides. The hard-packed earth radiated warmth into
the soles of her feet.

Just beyond the trees a lazy stream widened into a clear
turquoise-green pool, obscured by drooping cottonwoods
around the perimeter. Walks Dancing pointed, then un-
wound her braid, stripped off her buckskin dress and leg-
gings and plunged into the water.

Jessamyn gaped. On land the Indian girl moved in halting, labored steps. In the water she cavorted like a water
sprite.

Quickly she shrugged free of the rumpled plaid shirt
she'd slept in for two nights and unbuttoned her jeans. She
dipped her bare toes into cool, inviting water. Pulling off
her thin chemise and cotton drawers, she unpinned her hair,
letting the heavy tresses swing loose. She took a deep
breath and splashed into the water, wading out until it
reached her waist.

Walks Dancing swam in circles around her, chattering in
her strange tongue, while Jessamyn scooped handfuls of the
chilly water over her neck and chest. Finally she spread her
arms and submerged her entire body in the pool.

Cold stabbed her, then faded as she breaststroked in a
lazy arc. Following Walks Dancing's example, she ducked
her head below the surface, finger-combing her hair under-

water to wash away the trail dust. Swimming to the edge, she plucked her shirt and smallclothes from the bank and dunked them in the pool, as well.

Walks Dancing broke off a leafy cottonwood branch. Using a series of gestures, the Indian girl showed Jessamyn how to scrub the garments against a rock.

When she finished the task, she tossed the sodden shirt and underclothes onto the grassy bank and scrambled out of the pool after them. She spread the garments over a bush to dry, then stretched out full-length in the warm sun. Walks Dancing joined her, and the two lazed away the better part of an hour in companionable silence.

She must have drifted off to sleep, because the next thing she knew, a horse crashed through the tangled underbrush, blundering into the sheltered copse on the other side of the pool. Jessamyn glimpsed a dun-colored pony, a half-naked Indian brave on its back.

The horse stood, its sides heaving, and the brave slipped off. Unaware that he was being watched, he draped the animal's reins over an overhanging pine branch and loped off toward the camp.

Walks Dancing snorted a word into the quiet. Without a sound, she rose, dressed herself and went to rub the horse down with a handful of dry grass.

Jessamyn lifted her still-damp drawers from the bush. Ignoring the chill from the wet material, she pulled the garment on anyway, then donned her chemise and buttoned her shirt over it. She had just stepped into her jeans when Walks Dancing whistled to her. The girl pantomimed spooning food into her mouth. Was she hungry?

Jessamyn nodded. She was starving!

Her olive-skinned companion grinned, patted the pony's neck and slipped past her. Just as Jessamyn turned to follow, something caught her eye.

A metallic glint riveted her attention on the blanket roll tied on the pony. She moved forward. With careful fingers she lifted the cover.

A polished blued-steel gun muzzle poked from the woolen material. Jessamyn sucked in her breath. She'd been told the Indians had no weapons save for their lances and bows. What would a Klamath brave be doing with a rifle?

Walks Dancing called out, her voice carrying through the trees. Hurriedly Jessamyn shoved the gun back under the blanket. Had she been misinformed? Were the Indians now allowed to have firearms? If they were, why was the weapon carried as it was, concealed under the blankets?

A shiver crawled up her spine. Every instinct told her something was wrong. She didn't know what, just... something. She had to tell Ben.

She forgot all about breakfast. Wheeling in her tracks, Jessamyn headed toward camp and the man she'd left sleeping in the tipi.

Chapter Eleven

Ben studied the carefully expressionless face of the old Indian chief who sat across from him sharing a meager breakfast of baked acorn dough and sweetened tea. For the past hour he and Black Eagle had fenced in two languages trying to discover each other's secrets. Again and again the canny old man evaded Ben's careful, probing questions. The Indian knew something, but damned if Ben could wrestle it out of him.

In turn, Black Eagle queried him about one apparently unrelated thing after another. About Jessamyn—was she willing? How many times? How was it when he was with her? About his family, his brother, Carleton, and Ella, his wife. About plans for the railroad to the coast, about the Modoc people herded onto the reservation along with their enemies, the various Klamath tribes—how many warriors? How many women and children? About alfalfa and wheat yields from the valley ranches, then more questions about Jessamyn.

None of Black Eagle's circular conversation seemed connected. As the sly chief skipped from topic to topic with consummate skill, Ben wondered if he had inadvertently fed the Indian leader a crucial bit of intelligence without realizing it. But if he had, what in the hell was it? What was Black Eagle after?

Or was he mainly interested in Ben's relationship with
"his woman"? Over and over, Black Eagle asked about
her. Was she intelligent? Were her hips wide for child-
bearing? Did she cry out during the act? Ben clenched his
jaw at the sparkle of delight in the old man's eyes. His
neck muscles tightening, he worked to erase the frown of
annoyance he knew creased his brow. If Black Eagle suspected his guest's patience had worn thin, sure as beans
and bacon the old chief would use the knowledge to his
advantage.

But goddammit, no more about Jessamyn! He'd lain
awake most of the night throbbing with need for the Yankee lady who'd kept him off balance since the moment he'd
laid eyes on her. The last thing he wanted to think about
was her soft, pliant body curled in his arms all night, her
backbone pressing into his chest, her bottom snugged
against his thighs until he ached with desire.

"Pain," Black Eagle had told him years ago, "makes a
man think. Thought makes him wise, and wisdom makes
life endurable." Now the old man's words haunted him.

Ben's pulse pounded. He'd bet the old chief hadn't
meant that particular type of pain. This discomfort had
nothing to do with a man's rational thought process. Quite
the opposite. His brain would explode if he couldn't get
her out of his thoughts soon.

He shot a surreptitious glance at Black Eagle. How much
did the old man guess about Ben's real reasons for visiting
the Indian camp? Did he suspect Jessamyn was not really
his woman? That she accompanied him to discover something about her father's murder?

A smile quirked the chief's otherwise impassive coun-
tenance, and Ben sucked in his breath. Fathomless black
eyes surveyed him from under motionless shaggy brows.
The Indian was a master at deception.

"You dance well, my friend," Ben said, keeping his
voice even. "The music of your mouth is as subtle as your

footsteps. In these many hours I have learned little of importance."

Black Eagle nodded. "Tell me then what you wish to discover."

Ben laughed softly. "I grow weary of this game, Black Eagle. I speak plainly, yet you reply in riddles."

"Ho!" The old man chuckled. "A man has a tongue with which to speak, and words to hide his thoughts. Your tongue, my friend, is as nimble as a young deer."

Ben shrugged. "My tongue grows numb with wagging."

"It is necessary." Black Eagle made a show of sipping from the soapstone tea bowl, but a shadow fell across his face. "The Indian way of life is dying." His voice dropped to a throaty whisper, and he sipped again. "As a nation, we grow old. Soon we will pass away forever."

Ben's gut twisted. He knew what Black Eagle felt. He himself had experienced the same grinding sense of loss in Carolina after the war. An entire era, a civilization he had known and loved, had been wiped from the face of the earth. The old Indian was fighting for survival against an inexorable force with the only weapon he had left—his wits.

Ben laid his hand on Black Eagle's bony, buckskin-sheathed arm. "Old friend, I would aid you if I knew how."

"Tell me, then," Black Eagle replied quietly, "how are we to save ourselves? We have little food. Our women grow too weak to bear healthy sons. Our enemy, the people of the Modoc, ride from the south to count coup against us and steal our children. How are we to protect ourselves?"

Ben's heart faltered. That was it! Black Eagle needed weapons. Guns. But the chief knew guns were forbidden to the Indians. Did Black Eagle think Ben would supply him with illegal rifles?

Impossible. But for the moment, he wouldn't tell that to the chief. First he would use it as leverage to pry loose the information *he* needed—who was rustling cows from Wild-wood Valley ranches?

It was not Black Eagle, that much Ben knew. But he'd bet a dollar the old chief's scouts knew who it was. The sharp-eyed Klamath tribes knew everything that went on in these mountains. A sixth sense told Ben the chief knew more than he was telling; that piece of information had to link in some way with Thad Whittaker's killer.

He raked his fingers through his hair. Time was running out. He didn't like the way the chief's interest returned again and again to Jessamyn. For all he knew, one of Black Eagle's braves would offer to buy her, or—worse—would kidnap her. He had to get her out of camp.

And that meant he'd have to push Black Eagle a bit. Scratching the stubble on his chin, he purposefully un-crossed his legs and made as if to rise.

"Wait!" The chief's dark eyes expressed what the proud old man could not utter. His people were desperate. Black Eagle was ready to trade information—it was the only thing of value he had left.

Ben hesitated. "I will wait but one hour, old friend. And I will listen. What is it you would say?"

Black Eagle gestured, palms up. "There is one—"

The chief broke off. Jessamyn burst from the trees, strid-ing toward them with determined steps. Her bare feet made no noise, but her hard breathing was audible. She'd been running.

Ben raised his head and stared at her, then sucked air into lungs that seemed suddenly paralyzed. Good God, her hair...

A riot of dark chestnut curls tumbled almost to her waist. In the hot morning sunlight, red-gold highlights gleamed like a nimbus about her head and shoulders. He couldn't take his eyes off her.

"Ben," she panted. "I—I must speak with you!"

He looked away. "Later." He growled the word over his shoulder.

"No. Now."

Now? What the hell was the matter with her? Couldn't she see that he was busy?

"Ben, it's important."

Across from him, Black Eagle folded his gnarled hands into his lap and grinned. "Not beat her enough," he said in Yurok. The old man's shoulders shook with laughter. "Or maybe she is again willing?"

"Ben?" Jessamyn tugged on his shirtsleeve. "Please. Come with me—I have something to show you."

Black Eagle snorted. "Long legs and a smooth belly," he said in his native language.

Under his breath Ben cursed them both, Black Eagle for his suggestive words—words that called up a vision of Jessamyn naked beneath him, her skin hot and silky—and Jessamyn for her artless blundering into his intelligence negotiations with the Indian chief.

Exasperated, he sent Black Eagle a look of resignation. At the amused look on the old man's face, Ben narrowed his eyes. Why, the old fox relished his discomfort! The chief couldn't have engineered a delaying tactic any better if he'd planned it himself.

Furious, Ben slapped his palms on his knees and rose to face Jessamyn. "Say it and be quick about it."

"Not here." She plucked at his shirt. "Come with me," she breathed. "Hurry."

Black Eagle laughed out loud.

Ben groaned. He gripped Jessamyn's upper arm and pulled her toward the tipi. Her shirtsleeve was damp. Dark tendrils of her hair brushed against his hand as she moved. It, too, was wet. He inhaled the faint scent of sweet woodruff and clenched his jaw in sudden fury.

"What the hell have you been doing?" The fragrance of her hair made his insides feel weightless.

"Swimming," she said, catching her breath. "With Walks Dancing. You were asleep, so I—"

With his free hand, Ben reached for the deerskin flap.

"No!" she blurted. "Not in there. In those trees over there," she whispered.

Ben stilled. Behind him, Black Eagle's throaty chuckle rose as he slurped from his tea bowl.

"What a woman!" the Indian muttered in Yurok, just loud enough for Ben to hear. "She cannot wait more than one hour. No wonder you look so tired, my friend. You will have many sons!"

Ben gritted his teeth. He walked Jessamyn none too gently into the stand of sugar pines at the edge of camp. Once beyond Black Eagle's sharp eyes, he pulled her about to face him. "Talk!" he ordered.

She turned out of his grasp and led him to a tired-looking pony, its tail braided in the Indian fashion. Jessamyn flipped back one corner of the blanket tied behind the saddle. "Look."

Ben stared. "Well, I'll be goddamned."

"This Indian man rode in while we were swimming," Jessamyn whispered. "He didn't see us. After I got my clothes, I saw something shiny, like metal. So I looked."

Ben released the breath he'd been unconsciously holding and slipped the rifle partway out of its covering.

A Spencer repeating carbine. Brand-new. Lord God, what a war-hungry Indian could do with such a weapon. He slid the gun back into its hiding place. A brave didn't carry a rifle. No Indian he ever knew had owned a rifle. Here, right before his eyes, was the piece of information Black Eagle had withheld.

Ben stroked his chin. "Looks like someone is supplying guns to the Indians holed up in these mountains."

"In exchange for what?" Her quick question startled him. Of course, it would have to be a trade. But the tribe had no money, nothing of value besides a few warm furs and some cooking pots. The only thing the Klamath had now was his eyes and ears and—if he was lucky—his scalp.

His fury evaporated. Weighing the implications of what she'd discovered, his brain made the connection. Black Eagle needed weapons to protect his people from their traditional enemy, the Modocs. In exchange for rifles, Black Eagle was maintaining silence about something he knew, something about the cattle rustling going on in the valley. The chief must know who was behind it. He kept quiet to avoid jeopardizing his supply of weapons.

"Ben," Jessamyn whispered. "You look so odd—what is it? Are you angry?"

He drew her away from the pony. "I'll admit I was ready to strangle you not more than two minutes ago, but not now. Not after what you showed me."

"Oh, good," she said. "Because I'm dying of hunger and I know you've got some jerky hidden somewhere."

Ben had to laugh. She was completely unaware of the service she'd done him by discovering that rifle. Now at least one piece of the puzzle fit. All he had to do was pick up the trail of Black Eagle's scouts; eventually it would lead him to the cattle thief. Whoever it was probably sold the beeves on the hoof in Idaho and used the money to buy rifles from some corrupt army quartermaster at Fort Klamath. Or, more likely, Fort Umpqua.

Ben didn't realize how swiftly he was moving back toward camp until Jessamyn's ragged breathing told him she couldn't keep pace with him. Not with bare feet, anyway. Without thinking, he turned and scooped her up into his arms. She gave a little yelp, but he silenced her with a single hissed word. "Hush!"

He strode into the camp clearing to find Black Eagle sitting exactly where he'd left him. The old chief regarded Ben and Jessamyn with twinkling black eyes. Nodding his head and grinning, he motioned them toward the tipi and made a covert obscene gesture.

Unaccountably, Ben found himself grinning back. No harm if the chief entertained lascivious thoughts at this moment. Acting as if Jessamyn really was "his" woman would mask his discovery of the rifle. He chuckled. He'd managed to beat Black Eagle at his own game. With Jessamyn's help, he acknowledged.

A weight lifted from his shoulders. Now he knew how to proceed. The first thing he had to do was get Jessamyn safely away from Black Eagle's camp and back to town. Then he'd load up a week's worth of supplies and search the mountains for a hidden cache of army rifles. One of Black Eagle's scouts would unknowingly lead him right to it.

A heightened state of awareness washed over him, based on a combination of a sleepless night and euphoria over his success. He moved toward the tipi, Jessamyn clasped hard against his chest.

For just a moment he found himself actually looking forward to getting her alone, pretending she did belong to him. God, would he ever stop thinking about her?

The other thing you have to do, an inner voice reminded as he reached the shelter, *is get Jessamyn out of your arms.* He set her down at the entrance. He'd stay inside the tent with her for about an hour—just long enough to satisfy the imaginings of Black Eagle. Then he'd saddle their horses and depart with the old chief's blessing. His heart sang. Lord God, he could kiss her!

Jessamyn lifted the deerskin flap and stepped inside. Ben worked to keep his gaze off her gently rounded backside.

Inside, she turned to face him. "Ben, for heaven's sake, are you going to feed me?" she murmured.

Feed her! His pulse leaped. She didn't mean it the way he took it, but he had to crush the image that bloomed in his mind. Lord almighty, he was beginning to think like Black Eagle.

"Here. In my pocket." He felt for the strip of jerky, handed it to her along with his jackknife.

Jessamyn sank onto the soft fur at his feet. The elusive fragrance of her hair wafted upward, and his groin tightened. God help him, he wanted to do more than just kiss her.

From the way she attacked that strip of venison, she could probably spend the entire hour eating. He watched her tongue slip out from between her teeth, her mouth open for the slice of dried meat.

Damnation! He sat down opposite her. He hadn't planned on this, hadn't ever dreamed he could be so drawn to a member of the female gender. He wanted her. But he knew bone-deep he was too vulnerable. He couldn't afford the risk, wouldn't admit even to himself how soul-deep his hunger ran.

He clenched his jaw until his teeth ached. What the devil was he going to do for the next sixty minutes?

For an entire hour Ben watched Jessamyn gobble down sliced jerky. While she ate, she bombarded him with incessant questions. Her head cocked to one side, she scribbled in her notebook as fast as he could talk.

"What do you think about Indians having firearms?"

"Damn dangerous," he growled.

"How did you and Black Eagle get along when you served as the Indian agent?"

"We were blood brothers. We trusted each other."

"Do you notice any difference now in the chief's regard for you?"

Ben hesitated. There was a difference; he just didn't want to explain it to Jessamyn. Mercifully, she did not ask what Black Eagle thought of "his" woman.

Ben himself did not know what he thought of Jessamyn at the moment. The stubborn, overstarched Northerner, sheltered all her life in civilized Boston, had certainly made an impression on Black Eagle. And despite the language barrier she had befriended the Indian chief's daughter, Walks Dancing. Both things surprised him.

He shook his head. City lady or not, another day in camp and she'd have the whole band of Indians eating out of her hand. *He* was the only one she didn't seem to cotton to. Only when her otherwise valiant spirit flagged after hours on the trail, or after the emotional shock of eating a supper of roasted dog meat did she turn to him for help. Then she was like the feisty little banty rooster he'd once accidentally shut out of his sister-in-law's henhouse. Head up, squawking, but with feathers that drooped in the mud, the bird had glared accusingly at him with a hard, unblinking eye.

Jessamyn Whittaker had that same fighting spirit. And, Ben noted with an inward chuckle, she had emotional depths she herself was unaware of. He would never forget how she had wept during the audible lovemaking session Black Eagle and his wife had indulged in last night. What an astounding reaction for an unworldly woman of delicate sensibilities.

No doubt about it, Jessamyn was a decidedly uncommon woman. Ben watched her pare off another slice of dried venison, wash it down with the bowl of hot sassafras tea Walks Dancing had set just inside the tipi entrance. He knew he had to get her out of camp as soon as she could ride. Black Eagle had taken too much of a fancy to her.

"Soon as you've finished eating, pack up," Ben muttered over the tightness in his throat. "We're leaving." He rose to his feet, his head brushing the top of the shelter.

Jessamyn stuffed another piece of jerky into her mouth and shoved her notebook into the saddlebag. Snapping his pocketknife shut, she handed it back to him, along with the remains of the dried meat. She pulled her boots on over her thick wool stockings and stood up.

"I'm ready."

Ben eyed her. "No, you're not. Pin up that hair."

Jessamyn's eyes widened and her hand flew to her head. "Oh, my, yes, I'd forgotten all about it. Wait—my hairpins!"

She rummaged in the saddlebag, withdrew a handful of bent wire pins and a tortoiseshell comb. Raising her arms, she began to twist a handful of her thick, dark hair into a loose roll. Ben caught his breath as her shirt pulled tight across her breasts. He couldn't watch and not want her.

Lord, how was he going to stand the two-day trek back to Wildwood Valley with her?

He turned away, angry at himself for being so intrigued by this annoying bit of single-minded womanhood. Grumbling to himself, he strode outside to saddle the horses.

The entire Indian encampment gathered to see them off. Jessamyn followed Ben to their saddled mounts, letting her gaze roam over Black Eagle's little band. Everyone was here—the old woman, silent warriors, wide-eyed children. And not one single dog, she noted with a twinge of pain. Also absent was the brave with the hidden rifle. She quietly called that fact to Ben's attention, and he nodded.

Just as she settled herself on the mare's back, she spied Walks Dancing limping through the crowd, her undulating steps agonizingly slow. Pausing next to Jessamyn's horse, the Indian girl handed up a beaded deerskin pouch. Inside lay a beautifully carved comb made of polished bone. Jessamyn's heart swelled. A gift.

Touched, she withdrew the tortoiseshell comb from her hair and presented it to the young Indian woman. Then, with a final smile, she nudged her horse up the trail after Ben's gelding. At the first bend she twisted in the saddle to look back. Walks Dancing waved until she was out of sight.

Jessamyn's throat swelled. She had made a friend in the Indian camp. Though they could not talk directly with one another, a bond had grown between the two—a shared understanding. Words were not needed.

Ahead of her, Ben urged his horse into the rock-walled cavern. Jessamyn followed the hollow clatter of hoofbeats into the shadowy opening that led down to Wildwood Valley and civilization.

It was dark before the sheriff called a halt. Parched with thirst, her skin dry and tight from the hot wind, Jessamyn slid off the mare.

"Are we going to cook supper now?"

"Not tonight."

Her stomach contracted. She'd eaten cold jerky for breakfast, and since then she'd had only two dried-out biscuits from Ben's pocket. Now she faced a cold, meager supper, as well.

"Don't turn around, Jessamyn. Gather some wood. Someone's following us."

Her blood turned to ice water.

Ben dropped his saddle a good distance from the fire pit he'd fashioned. "Just keep moving around."

"Who is it?" she ventured. Her voice sounded tight and scratchy.

"They've been trailing us since noon. I wouldn't put it past Black Eagle to—"

He broke off. "Jess, don't turn around. Come over here to me."

"Wh-what is it?" She tried to keep her voice steady.

"Nothing, yet." He slipped one arm behind her shoulders and pulled her back against his chest. "See that ledge up there?"

She nodded. A lopsided boulder jutted from the rimrock above them.

"I'm going to stake the horses beyond the fire. Make it look like we're camped a ways off."

"Oh," she said in a small voice. "That's a g-good idea."

"Stay close beside me. If anything moves up there, you let me know."

Again Jessamyn nodded. Fear turned her mouth sour. She swallowed hard. Her saliva tasted like unripened grapes.

Ben moved to the stones he'd laid out in a ring, knelt and flicked his thumbnail against a match head. A flame flared and guttered. He touched it to a twisted wisp of dry dockweed.

Jessamyn watched the grass shrivel and curl as the fire licked at the tinder. She flicked a glance up at the ridge above them. Nothing moved.

Instinctively she moved toward the comforting warmth of the fire, but Ben laid his hand on her shoulder.

"Stay here. Out of sight." He gestured to her bedroll. "When it gets good and dark, unroll it next to mine and lay your head on my saddle."

Without waiting for her assent, he gave her shoulder a quick squeeze. Then he picked up her saddle and a single blanket and moved toward the fire pit. Dropping the leather saddle near the flames, he artfully arranged a blanket over three rounded rocks to resemble a sleeping person.

He disappeared into the shadows, then returned leading both horses. He picketed the animals between Jessamyn and the snapping flames, then turned to her. "Roll up in the blanket. There's food in my saddlebag."

"But—"

He tossed the blanket over her shoulder and turned away. "Don't argue, Jess. Eat. Then get some sleep."

"What about you?"

"I'll keep watch. Save me the last of that jerky." He settled himself on the ground beside her, putting his back against a flat rock. Grabbing her hand, he pulled her down next to him.

Trembling, she rolled herself up in the woolen blanket and stared hard at the rocks above them, trying to penetrate the thick darkness by squinting her eyes and not blinking. She watched so long her eyes stung.

Ben touched her blanket-swathed shoulder. "Cold?"

"N-no. Just scared, I guess."

He extricated his pocketknife from his pants and laid it and a strip of jerky within reach.

"Eat something," he ordered. He crawled to the fire,

added more wood and returned with something chunky in his hand.

"Here." He shoved a large fire-heated rock under the blanket next to her body.

Jessamyn curled her shaking form around the warm object and slipped a round of venison into her mouth. Little by little her shaking lessened. Wary, her senses overactive, she lay still.

Below them, a coyote howled. An owl hooted once into the quiet. Jessamyn thought of Black Eagle and his wife, the sounds they made inside their tipi. Mating sounds. Natural sounds.

She nibbled another piece of jerky and turned her gaze on Ben, watched him slip his pistol out of the holster he wore strapped low on his hip. He laid the gun in his lap, his palm resting against the butt.

A cricket scraped a series of off-key notes, lapsed into ominous silence, then began again. Ben's breathing slowed to a steady rhythm. Jessamyn chewed the lump of dried meat and considered the man at her side.

It was odd how she and Ben Kearney had become…well, almost friends on this journey. They certainly hadn't started out that way. She doubted that Ben had many friends outside of Jeremiah and perhaps her father. Women she could imagine the sheriff having—women in large numbers, in fact, given his handsome, even arresting face and those smoky blue eyes. But a woman *friend?*

Now he was protecting her, taking precautions to keep her safe from an unseen enemy. She laid the open pocketknife and the jerky strip next to Ben's empty holster.

"Thanks," he said. The quietly spoken word calmed her jittery nerves. She forced herself to plan a newspaper layout, compose headlines in her mind, make up lead paragraphs—anything to keep her thoughts off the danger she sensed. And off her growing respect for the taciturn, enigmatic man beside her.

She wondered if her father had ever been afraid. What would Papa have done if he'd been in danger?

Jessamyn drew in a shuddery breath. She already knew the answer. He'd have gone right on with the business of publishing his paper. That's probably what got him killed.

Tension knotted her stomach. She closed her eyes, then snapped them open again. Ben sat motionless in the shadows, his head resting against the rock, his Stetson tipped down over his forehead. Underneath the brim, his eyes were alert and hard.

"Go to sleep," he said, his voice quiet.

Her lids drifted shut. After a long moment she let them flutter open. It comforted her to watch him.

A movement caught Ben's eye. A glimmer of firelight glinted off something—a knife? A rifle? A cold calm settled over him. He slipped his forefinger into the trigger guard.

A twig snapped and an Indian brave stepped into the circle of firelight.

"Running Elk," Ben said, his voice even. He spoke in Yurok. "I have been waiting."

The brave grunted. "Iron Hand will sell me the woman?"

"Iron Hand will not." He switched to English. "This woman is not for sale."

"How if I take her, then?" The Indian took a step toward the lumpy blanket before the fire.

"You will not take her. I will kill you if you take one more step."

Running Elk hesitated. "She is worth much, then?"

Ben slid the gun barrel on top of his thigh and aimed it. "She is worth much. Many horses."

At his side, Jessamyn's blanket twitched.

The brave spat out. "Iron Hand knows I can get many horses."

"Iron Hand does not need horses."

"Guns, then." The Indian's eyes gleamed suddenly. "Rifles."

"Nor guns. The woman belongs to me."

The blanket jerked again. Deliberately, Ben rolled one booted foot sideways until it touched the reclining lump at his side. When he felt his foot rest against something solid, he pressed, slow and hard.

The blanket stilled.

"You are an old man, Iron Hand. She is young and strong. I will give her many sons."

"I am thirty seasons and six. I will give her my own sons," Ben heard himself reply. "You will give her nothing. Take your companions and ride back to Black Eagle. Tell him Iron Hand does not bargain for what is already his. Tell him also that I make a gift of the life of his brave, Running Elk. Go now, before I change my mind."

The Indian peered into the darkness toward the sound of Ben's voice. Slowly he turned away, then grabbed for the blanket covering the stones.

Ben's gun blazed a streak of red-orange fire, and Running Elk cried out and clutched his wrist.

Ben raised the pistol and sighted over the man's heart. "Running Elk's life ebbs like sand emptying from a seashell."

The brave pivoted. "Iron Hand does not fire at a man's back."

Ben chuckled. "Iron Hand values this woman. He will shoot if you remain until he counts to three fingers."

Running Elk muttered an obscenity in Yurok.

"One," Ben called.

"Two."

"Thr—"

The Indian vanished into the dark.

Ben breathed out a long, slow breath and lowered the pistol. "Jess?"

A muffled word from under the blanket.

"Let's go."

Jessamyn's head emerged from under the folds of tan wool, her eyes wide. "Go?"

Ben nodded. He grabbed his saddle from under her head. "Mount up. He'll be back. We've got to beat them to the river crossing."

Her mouth dropped open. "But that's miles from here!"

"Exactly." He tossed his saddle on the gelding, then went to retrieve hers. "Now, mount up."

They rode all night. After the first few hours Jessamyn gave up trying to see in the dark and let the mare have her head. Gus at the livery stable was right. On rocky ground, horses were smarter than humans. The mare stepped daintily after Ben's gelding, her footing solid and sure. Jessamyn gripped the saddle horn so tightly her hands ached. Every mile of the way she expected something or someone to jump out at her. She'd never felt so defenseless in her life.

Just as the sky began to lighten, Ben pulled the gelding up short. Quickly he slid out of the saddle and studied the ground. When he climbed on his horse again, he turned hard to the right.

Even at night, Jessamyn knew this wasn't the way they'd come. The trail narrowed, twisted along the hilltops instead of zigzagging down to the river she could faintly hear rushing far below them. They were moving away from it. The mare's hooves rang against the rock-strewn trail cut into the hillside. Ben raised one arm and pointed downward.

Jessamyn drew up her horse and peered over the mare's neck into the canyon below. For a moment she saw nothing, and then her throat closed. The river looked like a rumpled black ribbon in the faint light of dawn. The white spume on the water told her it was swift and treacherous.

And Ben was headed straight for it.

Chapter Twelve

The sheriff stepped the gelding along the rock-strewn riverbank. "We'll take the shortcut. Cross the river north of the ford." He pointed upriver where the river boiled around a bend.

Jessamyn blanched. The water shone like burnished metal in the first rays of early-morning sun. It surged over boulders the size of a small house, swirled with terrifying force along the uneven bank.

"There," Ben shouted over the roar of the water. "It's not as shallow as the ford where we crossed before, but here there's no Indian reception committee waiting for us."

He pointed out a section where the riverbed curved, the water eddying into a frothy lacework of silvery foam. "The current slacks about where that fallen tree lies."

Jessamyn stared at the gnarled black roots of a massive upended fir. Oh, no. She wasn't about to willingly risk drowning Cora's mare, much less herself, in that swift-sliding dark water.

"Isn't there some other place we could cross?" She had to yell to make herself heard.

Ben shook his head. "Got no choice," he shouted. "Have to cross before daylight. Otherwise, Running Elk will spot us. He's downriver now, waiting."

Jessamyn struggled to grasp their dilemma. "But he'll follow us, no matter where we cross, won't he?"

"He can't cross to the west side of the river for fear of being captured and sent to the reservation. He expects us where we forded before, not here." He glanced at the flaming sun, now crawling over the mountain peaks behind them. "Come on! We can't waste time."

Ben pulled the gelding about and edged down to the riverbank. Turning his face toward her, he shouted something Jessamyn couldn't hear over the rushing water. He nudged his horse forward, motioning her to follow.

She balked. She couldn't walk her horse into that raging water—she'd be swept away in an instant, along with the mare. She couldn't make herself kick the animal into motion.

"Ben!" she screamed. "I can't do it! I can't!"

He didn't hear. Only when he reached the water's edge did he glance back at her, frozen on the mare's broad back.

He wheeled and rode toward her. Grabbing the mare's bridle, he yanked the animal forward. He caught the reins out of her hands, looped them around his wrist and started forward.

Water spilled over her boot tops, soaked her trouser legs. Numb with fright, Jessamyn clung to the saddle horn and felt the animal bump into the river, then abruptly strike out with its legs and begin to swim.

Icy blue-green water sloshed at her waist, rose to her midriff. She kicked her feet free of the stirrups and fought to keep her balance.

No use. The mare plunged sideways, and Jessamyn toppled out of the saddle. With one hand she grabbed at the horse's mane, tried to knot her fingers into the long hair, but the flowing strands were wet and slick. She couldn't hold on.

She went under, thrashed to the surface, then sank again. *God help me, I damn well won't die before I put my first newspaper to bed!*

She kicked violently against a submerged rock and came up spluttering. Her hat floated away. She reached out and snagged it. Cora would never forgive her if she lost Frank Boult's favorite Stetson.

Clutching the sodden mass of felt in one fist, she struck out for the opposite bank, breaststroking slowly, oh, so slowly toward a stretch of calm water. Ahead of her, Ben's gelding and the gray mare swam in tandem.

Jessamyn caught the mare's tail and hung on.

At last her feet scrabbled on the rocky bottom. She stumbled. Coughing up water, she released the horse's tail and tried to stand up.

The mare scrambled up the bank and stood facing her, trembling violently. She couldn't reach it! Her chest ached with a cold, tight feeling, as if an iron band squeezed the air out of her lungs. She tried again, slipped to one knee as she lost her balance.

"Jess!" Ben rode toward her, pulled her upright and pressed her clawed hands around the edge of his saddle. "Hold on!"

He leaned down over her, his body pressing her face into his thigh, and grabbed her waistband. Hooking his thumb inside her belt, he pulled her up and began walking the gelding out of the riverbed. Jessamyn's weakened legs scraped over the tops of the shore rocks.

When he released her, she crumpled on the spot. Ben slid off the horse and was beside her in an instant.

"Jess! Stand up!"

Stand up? Was the man crazy? She couldn't draw breath, much less stand up!

She gasped for enough air to tell him what a stupid, inconsiderate, loutish order he'd just given. A gulp of air whooshed in. Oh, thank God. She could breathe. She was safe! Despite her resolve, she began to cry. Great heaving sobs racked her frame.

"Jess! It's all right. We made it! Running Elk has turned back—I can see him on the ridge behind us."

"G-good," Jessamyn sobbed. She struggled to her feet and Ben pulled her into his chest, pressed her head into the hollow of his shoulder. Long tendrils of dark, wet hair straggled down her neck.

The warm rays of the sun on her back eased the tight, aching knot in her rib cage. She felt warm and safe here in his arms. She wanted nothing more than to just stand here with him, feel his strong hands at her back, listen to the thrumming of his heart through the wet canvas shirt. She wanted to feel him tight and hard against her.

Ben wrapped both arms around the trembling woman before him, steadied her against his body. They'd done it—outrun Running Elk, crossed the river just in time. A heady joy at being alive and in one piece coursed through him, kicked his pulse into a gallop. He felt giddy with happiness.

He was alive. And Jessamyn was alive—very much alive, judging from the trembling warmth enfolded within his arms. He and Jessamyn together had outfoxed both Black Eagle and his scout, Running Elk. He and Jessamyn—that proper, petticoated, steel-spined Yankee who wouldn't take No for an answer. Who now wept in his arms like a frightened child.

But she was no child, he acknowledged. No child—or woman, either—had ever made him feel this way, simultaneously exasperated and protective, admiring and infuriated.

And no woman before her—not even back in Carolina—had felt this good pressed hard against his body.

A kernel of heat in his belly exploded into an inferno of need. He inhaled the scent of her thick hair coming loose from the prim bun, clinging to his shirt, teasing his chin, gazed at her wide, soft-looking mouth so near his. He licked his lips. My God, he had a three-day growth of beard. If he had any sense...

Jessamyn stirred and tipped her head to look up at him with drowsy green eyes. Before he knew what he was doing, he tilted her chin up and covered her mouth with his.

Behind his closed lids, scarlet and gold sunbursts faded to black velvet as his lips tasted hers. She jerked and then went still.

Her heart fluttered like a bird's wings against his chest. Warmth washed into his groin. He pulled her closer, moving his mouth on hers, his breathing growing ragged.

He deepened the kiss, deepened it again as she began to respond, moving unconsciously into the rhythm that pulled at his body. She made a small sound in her throat, and a strangled groan escaped him.

Goddamn. He wanted her so much he felt dizzy. He caught her buttocks, lifted her to meet him, to fit.

A shaft of hot sunlight on his closed eyelids reminded him where he was. And who he was. Who she was. Jessamyn Whittaker was *not* his woman.

He released her. Bringing his hands to her temples, he loosened the wire hairpins, threaded his fingers into her thick hair. "Jessamyn. *Jessamyn.*" He barely recognized his own voice. He breathed in the sweet scent of her and worked to keep his hands still.

Jessamyn thought her body would melt when Ben's lips touched hers. His mouth was dark and silky, mysterious, his tongue wicked and wondrous as it teased her lips open. He moved—oh, how he moved!—as if he knew her intimately, sensed what she wanted before she knew it herself.

A needle of white-hot pleasure pricked her belly, settled lower, lacing her senses into a flame-licked net of desire. His tongue flicked across the tip of hers and a jolt of sweet aching sensation tightened her loins. With drowsy abandon she let him lift her, position her hard against him. She ached, *ached!*

Dear God, she wanted him inside her, hard and deep.

She groaned, felt his body tremble. Her hands fluttered toward the top button of her shirt. She wanted to be naked against him. Now.

She wanted—

His hands found her hairpins, discarded them. She

couldn't move for the pleasure of it, his fingers deep in her hair, stroking, stroking. He spoke her name, his voice thick, and something within her twisted with longing.

Hot and wet, she reached up for his hands.

"Ben. Ben, stop." Jessamyn's voice shook. She had to put an end to this. As much as she wanted what was happening, she knew it had to stop. Ladies did not lose their heads after just one kiss.

She settled his palms at her waist and bent her neck until her forehead pressed against his chest.

"Jess," he breathed. "I'm sorry. I had no right."

"Don't talk, Ben. I wanted you to." The confession surprised her. Accustomed to speaking her mind, she now blanched at her unladylike blurting of the truth.

But she *had* wanted it. She still wanted it. She hadn't wanted him to stop.

"It won't happen again," he said in a careful, throaty voice.

Disappointment niggled at the back of her mind. "I—I'm not offended. But I don't mean to…to suggest…"

"You didn't."

"Then I hope you won't dwell on what just…occurred between us."

"I wouldn't think of it," Ben lied.

"I was just so glad to be alive, and safe, that I lost my head."

Ben nodded, his chin brushing the top of her head. "Sure, Jess. Happens all the time."

She jerked away. *"All the time?"* Frost tinged her words. "You mean this has happened before?"

Ben gazed down into eyes so green and hard they shone like polished agates. "No," he said truthfully.

"Oh." The silence lengthened. Ben remained motionless, his hands at her waist.

The pull of the tension between them drove all rational thought from her mind. She didn't want him to move. She wanted him to—

"Time to mount up," he said quietly.

"Yes."

"Should reach town by afternoon."

Jessamyn hesitated. "Yes," she said again.

Ben chuckled. "I'll bet my spurs you're dying for a hot bath." He made no attempt to move away from her.

"Cora's probably heating the water right now," she murmured. "But after crossing the river back there..." Her voice trailed off. She did long for a bath in Cora's cozy, savory-smelling kitchen. But just the same, she hated this journey to end, hated the adventure—all of it, right down to Ben's heart-stopping kiss—to end.

She wrenched her mind away from the glorious experience. She thought of Papa, of his life out here in the West. He must have had plenty of excitement in this rough, untamed place. He'd written in the *Wildwood Times* about some of his adventures. His editorials were full of fascinating events and places, captured in vibrant detail.

She'd do exactly the same, she resolved. She had to focus on her newspaper, not on Ben Kearney. She'd work hard, make every issue of the *Wildwood Times* sparkle with interesting vignettes, move her readers to tears with heartfelt descriptions of people and events in Douglas County.

But to do that, she had to get her mind off the man who still held her in his arms. She had to ride back to town and set some type.

She spun on her heel and made her way to the gentle gray mare waiting patiently beside Ben's big-boned gelding. Without looking at Ben, she hooked her toe in the stirrup and hoisted herself up into the saddle.

For the next hour they rode in tense silence, following the snakelike course of the river. They skirted fences enclosing green alfalfa fields and rolling pastureland so lush it looked like dimpled velvet. Eventually, they picked up their original trail. Side by side they drew inexorably closer to Wildwood Valley and civilization.

Part of Jessamyn rejoiced at their return. She wasn't a

horsewoman, she was a newspaper editor. She had her notes, and her ideas for her lead stories, and she itched to get to work. Another part of her longed to just keep riding beside the tall, quiet man who had coaxed her body into aching response just a few miles back.

Now his touching her, kissing her, seemed unreal, like a dream she must have fashioned out of relief and exhaustion. She gave herself a mental shake, then settled into the memory again. Real or not, she knew she would never forget the feel of Ben's warm mouth on hers, his shaking fingers laced in her hair.

She shivered with delight, and an odd sense of loss swelled inside her. She snatched off Frank's hat, tossed her hair loose in the hot sunlight. She wanted to see that same expression kindle in Ben's eyes—that indefinable look of hunger tinged with fear. She cast a covert glance at him.

Ben's attention was not on her. Instead, his smoke blue eyes focused on something far off in the distance, ahead of them. With a swift intake of breath, Jessamyn followed the direction of his narrowed gaze.

Riders. Two of them, judging by the size of the dust cloud kicked up by their horses.

And coming fast.

"Wait here," Ben ordered. He spurred his mount forward to meet the two men at a jog in the trail. Pulling the gelding up short, he raised his hand in greeting.

Jeremiah touched two blunt fingers to his hat brim. "Got trouble, Ben."

Silas Appleby glowered at him from under his Stetson. "Forty more head gone, just like that!" He slapped his leather gloves against his palm. "Forty head! Goddammit, Ben, whoever took 'em must have known you were gone. I'm positive it's those Indians."

Ben sat back in the saddle and pulled one knee to rest on the saddle horn. Leaning over it, he eyed the angry rancher. "Positive, are you?"

"Damn right! I wanted to round up a posse, but your

deputy threatened to put me in jail if I so much as opened my mouth.''

Behind the sandy-haired rancher, Jeremiah shrugged his broad shoulders, his palms turned up.

Ben shook his head. ''It's not Indians, Si. I've been in their camp the past two days. Not one of them's been rustling any cows from around here.''

Jeremiah grinned. ''That railroad fella's in town again,'' he said after a moment. ''Larsen, remember? He's talkin' posse, too.''

Ben lifted his hat, wiped the sweat from his forehead with his shirtsleeve and raked a hand through his hair. ''Larsen's worried about his investment.''

''Well, hell, Ben,'' Silas retorted. ''So'm I! All tallied up, that makes near a hundred head taken right under my nose!'' He rolled a cigarette with shaking hands, offered it to Ben and started on another. ''I'm not stupid, Ben. And I'm not blind. How the devil—''

''Don't know how, Si,'' Ben interjected. ''Might have an idea as to *who,* though.'' He watched the rancher's eyes come alive with interest.

''Yeah?'' Silas exhaled a puff of blue smoke into the dusty air.

Ben studied Silas's freckled face. ''Yeah. Could be somebody right here in the valley.''

The rancher's eyes widened. ''What? Why, that's crazy. Why would—''

He stopped short as Jessamyn rode up on her mare. He touched his hat. ''Ma'am.''

Ben didn't like the light that flared in Silas's eyes as he took in the tumbled mass of wavy hair sheathing Jessamyn's shoulders. The rancher gazed at her like a moonstruck puppy.

Jeremiah moved over to make room for her mare. ''Miss Jessamyn. You're ridin' pretty good now.'' His dark eyes twinkled. ''I expect Ben kept you pretty saddle-weary.''

"Yes, he did, Jeremiah. But I did learn to ride, didn't I?"

The deputy chuckled. "You surely did, Miss Jessamyn. Look mighty fine on a horse now. Just like a fine-trained Carolina lady." He shot a quick look at Ben, engaged in a heated exchange with Silas Appleby. "Yessir, mighty fine."

"Jeremiah, the truth is, I learned a lot more on this trip than how to ride." She smiled at the deputy. "And *none* of it was easy."

"Yes, ma'am. Seems like nothin' worthwhile in life ever comes for free." A somber look passed over his face, then he chuckled again. "Come on. Miz Boult's got a hot supper waitin' for you. We been expectin' you for the last day and a half."

The deputy pulled his horse abreast of Ben's gelding. "Ben, didja see Walks Dancing?"

"Yeah. Didn't talk to her much, though. Black Eagle keeps a close watch on her."

"She married yet?"

"Not yet. Soon, though. The chief's getting on in years. He needs sons, grandsons to follow him."

Suddenly serious, Jeremiah shook his head. "Yeah. Like I figured. Thanks, Ben." He turned his mount toward town.

Jessamyn fell in beside him, only half listening to the continuing dialogue between Ben and Silas Appleby. She couldn't wait to get home, breathe in the wonderful scents in Cora's kitchen, run her hands over the polished mahogany banister, the cool, smooth sheets she knew Cora would have put on the bed in her yellow-papered bedroom. Her own bedroom. In her own house. Pride and gratitude for the gift Papa had left her bubbled in her breast.

And her newspaper. After a bath and some supper, she'd walk over to the *Wildwood Times* office and start composing her first story. Provided, she admitted to herself, she could concentrate on the words long enough to make coherent paragraphs. The story was already sketched out in her notebook; all she had to do was refresh her memory and follow the outline she'd written down.

She sucked in a shaky breath and kicked the mare into a canter. All she had to do was stop thinking about Ben Kearney, stop remembering the low, rumbly sound of his voice, the unsettling male scent of his body, heavy with horse sweat and pine soap.

She rode out ahead of the three men. If Ben disturbed her, well, then, she'd have to find something to take her mind off him. Publishing her first edition of the *Wildwood Times* should do just that. No matter how compelling his presence, Ben was merely an attractive but transitory interest.

Her newspaper was her whole life.

Chapter Thirteen

"Child, child!" Cora Boult pulled Jessamyn into a bosomy hug. "If you don't look a sight!"

"Oh, Cora, it's so good to be home. And I'm so hungry!"

"'Course you are. I've got a nice stewed..." The housekeeper hesitated at Jessamyn's quick intake of breath.

"Chicken," she finished.

"Oh, thank God," Jessamyn murmured.

"Say, what's the sheriff been feedin' you, anyway?" Cora huffed. "You look positively peaked."

"Don't even ask," Jessamyn managed.

The housekeeper grinned. "If you say so. Say, lookee there, on the table."

Jessamyn swept her gaze to the bouquet of pearly pink roses jammed into one of Cora's glass canning jars. She bent to sniff the fragrant blooms. "Oh, they're lovely. Bathwater must be a special elixir for your roses. They smell extra nice—spicy, like vanilla cookies."

"Ain't any roses I grew, honey. Gus, down at the livery stable, brung 'em. Said they was 'Male Mason,' or somethin' like that."

"Malmaison," Jessamyn pronounced.

"You know, I think Gus is kinda sweet on you."

Jessamyn started. "Sweet on me! Whatever for?"

Cora propped both hands on her ample hips. "For court-in', that's what. You want to stay an old—a maiden lady all yer life?"

"I never thought about marrying," Jessamyn said slowly. "All my life I've planned to run a newspaper."

"Humph. 'T'ain't natural. I never seen Gus take roses to anybody else before. Don't make no nevermind that he runs the livery stable, he's a fine man, Gus is. He was an officer in the Union army, you know. That's how come he lost his eye. Don't never mention it, though. He likes horses, is all. When he first rode into town he didn't like how the blacksmith was treatin' the animals, so he up an' bought the place. Paid cash, too. You listening, child?"

Jessamyn sighed. "I'm listening, Cora."

"Anyway, he's been here in the valley ever since. And I never saw him take anyone roses before."

Cora moved about the kitchen, continuing her recitation as she clattered pot lids and iron spoons, but her voice faded from Jessamyn's consciousness. She didn't want to think about roses or Gus or anything beyond filling her growling stomach and settling herself at Papa's big oak desk over at the newspaper office. She especially didn't want to think about courting.

"Yes, Cora," she said absently. "Mmm-hmm. And roses... Yes, lovely." One thing in particular she didn't want to think about was Wildwood Valley's tanned, long-limbed sheriff.

"...are you?" Cora finished on a question.

Jessamyn started. "Am I what?"

Cora drew herself up. "Are you gonna eat your supper in them duds, or are you wantin' to get back into proper petticoats again?"

Jessamyn had to laugh. She gave the older woman a quick hug and planted a kiss on the lined cheek. "It doesn't matter. I'm so hungry I could eat stark naked!"

At the housekeeper's startled expression, Jessamyn un-hooked her wide leather belt and pulled the rumpled red shirt free of the waistband. The moment she began to unbutton the plaid garment, she thought of Ben. Her fingers stilled.

Ben certainly wasn't courting her, as Cora termed it. The sheriff had barely tolerated her for most of their journey together. It took days for him to even be civil until the end, and then he'd...

She closed her eyes at the memory of his hands moving over her back, the taste of his mouth. Maybe she didn't want a man to come calling, bringing her roses and making polite talk. All she wanted was Ben Kearney to kiss her again.

She snapped open her eyelids. She'd die before she'd admit such a thing to Cora, or anyone else. It was unsettling enough to acknowledge it to herself.

By the time Jessamyn arrived at the front door of the *Wildwood Times* office, darkness blanketed the town's main street. Even Charlie's Red Fox Saloon was unusually quiet. Maybe, she reasoned, because it was Friday, and the ranch owners and cowboys who caroused with boisterous abandon on Saturday night reined in their high spirits until then. Or maybe their wives—the ones who had wives—insisted their menfolk accompany them to evening prayer meeting.

The sound of singing rose from the painted clapboard church at the far end of town, floating on the soft June air. Jessamyn hummed along as she unlocked the office door, propping it ajar to enjoy both the hymns and the warm, honeysuckle-scented breeze.

"Rock of ages, cleft for me..." She lit the oil lamp, draped her blue paisley shawl over the desk chair and ducked into the back room where sectioned type cases lined the wall behind the wide, slanted worktable.

Her pulse tripped. She couldn't wait to compose her story, lay the completed type stick into the frame and lock it up. But first she had to get the words down on paper. She turned toward the desk. With deft fingers, she tied a starched work apron over her blue striped gingham skirt, then searched her pocket for the notebook she'd filled on her journey into the mountains. Settling herself at her father's battered desk, she flipped the pad open.

Merciful heavens! Jessamyn stared in dismay at the pages of fuzzy, water-washed writing. She'd carried the pad in her shirt pocket all during the trek with Ben. Now, after her unplanned dunking while crossing the river, she couldn't decipher one single word.

She snapped it shut and groaned aloud. All her notes—visual impressions of Black Eagle and the Indian camp hidden high in the mountains, all Ben's thoughtful, careful answers to her probing questions—gone. Washed away by the river's swift current.

Dumbfounded, she stared at the ruined pages. She'd have to start from scratch, draw on her memory to re-create her story.

Close to despair, she bent her head. After a moment she slid open the top desk drawer, closed her fingers around a thick pencil. If she worked all night and through tomorrow, she might still be ready to go to press on Tuesday.

Her thoughts churned. She sat motionless for a long minute, then drew in a deep breath, smoothed a sheet of scratch paper onto the desk top and began to write.

Sheriff Kearney On Trail Of Cattle Thief
Douglas County Sheriff Benning Kearney suspects the cattle thief raiding Wildwood Valley herds is in league with someone supplying illegal firearms to the Indians. Kearney concluded this following a recent trip into the Calapooya Mountain country....

She finished the paragraph and read the final sentence out loud. "It remains for Sheriff Kearney to unravel the mystery, but one thing is now clear. Identifying the thief is only a matter of time."

Jessamyn sighed in satisfaction. Bustling toward the composing table, she reached for her type stick.

Ben lifted his niece's small frame out of his saddle where she'd sat the past quarter mile and set her carefully on the bottom porch step of his brother's ranch house.

"Go on in now, Alice. Tell your mama I'll be along to supper after I feed old Blackie here and wash up at the pump."

The child bolted up the steps, and the door slammed behind her. Ben shook his head.

A part of him—a part he barely recognized it was so rusted over from years of denial—longed to share in the easy laughter and affection between two people who loved each other.

He'd had to force himself to saddle the gelding and ride out here today. The painful contrast between his brother's full life with the woman to whom he'd pledged his life and Ben's own existence—that of a hardscrabbling soul trying to find itself again, as Jeremiah put it—was all too sharp.

Sunday nights after supper at the Double K Ben slept badly, tossing on the hard, narrow cot behind the sheriff's office until Jeremiah grumbled about being awakened.

"You don' need this, Ben," the deputy always observed. "You need a woman—a permanent kind of woman. You gave up on Miss Lorena back home, but you'd best get on with your life pretty quick now, or it'll be too late. No sensible woman wants a burned-out ol' soldier with a busted heart on his sleeve."

Ben swore out loud just thinking about his deputy's oft-repeated litany. Hell, he'd worked hard to "get on with his life" after the war. After Lorena. When his right arm had stiffened up from the wound near his shoulder, he'd taught himself to eat and write, even shoot left-handed. Over the years, he got to where he could put a bullet between a man's eyes at twenty yards.

But let a woman get close? Never again. In the first

place, he *was* old. And tired. At thirty-six, after years surviving on battlefields in the South and then in Dakota, he was burned out. He didn't have an interest in courting a woman.

Or the courage.

A calico queen he could tumble into bed and forget the next morning. A lady was another matter. For one thing, he'd never met one he could stand listening to more than an hour. Charlie's calico girls didn't talk much. They did what was needed, and that was that. The act might be pretty perfunctory, but it was safer than getting tangled up in the clutches of some clinging vine.

Like Lorena. Damned spoiled and self-centered. He hoped she was happy with the rich carpetbagger landlord of a husband she'd married after he left. He wondered if she would tie up another man's heart, and his confidence, and make mincemeat out of them, too.

Ben gave the pump handle two vicious strokes and stuck his head under the water to cool off. Why was he dredging all this up again? He shook the water out of his hair, rubbed his wet hands over his face and blotted his cheeks against his sleeve. He had to get his mind off women.

The memory of Jessamyn Whittaker, her chestnut hair tumbled about her shoulders, her soft mouth lifted to his, would fade with a good supper and some ranch talk with Carleton and Ella.

He couldn't wait to ride into the mountains again. Tracking always distracted him from other things weighing on his heart. If he was on the trail, he wouldn't have to see her, wouldn't ache to kiss her again.

With a last swipe at his hair, he clapped his hat back on and strode toward the porch.

So tired she could barely stand, Jessamyn pulled the last sheet of newsprint off the press and held it up. Jeremiah released the lever arm and moved to read over her shoulder.

"Looks mighty fine, Miss Jessamyn," the stocky man

remarked. Nodding his head, he scanned down the page, his broad forehead creasing into a frown. "Gonna rile up some folks, though. But I expect you know that. And surely does look mighty fine."

Jessamyn's heart swelled with pride. Despite her exhaustion, her pulse quickened as she examined the still-damp copy of her first issue. The print was sharp and clear, none of the headlines were tombstoned, and the stories beneath were broken into readable paragraphs. The articles ranged from local doings to statewide and national events reported by the wire service and delivered on horseback from Steamboat Landing.

Papa would applaud her debut effort. All during this long night, the second in as many days she had labored at the newspaper office, Jessamyn had felt her father's spirit hovering near, guiding and encouraging her. She could almost hear his voice in her ear. *"That's my Jess!"*

Her hand shook so violently the paper rattled. "We did it, Jeremiah." She looked up at the deputy beside her. "Just think, by breakfast time we'll have fifty copies ready to deliver."

"You did it, Miss Jessamyn. I jes' helped out a bit here'n there."

Jessamyn shook her head. Jeremiah had sneaked over from the sheriff's office last night after Ben had retired, and stayed until the sun rose, helping her lock up the frames of finished type and pulling the heavy press lever for her when her arm gave out.

"I couldn't have done it without your help, Jeremiah. You're a good friend."

The deputy's toothy grin flashed. "We're not out of the woods yet, Miss Jessamyn. You don't have fifty copies— only got thirty-eight. We used the last of the paper a while back."

Jessamyn's heart sank. "No more newsprint? But my order at Frieder's isn't in yet!"

Merciful heavens, what would she do now? She massaged her temples with her fingertips. *Think!* she ordered her tired brain. She was out of newsprint and twelve copies short. She gave a little moan of despair.

"Aw, Miss Jessamyn, please don' cry. I can't stand it when a lady cries. Lordy, when Miss Lorena—"

Jeremiah caught himself and stopped short.

Jessamyn's gaze locked with the sober-faced deputy's. "Jeremiah, tell me. Who is Miss Lorena?"

Jeremiah ran a blunt forefinger around the inside of his shirt collar. "Miss Lorena was…well, uh, she was Ben's lady, back in Carolina. And, well, seein' as how Ben and me and Lorena, we grew up together, I sorta liked to imagine she was my lady, too."

"You were in love with her, weren't you?" Jessamyn remarked, her voice soft.

The deputy's eyelids closed momentarily. "Yes'm. But I never spoke out to her. Didn't have the right. I was just the overseer's son, and we were mighty poor folk. I couldn'a bought her pretty dresses and fine horses like she'd expect from a man. And Ben…well, Ben was more what Miss Lorena wanted. So I never said nothin'."

"And Ben never knew, did he?"

"No, ma'am." The deputy tapped his well-developed chest. "It's been locked in here for these twenty years."

A silence dropped over the room. For a moment Jessamyn's newspaper problems seemed insignificant compared with the lifelong ache in a man's heart for something he couldn't have. Lord knew she'd felt a similar longing for her father all those years he'd been gone.

"I am sorry, Jeremiah. Truly I am."

Jeremiah started as if roused from a dream. "Oh, I'm not so heart-laden I can't appreciate a fine-lookin' woman. Sorta like hair of the dog, you might say—it's good for a man."

Jessamyn studied the solid, square-faced man before her. If she wasn't mistaken, her sharp eyes had already identified the deputy's choice. The look in Jeremiah's soft brown eyes that day Walks Dancing had ridden into town told her the deputy might be well on the road to recovery.

Jeremiah cleared his throat. "Now, then, 'bout your paper supply. Your pappy ever smoke ceegars?" he inquired in his soft drawl.

"Cigars?" She stared at him. Jeremiah's shift in subject matter pulled her attention back to the newspaper. "Are you suggesting that smoking a cigar will help me think what to do?" She choked down a bubble of laughter at the thought.

"No, ma'am, surely not. But ceegars come packed in big boxes, and those boxes are wrapped in fine big sheets of paper. Kinda tan colored, but we could iron out the creases and—"

"Jeremiah, you're a genius!"

"Yes, ma'am," the deputy said modestly. "I'll just go rouse up Mr. Frieder and see what kind of ceegars he's got in stock."

Jessamyn watched the stocky man march through the doorway, her mind racing ahead of him. An iron! She'd need an iron. And a fire in the stove to heat it on. She could smooth the wrapping paper out on the desk.

Before she could dash over to beg the use of Cora's sadiron, Jeremiah was back, a roll of wide wrapping paper in one hand and a small flatiron in the other.

"This here's my special pressin' tool. Works just fine on Mr. Ben's shirts, so I figured—"

He broke off as Jessamyn gave him a swift hug. "Jeremiah, you're not only a genius, you're a newspaperwoman's gift from heaven!"

Jeremiah's grin flashed again. "Yes, ma'am."

Jessamyn swore a blush tinged the deputy's tanned cheeks. "Come on, Jeremiah. Another hour and our paper will hit the street, as they say in Boston. Oh, isn't it exciting?"

Jeremiah's bushy eyebrows rose. "Yes, ma'am." If she only knew. He'd almost choked when he'd heard old Mrs.

Henson's rooster crow at five this morning and realized
he'd been at the news office all night. Then he'd had to
rouse Otto Frieder and his wife out of a sound sleep to
rustle up the cigar-box wrapping paper. Otto had sworn a
blue streak all the way to the mercantile front door.

"Yes'm, Miss Jessamyn, it surely is exciting."

Jessamyn flitted away to the back room with the nickel-
plated iron in her hand. Jeremiah spread the roll of wrapping paper out on the desk.

At half past six that Tuesday morning, fifty neatly folded
copies of the *Wildwood Times,* editor J. Whittaker, were
completed. They had printed the final four copies on
squares of clean muslin sheets that Cora had reluctantly
agreed to cut up as the deadline approached.

Jessamyn flew up one side of the street and down the
other, delivering her papers. She left copies on the Dixon
House hotel desk, on the table just inside the door of Charlie's Red Fox Saloon, at Frieder's Mercantile and the barbershop. She would hand-deliver the paid subscriptions
later this morning, after some breakfast.

Jessamyn watched her helper and mainstay through the
endless, exhausting night sprint across the street and disappear into the sheriff's office. Feeling enormously pleased,
she pulled the front door shut, locked it, then headed for
the two-story white house and the soft bed in the yellow-
papered room at the end of the upstairs hallway.

It was a good issue, she thought with pride. A good beginning. She could almost hear her father's voice. *"Well
done, daughter!"*

She hoped Ben wouldn't be too angry when he read the
story about him on the front page. She drew in a tentative
breath and held it. Closing her eyes, she fought down a
tremor of alarm, remembering Jeremiah's frown when he'd
scanned her lead article.

Chapter Fourteen

The sheriff's office door banged open, then slammed shut. "Ben!" a furious voice bellowed. "Ben Kearney, where the hell are you?"

"Putting on my pants," Ben said quietly as he emerged from the sleeping quarters. He cinched his belt up, moved to meet the short, wiry man dancing a jittery path toward him.

"What are you doing up so early, Jack? I thought railroad barons lived a life of luxury."

"Luxury!" Jack Larsen sputtered. "Don't you know what's happening? They're talking about changing the railroad route to the coast. Hell, if they do that, I'll be flat broke in a week!"

Ben looked the man in the eye. "I warned you to wait. Only a fool would rush out and buy up all that property on sheer speculation."

"Ben, it was a sure thing." The man's impeccably groomed mustache twitched with fury. "I had Senator Tiel eating out of my hand. If it wasn't for that goddamned newspaper—"

"Thad Whittaker's dead, Jack. You know that."

Larsen's small black eyes narrowed. "Yeah, well, the newspaper isn't. You seen it?"

"Seen what? The paper? No, not yet. I know Jess—the

editor's been working on it. Last I heard she hadn't gone to press. Nobody's seen a printed copy yet.''

"Like hell." Larsen withdrew a rumpled page from inside his vest and slapped it down on Ben's desk. "Read that!''

Ben studied the words printed on the odd-colored paper. A faint design showed through the typeset copy—a huge, floppy petaled flower with the word *Havana* beneath it. Disregarding it, he scanned the articles. Activities of Mrs. Ellis's church quilting society. A formal birth announcement for Henry Winchester and Lyle Coulter Bartel, Rufus and Lizzie's twins. Ah, there! At the top of the last column.

"Legislature Reassesses Railway Route," Ben read out loud.

Jack Larsen rocked back on the heels of his black leather boots. "It's all over town. I got the last copy over at Charlie's saloon.''

Ben eyed the man before him. "What's all over town?''

Larsen snapped his jaw shut, then cracked his thin lips just enough to speak. "Senator Tiel thinks the original route—*my* route—is unsafe. Rock slides or some damn thing. Hell, Ben, another article like this one could ruin me!''

Ben nodded. If he was going to get any breakfast this morning, he'd better smooth Jack's ruffled feathers. Otherwise, the irate investor would talk his ear off all morning complaining about unfair news coverage and biased editorials, shooting off his mouth before he thought things through.

"Write a rebuttal, Jack. Maybe a letter to the editor making your views known. If you're convincing enough, you might even change the senator's mind. And coherent enough," he added as an afterthought. Jack Larsen was always going off half-cocked and doing something crazy. The attribute annoyed Ben. He'd watched Thad Whittaker punch holes in Jack's outrageous accusations for years; it was like popping a hatpin into an overinflated balloon.

"Talk to Jeremiah when you've calmed down," Ben advised. "My deputy's good with words."

"Yeah, Ben, maybe I'll just do that." The tightness in the railroad man's voice eased. "I'll just do that. As my daddy used to say, there's more than one way to skin a cat." His narrow, pinched face lit up with a secret smile. "Or an editor."

Ben hustled Jack out the front door ahead of him. The last thing he saw as he made his way to the Dixon House dining room for his breakfast was Jack Larsen's black-jacketed backside disappearing into the Red Fox Saloon.

Ben frowned. Not only was the man a damn fool, he was not trustworthy. Not for one minute did he believe the investor had Senator Tiel eating out of his hand. More likely that was some puffery designed to mollify Larsen's co-investors. Now the railroad investor was mad as a hornet because his lie had been exposed. When he went back up into the mountains tomorrow, he'd ask Jeremiah to keep an eye on Larsen.

At Dixon House Ben hung up his gun and ordered coffee and the usual steak and fried eggs, then slid into a chair at one of the unoccupied tables. A copy of the *Wildwood Times* lay on the next table. Ben picked it up, opened it to the front page.

"Goddammit to hell!" His fist crashed onto the wood surface.

Ben ran one hand through his hair as he scanned the front page. There before him, in bold black type, was exactly the information he needed to keep quiet—the link between cattle rustling and providing guns to the Indians. God almighty! The minute whoever was responsible read this, he'd know the sheriff was on to the scheme.

Ben gritted his teeth. The first thing an outlaw would do would be to go underground. Disappear. Damnation! He'd lost the only advantage he ever had—surprise.

"Jessamyn," Ben muttered. "You damned little fool." She'd forced his hand. Now he'd have to saddle up this very morning to get the drop on his quarry before the news spread.

Ben gulped the scalding coffee, grabbed his pistol off the hook and moved toward the door.

"Rita?" His voice rang in the empty dining room.

The waitress poked her head out from the kitchen.

"Cancel that steak, will you?"

Miss Whittaker, if I live through this, I'm gonna tan your backside so hard you'll stand up for a week.

Ben strode through the door into the hot June sunshine and headed for the sheriff's office. He had to let Jeremiah know he was going back up into the mountains.

Jessamyn rolled over in her narrow bed and pulled the sheet over her head, trying to shut out the morning light that flooded the upstairs room. No use. Exhausted as she was, she was too keyed-up to sleep any longer. She had to hear firsthand the townspeople's reaction to her first issue.

She sat up, easing her pantalet-covered legs off the edge of the bed. She had to know Ben's reaction, too.

She splashed cool water from the washstand basin onto her face, scrubbed her teeth with baking soda. She wouldn't bother with her corset, she decided. She was in too much of a hurry to take the trouble to snap herself into it and cinch up the laces. Hurriedly she pulled two crisp, starched petticoats on and tied them at the waist over her chemise.

Twisting her hair into a loose bun, she jammed seven wire hairpins in as fast as her fingers would move, then buttoned up her shoes and grabbed her parasol. She was down the stairs and out the door in a twinkling. Cora didn't even look up from the kettle of fragrant strawberry jam bubbling on the stove.

The morning air smelled of dust and Cora's prize damask rose blooming in the side garden. Jessamyn flew past the livery stable and up the street toward her office.

Dr. Bartel tipped his hat and smiled his thanks for the birth announcement. Then Addie Rice hailed her. Could the seamstress place another ad for dressmaking and one for millinery in next week's issue?

In front of the mercantile, a beaming Anna-Marie Frieder waddled out the front door with a small paper sack of ginger drops. "You write about our baby, too, when it comes next month?"

Of course she would, Jessamyn assured her. Birth announcements and obituaries were the staples of the news business, along with political advertisements. How glad she was this was an election year—her coffers would be running over by voting day in the fall. Already some senator from Portland had written to inquire about her rates.

Her brain hummed. Next week's issue would include the church choir director's plea for men's voices and an editorial on sprucing up the buildings along the main street in time for the Fourth of July.

But just think, she had readers! Already supporters flocked to subscribe. Silas Appleby had ridden in from his ranch just yesterday to offer a year's payment in advance. He'd gazed with interest at her frenzied activity at the composing table and gallantly invited her to supper. She'd declined, but even so, the sandy-haired rancher had insisted on paying for his subscription then and there.

Oh, it was wonderful, all of it. She knew why Papa had loved it so. A newspaper was an important contribution to a community, an economic and cultural asset to the county. The process—and the heady sense of connectedness she gained—were as intoxicating as fine brandy.

Just as she reached the door of the *Wildwood Times*, Sheriff Ben Kearney appeared on the opposite side of the street. He pivoted, spoke over his shoulder to his deputy and lifted a saddlebag onto his shoulder.

Ben was going away? So soon after…

He caught sight of her and stopped still for an instant, then started across the street toward her. Jessamyn swallowed as his long legs brought him closer and closer. His angular face looked grim, his well-formed lips compressed into a hard line, his stride unrelenting. Watching his loose-jointed gait, the long, powerful legs flexing in her direction, she felt mesmerized by the sheer animal magnetism of the man.

Blood surged into her face. Dizzy, she wrenched her attention away, jiggling the key in the front door lock. His footsteps echoed on the board sidewalk behind her.

"Lift it up," Ben breathed at her back. He reached around her, maneuvered the sticking door open. "Now, lock it behind us. I want to talk to you."

Unsteady, Jessamyn swung the door wide. Her heart pounded erratically. Ben swept her through the opening and kicked the door shut with his boot. Then he turned the key, locking them inside.

"No one can get in," Jessamyn ventured.

"Exactly."

"What about my subscribers?" She made a half turn away from him to peer out the front window. "Some of them might want to pay—"

"Later." Ben dropped his heavy saddlebag where he stood and took two steps forward. Grasping her shoulders, he spun her to face him.

"Just what in the hell do you think you're doing?"

Jessamyn stiffened. "Publishing my newspaper, that's what."

"Have you any idea... I thought we agreed you'd keep your nose out of my investigation."

"You agreed," she reminded him. "I didn't. I said I wouldn't interfere. I never said I wouldn't report on it."

"Semantics!" Ben growled. "You're just like Thad, all brains and ideas but no common sense." He tightened his grip on her shoulders.

"So now," he continued, "I've got a wild bull by the tail. When you made sure your readers heard about that rifle we found at Black Eagle's camp, you blew my only cover to hell."

"C-cover?"

"Well, I've got to find those carbines. There has to be a cache of them hidden somewhere up in the hills. Except now—thanks to you—instead of hunting slow and sure, with time and secrecy on my side, I've got to ride hell-for-leather and try to find those guns before whoever's stashing them finds me first."

"Oh, Ben, I—"

"Jessamyn, why couldn't you just keep your mouth shut?"

Jessamyn stared up into smoky blue eyes that now glittered with anger. Her breath choked off as her heart thumped to a stop and then jerked into a new rhythm.

"News," she blurted when she could trust her voice, "is what's *new*. Any good journalist knows that. And I'm a journalist."

"You're a damn fool."

"I am not! I worked hard on that story. It's factual, and it's accurate. It's well written."

"It's most likely going to get me killed."

Jessamyn opened her mouth, thought for a long moment, then closed it. "Ben, I don't know how to say this. I'm not sorry I printed an important piece of hard news—that's my job as a newspaper editor."

"That's what I thought you'd say. Goddammit, Jess—"

"I'm not finished." She drew in a shaky breath and closed her eyes, then flicked them open and looked up at him. "Ben, believe me, I am sorry if my newspaper has put you in danger."

Ben relaxed his hold on her. "Wouldn't be the first time. Thad and I had similar talks after every issue he printed. Nosy old coot."

Jessamyn bristled. "He's not a nosy old coot! He's my father, and he was a wonderful—"

"Nosy old coot." Ben's voice softened. "Hell, Jess, I loved him as much as you did. That doesn't keep me from speaking the truth as I see it. Thad was a fine newspaper editor and a thorn in my side from the day I rode into town and took on this job. I suspect you're not going to be any different.''

Jessamyn stifled a nervous laugh. "You think I'm a 'nosy old coot' too, is that it?''

"I think you're a nosy young...woman.''

Suddenly aware of his hands still on her shoulders, Ben let them fall away. A silence stretched between them, the air so charged it almost sang with tension. Very deliberately Ben replaced his hands.

Jessamyn's head came up. She stuck her proud little pointed chin in the air and spoke quietly. "You're right, Ben. I'm a nosy old maid. But it's all I've got.''

"Jessamyn...''

"Don't stop me now. I'll never have the courage again.''

"Courage for what?''

"I've never said this to anyone, not to Papa or Mama or anyone.'' She shut her eyes momentarily, ran her tongue over her lips. "I'm frightened underneath. Afraid my life doesn't matter. That *I* don't matter. Sometimes it makes me angry. If I can get angry enough, it feels cleansing. Clarifying. When I'm so angry I don't care what happens, I feel stronger. N-not so scared.''

Her voice broke. She took another deep breath.

"The newspaper—Papa's legacy for me—makes me feel I'm worth something. So I don't think—I write. And writing eases my fear.''

Ben felt as if he'd been poleaxed. He couldn't utter a word. For one thing, he couldn't think what to say. But more than that, he wasn't reacting to her verbally at this moment; his response was strictly visceral. He wanted to crush her against him, take her mouth in a hot, slow rhythm. Some part of Jessamyn's inner being, her real self, had spoken to him so honestly he felt humbled. He didn't know how to respond.

But he did know one thing—he didn't want to get killed. He wanted to come out of the mountains whole in body and in spirit. He wanted to come back to her.

But right now, God forgive him, part of him wanted to strangle her pretty little neck, and part of him wanted to lay her down in that sun-warmed patch on the floor, pull off those soft, ruffly garments, and stroke her until she wept.

He stood perfectly still, aware his body was trembling. "I'm frightened, too, Jess. I don't trust anyone, not even my family. It makes me crazy sometimes. It makes me...hurt inside."

His belly went cold. He'd revealed too much. Not even to Jeremiah had he admitted these things. Until this moment he had not admitted this much even to himself. He felt himself sucked into a vortex, then became aware that his mind was beginning to float, disoriented. God, what was happening to him?

Without conscious thought, he drew Jessamyn forward until her warm breath gusted against his neck. "Look at me," he commanded, his voice quiet.

Mute, she shook her head.

"Kiss me, then." He pulled her upward, half lifted her onto her toes and bent his head. When his mouth touched hers, his heart seemed to explode. Heat spiraled into his chest, his belly. "Jessamyn." He spoke her name in a rough whisper. "Jessamyn."

She opened to him, her mouth like black silk. He explored, went deeper, withdrew to gasp for breath. He kissed her again, too forcefully he knew, but he couldn't stop. God, he wanted her.

She moaned under his lips.

He had to stop, had to ride into the hills before the day got any older. He lifted his mouth from hers and set her apart from him.

"Ben," she breathed. "Don't go."

"I have to, Jess. The sun's up good and high—I can't wait any longer."

"Don't get killed," she said in a trembling voice. "I'll never forgive myself."

Ben chuckled. "Neither will I. Jess, I'm sorry I—"

"No, you're not," she said. "Don't lie to me."

He laughed out loud. "You're right, I'm not."

To prove his point, he kissed her again, long and slow and deep. Then he pivoted away from her, grabbed the saddlebags up off the floor and strode to the door.

Shaken, Jessamyn watched his tall form step out onto the plank walkway and move past the front window toward the livery yard. She listened to the rowels on his spurs spin until the sound faded into nothing.

For the first time in her entire life she didn't know what she wanted most—another first-rate issue of the *Wildwood Times* or Ben Kearney's safety.

"Saddle up Blackie, would you, Gus?" Ben shifted the saddlebag to his other shoulder as he spoke to the liveryman.

The tall Norwegian trained his one blue eye on the sheriff. "How long you gonna be gone this time, Colonel?"

Ben winced inwardly at the man's unconscious use of the military title. Gus had served as a major in the Union army. His observation of Ben's superior military rank reminded Ben that—for Gus, at least—the war was over.

For Ben, the war would never be over. The battle inside himself between his hunger for human connection and his gut-level fear of loving another woman ate at his soul. Wanting a woman the way he had wanted Jessamyn not five minutes ago—the way he wanted her still—like a dying man seeking light, shattered his equilibrium. If he let himself love her, he would suffer.

As he eased the saddlebag off his shoulder and onto the ground, he resolved he wouldn't think of her. Wouldn't want her. Wouldn't remember her scent, the feel of her silky hair tangled in his hands.

"How far you goin', Colonel?" the wrangler repeated.

Ben jerked his attention back to Gus. "Don't know yet.

Be gone three, maybe four days. Maybe a week—it depends.''

"Depends on what?" Gus gazed at him, a quizzical look in his one good eye.

"Hell, Gus, you know I'm not going to broadcast my plans to you or anyone else. No offense, but I'm still the sheriff around here, and I've got a bunch of missing cows and an unsolved killing on my hands."

The husky man grinned and shrugged his massive shoulders. "No harm done, Ben. I'll saddle your horse."

Gus tramped away toward the stable, leaving Ben with an uneasy feeling gnawing at his gut. The tall liveryman always wanted to know Ben's travel plans. Could Gus want to keep track of his comings and goings for his own reasons?

By agreement, Gus covered Ben's tracks each time he headed out on a job, telling anyone curious enough to ask that Ben rode east when in fact he headed west, and vice versa. Outside of Jeremiah, Gus alone was privy to the truth of Ben's whereabouts.

The wrangler tramped over to Ben, leading the gelding. "Here he is, Colonel. He's been kinda restless these past two days. Could be the old boy's ready for some new adventure."

"Could be." Ben checked the rawhide thongs securing his bedroll and slung his heavy saddlebags over the animal's back. He'd packed more supplies than usual, including extra dried beans and coffee. For all he knew, he might be on the trail a week or more. He had a hunch about an old abandoned miner's cabin in Copperblossom Canyon. Few people knew about it outside of Black Eagle and one or two of his braves. It would serve as a perfect hiding place for outlaws. Or, Ben thought with a grim smile, a cache of guns.

He hoped it would be the latter. If he could discover such a cache, he could stake out the place and let his quarry walk into a trap.

"Which way you ridin', Colonel? Officially, I mean."

Ben stepped into the stirrup and swung himself into the saddle. "South."

"South." Gus grinned up at him, his one good eye widening with interest. "Sure thing. Same as last time, huh? South."

Ben kneed the horse, turning him toward the corral gate. "Take care of yourself, Major."

"That I will, Ben."

The moment the sheriff turned north on the river trail, Gus smiled to himself and nodded his head in satisfaction. "Yessir, Colonel. That I will."

By midday Ben had covered more than half the distance to Copperblossom Canyon. He rode steadily, his brain working to sort out the puzzle pieces he needed to fit together. If he'd guessed right, whoever was rustling cattle was also supplying guns to the remnants of Black Eagle's tribe holed up in the mountains. At the very least, Black Eagle would know who was supplying the guns.

The connection with Thad Whittaker's murder was even more tenuous, but a sixth sense told Ben these events were also linked. The outspoken newspaper editor had been his own worst enemy.

Ben's heart stopped. *Oh, God, Jessamyn!* She was as forthright—and as foolhardy—as her father. She'd picked up right where Thad had left off, sticking her editorial finger in controversial pies all over Douglas County. The railroad. Indian rights.

Plus stolen cows and illegal rifles. That meant Jessamyn might be in as much danger as Thad had been. God almighty, she might be—

Ben swore under his breath. He'd left Jeremiah with instructions to keep a sharp eye on her. He knew his deputy would do so anyway—nothing could keep him away from the newspaper office. Jeremiah was drunk on printer's ink. Ben knew he'd sneaked out last night to work until dawn helping Jessamyn get the first issue of the *Wildwood Times* to press. There was nothing Jeremiah wouldn't do for someone who could teach him more about the printed word.

Still, Ben felt uneasy being away from her. She was just headstrong enough, still enough of a tenderfoot in this wild country to get herself into trouble up to her neck.

After another three hours on the trail, he brought the gelding to a halt. He'd camp here, in the tiny grass-covered meadow that opened before him. The site was remote, accessible only by the trail he himself had followed. The place was so well hidden he'd even risk building a fire. Surrounded by rounded granite boulders the size of steam locomotives, a campfire wouldn't be seen unless someone magically scaled the rocks above him. He chuckled. Not even Running Elk could fly!

Ben dismounted, unsaddled the gelding and lifted the saddlebag and bedroll off the horse's sweaty back. He took his time building the fire. While it slowly kindled to life, he removed the bit from the animal's mouth and held a double handful of oats under the broad lips. Finally, he rubbed the gelding down with a handful of dry quack grass. The floppy seedheads of the plant whispered against the horse's warm, black hide. An echoey whisper bounced off the rocks.

Or did it?

"There now, boy," Ben said. He smoothed his hands over the gelding's twitching neck muscles. "Easy, fella." He worked the grass clump down the horse's withers, listening intently to the sound behind him.

Ben turned from the horse and tossed the dry grass onto the flames. The blaze mounted.

Maybe it was a coyote. Or a mountain lion. Whatever it was, it was trying to keep quiet. Ben drew in a careful breath.

And it didn't move away when the fire flared. It was not an animal, then. It was a man.

His steps purposeful, Ben dug a sack of dried beans out

of his saddlebag and positioned himself between the fire and the unidentified sound. He filled a pan with water from his canteen, dropped in a handful of beans and shoved the pan into the flames.

If it was an Indian, one of Black Eagle's scouts, the redolent smell of the cooking beans might bring him out. If it wasn't...

Certain now that he was being watched, Ben turned sideways to the fire and with his left hand eased his revolver out of the holster. Holding it to his body with one elbow, he lowered his frame to the ground and settled back against a smooth, gray rock. With his right hand, he stirred the beans with a bent metal spoon. His ears strained for the slightest sound.

Nothing. The gelding shifted, gave a low whinny and began to crop the lush grass at his feet.

Ben waited. Sweat started down his forehead. Deliberately, he crossed his boots at the ankles and stared out past the fire at the impenetrable wall of darkness.

There! A slow, indrawn breath, barely audible as the horse munched and gusted air in and out of its nostrils.

Ben stopped breathing. *Move, damn you! Make a noise!*

Surreptitiously he slid his hand around the gun butt, positioned his forefinger against the trigger. He raised the weapon a scant inch and aimed it into the darkness, chest high.

"You can come out, now," he said quietly. "Make it slow. You're dead center in my sights."

For a long, agonizing minute, nothing happened. The gelding stopped grazing suddenly and lifted its head, attentive. Its tail switched nervously back and forth.

Ben tightened his finger on the trigger.

Chapter Fifteen

Cora Boult wrung the rinse water from the last embroidered pillowcase in her Tuesday white wash and tossed it onto the tower of wet linen in the wicker laundry basket. She hefted the bulging container off the bench, grunting at the renewed ache in her lower back, and staggered to the rope clothesline strung from the back porch to the sweet gum tree.

Dropping the basket, she straightened and surveyed her morning's work. Before she could throw a single sheet over the line, Dan Gustafsen clumped up the garden path.

"Mornin', Cora."

"Morning, Gus." Cora surveyed the tall man towering over her. Up close, the black patch over his left eye always unnerved her. For some reason, when she conversed with the soft-spoken liveryman, she couldn't help focusing on the patch rather than his one good eye.

"Miss Jessamyn at home?"

"I expect Jessamyn's down at the newspaper office. Subscriptions are rollin' in today, prob'ly because her first issue's been printed and delivered. She's either there or over to the bank."

Gus frowned. "It's a fine newspaper. She's...uh...a mite outspoken for a lady, but I guess she'll learn." He hesitated.

Cora seized the opportunity to toss her wet sheet over the line and tug the corners straight. "Something on your mind, Gus?"

"I...well, no. I guess not. She's not at the newspaper office, though. I was just there. Wanted to give her these."

From behind his back he produced a bouquet of peach-blushed yellow roses clutched in one beefy fist.

"Oh, my," Cora breathed. "Aren't they something! Just look at that color. And no thorns! I do believe I'll have to have a start of this one, Gus. I never seen one like it in all my born days."

"It's my new rose. A climber," Gus added. "Would... would you give them to Miss Jessamyn, like you did the others? Blazes, I sure hope she likes roses!"

Cora stared into the Norwegian's craggy, anxious face. Poor lovestruck man. Why, he looked positively green-apple sick. It made no sense to her why being sweet on someone made people feel the mis'ry. She'd loved Frank Boult until the day he died and never had a pecky day in her life.

Gus coughed self-consciously. "Could I maybe call again this evenin'? Maybe Miss Jessamyn'd fancy takin' a walk down to the river."

"Dunno 'bout that, Gus." Cora pinned a huck dish towel on the clothesline, drawing a wooden clothespin out of the cloth bag at her waist. "Jessamyn's been down at the shop for the last two nights, workin' on the newspaper. She'll likely be dead on her feet by tonight."

Gus's brows lowered. "Anybody else ask after Miss Jessamyn lately?"

Cora removed the clothespin she held clamped between her teeth. "Now, that's an odd question, Dan Gustafsen. Exactly what do you mean, 'ask after her'?"

"I...uh...mean does anyone else—any man, I mean—know where she is?"

Cora laughed. "You think you can keep her other admirers away from her, is that it?" she huffed. "Gus, I'm plumb surprised at you. A man don't own a woman until he's bought and paid for her, so to speak.''

"So to speak," the bulky livery owner muttered, his low baritone voice dropping even lower. He thrust the bouquet at Cora. "I'll call back tomorrow."

Cora watched the big man pivot and stride through her back gate, his huge feet crunching on the river-rock path. "Lord love him," she mused out loud. "A love-smitten giant who grows roses."

She pinned up the remaining towels, then spilled the rinse water out on her prize damask rosebush. *And such roses!* She'd give her eyeteeth for that gold-tinted climber with the blush of peach on the petal edges.

Ben stared into the murky dark until his eyes burned. "Come on and show yourself," he said in Yurok. He repeated the words in English. "Get it over with—my supper's getting cold."

A figure emerged from the inky blackness, and Ben leaped to his feet. "What in the bloody hell are you doing here?"

Jessamyn moved unsteadily into the circle of firelight. "I—I was frightened."

"Frightened!" He spit the word out, jammed his Colt back into its holster. "You ride up here alone—I assume you're alone—on an unfamiliar trail, at night. Why the devil shouldn't you be frightened?" His voice rang like steel. "For Lord's sake, you don't have the sense God gave an ant!"

Jessamyn nodded in silence.

"Well?" Shaking with barely controlled fury, Ben paced around her like a prowling mountain lion. "You could have fallen or been thrown. Gotten lost. God, I don't know— died of thirst! Why, Jessamyn? *Why?*"

"S-someone threw a rock through the window of the newspaper office. I was standing right in front of it, and

the glass just exploded. There were little p-pieces of it ev-
erywhere, and I—"

"A rock, huh? Even so, I ought to tan your backside,"
Ben muttered. He stopped pacing long enough to rotate the
pan of beans in the fire. "What makes you think you're
safer up here than tucked up cozy in Cora's house in
town?"

"*My* house," she said wearily.

"All right, *your* house. Dammit, that's not the point."

"No," she agreed. "It's not." Her voice came out thin
and shaky. "I thought I'd be safer up here because...
because you were here. I wasn't thinking clearly, I guess."

"You bet your boots you weren't thinking!" he snapped.

"Ben, please. I had glass all over me, in my apron pock-
ets, in my hair. I know I shouldn't have come. It's just that
I was so unnerved..." Her head drooped. "I'm terribly
sorry."

"Where's your horse?" he growled.

"Down the trail about a quarter of a mile. I came up the
last part on foot to make less noise."

"Stay here. I'll go down for him."

"Her. It's Cora's mare. Lady."

He swung toward her. "Cora let you do this harebrained
thing?"

"No," Jessamyn blurted. "Cora won't know I'm gone
until tomorrow morning. She thinks I'm still at the news
office, cleaning up the press. And—" her voice trembled
"—all that glass."

Without a word, Ben turned and strode back down the
trail after her horse. He found it tethered to a scrub pine, a
bedroll inexpertly tied in back of the saddle. No saddlebags,
though. Which meant she hadn't brought food or extra
clothing. Damn scared little fool. He'd like to throttle her
for the fear she'd got pumping through his veins. His body
shook like a schoolboy's. Every inch of his skin felt

prickly, as if thousands of red-hot needles were branding him.

When he returned to camp, Jessamyn was sitting right where he'd left her. "Didn't Gus try to stop you?" he snapped.

"I didn't give him a chance. He said you'd gone south. That's what he said the last time, so I figured you'd gone north, instead. Into the hills, as you did last time. I sneaked home to change clothes, and when I got back to the stable, Gus was gone. I saddled the mare myself and—" Her voice faltered. "Ben, could we please stop arguing? I'm so tired."

His gut twisted. "I'll just bet you are." Despite his twinge of sympathy, he growled the words out like an enraged bear. Stalking behind her, he picketed the mare next to his gelding.

"I followed your tracks, Ben. I guessed they were yours, anyway."

"My God, you could have trailed some damn cowhand all the way to Lane County! How did you manage to cross the river?"

"At the ford, where we crossed before, on our way to Black Eagle's camp. I walked the horse across the shallow part."

She knelt by the fire and began kneading her thigh muscles. "I did a lot of thinking on the trail today, Ben. I know I shouldn't have come, and I'm sorry, really I am. I know you're the sheriff and you've got a job to do, and I'm just in your way."

Ben nodded his assent, tried to calm the pounding of his heart.

"I don't want to…to be a trial. Just let me stay the night, will you? I promise I'll go back in the morning."

Ben studied the young woman who crouched at his fire. Firelight licked her dark hair, highlighted the delicate, sunburned cheekbones. She wore a different hat—a plain black felt with a braided cord around the crown. New, from the look of it. Probably didn't dare ask Cora if she could borrow Frank's old Stetson, so she'd bought this one at Frieder's on her way out of town. At least she'd thought that far ahead. No one traveled in this country without head protection.

Except for the way she filled out the red plaid shirt and skintight jeans, she looked like a tousle-haired kid playing cowboy.

"Are you hungry?"

Her green eyes widened. "Oh, yes. I found some cookies in Cora's cookie jar, and I ate them along with some blackberries I picked along the trail, but it wasn't very much. I'm starving!"

Ben rose to get another spoon from his saddlebag. "Any idea who threw that rock through your front window?"

"No. I was cleaning the press. My back was to the street."

"Did you hear horses? A voice?"

"N-no."

Dragging the pan of bubbling beans out of the fire, Ben maneuvered it onto a flat rock to cool. "Listen, Jessamyn. I'm not sure whoever did it really meant to harm you. Maybe they just wanted to scare you."

Jessamyn pulled her knees up to her chest. Wrapping her arms around both legs, she rocked her body back and forth in jerky motions. After a moment she laid her forehead on her knees.

"You know, it's an odd thing," she began in a low, tight voice. "I was actually beginning to feel at home out here in the West. I like it. It's different. Free."

She raised her head and looked into Ben's eyes. "But it's also dangerous, isn't it? And violent."

Ben grunted.

"Do you really think that rock was meant to warn me about something? Something I printed in the newspaper?"

Ben nodded. "On the outside, the country looks peaceful enough, since the war's over. But deep down there's a good many issues people out here are touchy about—Indians, for one. Railroads, for another. Getting the vote for women. You hit them all.''

"Oh," she said in a small voice.

"I'd guess you got too close to some piece of information somebody doesn't want known. Or you might have touched too hard on a sensitive issue.''

Jessamyn let out a long sigh. "Now I have to decide what to do next. Should I print only what my readers approve of? The news Douglas County ranchers and townspeople want to hear? Or should I report the news that actually happens?''

"I can't answer that, Jessamyn. I can give you a lot of good advice, but in the end, you've got the same problem Thad was stuck with—you're the editor.'' Ben stuck the extra spoon into the beans and laid one finger against the metal pan for a split second. Satisfied it wasn't too hot to pick up, he lifted it and held it out to her.

"Supper.''

She grasped the spoon, tested a bite on her tongue and gobbled a double mouthful while Ben held the pan steady. When he got a chance, he shoveled a tasty bite into his own mouth.

"I feel like such a fool," Jessamyn murmured when the pan was empty. Her voice was so low it was barely audible. "Without even thinking, I ate almost all of your dinner.''

"Yeah," Ben said gently. "You're a real thorn in my side." He rose abruptly, rinsed the pan with water from his canteen, then refilled it. Adding a scant handful of coffee, he set the container among the coals.

"I've caused you no end of trouble, haven't I?''

"No more than some. Listen, Jessamyn—''

Her chin drooped almost to her shirt buttons. "Well, I want you to know I'm sorry.''

Ben hesitated. He couldn't believe the words that sprang to his lips. He had to choke them back. *I'm not sorry!* Despite the difficulty of backcountry travel with a greenhorn, he wasn't sorry for her company. He wasn't sorry about any of it!

And that, he reasoned, would take some heavy thinking to sort out. All he knew was that Jessamyn was here with him now, and she was safe. Inexplicable as it seemed, he was glad on both accounts.

God almighty, what ailed him? Had he fried his brain in the sun today? He didn't want to be saddled with her tomorrow, or any other day, for that matter. He didn't want to have to watch over her, worry about her falling off that damned underexercised mare of Widow Boult's. He didn't want to see her wake up in the morning, see her hair tumbled loose about her face, her eyes soft and dewy with sleep.

But it wasn't safe to send Jessamyn back to town now. It would be irresponsible to turn her loose, alone, on the trail he'd ridden to this point. On *any* trail. By now, whoever had harassed her earlier would know she'd ridden out of town, would probably know which direction she'd gone. He couldn't risk an unknown assailant finding her, alone and unprotected.

With a forked stick Ben raked the pan of boiled coffee away from the coals.

"You can't go back," he said. He sipped the black brew from one side of the pan, then offered it to Jessamyn.

Jessamyn placed her small, cool hands over his and angled the container toward her. "I can't keep up with you, Ben."

"If you can't go back, and you can't keep up..."

She pushed the pan of hot coffee back toward him. "You'll have to slow down," she said, her tone matter-of-fact.

Ben blinked. "Slow down? Hell, lady, I'm tracking what may be your father's killer and you want me to slow down?"

Jessamyn gave him a level look. "You can track him

slowly, can't you? Besides, I handle the mare much better now. Maybe I can ride faster.''

Ben bit back a chuckle. "Maybe. Maybe not."

"Maybe I could even help."

"Like hell."

"After all, Sheriff Kearney," Jessamyn continued, "it was I who discovered that Indian's new rifle, remember?"

Ben choked on a mouthful of coffee. He remembered, all right. She'd come within an ace of getting caught red-handed snooping through a Klamath brave's private effects. To Black Eagle, that would have been a serious breach of honor.

"I'll try not to slow you down or get in your way. I won't talk on the trail, either, because by now I know you hate that."

"You do," he echoed, his tone disbelieving.

She looked him straight in the eye. "You're going to send me back, aren't you?"

"I wouldn't think of it," he said truthfully. "It's against my better judgment, but I don't see any other way. You'll have to come with me."

Her tired eyes widened, then shone with renewed life. "Really?" She sent him an unsteady smile. "Ben, I promise you, you won't regret it."

Ben groaned inside. Oh, yes, he would. He regretted it the instant he uttered the words. At the thought of spending another night alone with her up here in the high country, the unsatisfied gnawing in his gut returned.

He shot a glance at her. The pleased, little-girl look on her face reminded him of his cat, Shiloh, lapping up a saucer of cream.

He untied his bedroll, rolled himself in a cocoon of tan wool and closed his eyes. "Get some sleep, Jess. Tomorrow's not going to be any picnic."

She made no reply. He heard the swish of liquid, then the bean-and-coffee container thunked onto a rock. A breath of air whooshed over his face as she unrolled her own blanket. With a soft sigh, she stretched her body out beside him.

Ben clenched his jaw. He could reach out and touch her if he wanted. They were high up in these ancient, silent mountains, far from civilization, away from cares and the small daily events of life.

And, he acknowledged as his groin tightened into an ache, they were completely alone.

Ben worked to keep his mind off Jessamyn, focusing instead on the night sounds around their mountain campsite. The fire snapped sporadically. Far off in the hills, two coyotes called to each other.

He laced his hands behind his head and gazed up at the stars overhead, brilliant as gems. How simple life seemed in the wild. He'd learned much from his years dealing with Black Eagle, things that had steadied him after the war, given him something to hold on to when his bitterness threatened to overwhelm him.

He closed his eyes, remembering. Those years had been instructive. Not only were the Indians—Klamath and Modoc alike—treated badly by the government, the tribes themselves fought each other with vicious efficiency. Then, despite all Ben's efforts, the captured members of rival tribes had been sent to the same reservation—a bungled move, if ever there was one.

Still, those years had been lifesaving for Ben. Black Eagle had been both friend and surrogate father. But one thing the wise old chief had not taught him about was being with a woman. Not just any woman, but a woman of depth and substance. A woman of value. A woman like Jessamyn.

Ben closed his eyes, listening to the gentle sound of her breathing beside him. He knew she wasn't asleep. He wondered what she was thinking.

As if in answer to his thought, her drowsy voice came to him over the rustle of night birds in the pine branches above. "Ben?"

He kept his lids closed. "Yeah."

"Are you awake?"

He chuckled. "Have I ever talked in my sleep?"

A soft laugh escaped her. "As a matter of fact, you have. That night in the tipi. You said 'Stop, damn you,' and mumbled a woman's name."

Ben said nothing. He didn't want to know any more. But he knew it was true. Jeremiah always claimed that he muttered things in his sleep. Ben didn't mind if Jeremiah overheard him—there were few things his deputy and lifelong friend didn't know about him. Jessamyn, however, was another matter. His mind recoiled against feeling exposed, vulnerable, to another human being.

"Ben?" she whispered again.

"Yeah." The tight feeling in his groin spread to his chest.

She waited a long minute before speaking again.

"Ben, why did you kiss me that day at the river?"

His lids snapped open. God almighty, he wished he knew. "I guess because I thought I'd like it," he said without thinking.

Another long silence.

"Did you? Like it, I mean? Is that why you kissed me again at the newspaper office?"

He thought a minute. "Jessamyn, why are you asking this?"

"Just tell me—did you like it?"

Ben swallowed. "I did. Quite a lot, as a matter of fact."

Silence. Then in a very soft voice she said some words that turned his heart over.

"I'd never been kissed before. Not like that, anyway. Before, back in Boston, it was…different. A man—even a beau—didn't…" She hesitated, groping for words. "Didn't…well, it didn't mean anything."

Ben attempted to translate. "Are you saying it wasn't a serious thing back in Boston?"

"I guess so." She waited three full cycles of coyote calls before continuing. "It felt...serious with you."

Ben jerked. *Serious!* It was all of that and more. He'd been downright awed. Not only had he been surprised at his action in the first place, he was appalled at his gut-level reaction. And hers, as well.

A burst of purely masculine pride warmed his chest. He'd bet Jeremiah, for all his uncanny insight, didn't know *this* about him!

"Well, were you?" Jessamyn prompted. "Serious, I mean?"

"Hell, yes. And scared to death halfway into it," he blurted. *My God! What is it about her that goads me into opening my mouth and letting the truth escape like so many pebbles?*

"Oh," she breathed.

Ben's brain tumbled over itself trying to make sense of their conversation. Over the past week, he and this unlikely, unpredictable Northern lady had somehow become friends. Maybe more than friends. Never before had he longed to possess a woman—even Lorena—as desperately as he wanted Jessamyn. Lord God in heaven, what was happening to him?

If you don't know, said a voice inside his head, *you're a damn fool!*

Oh, hell, he knew, all right. She'd given him a flick of her petticoat and a glimpse inside the genuine person behind the facade of starched lace and good manners, and he'd fallen like a sack of potatoes.

Goddammit, he was in love with her!

After a long, long silence, he heard her voice again. "Ben?"

"Go to sleep, Jessamyn," he growled.

"But—but I wanted to ask—"

"Jessamyn?" His voice came out gravelly.

"Y-yes?"

Ben rolled toward her, reached one arm around her middle and pulled her, blanket and all, back against his chest.

"Shut up," he whispered against her temple. "Just shut up and go to sleep."

Jessamyn awoke to a cold rain pelting her face. Instinctively she ducked her head, pulling the scratchy wool covering up to her eyebrows, and snuggled her backside toward Ben's warm body.

He wasn't there. She popped her head up and gazed about the campsite.

Ben turned away from the horses and came toward her in long, graceful strides. He'd saddled both mounts, she noted. Already his saddlebags were loaded and tied in place. She groaned. No breakfast, then. Just more riding.

She watched him pack up his bedroll and return to the horse. He tied the blankets behind the cantle with quick, careful fingers, taking extra time to murmur some words to the gelding and smooth his hands over the animal's dark hide.

She respected Ben, she acknowledged. He was remote, even brusque at times, but she sensed something else beneath his impassive exterior—a courageous heart and a depth of spirit few men she'd ever known had had. She trusted him. And she liked him. A lot. So much, in fact, that when his mouth had touched hers, a part of her had come alive, a part of her she'd never been aware of before. She'd given herself up to him, accepting him as a man, acknowledging herself as a woman.

The feeling of his lips on hers was unsettling. In all her twenty-six years, she'd never felt that way about a man.

Slowly Jessamyn slid her aching limbs out of the warm blankets and stood up.

Ben kept his back to her. "Weather's turned," he observed without looking in her direction. "Mount up."

* * *

They rode all day as rain poured out of the thick mass of gray clouds hovering above them. After the first few minutes, Ben unpacked his poncho and pulled it over Jessamyn's rain-soaked hat. In silence he settled it around her shoulders and draped the folds over her knees. Then he shrugged the collar of his sheepskin jacket up to his ears and remounted.

Behind him, Jessamyn watched beads of water roll off the gelding's rump. In her effort to keep up, she followed so close behind the other horse that occasional switches of the gelding's wet tail sprayed stinging droplets into her face.

She gritted her teeth and said nothing. She was cold and hungry and wet. But, she vowed, she would not deter Ben from whatever he had to do. Not even if she drowned in the process.

She flicked the mare's reins, urging her slow-footed mount forward.

What was it Ben had said he was looking for? An old miner's cabin?

She gazed at the terrain around her. Sparsely forested mountainsides rose around them, broken by outcroppings of black rock and tree stumps split wide by lightning. An occasional rocky canyon opened up between peaks that disappeared into the clouds and mist overhead. Hardly a likely location for a shelter.

Jessamyn shivered under her rain gear and pressed the mare onward. The trail descended, then climbed again. Now they were exposed on the rounded crest above the timberline.

Thunder boomed over her head. The mare jerked her neck up, then lowered it and plodded forward. "Good girl," Jessamyn crooned. She herself had lifted out of the saddle at the earsplitting sound. She tried not to let the horse sense her fear.

The sky darkened to an ominous charcoal gray. Lightning flickered over her head, followed immediately by a deafening clap of thunder. Jessamyn's ears rang. She cried out, but the sound was swallowed up by another thunderous crash. An odd, sharp odor filled the air.

In the next instant the entire sky lit up as a jagged bolt of white light stabbed downward. Directly ahead of Ben, a sugar pine exploded and crashed into another tree on its way to the ground.

Ben twisted in the saddle and shouted something, but pounding rain obliterated his words. He dismounted and slogged back along the muddy trail toward her. "Get down!" he yelled. "Get off your horse!"

Frozen with fear, Jessamyn stared at him.

Ben grasped the mare's bridle, then hauled Jessamyn out of the saddle. Steadying her against his shoulder, he shouted into her ear.

"Can't ride," he rasped. "Too dangerous. Walk your horse and keep your head lower than the saddle."

She nodded. Icy rain slashed against her cheeks. "How far?"

Another lightning bolt, closer this time, followed by rumbling peals of thunder.

"Don't know," Ben yelled. "Can't be far. I found it once before, but it was years ago."

He gestured ahead with one hand. "Down there, maybe."

Jessamyn peered down into a dark canyon thick with vine maples and tangled brush. It didn't look promising as a cabin site.

The rain gusted, blew under her poncho, soaking her shirt and jeans, and she shivered. Even the canyon looked safer than the exposed trail they followed.

"Let's go!" She screamed the words into his ear over the whine of the wind. "Even a cave would be better than this—I'm wet to the skin!"

He gave a short nod, laid the reins in her hand and pressed her body close to the horse's shoulder. Striding away from her, he started on foot down the long series of switchbacks leading to what she prayed was Copperblossom Canyon.

Chapter Sixteen

Jeremiah lifted his high-crowned felt hat and combed restless fingers through his hair. The deputy's bones told him something was up. Ben's secretiveness about his visit to Black Eagle's summer camp, the rock heaved through the window of the *Wildwood Times* office this morning—none of these things augured at all well.

A long, worried sigh hissed out between his teeth as he locked the *Wildwood Times* door behind him. Yessir, Mr. Ben and Miss Jessamyn were two of a kind—smarter than most and twice as stubborn. Resolutely he tramped across the street to the sheriff's office to go through the mail.

Toward evening, Jeremiah settled his muscular frame onto the battered oak chair on the plank walkway outside, tipped it back and propped his boots on the hitching rail. His nerves on edge, he smoked one cigarette after another, watching the dusty street from under his drooping hat brim. His throat was dry and scratchy from answering the townsfolks' questions all day long. He longed for a shot of whiskey. But in Ben's absence, he was on duty.

Charlie's Red Fox Saloon was unusually quiet except for the piano player, idly plunking out a made-up variation of "Aura Lee."

Jeremiah shut his eyes. "Aura Lee, my Aura Lee, maid of golden hair..."

His throat closed. A man was fortunate to have had a sweetheart once in his life. He always wished he'd been the kind of man Ben was, a gentleman, born to land, educated to rise above common folk, to marry a real lady like Miss Lorena. But even if he, and not Ben, had been born in the big house, would it make a difference now?

He thrust the thought away. What woman with all her senses would look twice at a scarred-up old gunfighter like himself? Miss Jessamyn, now—she treated him real nice. Miss Jessamyn saw the person beneath his rough manners and uncultured speech.

But to everybody else, it seemed he didn't count for much, really. Most of the time he felt invisible next to Ben, a mere shadow of his lifelong companion. Except for the sheriff, and maybe some of Black Eagle's bunch, half the time people acted as if he wasn't even there. "Tell your deputy," they'd say to the sheriff with Jeremiah standing a scant arm's length away. "Tell your deputy..."

"Love and light return with thee..." He hummed a snatch of the melody. Yessirree, a man was lucky to have a woman, even for a short while.

A horse stepped slowly up the street. Jeremiah didn't move, didn't even open his eyes. Instead he tipped his hat over his face and concentrated on Charlie's piano music.

The hoofbeats came closer. Almost opposite him now. And then they stopped.

A footstep so quiet he had to strain to hear it sounded on the hard-baked street. Then another, the rhythm uneven. He sucked air into his lungs. He knew that step. With one careful finger he pushed the Stetson up off his face and cracked open his eyelids.

Walks Dancing.

Jeremiah ground out his smoke and rose to meet her. Try as he might, he couldn't seem to get his breath. "Ben's not here," he managed at last.

"It is not Iron Hand I seek," the Indian girl replied. "It is you I have come to speak with."

Jeremiah swallowed. "Come." He gestured toward the sheriff's office. His Yurok was so rusty he couldn't think of anything else to say. Instead, he stepped into the street and grasped Walks Dancing's elbow. He let her move at her own pace, but when she reached the sidewalk step, he dropped behind her, placed both hands at her waist and lifted her up onto the plank walkway.

She limped toward the door. Jeremiah turned the knob, pushed it wide, then followed her inside. Shooing the cat out of the desk chair, he pulled it toward the laboring girl and gestured for her to sit. He snagged another chair, pulled it around and seated himself opposite her. The sleek feline leaped into his lap.

Walks Dancing watched his hands smooth the purring animal's fur. "You are a good man, Horse Talker," she observed quietly.

Jeremiah's heart skittered to a stop.

"That is why I have come." Her fine, black eyes looked straight into his. "My father, Black Eagle, wishes me to marry. To bear sons."

Jeremiah's hand stilled. He knew it! That crafty bastard Black Eagle might marry her off before Jeremiah could ask for her. He clamped his jaw shut so hard his teeth ached.

"Marriage," Jeremiah began, working to sound matter-of-fact, "is a fine thing."

Walks Dancing shook her head. "I do not wish this."

He studied the girl's delicately chiseled face, let his gaze drop to the small, capable hands clasped in her lap. "Who is the man?"

"Four Moons. I do not like him. He is unkind. He mistreats his horse. He will mistreat a wife, as well."

"Black Eagle is your chief, as well as your father. Can you refuse?"

She hesitated. "If I refuse Four Moons, I must leave the tribe."

Jeremiah found he could scarcely draw breath. "Could you marry another?"

Walks Dancing remained silent so long he imagined he could hear ants scratching beneath the wood floor.

"My life has been torn apart," she said at last. "My body, as well. Because of this, I must do as my father asks. Four Moons will pay the bride price. He will kill any other man who claims me."

Very slowly Jeremiah lifted the cat off his lap and set it on the plank floor. "My momma always said when your life is cut in two, you gotta fill the split with good things."

Walks Dancing's dark eyes shone with tears. "I cannot."

"Yes," Jeremiah said, "you can." He stood up. "Four Moons will not have you. And he will kill no man. You will marry me. Black Eagle and I have spoken on it."

Amazed at himself, his heart hammering against his ribs, Jeremiah waited for the Indian girl to speak. He had loved Walks Dancing since the day he first saw her. She had been more dead than alive the night he and Ben had found her, her limbs mangled and broken. They had carried her to Black Eagle's camp. Crazed with pain, she had opened her eyes once and gazed up into Jeremiah's face and smiled. He had loved her ever since.

Now, afraid to breathe, he waited for her answer.

"You are a good man, Jeremiah," she said at last, her voice quiet. "I will be your wife if you wish it. As long as I live, I will hold you in my heart."

His thoughts tumbled about his brain like loose grapeshot. He would not send her back to Black Eagle. He knew what Black Eagle wanted—weapons. The bride price. If he just kept his head, maybe he could get the old chief what he wanted.

Jeremiah bowed his head. Dizzy with happiness, he dared not utter one word. He held Walks Dancing's slim hand in his own and stared at her in a haze of joy, afraid he would wake up any moment and find he was dreaming.

On foot, Jessamyn led her mare through the steep switchbacks zigzagging down the mountainside into a seemingly bottomless canyon. Needles of icy rain stung her face as the wind gusted, buffeting her chilled body. The mare whinnied nervously. Step by halting step, Jessamyn guided her mount down the wide, mud-washed path. It must have been a wagon trail once, though she couldn't imagine how a miner's buckboard would make the tight turns.

Her descent was agonizingly slow. At each twist in the trail, the normally surefooted animal hesitated, placing her hooves with maddening care on the slippery surface. Jessamyn had to tug hard on the bridle to make any headway.

Ahead of her, moving with steady, sure steps, Ben walked beside the gelding, his body hunched forward, the collar of his sheepskin jacket turned up to his ears. An hour ago he'd tied a bandanna over his Stetson to keep it from blowing off. Jessamyn tried to do the same, but at each attempt, the blustering wind snapped the kerchief out of her hands. At last she gave up and stuffed the sodden hat into her jacket pocket.

Water sluiced across her forehead, down her neck. Strands of wet hair plastered themselves across her face, blearing her vision. In vain she worked to brush it out of her eyes, but the hairpins securing the soaked bun had begun to loosen. The heavy knot of hair drooped lower and lower, then at last broke completely free. Flying dark tendrils slapped against her cheeks.

Merciful heaven, she was so cold! Inside the leather gloves, her fingers stiffened until she could no longer feel them. At each step, the toes of her right foot stung. They had to find that cabin soon. She couldn't go on much longer.

Ahead of her, the gelding's dark rump rocked steadily forward. Jessamyn concentrated on counting the animal's steps. When she reached two hundred, a hoarse sob escaped her, and she lurched to a stop. She was at the end of her strength. She clung to the bridle while her body shivered uncontrollably. *Dear God, don't let me die like this!*

A shout reached her, the sound muffled and far away.

Another shout, closer this time. Then Ben's arm around her shoulders, pulling her forward.

"Just ahead," he yelled near her ear. "Cabin."

Cabin! Had he really said that? She tugged on his sleeve to get his attention. She couldn't make him hear her voice over the shriek of the wind, so she pointed ahead, hoping he would understand.

He nodded at her, a grin splitting his water-washed face.

"How far?" she screamed.

He nodded again, and the rich sound of his laugh rolled over her. She caught just one word. "Safe." Her chest squeezed so tight she thought she would burst.

Safe. *Alive!*

Desperate to keep her numbed feet moving, Jessamyn gritted her teeth and plodded on. She counted fifty steps, then another eighty, then...

Ben gave her shoulder a squeeze and gestured with his chin. A squat wooden structure nestled between two thick stands of pines on the side of the canyon wall. A blackened metal stovepipe jutted at an angle from the split-shake roof.

Tears stung, spilled over her lids and down her cheeks. She'd never seen anything so beautiful in her entire life! With renewed determination she bent her head and moved forward.

The cabin looked smaller than Ben remembered it. Thank God it had been deserted for years. He didn't fancy the idea of negotiating for territorial rights in the middle of a freezing rainstorm.

And, he added as an afterthought, with a woman on his hands. A wet and very cold woman, from the look of her. The shuddering of Jessamyn's slight frame had increased in the past half mile. She needed to get out of her wet clothes and warm herself up, fast. Already her movements were lethargic, her limbs stiff-looking and uncoordinated.

He prayed she wasn't one of those women with weak lungs. Thad, he remembered, claimed he had never sneezed in his life. Still, he'd seen strong men succumb to pneu-

monia in warmer weather than this. Hurriedly he pulled
both horses down the hillside to the leeward side of the
shack, out of the wind, and tethered them to a post. He'd
return and give them extra rations of oats when he'd gotten
Jessamyn inside and built a fire.

He didn't waste time picking the padlock on the cabin
door; he blew it off the hasp with a well-placed bullet.
Shoving the wide pine plank inward, he half dragged, half
carried Jessamyn inside.

Damn, she was cold! Her straggling hair dripped icy water onto his wrists. He yanked off her wet poncho, tugged
off the leather gloves and dropped them in a pile on the
floor. Her fingers looked abnormally white and she had
trouble flexing them.

"Strip!" he ordered. He turned away toward the stove.
A waist-high stack of split dry logs stretched the length of
one short wall. Kindling filled a box by the crude kitchen
table.

Ben's heart stopped. Someone was using the cabin. The
cast-iron stove was stone cold, but the kindling smelled
piney. Freshly cut, he guessed. Less than a week ago. Pitch
oozed from the stacked logs.

A prickle zinged up his spine. He prayed whoever it was
would not return tonight. Or tomorrow, for that matter. The
storm outside showed no signs of letting up. Until it did,
he and Jessamyn were stuck here.

He piled kindling and small logs onto his arm and strode
toward the stove. Jessamyn stood in the center of the small
room, unsteady on her feet, the puddle of water beneath
her boots spreading. Ben brushed by her with the load of
wood.

"I said strip, dammit! You want to catch pneumonia?"

He knelt before the stove, yanked open the iron door and
laid dry sticks and small branches on the bed of ashes. He
touched a match to the dry pine needles, and the fire flickered to life.

He heard Jessamyn's waterlogged jacket smack onto the

floor behind him, followed by the plop of a lighter garment—her shirt, he guessed.

He straightened and turned to face her. Her damp camisole stuck to her skin, revealing the outline of her breasts
underneath the thin material. She seemed unaware of his
perusal. Very slowly she bent to remove her boots, fumbling at the slick, wet leather with cold-stiffened hands.
Finally she gave up with a shrug.

. Ben sucked in his breath. She acted confused, disoriented. He had to get her dry and warmed up in a hurry.

He moved toward her. "Hold on to me," he barked.
Dropping to the floor, he tugged off one boot, then the
other, while she steadied herself against his shoulder.

"Now undo your trousers."

She gazed at him, her eyes distant.

"Jessamyn, help me! Take off your—"

"Can't," she said, her tone dull. "Fingers won't..." Her
voice trailed off.

Ben reached up and undid the metal button at her waistband. A glance at her face revealed the whiteness around
her mouth, an odd, removed look in her eyes. She was
drifting.

He'd have to do it for her.

"Jess, come over here."

When she obeyed, he laid his hands on her hips and
rotated her body so her back was close to the stove. Her
hands dangled idly at her sides. He lifted them to his shoulders. When she could stand without wobbling, he began to
undo the buttons at her fly.

Her frame shook, whether from cold or fear he neither
knew nor cared. He did know that if he didn't undress her
this minute and warm her up, she was a dead woman.

Two buttons free. Then three. He heard her breath hiss
inward, but he did not look up.

Four. She exhaled in a shaky sigh that unnerved him.
Heat pounded into his chest, his groin. Behind her, the
stove crackled and spit as the pine pitch heated.

One more button and she could step out of her jeans. His fingers trembling, he slipped the last metal disk through the buttonhole. The top of her white underdrawers showed where the trousers separated across her belly.

Ben tore his gaze away from the thin material and slid the denim jeans down over her hips. Her hand came to rest on his shoulder. The chill penetrated clear through his shirt. He guided her fingers over his collar, pressed them against the warm skin of his throat.

"Jess," he said. His voice came out gravelly. "Step out of your denims."

She did not move.

"Come on." He reached his hand behind one knee and pushed it gently forward. "One foot at a time."

When her foot came up off the floor, he pulled the trouser leg free.

She said nothing. In the quiet, all he heard was the sporadic snap of the fire and her uneven breathing. He repeated the operation, freeing the other leg. The sodden denim he pulled off was ice-cold. Tossing the jeans onto the growing pile of wet clothes, Ben rose. "I'll get you a blanket."

Her dulled eyes looked up into his for an instant, then shuttered.

Taking her by the shoulders, he turned her toward the stove. "Get warm."

She nodded, tried to speak, then gave up. Tears shimmered at the edges of her lids.

Ben strode to the door and plunged out into the slashing rain. Lightning flashed overhead, followed by the crack and roll of thunder. The horses danced uneasily as he lifted off both saddles and slung the oilcloth-wrapped bedrolls and the saddlebags over one shoulder. Staggering under the weight, he reentered the cabin and dumped the gear onto the floor. Untying both bedrolls, he shook out three warm woolen blankets. He tossed one at Jessamyn's feet.

"Take off your underthings and wrap up in that."

He didn't wait for her assent. He wheeled and again

made his way outside to the horses. He snugged the two animals close together under a densely branched cypress and spread one tan blanket over them both. Reaching into his pocket, he withdrew a handful of grain and held it out to the tired gelding. Another handful for the mare, and he tramped back into the cabin.

Jessamyn stood with her back to him, the blanket wrapped tightly around her shivering body. Two delicate-looking white garments graced the pile of wet clothes on the floor like frosting on a lumpy cake. A shard of heat pierced his belly, and he tore his gaze away.

He chunked two more small logs into the flames, and with quick motions began to remove his own clothes. He dropped his jacket over the back of a rickety homebuilt chair, pulled off his boots and shed his shirt and jeans. Last, he stripped off his soaked underwear and wound a blanket around his waist, Indian fashion.

He hadn't realized how chilled he'd gotten until he felt the blanket's enveloping warmth. His sluggish blood surged to life as if hot, slowly dripped honey spread over him. Savoring the sensation, he listened to the thunder roll overhead. It would be dark in an hour. He'd better see about some food.

Jessamyn turned slowly. Keeping her backside to the warmth of the stove, she hooked a chair with one bare foot and dragged it closer. She settled herself onto it, then smiled up at Ben.

"Isn't this wonderful?" she said in an unsteady voice. "This little stove is almost glowing!"

Ben chuckled. Relief at her attempt at normal conversation made his knees weak. She was safe and warm. They were alive.

And alone.

"I'll get some hardtack out of my—"

"There's food here," she interrupted. "Look!" She tipped her head to indicate the wall behind him.

A crude shelf had been attached to the split cedar logs;

tins of tomatoes, beans and corn crowded the entire length. His gaze followed the line of foodstuffs until it rested on a brown glass bottle with a shiny gold label tucked in one corner. Child's Premium Whiskey.

Ben laughed out loud. Just what two half-frozen refugees needed!

Heartened by his discovery, he scanned the rest of the one-room shack. In the opposite corner—

Holy God! Two oblong wooden crates sat under the single barred window. Ben swore under his breath. He'd seen such containers before.

Rifles.

The instant he lifted the lid a long, low whistle escaped him. Spencer repeaters. Army issue.

His belly tensed into a hard knot. He'd found the cache of guns. He'd also uncovered the hideout for whoever was supplying the weapons to Black Eagle's Klamath Indian braves. Maybe to the Modoc, as well.

Goddammit all to hell. Arming both sides of warring Indian nations invited an Indian war for sure. Someone was playing one side against the other for maximum profit.

But who? His brain turned over the possibilities.

Someone who would kill to keep his dirty little operation a secret. Thad's killer and the man Black Eagle was protecting might be one and the same. That was why the Klamath chief had said nothing about either the cattle rustler or the rifles—he couldn't afford to.

Ben raked his fingers through his damp hair, and then he smiled in satisfaction. Whoever it was, he had him now. All he had to do was bide his time and the outlaw would stumble right into his trap. Except for the storm raging outside, he couldn't have had better luck.

He lifted a tin of tomatoes and another of beans off the shelf, tucked the whiskey bottle under his arm.

The only thing I ask, Lord, is that the bastard doesn't make an appearance tonight. Tonight he had better things to do than chase an outlaw in the rain. At the moment, survival was more pressing than catching up with a rustler, or even a murderer.

Years of caution made him pause to take stock of the situation. Had he taken adequate precautions against an ambush in case the outlaw did return tonight? He doubted he could hear an approaching horse through the noise of the storm, and even though their own mounts were hidden behind the shack, chimney smoke would signal their presence.

On the other hand, Ben reasoned, no Indian would travel in this weather. And no white man, either—unless he was foolish or just plain crazy. And most outlaws, he knew from experience, were neither. As long as the storm kept up, they were safe for the night.

He bolted the door, and the tension knotting his belly eased. For now, he had more basic worries. He had to make sure Jessamyn was all right. He needed to fix them both some supper and dry their clothes by the fire. He needed—

A rush of pure pleasure welled up inside him. All he had to worry about for the next ten hours was Jessamyn and himself. Life, pared down to its bare essentials, lived second by second in small, lucid moments such as these, was simple. Beautiful.

And alone with Jessamyn in this remote cabin for an entire night, it would be as unnerving as hell.

Chapter Seventeen

Jessamyn let the stove's heat soak into her bones, relishing the soothing warmth as her numbed body gradually returned to life. All her toes and the thumb and index finger of her left hand throbbed as the heat penetrated. As feeling returned, pain pounded with each heartbeat. It was a miracle she hadn't frozen to death!

A languorous feeling of well-being stole through her. Idly, she watched Ben open a tin of beans with his pocketknife and dump the contents into a deep-sided skillet hanging by the stove. He added a second can—stewed tomatoes, she guessed from the plopping sound they made—stirred the mixture with a fork and set the pan atop the black iron stovetop. It smelled heavenly.

"I can help," she offered. She tugged the blanket around her and tried to stand up. Needles of fire shot through her feet.

"Sit," Ben ordered. "It'll pay to warm up slowly before you move around too much."

Jessamyn sank back onto the chair. Maybe he was right. The thought of taking a single step on her oversensitive feet made her cringe. "What about you?"

"What *about* me?"

"My toes feel prickly. Are your feet numb, too?"

"Some. Not as much as yours. Besides, I've been moving around. Keeps the blood flowing." He began to whistle "Oh, Susanna" as he set two tin plates on the scarred kitchen table.

Jessamyn wondered how he kept the blanket tucked so neatly about his waist. She eyed the pile of wet clothes in the center of the rough plank floor. What did he have on underneath? Was he stark naked, as she was, under the woolen wrap? Aghast at her turn of thought, she felt a wave of heat flush her face.

Pivoting toward a crude shelf attached to the split-log wall, Ben reached for mugs and eating utensils. The muscles in his bare back rippled as he raised his arm. His skin looked smooth and warm, like brown velvet. Tanned by the sun from working without his shirt, she supposed. All at once she wanted to run her palms over it, from shoulder to waist, just to see what it would feel like. Oh, what a wanton notion! Miss Bennett would have apoplexy!

Miss Bennett, an inner voice reminded, *might not be so prune faced and disapproving if she'd ever allowed herself such a thing.* Surely it was natural for a man and a woman to touch each other? Otherwise, how would the world keep itself populated? It was one of nature's principles, was it not?

But, she acknowledged, not a principle Miss Bennett would ever allow to be taught at her young ladies' academy. Butterflies and birds, not human beings.

Well, she wasn't a butterfly or a bird. She was a creature of flesh and blood. She liked looking at Ben. Liked his broad shoulders, his lean upper torso. A little rush of pleasure settled in the pit of her stomach.

He made a quarter turn toward her. She liked his sunbronzed, muscled chest, his long, sinewy arms. Not even the crooked purple scar that snaked from his jaw to his taut midriff spoiled the symmetry of the man's form.

And his hands... An odd, sweet pain lodged below her belly. His hands were extraordinary, the fingers lean and skilled. Capable. They moved surely, swiftly, like an elegant bird of prey.

Suddenly she shivered.

"Still cold?"

His voice startled her. "N-no." Quite the opposite, in fact. Perhaps she was too close to the fire. She hitched her chair away from the glowing stove.

Ben moved toward her on noiseless feet. Leaning down, he folded her fingers around a chipped china mug. "Whiskey," he said. "Sip it slowly."

She swallowed a mouthful of the clear amber liquid and choked. Tears sprang to her eyes as the alcohol seared its way down her throat.

"I said 'sip.'" His voice, tinged with laughter, set her nerves on edge.

Jessamyn coughed, gasping for breath. Finally she sputtered out a hoarse word. "Burns!"

Ben laughed. "Damn right. That's the point. Try another *sip.*" He accompanied the word with a significant look.

Hesitant, Jessamyn stared down at the mug in her hand. It did feel good, once it got where it was going. The soft circle of warmth in her belly was comforting. She tipped the cup to her lips and let a minuscule amount dribble past her teeth.

She sipped again, watched Ben gather up the wet garments and wring them out in the wooden sink. When he lifted her drawers and lacy camisole and shook them out with his fine, strong hands, the sweet ache in her body blossomed into fire. She wanted him to touch her, as well. All over.

Hurriedly she averted her eyes as he hung her smallclothes up to dry. The whiskey must be addling her brain. She felt safe and warm, even oddly comfortable with this man, despite their state of undress. In fact, she realized, ever since that first night alone with Ben in Black Eagle's guest tipi, she had felt different about him. During everything they had been through together, the unspoken bond between herself and the Douglas County sheriff had grown steadily stronger.

When he had kissed her that day after the river crossing, something inside had blazed into white-hot awareness— knowledge of herself as a woman. Not a newspaper editor, not Old Maid Whittaker as she was known back in Boston, but a purely female creature of longing and bone-deep instincts. Later, in the *Wildwood Times* news office, when Ben had kissed her again, the feeling had returned tenfold. She wanted him.

Miss Bennett, she thought with sudden clarity, *you have missed the point of life!* The point of life was to be involved, to feel. And feel she did. She sipped again. Ben's steady, smoke blue eyes met hers over the rim of her mug. "Hungry?"

She nodded.

"I'll dish it up if you can walk to the table without—" He cleared his throat. "Without losing your blanket."

She rose, gathered the folds of wool about her. Clutching the mug of whiskey, she edged forward. At the battered table she sat down at the place he indicated.

"Bean stew," he announced, ladling half the skillet's contents onto her tin plate. "Or, if you prefer, stewed tomatoes with beans. Either way, it's hot and we're hungry."

His quick smile dazzled her. Her heart seemed to fill with light.

"I feel like saying grace," she heard her voice say.

Merciful heavens, she hadn't spoken a blessing for fifteen years! What had come over her?

She watched him settle his tall, blanket-clad frame onto the chair opposite her. A wellspring of joy bubbled within her at simply being alive. For that, she would give thanks.

Ben gazed at her for a long, quiet moment. "I haven't felt much like offering thanks since the war."

The rasp in his voice told Jessamyn more than his words. He was scarred—not just on the outside, but inside, as well, where healing was more difficult. Inside, he was dried-up, like a spiny thistlehead. Just as she was, she admitted. Or had been before Ben's mouth had sought hers that day.

Without thinking, she hitched her blanket around her shoulders. When it was secure, she reached her hands across the table to him.

She bowed her head. "Dear Lord," she began. "I—we thank you for…"

Ben's hands gripped hers, his fingers warm and strong.

"For this food, and for this safe haven from the storm." She wondered at the tiny catch in her voice. "And for our horses outside, and…for this whiskey."

Ben's fingers clenched. After a second's pause, he gently squeezed her hand.

"And," she heard herself say over the sudden thudding of her heart, "Lord, I thank you for this man, Ben Kearney, who has saved my life."

She raised her head to find Ben staring at her. Fear and distrust warred with a smoldering fury in his eyes. From somewhere inside her she summoned the courage to smile at him. "Let's eat, Ben. The food will get cold."

She withdrew her hands from his and reached for the spoon beside her plate.

They ate in tense silence while the stove spit and the rain drummed onto the roof. Jessamyn's throat felt so tight she could barely swallow. It wasn't his anger she feared; it was her joy in simply being near him.

Ben ate slowly, moving his spoon mechanically up and down from the tin plate to his mouth. Jessamyn sipped her whiskey and watched him surreptitiously. Finally he seemed to shake himself free from whatever preoccupied him. His spoon halted halfway to his lips.

"Did you notice those boxes in the corner?" He gestured behind him with his head.

"No, I didn't. Not until now. What's in them?"

"Rifles." A glimmer of a smile settled across his mouth.

"Rifles! For Black Eagle?"

He nodded.

"Oh, Ben, that's what you hoped to find, isn't it?"

"It is."

"Why...why, that's grand!" A wave of dizzying heat washed over her. "It's just grand, isn't it, Ben?"

His smile broadened. "It is." A light danced in his eyes as he studied her. "I think there's a connection between these guns and your father's killer."

Jessamyn sucked in her breath. He continued, his voice quiet.

"Cattle rustling is part of it, too, the way I figure it. That's what got Thad in trouble in the beginning. Then, later, he must have stumbled onto the real meat of the matter—supplying guns to the Indians. Whoever's doing it had to cover it up. Couldn't afford too many questions. And Thad," Ben said in his soft drawl, "always asked a lot of questions."

"Who is it?" Jessamyn blurted.

Ben tipped his chair back on the two rear legs. "Whoever's using this cabin."

Jessamyn watched him lift his whiskey and bring it to his lips. A thrill shot through her midsection, whether from Ben's words about her father or the sight of his fingers caressing the china mug, she wasn't sure.

"Guess I should have included this bit of information when you said grace for supper," he said with a chuckle. "Come to think of it, I'm feeling pretty damn good about how things are working out!"

Jessamyn took another tiny taste of the whiskey remaining in her mug. "I'm feeling good, too. Warm and safe. We have lots to be happy about."

"Yeah? What's so joyful about riding miles half-frozen through a summer squall?"

Jessamyn noted he was grinning again. A satisfying sense of accomplishment swept over her. "You're going to capture him—whoever it is, aren't you?"

"In time, yes. I don't figure he'll turn up here tonight, but he will soon. When he does, I'll be waiting for him."

"And I helped, didn't I, Ben? Not the newspaper story, I mean. I know that only made things worse for you. But finding that rifle in the first place, the one at Black Eagle's camp. Didn't that help?"

"You helped," Ben conceded. His voice sounded warm, almost gentle.

Jessamyn gave a little squeak of joy. It felt wonderful to be part of things—important things—like catching a thief and identifying her father's murderer. Pride puffed her chest out.

Ben laughed softly. Rising, he drained his mug, then began gathering the dishes.

"Let me!" Jessamyn reached for a plate, and the blanket slipped off one shoulder. She hitched it up, held it together across her body with one hand while she stacked her plate onto his.

Ben watched her a moment, then stepped to her side and lifted the tin dishes and the spoons out of her hand. "I don't think you should do any walking around that you don't have to, seeing how you're...encumbered."

"What? Oh, you mean my blanket. Well, it is hard to keep closed."

"So I noticed." Ben shot her a quick look. "I'll just set these plates outside the door—let the rain wash them clean."

He had to admit he'd enjoyed watching her struggle to keep the tan wool covering over her shoulders and chest. In fact, he'd been preoccupied with her nearness for the past hour. Not many women could ride—or walk—all day in a driving rain and end up looking as unconsciously alluring as she did, draped in that army blanket with her hair hanging loose.

He took another long, careful look at her. Not many women could measure up to Jessamyn Whittaker, no matter what the weather. Yankee or not, this lady was one of a kind.

And, he reminded himself, none of his goddamned concern beyond keeping her warm and safe for the next twenty-four hours.

Night came quickly. Except for the glow of firelight from the window in the stove, the interior of the old shack was cast in shadow. Hunched in her chair by the stove, Jessamyn watched Ben prowl about the tiny cabin searching for candles to dispel the darkness.

He flipped over the two pairs of jeans spread out on the floor and ran his hand across the smaller garments—shirts, underdrawers, her frothy camisole—feeling for dampness. Almost dry. Soon she could get dressed, or at least partly dressed. Enough to sleep in, anyway. The thought made his groin tighten.

On four different nights now, he and Jessamyn had shared sleeping quarters. Each time was more strained than the last. It was getting difficult to be around her, watching the little feminine things she did before bed—taking down her hair, scrubbing dirt off her face with a dampened bandanna. He wanted to reach out and smooth her cheek with his thumb. When she rolled against him during the night, snugged that soft, round little derriere into his groin, oh, God. Every bone in his body ached for her. He hadn't had a good night's sleep since she'd come into town on the stage.

He found the remains of a tallow candle and touched a flaming pine sliver to the wick. Soft light pooled about him. He sensed more than saw Jessamyn move toward him out of the darkness.

"Are our clothes dry?"

"Not yet. Maybe another half hour." He bent, tugged her jeans closer to the stove. "The...uh...smaller things should be wearable, though. What do you need for sleeping?"

"The small things," she said after a moment. "And my shirt. Over there, on a nail." She gestured behind him.

Ben turned to retrieve the garments, leaving Jessamyn in

shadow as he raised the candle to illuminate the wall. Wind-whipped rain splatted against the single window. Water sluiced onto the roof in erratic bursts, now drumming hard on the surface above them, then subsiding into a whispery wash of droplets. The wind moaned around the eaves.

He lifted her shirt and the lacy white drawers from the nails where he'd hung them and held them out to her. When she took them, the tips of her fingers brushed his knuckles. His heart thumped as if a horse had kicked it.

She retreated to the far corner of the room, away from the candlelight. Ben turned away, concentrated on the sound of the storm raging outside. His body tense, his blood pounding with need, he thought about the woman he had come to know these past few days.

The truth was, he was afraid to be alone with her. He didn't dare risk reaching for what his body hungered for, didn't dare because his heart hungered, too. He didn't trust the emotion. It seemed a lifetime since he'd opened himself to another human being, and now he had nothing to give a woman save a weary, battle-scarred body and a spirit that life had sucked dry.

It was not enough. It would never be enough. But, God in heaven, he wanted her.

He did not hear Jessamyn's noiseless footstep behind him.

"Ben?"

He jerked at the sound of her voice.

"Ben?" she repeated.

"Yeah?" Fear tightened his throat. Even to him, his tone sounded brusque and unfriendly.

"Where do you want me to sleep? Next to the stove or—"

Want? *Want?* He wanted her beside him, in his bed. In his arms.

"Over there." He pointed with the guttering candle toward the stove. "Lay your bedroll out close to the fire."

She hesitated. "What about you?"

He listened to her soft breathing in the darkened silence, heard the thunder growl and rumble overhead. He ground his teeth in frustration, wanted to lift his head and howl into the night, his longing for her was so sharp. Instead, he heard his own voice respond in an almost normal tone. "Between the stove and the door. I'll sleep with my rifle ready," he added. "Just in case."

Jessamyn shivered. "Do you think anyone…"

"No, I don't. But I won't take chances, either." He knew he'd spit the words at her. Inwardly he winced.

She bent to arrange her blankets, then straightened and stepped forward into the circle of light shed by the candle he held in one hand. "Something's wrong, isn't it, Ben? I can tell by your voice."

"Nothing's wrong," he lied. "I get moody sometimes. Just ignore me."

"No, I won't. I can't." Her gaze held his for a heartbeat, then dropped to her toes. "The candle is dripping wax onto the floor."

"It's happened before."

She cocked her head. "And over your hand," she observed quietly.

"That, too."

"But don't you feel it? Doesn't it burn?"

He felt it, all right. He concentrated on the discomfort, hoping it would take his mind off other things. "Not if I don't think about it. Pain is relative. Some kinds are worse than others."

She stared at him. In the flickering pool of light, her green eyes widened. "What pain? What are you really talking about, Ben? Tell me."

He realized how much he had inadvertently revealed. Anyone else would have taken his remarks at face value, but not Jessamyn. Not a lady reporter with a printing press where her heart should be. Inside, he had to laugh. Her damned guileless curiosity about life, about him, was part of what made her the way she was—perceptive. Sensitive. Maddeningly alive.

"What pain?" she repeated, her voice gentle.

He turned away from her. "I was wounded in the war." He lugged his bedroll over to the stove and spread it out opposite hers.

"I know. I've seen your scar."

"The scar isn't all on the outside," he said without thinking. He wished he hadn't spoken. He wanted no one, not even his old friend Jeremiah, to see inside him. He felt transparent as a cold winter stream when he revealed his feelings. If he were seen—known and understood—he could be hurt.

"I know that, too," she said softly.

Caught off guard, Ben laughed. "For a maiden lady, you seem to know a lot about men."

He regretted the comment the instant he said it. He'd blurted it out in an attempt to reestablish the protective shell he felt cracking with Jessamyn's every statement.

She faced him, her fine, dark eyebrows lifted. "Yes, I do. I've spent my whole life observing the males of this world at close range. It's a rare man who shares his real feelings. Papa never did. Not with Mama, anyway. And not with me. It made me lonely all my life."

Ben's insides turned cold. "You're wrong, Jessamyn. If you've been lonely, it's because you chose to remain single, not because Thad abandoned you. But I'm sorry for the 'maiden lady' remark. I'm sorry I snapped at you, but you're just…wrong."

Inexplicably, she gave a low laugh. "I'm not wrong, Ben. And you know it." She turned away, spread over her pallet the blanket she'd been wearing. In the firelight her long hair gleamed like satin.

A wave of heat swept into Ben's throat, moved through his chest. "Jessamyn, you are the goddamnedest woman…"

"Yes," she said with a sigh. "I know. I'm stubborn and I can be difficult, I'm sure."

She drew in a deep breath, straightened her spine. "But you like me, Ben. I know you do."

Dumbfounded, Ben stared at her back as she tugged her blankets into place. "I do," he echoed.

He was more than surprised by her matter-of-fact statement. He was completely undone. One thing about Jessamyn he'd never get used to was her candor, her complete lack of artifice. She reminded him of his mother. A more soft-spoken, proper lady he'd never known, yet Kathleen Kearney's mind had been as logical as a lawyer's, and she'd expressed herself with the quiet eloquence of General Lee addressing his troops. In spite of his fraying nerves, he found himself chuckling at the similarity.

Jessamyn spoke over her shoulder. "It's because of Lorena, isn't it?"

His entire body froze.

"Jeremiah was in love with her, too," she continued, her voice gentle. "Or did you know that?"

Ben jerked. "Jeremiah? He told you that?"

"Actually, he said very little. I guessed most of it."

"You guessed it," Ben repeated, his voice hardening. Part of him was relieved that he didn't have to explain. Part of him wanted to thrash her for delving this close to the core of his wounded spirit.

"Ben, that—Lorena—was years ago."

"Yeah." He busied himself checking and positioning the rifle on the floor within easy reach of his bed.

"You know that Jeremiah's smitten with that Indian girl, Walks Dancing?"

"I know. He'd like to marry her."

"Well, then, why doesn't he?"

"When a man wants to marry an Indian girl, especially the daughter of a chief, he has to pay her father a price. Black Eagle's price for Walks Dancing is plenty high." He paused to draw in a shaky breath.

"Jessamyn, why all the questions? Why tonight, when we're cooped up in this damned cabin with a storm blowing outside and no way to get out until morning?"

"Because I... Well, because we're here together, alone, and... Well, I've never been alone—really alone—all night with a man before. I wanted to know some things about you."

His heart leaped. He knew she relied on him, depended on him. Trusted him. Was it possible she *liked* him, as well? As a man?

The thought made his palms sweat. Being with a woman he didn't care about was one thing. If she meant nothing to him, he could not be hurt. Rejection would not matter. But being with a woman who mattered—a woman like Jessamyn—was different.

"Why, Jess? Why do you want to know things about me?" He resisted the urge to step toward her. Touch her. He studied her face in the candle glow.

"Because when you kissed me the other day at the river, I—I liked it," she blurted. "And—"

As if suddenly aware of what she had said, she stopped short. A flush of crimson washed up her neck to stain her cheeks.

"And?" he queried, his voice low and hoarse.

"Ben, I..." She licked her lips.

"And?" he repeated. "Answer me, Jess."

"Oh...oh, bother!" She gave a little moan of embarrassment and angled her face away from the light. "Don't look at me, Ben. I know I'm blushing—I turn red at all the wrong times. Please, just don't look."

Quick as a frightened bird, she dipped her head and puffed out the candle flame. In the darkness Ben heard her suck air into her lungs.

"Oh, dear," she whispered. She swallowed audibly.

Ben imagined her soft pink tongue again rimming her lips. He clenched his hands into fists, concentrated on keeping one closed around the candle stub, the other at his side.

His knuckles brushed against the blanket he wore about his waist. Suddenly he became excruciatingly aware of his lower torso, his bare thighs and calves, his hips, his manhood touching the soft wool. His entire body seemed bathed in flames.

A breath of air against his chest told him Jessamyn had spun away. Before he could stop himself, he reached out for her.

His fingers closed on her bare forearm. Very, very slowly, he pulled her backward toward him until her spine pressed against his rib cage. Barely able to breathe, he waited.

For a long moment neither of them moved. The sound of the rain drummed in his ears. By the dim light cast by the stove, he could see the outline of her breasts.

He dropped the candle stub and took hold of her shoulder with his hand. Her head came up, tumbling her hair against his bare chest.

"Ben."

Her voice was no more than a sigh, but he reacted as if a cannon had been fired inside him. A searing hunger surged through his body. He bent his head until his lips found her warm neck.

"Jessamyn." He murmured the word at her ear, moved his mouth to the smooth area beneath her cheekbone and blew his breath out against her skin.

She stiffened. After a long minute, she let her head roll back against his chin. Oh, God. Her hair, thick and warm against his skin, spread across his chest like a mantle of silk. He opened his mouth, inhaled its fragrance.

"What did you want to ask me, Jess?" He kissed her hair, her earlobe. "Tell me now."

"I... N-nothing. Nothing."

"You're lying," he said gently.

"Yes," she whispered, her voice so soft it was barely audible. "I know I am."

Ben lifted his head, smiled up at the roof over their

heads. Water pounded down in irregular bursts like volleys of rifle fire. He closed his eyes, remembering the sheer terror of battle, of risking everything in a desperate pitting of life against death. Despite the fear, he had moved forward, led his troops to safety and a renewed belief in their cause and their own survival. God knows how he had managed it, but he had.

In a way, he was facing the same thing now. He wanted her. He wanted her as he'd never wanted a woman before, as if something inside would shrivel and die if he couldn't have her. The feeling, hot and sweet and urgent, drove out the hard ball of fear he'd carried for so long, made him tremble with the joy of being alive. Something buried within him broke free.

"Jessamyn," he breathed against her temple. "Walk away from me if you don't want this."

For a long moment she remained motionless. Then she murmured a single word. "Ben."

In the dark, her ragged breathing told him everything. Very deliberately, he lifted his hand from her shoulder, moved it in front of her, across her chest, and curled his fingers around her upper arm. With a little twist, he turned her to face him.

She tilted her head to look up into his face. "Ben," she said again. Hearing her trembling voice speak his name fired a hot ache into his loins.

He'd make it good for her, slow and sweet and easy. He wanted it to be beautiful, something she'd never forget.

Very gently, he pulled her into his arms. When her body pressed against his bare chest, he bent his head and spoke near her ear. "We don't have to do this, Jess. You know that, don't you?" His own voice shook.

She nodded, her hair brushing his skin.

"Up to a point, you can tell me to stop. After that, though, I can't promise…"

"How will I know?" she whispered.

Ben smiled, his lips caressing her hair. "I'll tell you when."

Silence. Then her voice, low but steady. "Ben?"

"Yeah?"

"Kiss me."

He found her mouth, warm and slightly open under his. His senses reeled at the heat of her, the fire she kindled in his blood. He kissed her once more, deeper, and then he couldn't stop.

She arched against him, moved her hands to his neck and clasped them behind his head. Ben groaned. She was like honey and flame mixed up together—sweet and hot, and so strong, so alive.

She uttered a little moan. His heart thrumming, he broke contact. "We're at that point now, Jess," he said in a ragged voice. "Tell me to stop or…"

She stared into his face for so long he thought maybe she didn't understand. Then she astounded him.

"I want you," she murmured. She met his lips, opened her mouth under his.

Blinding happiness washed through him, like a flood of white light shining into his dark soul. "Jessamyn," he whispered. He kissed her again, let his tongue taste the sweetness of her mouth. When he broke free, she kept her eyes closed.

"Don't stop, Ben," she murmured. "Don't…just kiss me."

He gathered her close, his mouth hungry, then forced himself to slow down. Lifting his lips from hers, he kissed her neck, swept his tongue into the hollow at the base of her throat.

She gave a little sigh, and he swirled his tongue into the shell of her ear. She sucked in her breath and stiffened. Then with a low cry, she laid her palms against his chest and arched her neck back.

Ben slipped the top button of her shirt free, then slowly worked downward, one button at a time. Parting the fabric, he slid one camisole strap off her shoulder, moved his hands down her rib cage to her lower back. Curving his fingers under her buttocks, he lifted her against him.

He bent his head. With his tongue he circled the nipple straining under the thin fabric of her camisole. She cried out, and he continued until the spot was wet.

Half sobbing, she called his name.

"Jess, Jess," he whispered roughly. "I want you."

"Yes." She moaned the word. "Yes."

He picked her up, walked to the bedroll spread near the glowing stove, and laid her down.

Then, while she watched, he freed the blanket wrapped at his waist and let it fall away.

Chapter Eighteen

In the faint glow of the firelight, Ben's eyes burned into Jessamyn's with an intensity that stopped her heart.

Was this what loving a man was all about, this inexplicable joy tearing at her insides, pushing at her, compelling her toward some kind of completion? No man had ever made love to her before, kissed her until she was wet and aching between her thighs, stroked his tongue in secret places. It was the most glorious thing she'd ever experienced. Waves of exquisite sensation pulsed through her body until she thought she would die of pleasure.

This must be what Black Eagle and his wife were doing that night in the tipi. Oh, the wonder of it, a man and a woman together! The sweet, sweet wonder. Dizzy with longing, she lay back on the soft pallet and waited for him.

He knelt beside her, and she caught her breath. His body was lean and hard and warm. The heat of his skin drew her, almost against her will. She reached out one hand, touched his taut belly.

Ben captured her fingers and gently repositioned them at her side. "Not so fast," he murmured.

He eased her shirt off. Already unbuttoned down the front, it was just a matter of slipping her arms out of the sleeves and pulling the garment down off her shoulders. Next he slid her camisole straps down, untying the neck ribbon she had carefully knotted not twenty minutes before. He stripped the lacy garment off over her head, brushing the tips of her breasts with his fingers.

A thrill spiraled into her midsection, coiled below her belly. She wanted him to touch her again.

Instead, he loosened the drawstring tie of her underdrawers, then paused, his hand resting at her waist.

"Jessamyn, listen to me. There's risk here, more for you than for me. I have to know—are you really sure you want this?"

She could not help the smile that tugged at her lips. "I'm sure, Ben." She lifted her mouth to his. "Very sure."

He gave a low, choked laugh. "Thank God," he murmured. He reached for the top of her drawers, tugged them down over her knees and ankles. "Even if I wanted to," he said in a hoarse voice, "I'm not sure I could stop."

He smoothed his hands over her breasts, grazed his thumbs lightly over the swollen peaks. "I haven't loved a woman in a long time."

Jessamyn's heart soared. Wherever his fingers rested, fire licked her skin. She drew in a deep, ragged breath, expelled it in a shaky sigh, drew in another. Ben breathed in rhythm with her. His controlled, purposeful movements contrasted with the sound of his uneven inhalations, and she found herself panting as she listened to him.

The sound of their breathing in concert sent a thrill through her. She was the cause of his hunger, the focus of his struggle for control. In the same way, she admitted, he was responsible for the swelling, soaring ecstasy that flooded her being. She mattered to him.

And, she knew now, he mattered to her, mattered more than the risk of letting him take her in the way a man possessed a woman. She was frightened. Yet, slowly, deftly, he soothed away her fear.

He drew his tongue between her breasts, then beneath them, circling purposefully up and around her flesh until he reached the erect nipples. Her fingers curled and stiffened as he stroked in languid spirals over the engorged peaks, repeating the process again and again until she thought she would scream.

She gasped his name. He lifted his head, then moved lower, across her belly, then lower still. Instinctively, she raised one knee. He spread his fingers near her inner thigh, held them there for a heartbeat. Then, very slowly, he dipped his tongue into the private place between her thighs, stroking back and forth as she cried out.

She listened to the uneven rasp of air pulling in and out of his lungs, her own unsteady breaths matching his. How exposed they were to one another—naked and defenseless. A shiver of apprehension rippled through her.

She had no experience, did not know what to do, or even what to expect. But in the next moment he groaned deep in his throat and murmured her name, his voice close to breaking.

He was shaken by what was happening between them, just as she was! A delicious languor filled her. She lifted both arms over her head and gave herself up to it.

His tongue grazed her heated skin, explored, making subtle variations in its path among the folds of her sensitive flesh. God in heaven, what ecstasy! Behind her closed lids, crimson stars floated against black velvet.

He thrust his tongue inside her, and she arched. Withdrawing, he inserted one finger, slipping it deep, curving upward to touch an undreamed-of secret place. The sensation he elicited set her afire. She moved against him, her mouth opening on a sob of delight.

He withdrew, then rose over her and entered her, a slow, steady pushing in to her center. It felt hard and full. Instinctively, she closed her inner muscles around him and heard him gasp.

His entire body trembled. He withdrew once more, then sought her mouth. She opened to him, felt his tongue touch hers, his hard, swollen member pause at her entrance. And then he slid one hand under her hips and lifted her to meet him.

He drove deep inside, his mouth covering her cry.

He shouted her name with his release, and at that moment violent waves of pleasure rolled through her. The exquisite spasms went on and on, convulsing her body, her entire being. Ben held her until it was finished and she lay panting in his arms.

"Jessamyn?" His voice was hushed, unsteady.

She reached her arms around his body and pulled him down on top of her.

"Are you all right?" he breathed.

She felt like laughing, weeping, even singing. "Yes. I am very all right. I didn't know it would be so...so wondrous. So beautiful. Did you?"

"No," he breathed. "It's never been like this before."

Jessamyn laced her fingers through his dark hair and smiled up at the ceiling. "Good," she said. She sighed with satisfaction. "I like surprising you."

She closed her eyes, tightened her arms around him. "Stay with me," she murmured, her voice drowsy.

Ben held her close. He didn't want to crush her with his weight, yet he didn't want to break the connection between his body and hers. At last he compromised by rolling to one side, bringing her with him, held tight against his body. In less than a minute, her breathing slowed and deepened.

She was not asleep. To his astonishment, she caressed his chest with her fingertips, murmuring something—his name, and something else. A word. "Again."

He stopped breathing, strained to be sure he had heard correctly.

"Again, Ben. Please."

He'd do anything—*anything!*—for her. He'd bring her the moon if she asked. After what she'd given him, no request, however unattainable, however unmeasurable, was impossible.

He turned her over, hovered above her while he caught

her mouth under his. He felt her hands move slowly up his arms, over his shoulders to his neck, felt her fingers lace themselves into his hair. When he touched her, she opened her thighs, moved her hips to meet him.

He entered her slowly, his member hard, throbbing again with need. She felt like hot, wet silk. He pressed deep, deeper, and she closed around him.

"Ben. *Ben.*" Her hands fluttered at his back like birds' wings.

A transforming joy pumped through his veins, demanding culmination. Completion. He moved within her, took pleasure in the sounds she made, words whispered brokenly for his ears alone, for him only. "Ben, I want to be yours...now. Make me yours."

It was not the gift of her body that meant so much, but her allowing him to find himself, with her. In her. For him, it was a resurrection of his belief in his own value, his own inner wholeness and strength. He knew he would never forget this night. God in heaven, he would never be the same.

Toward morning, the storm blew itself out. Moonlight bathed the pallet where Ben lay, Jessamyn curled in his arms. He had slept briefly, then lay thinking for the rest of the night hours.

He thought about the woman beside him. About himself. About Lorena and Jeremiah, and Walks Dancing. What Jessamyn had told him about Jeremiah and Lorena explained some of his deputy's inexplicable behavior over the past year. Some, but not all.

Why had Jeremiah hidden his feelings for Lorena all these years? He must have come close to hating Ben when Lorena had become engaged to him. Then, after the war, when he and Jeremiah had made their way home to Carolina, they'd found the woman they both loved had married someone else, someone with land and money. That winter, Jeremiah had steadied him through a private hell. Later, when he'd moved on to Dakota Territory with the U.S. Cavalry, Jeremiah had stuck with him.

Why? Jeremiah was the one person in the world Ben trusted with his life, even though—unknown to him all that time—the two friends had been rivals. It seemed odd that his lifelong companion would share his feelings about the Indian girl, Walks Dancing, but not about Lorena. Maybe Jeremiah had never come to terms with events as they had played out after the war. Chances were Jeremiah had never forgiven Ben for courting and then winning the beautiful heiress. And when she'd rejected him, he'd left her behind.

Ben rolled onto his side, laid his arm across Jessamyn's midsection. Her chest rose and fell as she slept, and he slipped his hand under the blanket covering them both, stroked the warm, smooth flesh of her belly.

He was in love with her, no doubt about that. He'd known for days, but he accepted the knowledge with trepidation. There was no room in his life for a woman. He would never be able to trust a female, even if he did love her. The only human being on earth he trusted, outside of himself, was Jeremiah.

Come morning, he and Jessamyn would head out. He'd found what he had suspected—a hideout and a supply of guns. He'd bet money the weapons were destined for Black Eagle's camp and the weary, smallpox-ravaged remnants of Klamath warriors. He'd also bet money that, sooner or later, Thad Whittaker's murderer would step over the threshold of this cabin and into the trap Ben intended to set for him.

At first light, he'd take Jessamyn back to Wildwood Valley and alert Jeremiah. With his deputy, capturing a killer on the run would be easy. God knew they'd done it half a dozen times before. In the meantime, he'd just lie here with Jessamyn beside him and plan his next move.

His lids snapped open at a sound outside. Horses!

He eased himself away from Jessamyn, slipped quietly from under the blanket and grabbed up the rifle. Naked, he moved to the single narrow window and peered out.

Pale moonlight illuminated the surrounding trees, the canyon ridge above them, the jagged trail snaking down the canyon wall. Two horses. The first, a roan, bore a single rider. The second was loaded with supplies. Swaying behind came a surefooted brown mule. Two crates of rifles were strapped across the animal's broad back, one balanced on each side. The trio descended slowly, picking its way among the jumble of rocks and mud deposited by the storm. The moon's silvery light barely outlined the edges of the trail where it hugged the sheer canyon face.

Ben stepped away from the window and bent over Jessamyn's sleeping form. "Jess!" He shook her shoulder. "Wake up! Someone's coming."

Catlike, she stretched and yawned. "What?"

"Get up, Jess. We've got company." He yanked the blanket off her and she sat up.

Ben gathered up her smallclothes and shirt, snatched her dry jeans off the floor and tossed them to her. Without a word, she scrambled off the pallet and hurriedly pulled the garments on.

"Who is it, can you tell?"

Ben snapped up his fly. "One man. Looks kind of familiar, but not a horse I recognize. Can't tell if he's armed, but at least he's alone." He stuffed his shirt into the waistband, shrugged into his sheepskin jacket.

"He can't see our horses yet. Thank God we let the fire die last night—the smoke would be visible for miles."

Jessamyn did not answer. Fully dressed, she tugged on her boots and jacket, then rolled up her bedroll into a tight wool sausage. When Ben did the same with his, she snatched them both up, jammed her still-damp hat over her tangled hair and followed him to the cabin door.

At the threshold, Ben paused. Catching her shoulder with his free hand, he pulled her close and kissed her, hard. "Keep low. Run for the horses."

She stared up at him for a split second, her face white, her eyes huge pools of emerald light. He wanted nothing more than to wrap both arms around her warm, pliant body and take her back to bed, but there wasn't time. Even with his necessarily slow, laborious descent into the canyon, any minute their visitor would spot them. He might forego questions and shoot on sight.

With an inward groan, Ben turned away, unbolted the door and edged it open. "Stay close," he ordered.

He slipped outside and headed toward the horses. Jessamyn moved in his shadow, her footsteps quiet and steady.

Overhead, a single star gleamed. Ben slapped a folded dry blanket on the mare's back, then threw on the saddle and cinched it tight. The bit and bridle were next.

When he'd saddled his own horse, he hastily tied the saddlebags and bedrolls in place, then turned to help Jessamyn.

She flashed him a quick, shaky grin from atop her mare. She'd mounted by herself. Spunky lady, he thought. Looked mighty dainty, but didn't need coddling. His heart swelled in admiration.

He spoke in a low voice. "If I remember right, there's an old Indian trail out the other side of the canyon. If we're lucky, we won't be seen."

Jessamyn nodded and lifted the mare's reins.

"Walk her," he said. "It'll be quieter."

He nudged the gelding past her mare, heading away from the cabin in the gray predawn light. Behind him, the clomping of hooves on wet earth grew louder. Birds began to twitter high in the dripping tree limbs. The mule hawed suddenly, and a deadly silence fell.

Gradually, step by muffled step, Ben led Jessamyn away from the danger along the unused Indian trail that wound down into a thickly wooded ravine. The minute they reached the cover of mist-wrapped cypress and pine trees, Ben released a pent-up breath.

Safe. For the moment, anyway. Now all he had to do was get Jessamyn out of Copperblossom Canyon and back to town. He shot a quick backward glance at her.

She met his gaze, lifted her mangled hat in a spur-of-the-moment salute, and smiled.

All the way out of the steep-sided canyon, Ben's throat ached with joy.

Chapter Nineteen

Jessamyn racked the type case and laid it on the slanted composing table. Her eyes aching from hours of selecting the tiny pieces of metal and slipping them into place, she slid off the high stool, untied her work apron and swept past the keg of printer's ink Otto Frieder had delivered that afternoon. Along with the ink, the beaming storekeeper had announced the birth of his daughter.

"Was early, but Dr. Bartel, he say she is fine baby," Otto had sputtered. "And—" He'd moved his two extended forefingers in toward each other. "So tiny. Like a china doll she looks!"

All afternoon and evening Jessamyn thought about the Frieders' new baby, the life a young girl and later a grown woman faced out here in the West—physical hardships and unending work. And there were other dangers, as well— emotional risks, such as men like Ben Kearney who turned her heart inside out with pleasure and then wrenched it with longing for something that could not continue.

With a sigh, she laid her apron over the battered oak desk in the front office. She had made love with a man, let him touch her in intimate places, and she had reveled in it. She had taken his body into hers at the height of passion, and—despite her mother's admonitions and Miss Bennett's training in propriety—she didn't regret one minute of it.

But she knew it couldn't go on. Ben was not the marrying kind and, to be honest, neither was she. Still, for a woman like herself, a properly reared single lady, now with a career as a dedicated newspaperwoman, there was certainly a limit to the boundaries she could overstep and still remain respectable.

Jessamyn turned down the lamp wick and puffed out the flame with a quick breath. She hadn't seen Ben since they'd returned to Wildwood Valley two nights ago. He'd left her with a quick, warm kiss and had vanished down the dark path. He hadn't been angry—his mouth, hot and sweet on hers for those few glorious instants, had told her that. But she knew he had other things on his mind—Spencer repeating rifles and her father's murderer. She wondered what he planned to do now.

In the next instant she knew the answer. When he found Jeremiah, the two men would buckle on their gun belts and ride back up into the mountains to capture an outlaw.

Her heart all but stopped beating. Merciful heaven, here was a hazard about life in the West she hadn't considered before—caring about a man whose life was in danger!

Hurriedly she locked the news office door and in the dusky light made her way along the plank walk, past the Dixon House hotel and Charlie's Red Fox Saloon. Both establishments were lit up like Christmas trees. The sheriff's office was dark. She supposed Ben had ridden out to his brother's ranch for supper, or maybe he and Jeremiah were both at the saloon. Jeremiah hadn't stopped in to visit at the *Times* office since Walks Dancing had come to stay with Cora. The deputy might be there at the house now, visiting the Indian girl.

She quickened her step. She wanted to ask Jeremiah's help when she put the next issue of her newspaper to bed. She covered the quarter-mile walk to the big white house preoccupied by the articles she had to finish for her next edition—the latest news about President Johnson and impeachment, the new plan for the railroad to bypass Jacksonville in favor of Medford, which would put that city in line for county seat. Bad news in good English, Papa used to say.

She would print nothing about the sheriff's closing the net around the cattle thief and her father's killer, at least not until Ben made an arrest. She would not, for a second time, compromise his plans for capturing the outlaw. Besides, if she held the news over, it would make a bigger splash to break the entire story at one time.

When Jessamyn entered Cora's warm, good-smelling kitchen, she found the elderly housekeeper rolling biscuit dough out on a floured board while Walks Dancing stood at the stove, stirring a kettle of simmering stew.

"Where've you been, child? I'd near give up on you gettin' home in time for supper, but your Indian friend here wouldn't eat without you." Cora stamped out rounds of dough with an upended jelly glass. "Beats me how you two can communicate—she can't say but two words in English."

Jessamyn flashed a quick smile at Walks Dancing and bent to sniff the stew. Turning, she noticed a bouquet of pale gold roses arranged on the kitchen table. The spicy perfume sent an odd, empty ache into her chest.

"Gus was by earlier," Cora said as she arranged the biscuits on a square tin pan. "Brought you more flowers. That man has the greenest thumb I ever did see! And," she continued, "he ain't the only one to come callin'."

From the stove, Walks Dancing sent Jessamyn a mischievous grin and held up two fingers.

Jessamyn stared at her. "Two? Two what?"

The girl assumed a studiedly serious facial expression and pantomimed a man's swaggering walk.

"Two men," Cora interpreted, sliding the pan of biscuits into the hot oven.

"Oh, no." Jessamyn shook her head at Walks Dancing. "You're quite mistaken. Not two at all! Not even one!"

"More'n two, if you ask me," Cora said with a laugh.

"Jes' look outside." She gestured at the window over the kitchen sink. "Looks like company for supper."

Jessamyn peered through the glass panes and caught her breath. Three horses stood in the yard.

Dan Gustafsen clutched another bouquet of roses in one meaty hand—this time creamy white blooms tinged with pink. Silas Appleby was empty-handed, but his gray hat looked brand-new and his boots gleamed like polished piano legs.

The third rider was Ben Kearney, looking bone tired and rumpled, his hat brim pulled low over his sun-bronzed face. Dust covered his dark leather boots. Jessamyn took one look at him and felt her heart contract.

"Might as well face it, child," Cora said as she patted the remaining biscuit dough into a lozenge-shaped mound on the cutting board. "Them's courtin' males in full feather."

Walks Dancing grinned and waggled three fingers in Jessamyn's direction. The housekeeper glanced out the window, then attacked the mass of dough with a flour-coated rolling pin.

"Look out there, Jessamyn," she commanded. "I'm gonna give you a lesson on how to judge a man as a potential husband."

"I'm not looking for a husband, Cora," Jessamyn said stiffly.

"Of course not," the housekeeper agreed. "But if yer gonna save up for a rainy day, you got to learn to recognize one!"

"Cora, I'm not saving—"

"Oh, well, then come and learn how to judge a man as a schoolteacher you may want to hire, or a foreman on a cattle ranch, or your banker. No matter what, come and watch."

Intrigued in spite of herself, Jessamyn looked out the window. Even Walks Dancing twisted to watch the activity in the yard outside.

"Watch what they do about their spurs after they get off their horses at the fence."

Jessamyn did as she was directed. Gus flipped his reins over the top rail and strode, spurs jangling, toward a wash-basin set on a bench beside a water pail and dipper. On a nearby post hung a huck towel, clean and white as lye soap could make it.

"Gus'll likely come to call with his spurs on," Cora said. "And he'll dry his face on the center of the towel. Don't marry him."

Gus and Silas walked together to the basin. Gus carefully put down his bouquet, then one after the other, they bent to splash their faces and hands, taking turns at the towel. Gus used the center, Silas all four edges.

"Either one of them might be trained to be a decent husband and maybe a father, but it won't come natural. Now, look at the one still at his horse. All of them loosened the cinch except him. What's he doing now?"

"He's leaning against his horse and talking. Now he's doing something with the bridle."

"Slipping the bit," Cora said approvingly. "Makes the wait more comfortable for the horse. Where's his spurs?"

"He's hanging them on the saddle horn. Gus and Silas are coming up the path toward the house."

"Silas is a handsome feller, ain't he? Two weeks ago, Silas was practically engaged to the Harber girl. Now, he ain't," Cora remarked. "But look at his boots if you get a chance. If they're good working boots, it might be worth it to smile at him, but if they're anything fancy, hold back. That last fellow isn't so polished up, maybe, but watch him wash."

In spite of herself, Jessamyn's interest rose. She watched Ben carefully empty the used water at the base of a rose-bush, ladle one dipperful of water into the basin and wash his face, neck and hands. After a critical look at the towel, he pulled a folded bandanna from his pocket and dried his

face. Then he again poured the water on the rosebush and
stepped up to the house.

A bud of inexplicable joy bloomed within Jessamyn's
chest. Without a word, she stepped to the oven and opened
the door. Folding a dish towel around the edge of the pan,
she slid the golden brown biscuits off the rack, then moved
to meet the sheriff. As she passed the stove where Walks
Dancing stood vigil over the steaming kettle of stew, the
Indian girl held up a single finger. Her fine, black eyes
sparkled as they met Jessamyn's.

Ignoring the gesture, Jessamyn flew out of the kitchen
and down the hallway to the front door. At this moment
nothing mattered except seeing Ben, hearing his voice,
watching his face change when he looked at her.

Near the doorway Gus thrust a handful of creamy pink
roses at her. "Evening, Miss Jessamyn."

Silas Appleby snatched off his hat and slicked back his
sandy hair. "Howdy, ma'am."

Jessamyn smiled briefly at each man but did not pause.
As the two strode on into the sitting room at Cora's invitation, Jessamyn continued toward the doorway. She inter-
cepted the sheriff just as he ducked his head under the door
frame.

"You're going back up into Copperblossom Canyon tonight, aren't you?" she said quietly.

Ben removed his hat and nodded.

The realization that he was leaving again so soon knifed
through her. A cold lump of apprehension settled in her
stomach.

"I could tell by the way you walk." She held up the
pan. "You'll want biscuits to take with you."

She scooped four fat biscuits off the baking tin and
stuffed two in each pocket of his sheepskin jacket.

He encircled her wrist with his warm fingers. "Come
outside, Jess." He pulled her gently toward the open doorway.

Jessamyn set the biscuit pan down on the oak hall rack

and followed him out onto the front porch. Resettling his hat, Ben turned to face her.

"I don't have a lot of words to give you, Jessamyn."

She inhaled a lungful of the warm, honeysuckle-scented air, watched the sky behind him flame rose pink and crimson. "I don't expect words, Ben. Least of all from you," she added with a soft laugh. "When something important happens, I've noticed you say very little."

His eyes, gray-blue with fatigue, widened for a split second, then flared with a hot light in their depths. "*Has* something important happened?"

Jessamyn let the question hang in the quiet, color-washed evening silence. Watching his face, she waited while she thought how to respond. She knew what he meant. It was clear that their night together at the cabin had been important to him in some way—she just didn't know *what* way.

"Has it?" he repeated.

A mockingbird trilled from the rose arbor. Endless variations of the song floated out, altering with each passing second. Like life, Jessamyn thought. One moment things were one way; then something would change and everything would be different.

"Yes," she said at last. "Something important has happened. Between you and me, that night at the cabin. Nothing will ever be the same."

"Jess, I don't know how—"

"Don't talk, Ben," she interrupted softly. "Just kiss me."

He wrapped both arms around her, enfolded her in his warmth. She lifted her face, felt his warm mouth move over hers. His breath caught as she began to respond, and he deepened the kiss, his lips saying what words could not.

An ache flowered in her throat. She could not say what she felt, either, but she could show him. Her mouth under his would tell him she valued him, wished him a safe journey—her kiss, and the biscuits she'd slipped into his jacket.

He broke free with a soft groan and set her apart from him. In the dying light she saw his face twist.

Jessamyn rose on tiptoe and pressed her lips against his one last time. "Jeremiah told me you did brave, courageous things in the field during the War of the Rebellion."

"The War Between the States," he corrected gently.

"Yes, the war. Don't do anything foolishly heroic this time," she whispered.

A low chuckle sounded in her ear. "I won't."

"And I hope..." She faltered. "I hope you weren't thinking I'd miss you, Ben, because I—"

"No," he breathed against her mouth. "I wasn't."

"And, Ben... Oh, Ben, you know this can't go on. Don't come back expecting...more."

After a long hesitation, his words whispered against her temple. "I wouldn't think of it."

He caught her hard against him, kissed her roughly and spun on his heel. He paused briefly to reattach his spurs, then mounted and turned the black gelding into the road. His rowels chinged musically as he rode away from her.

Long after the hoofbeats faded, Jessamyn fancied she could still hear the jingling sounds over the hammering of her heart.

"I told you, Jeremiah, I don't have a choice." Ben's throat was parched from filling in his deputy during the past hour at the Red Fox. He signaled the bartender.

"Another round, Charlie."

Jeremiah frowned at him across the scarred corner table of the noisy saloon.

Ben regarded his deputy in silence. Jeremiah seemed edgy. He guessed it was Walks Dancing's presence in town. Jeremiah probably worried that some young buck was going to sneak into town and steal her away the minute they saddled up. It was the only time Ben could ever remember his deputy's being skittish about a capture. Neither of them knew precisely the identity of their quarry, but that had never bothered Jeremiah before. Whatever the situation, his deputy was always steady under fire, quick to adapt to surprises.

"You're sure about all this, are you?"

Ben grinned at his deputy. "Not positive. Just sure. Only a fool believes everything his gut feel tells him."

"Only a fool'd try to smoke a man out the way you plan to, Ben. And you never been a fool."

"I'm not wrong very often, either," Ben responded in a matter-of-fact voice. "That's why we're so unpopular with the jailbird set."

Jeremiah studied the sheriff's sun-weathered face. "One big mistake is enough," he said softly. "I got a bad feeling about this, that's all. Wish I could talk you out of it."

"You'd rather not ride straight into Copperblossom, is that it?"

"Hell, Ben, I got to go!" Jeremiah swallowed. "Just not at night, maybe. Trail's faint, weather's changeable as a woman's heart, and…"

Ben grinned. "And Walks Dancing is at Widow Boult's. I know. For God's sakes, man, go tell her goodbye. We saddle up in an hour." He rose, slapped six silver coins onto the table and strode through the saloon's swinging doors.

Shaking his head, Jeremiah watched the tall man stride away. "Troublous," he muttered under his breath. "Just plain troublous."

Jessamyn laid her pencil aside, stretched her arms up over her head and massaged the tight muscles at the back of her neck. She'd been working since dawn, alternately writing stories out in longhand on pads of scratch paper and then, when her index finger cramped, moving to the high stool before the slanted worktable under the window, composing type in the stick and locking it into the frame.

The measured *tick-tick* of the wall clock sounded overloud in the quiet room. Almost midnight. She would not admit to Ben that she had again worked, alone, into the late evening hours. The sheriff had enough on his mind as it was.

Her nerves on edge, she rose and paced back and forth in front of her desk. Every creak in the plank floor beneath her leather shoes made her start. Her pacing took her into the back room, where she stretched out full-length on the cot.

With a sigh, she let her lids drift closed. A newspaper editor carried a heavy responsibility, she reminded herself. "A newspaper," her father had always said, "should be society's mirror and a force for moral improvement."

A tall order, Papa. Feelings among the ranchers and townsfolk ran high on most issues, and she knew in her heart that one editor could not go to war alone. That's what had gotten her father shot in the back.

Still, she couldn't give up. The philosophy of one century was the common sense of the next, she remembered Papa saying. Jessamyn believed every word. Tired as she was, and uneasy ever since that rock had crashed through her front window, she mustered up her reserve of courage. She'd just have to do the best she could under the circumstances.

Opening her eyes, she gazed at the ceiling. *What do I myself value most?*

The first image that floated into her mind was the two-story white frame house she shared with Cora Boult. Her own home. That represented security, the opportunity to be safe in this topsy-turvy world.

But after security, then what? She thought hard for a moment. She needed to work at something that mattered, something that made a difference in people's lives—not just today and tomorrow, but generations from now, when she would be dead and gone.

And then her thoughts settled on Ben Kearney, and a silent finger touched her heart. Tall and capable, blunt spoken, hurting on the inside yet oddly gentle, Ben Kearney was a man for all the challenges life offered. A man she—

A burst of gunfire and a crash from the front office brought her upright, one hand clutching the throat of her white lace blouse.

"In here," a gruff voice shouted. "Hurry it up!"

Jessamyn bolted off the cot and ran into the front office. Four men surrounded her printing press. With their hats pulled low, she didn't recognize any of them.

"Just what are you doing here?" she demanded in the loudest voice she could command.

The apparent leader of the band ignored her. "Load it, boys," he growled.

He'd been drinking, she realized. They'd *all* been drinking. The reek of whiskey hung in the air. One of the men could barely stand up.

"Get out of my office this instant!" Jessamyn ordered. She snatched up a type stick and took a step forward.

"Not so fast, ma'am. Me an' the boys here have some business."

"What business?" she snapped. She brandished the wooden stick in the face of the man closest to her. "The news office is closed. Now if you'll kindly—"

The click of a pistol safety catch cut her words short. Horrified, she stared into the barrel of a blue steel revolver pointed straight at her chest.

Her heart hammering, she closed her mouth and lowered the type stick. "What is it you want?" she said as calmly as she could.

"Your press, ma'am, if you'd be so kind as to step aside. The 'Talking Paper,' them Indians are callin' it."

"And what do you intend to do with it? Do any of you know how to run—"

She broke off as the gun barrel waggled.

"We're not gonna run it, lady. We're gonna get rid of

it! Lately it's been printin' some stuff certain parties don't want to hear about.''

Jessamyn jerked. "You can't do that. I own that press. I inherited it from my father. Just tell me what you men are upset about and I'll—"

"'Fraid you won't have a chance, ma'am." At the leader's signal, one man secured a rope around the black iron press and then three of them heaved and grunted until they got the machine through the doorway and into a dilapidated freight wagon.

Desperately, Jessamyn tried to memorize their faces. None of them looked even remotely familiar. The minute they were gone, she'd sit down and sketch their features. Of one thing she was certain—they weren't going to get away with this, not as long as she had breath in her body.

She watched the wagon rattle off down the dark street and disappear around the corner. Oh, God, they were heading for the river.

Heartsick and shaking with fear, Jessamyn grabbed up a notebook and a fistful of pencils, stuffed them in the pocket of her navy sateen skirt. She wasn't going to stay here one minute longer than necessary.

With trembling fingers she turned down the lamp wick, blew out the flame and marched out into the night air on legs that felt like rubber.

She stopped at the livery stable, where a light still shone.

"Gus," she said in a determined voice when the stable owner answered her knock, "first thing tomorrow morning, I need a team of horses to pull my printing press out of the river."

Chapter Twenty

Chewing one of the crumbly fresh biscuits Jessamyn had pressed on him, Ben urged his mount down the tortuous, rock-strewn trail into the upper end of the canyon, ominously quiet in the graying morning light. A niggling thought floated just at the edge of his mind.

Something didn't fit. What would a man gain by supplying rifles to Black Eagle? What profit could a gunrunner hope to reap from an impoverished band of renegade Indians?

Something was wrong. He didn't know what for sure, but over the years he'd learned to recognize the uneasy feeling in his gut when something didn't add up. Under ordinary circumstances, once he knew what he had to do, he shut everything else out of his mind until he got the job done. This time his brain kept trying to make a connection that hovered tantalizingly just out of reach.

If a man stole cattle, why not just sell them and pocket the money?

He shot a glance back at Jeremiah. The deputy appeared to be half-asleep on the surefooted mare, the shapeless brown felt hat obscuring his face. Ben knew he wasn't asleep. Underneath that battered hat ticked a brain more like a machine than a human organ. Jeremiah would be focusing his mind on the cabin layout, determining the angle of the sun when they got within hearing range, weighing the odds. He'd be figuring how many guns they might be facing, and what kind. Long ago he'd learned never to underestimate Jeremiah.

They took the cutoff, circling around on the unused Indian trail to approach the cabin from the back, unseen. Ben hoped the shack would be deserted. Then he and Jeremiah could take their time, move in and set up a trap.

The trail narrowed to a faint path snaking through ankle-high goosebush and quack grass, the delicate stalks doubled over by the recent rainstorm. Behind him, Ben heard Jeremiah's mare break into a canter, closing the distance between them.

"This place gives me the spooks, Ben. Always has."

"Yeah. Me, too. Another mile and we can see the roof. Check for smoke."

Jeremiah was silent.

"I saw only one rider," Ben continued. "Plus a pack-horse and a mule. Might have been more behind him, but I didn't wait to find out."

"Did he see you?"

Ben thought for a moment, nosing the gelding along with knee pressure as he twisted toward Jeremiah. "Don't know. Maybe. We were quiet enough, but he could have seen one of the horses. No woodsmoke, though. We didn't keep up the fire much past nightfall."

Jeremiah chuckled. "Didn't need it, most likely," he said dryly.

Ben let the remark pass. Some things were best kept private, even from his lifelong friend.

"Ben." Jeremiah brought his mount to a halt and pointed beyond Ben's shoulder.

A hundred yards below them, a lazy curl of blue smoke wound into the sky. In the next moment the blackened metal chimney came into view, just visible through the screen of cedars and sugar pines.

"How many, do you think?"

"Can't tell yet," Ben replied. "Just beyond that tree stump, you can see the back side of the cabin. The horses will be tied there. The window's around to the front."

Jeremiah grunted and stepped his mare forward.

"Cover me," Ben directed.

The deputy slid his shotgun out of the rifle scabbard and laid it across the saddle in front of him. Ben did the same. Then he nudged the gelding into motion.

Despite the evidence of smoke from the cabin chimney, Ben saw no sign of life, heard nothing but the raucous call of an emboldened blue jay and the nattering of a woodpecker in a sugar pine high above his head. He walked the gelding ahead a few yards, then dismounted. Jeremiah followed suit. With slow, deliberate footsteps, the two men crept noiselessly forward until the cabin came into full view.

Three animals—two horses and the pack mule—were tethered to a log hitching post. Ben breathed out in relief. Only one rider. They could take the man easily. He shoved a cartridge into the chamber of his rifle.

Motioning to Jeremiah, he crept around the side of the structure to the front wall and stationed himself beside the plank door. It was not bolted. The door hung slightly off center unless pinned from the inside by the thick iron rod.

Jeremiah moved into position, pulled back both hammers on his shotgun. Ben sucked in a lungful of air and held it. In the next instant he smashed one booted foot against the metal hasp and sprang into the entrance as the heavy plank door swung inward.

A dark, wiry man looked up from the weathered kitchen table as Ben strode into the room.

"Kinda early for a visit, aren't ya, Sheriff?" Jack Larsen's thin lips curled into a smile. "Sit down, why don'tcha, Ben? Coffee's still hot."

"I'll stand." Ben noted the three-day growth of dark stubble on the railroad man's narrow jaw. "Been here long?"

"Yeah. Came in after that storm. How'd you know that?"

Ben didn't answer. Instead, he gestured with his gun barrel at the four boxes of Spencer rifles stacked up in the corner.

"Where did those rifles come from?"

Larsen shrugged. "Beats me."

Ben nudged his rifle against the top button of the man's patterned silk vest. "Come on now, Jack. Give me some straight talk."

Larsen's dark eyes flicked to Jeremiah, then back to Ben. "I packed them in, goddammit."

"Where'd you get them?"

Nervous, Larsen eyed the steel barrel poking his chest.

"Where?" Ben repeated, his tone hardening.

"They're bought and paid for, Ben. What the hell does it matter where they came from?"

"It matters. Who bought them—you?"

Larsen shook his head.

"Who, then? Someone's in this with you. I want to know who it is."

"Can't say," the sharp-faced railroad man barked back. Again his gaze drifted from Ben to Jeremiah and back. Uneasy, he shifted position on the hard chair.

"Talk to me, Jack. Where were those rifles bought and who bought them? I think I know where the money came from—you rustled cattle from ranches all over the valley, didn't you? You, or somebody working with you, drove them to Idaho to sell, then used the money to buy guns."

He shoved the gun hard into Larsen's sternum. "Give me some answers, Jack."

Larsen squirmed. "Honest, Ben, I only took a few beeves at a time. I figured they wouldn't hardly be missed. Anyway, it wasn't my idea to buy guns. Hell, I needed the money for my railroad!" He sent a desperate look at Ben and then at Jeremiah, behind him.

"For your railroad," Ben echoed. "You damn fool. You turned cattle thief to finance a railroad?"

The thin face whitened. "I had to, Ben. I ran out of money, and... Well, there's twenty years of my life gone. I had to do something!"

"I'd say you made a very bad choice. You ended up with rifles, not railroad shares. I figure somebody pressured you to change your plans. Come on now, Jack—you know in the end I'm going to find out who it was."

"I—I got a partner, it's true. But that doesn't mean I got to go down on his ship, does it? If I tell you who it is, will you go easy on me? Maybe let me ride out of here?"

Jeremiah's gravelly voice rose at Ben's back. "Why, you lousy son of a— You oughtta be shot!"

Larsen flinched. "No! Don't shoot me! I—I...uh...won't say any more. But look at it this way, Sheriff." A crafty glint surfaced in the black eyes. "The dumber people think you are," he said, pronouncing each syllable with care, "the more surprised they are when you kill them." His gaze flicked to Jeremiah. "Isn't that right, Jeremiah?"

Jeremiah said nothing.

Ben swore under his breath. "You killed Thad Whittaker, didn't you, Jack?"

For a long minute, no one in the room moved. Then Larsen slumped forward, his face in his hands. "God help me, Ben, I didn't mean to. The old man just never stopped writin' those things in his newspaper. He was gettin' closer and closer to the truth—I had to shut him up. I was only gonna threaten him, but Thad went yellin' across the street to the sheriff's office, and—"

"You shot him in the back," Ben finished for him. "I've got to take you in, Jack. You'll hang for killing Thad."

Larsen's narrow shoulders sagged. "I'm not goin' alone, you hear?" he muttered. He looked up, staring at something over Ben's right shoulder. "There's two of us, only one of you."

Ben glared at the small man cowering at the table. It

made sense now. The pieces were falling into place. Larsen had a partner, someone who had blackmailed him into buying rifles instead of railroad stock. Someone who knew it was Jack who had murdered Thad Whittaker.

Something clicked into place. *There's two of us.* The other person, Jack's unnamed partner, was the one supplying rifles to Black Eagle. In exchange for what? The only thing the Indian chief had left of any value was...

He closed his eyes in anguish as the realization hit him. In that instant Larsen came to life, knocking Ben's rifle aside. He grasped the gun barrel and yanked it out of Ben's momentarily loosened grip.

Jeremiah. It was Jeremiah who was supplying guns to Black Eagle. Ben suddenly felt sick.

A shotgun pressed against his backbone. "I had to have her, Ben," his deputy rasped in his ear. "This was the only way."

Ben jerked. "God in heaven, man, it couldn't have been the only way. There's got to be more to it than that."

"Maybe," Jeremiah breathed. "Yeah, just maybe."

Larsen edged toward the open door, keeping the rifle pointed at Ben's heart. "I don't want to hang for Thad Whittaker's killing. Your deputy was there—he could'a stopped it, but he didn't. He let me walk away afterward, so the way I figure it, he's in it as deep as me."

He gestured with the rifle barrel. "So you just move on over to the stove, real easy-like."

Ben took a single step forward. A sickening sense of futility washed over him. Of what value was law, or truth, or even love if it could so easily be swept away by greed? Simply disregarded by someone willing to betray a friend for gain? What value then lay in the bonds of human friendship, the kind he had known with Jeremiah all the years of his life, if in the end one man turned against another?

Ben loved Jeremiah like a brother, had thought of him as family ever since they'd fished and gone swimming and learned how to read together back as boys in Carolina. His throat thickened. It was harder to swallow in some ways than Lorena had been.

He reached the stove and turned to face his deputy.

Jeremiah's soft, chocolate brown eyes shone with tears. "I'd give anything if I hadn'ta done it, Ben. God knows I never wanted you to hurt over it."

Ben studied the familiar square visage of his old friend. "It was because of Lorena, wasn't it? Because you loved her, too, and I— When she wouldn't have me, after the war, I left Carolina for good."

Jeremiah nodded, his face stricken. "I loved her all my life, Ben. I never once woke up in the mornin' without seein' her face, rememberin' how good she smelled."

He shook his head as if to clear away a memory. "I couldn't never have had her—I knowed that all along. I wasn't the man you was, Ben. My daddy was poor. Miss Lorena, she never looked twice at me, even when we was growin' up. You could'a convinced her to marry you, though. Stayed in Carolina after the war. And then I could'a just been near her sometimes, like when we was young."

Ben shut his eyes for a brief moment. "Lorena didn't want me after the war. She wanted land. Money. My God, how you must have hated me, Jeremiah. I never knew."

The stocky man drew in an unsteady breath. "I didn't hate you, Ben. God knows I wanted to—for years I wanted to. But I just couldn't. I guess I loved both you and Miss Lorena 'bout equal."

He lowered the shotgun. "Then we found Walks Dancing by the river that day, and Black Eagle said he needed rifles. I figured another woman'd help me get over Lorena."

Ben's chest tightened.

By the doorway, Larsen made an abrupt motion. "What the hell does all this talk matter, Jeremiah? Shoot him and get it over with!"

Jeremiah stiffened. "Shut up, Jack."

"One of us has to do it!" the wiry man snarled. "If

you're not up to it, I'll—'' he raised the rifle, pointed it at Ben's chest ''—do it myself.''

"Jack, no!"

Larsen's forefinger squeezed the trigger, and a blaze of orange fire erupted from the barrel. Frozen, Ben waited for his body to feel the bullet. At that range, he was a dead man.

A hot, white pain blasted into his chest. For a fleeting moment he felt relief. It was over now. He thought of Jessamyn, hoped desperately she had conceived his child. He sank to his knees and braced himself for death.

Instead, Jack Larsen crumpled to the floor, a bloody hole gaping in his throat. Smoke curled out of Jeremiah's shotgun.

The deputy hurled the weapon away from him and knelt over Ben. With his big, gentle hands, he stripped off Ben's shirt, ripped away the blood-soaked underwear and pressed his fist hard against the gushing wound.

Ben groaned. "Damn, that hurts!"

"Won't be the first time I tended a bullet wound in yer hide," Jeremiah muttered. Hurriedly he tore Ben's undershirt into strips and packed them against the flesh. Suddenly his large hand stilled. "But prob'ly be the last, won't it?"

For a moment Ben could not speak. His gaze locked with his deputy's. At last he nodded. "Jack?" he managed.

"Dead."

"Thanks for that," Ben murmured.

Jeremiah made no response. He bound Ben's shoulder and immobilized his useless arm using his own belt as a sling. "Can you ride?"

"Not sure," Ben replied through gritted teeth. "Maybe."

Jeremiah caught him under the armpits. "Try," he ordered.

Ben struggled to stand. A wave of dizziness drove him down to his knees.

"Again," Jeremiah demanded.

"Can't," Ben gasped. "Leave me here. Go for help."

The deputy snorted. "What makes you think I'd come back instead of skedaddlin' to Colorado?"

In spite of his pain, Ben gave a tight laugh. "You wouldn't dare. I know Colorado as well as you."

"You make it mighty hard on a man, Ben." Jeremiah's voice shook, and he hardened it before he spoke again. "Somebody hits me, I'm gonna hit him back, even if he is a friend. You know that, Ben."

"Shut up, man. You shot Jack to save my life—you're not going to let me die now. Help me stand up."

With a supreme effort, Ben pulled himself to an upright position. Leaning his weight on Jeremiah's solid shoulder, he struggled step by step out the doorway and along the west wall of the cabin. In a haze of pain he mounted his horse with a hefty boost from behind.

"Get me up out of this hellhole and make camp somewhere. I can last till then." He made a feeble attempt to kick his horse.

Jeremiah swung up onto the mare, laid the shotgun across his saddle and leaned down to grab the gelding's bridle. He tied the reins to his wrist. "We'll go out together," he rasped. "Maybe do some talkin'."

Ben tried to grin. "Maybe. Not much breath left."

Jeremiah shot a quick look at him. Ben knew he was sweating. His chest felt wet and sticky. It couldn't be all blood, he reasoned. He looked down and groaned. His underwear dripped crimson.

I'm not going to die, dammit. That bullet hurts less than finding out Jeremiah watched Thad die and turned a blind eye. That's what's tearing up my gut. But it's not going to take me. Oh, God, if I die, I'll never see Jessamyn again.

Ben stepped his gelding after Jeremiah's mare.

Hours passed. The deputy moved steadily up the steep, narrow trail. Ben could hear the raspy voice ahead of him, sometimes talking, sometimes singing in a croaky tenor, the way he'd done when they'd been at Rock Island prison together. Gradually, the trail leveled out. When Ben opened his eyes, he recognized the campsite he'd used two nights ago.

His shoulder throbbed as if it had been skewered with a red-hot poker. His head pounded. At each jolting step the gelding took, bile rose in the back of his throat.

Jeremiah stopped his rough rendition of "Shenandoah" and began to talk again. Ben could barely distinguish the words.

"I never been like you, Ben," his deputy said in his low, rough voice. "You wanted Lorena, but when she wouldn't have you, seems you could set her aside and get on with yer life. You believe in things. Me, I mostly done without much philos'phy. 'Bout the most precious things to me all my life were my momma and Miss Lorena. And you," he added in a softer tone. "I always been proud to ride beside you, Ben."

Ben released a careful breath. "You saved my life twice now," he said. "Once in prison in Illinois. Seems like a long time ago."

Jeremiah dismounted, a worried expression on his face. He led Ben's horse close to the rock fire pit, still intact after Ben's last use. "You rest easy. I'm gonna boil up some water and poultice that hole in yer chest with wet moss, like my momma taught me."

Ben let himself slip sideways onto Jeremiah's solid, muscular body, felt his deputy cushion his descent to the ground. Grateful for the presence of another human being— even the friend who had betrayed him—Ben whispered his thanks and let his eyelids drift shut.

Jeremiah was just a man, like himself, driven by his longing for a woman, by his own private demons. Just the same, he'd gamble that his deputy wouldn't turn on him now. He'd have to stake his life on it. Poor love-smitten bastard that he was, all Jeremiah had wanted was his own woman. Ben had just been in the way.

He must have dozed off. When he woke, Jeremiah had

a fire going and a pan of water bubbling between two flat rocks. The deputy cut away the sweaty, blood-soaked pieces of undershirt, dropped a relatively clean strip of fabric into the boiling water and stirred it with a short, straight pine branch. When steam rose, he lifted the material out with the stick and slapped it onto the ragged wound in Ben's chest.

Ben sucked air between his teeth. "Goddammit, Jeremiah!" He tried to twist away, but his deputy pinned his arms.

"Easy, Ben. Only hurts for a minute."

"A minute!" Ben's senses swam. "You got any idea how long a minute can feel when you're being boiled alive?"

"Must feel a little bit like goin' to hell, I guess," Jeremiah growled low in his throat. "Yessirree, I surely do know what that feels like."

He hesitated, then began to swish another square of Ben's underwear back and forth in the boiling water. "I thought for a long time about doin' what I did—buyin' those guns off the army post. Felt torn in two about it, like a man bein' ripped apart tied to a couple of Sioux ponies."

He lifted the cool cloth from Ben's chest, dropped a steaming one in its place. "Sorry, Colonel. If it don't sting, it ain't hot enough."

"Sting!" Ben repeated through clenched teeth. "You're lucky I don't shoot you."

Jeremiah fell silent. After a long minute, he exhaled an uneven breath. "In a way, Ben, I wish you would."

Ben shook his head. "You know I can't do that."

Jeremiah's jaw worked. He refused to meet Ben's eyes. "You gotta do something, Ben. I know it, and you know it. You can't let me go scot-free after what I done, and live with yourself. I know you too well."

Ben groaned. At this moment his deputy didn't know him at all. All day long in his lucid moments he'd chewed over what to do about Jeremiah. He doubted Jeremiah could guess how tempting it had been to overlook his perfidy. But his deputy was right—as the sheriff, he had to exact some recompense. Otherwise, the entire concept of a society based on law and order was undermined. But, God almighty, the idea ripped his insides open.

"You gotta, Ben," Jeremiah repeated. "You think on it while we ride back to town tomorrow." He slapped another hot pack on Ben's chest. "Just don't tell me what it's gonna be until it's time."

Ben nodded. "Sure, Jeremiah." He twitched as the poultice dropped in place. "You got any whiskey in your saddlebag? I could sure use some. I think—ouch! Dammit, man, be careful with that!"

When he could talk again, Ben continued. "Think this might be a two-glass night, Jeremiah."

"Yessir, Colonel," the deputy replied, his voice subdued. "Maybe even a three-glass night, seein' as it's prob'ly our last time drinkin' together."

Ben flinched. "Hell, man, I'm not going to die." He tried to grin.

"Damn right you're not. But, you know somethin'? I feel like *I* might. Sure feel awful."

Ben's heart squeezed in agony. Hell's fire, men were such damn fools. He couldn't condone Jeremiah's actions, but deep in his heart he could understand what drove him. A woman. Lorena, and then Walks Dancing. Jeremiah had grasped for what he wanted and paid the price. In the process, he'd lost everything, even himself.

Ben realized suddenly that he didn't hate his deputy. And he no longer hated Lorena. A glimmer of understanding flickered, illuminating the darker chambers of the human heart—Jeremiah's, Lorena's, even his own. Maybe it was because of Jessamyn.

She'd shown him something about life, about himself. It wasn't perfect. It didn't have to be perfect. Life, and the human creatures in it, were flawed—scarred by stupidity and greed, stubbornness and pain. Yet there were soaring moments of joy and meaning, as well. He'd felt it with Jessamyn that night in the cabin.

She had given him much more than just her physical self. At this moment he wanted nothing more than to hear her voice, feel her cool, gentle hand. If he lived, he'd tell her these things. He'd tell her how much more he understood now that she had touched him, inside and outside. In some indefinable way she had opened him up, made it possible for him to hear the words he'd held deep in his own soul all these years. Words of forgiveness. Words of love.

"Troublous," he pronounced over the choking ache in his throat. "Just like you always said, Jeremiah. But for all that, a woman is God's gift to a man's spirit."

Jeremiah started. His large brown eyes moist, he slapped another hot cloth on Ben's wound.

"Troublous," the deputy echoed. He bowed his head over the pan of simmering water.

Chapter Twenty-One

Ben awoke to the song of a meadowlark in the pine tree over his head. Lord in heaven, what a beautiful sound! A rush of pure joy surged through him. He was alive! He drew in a gulp of the sweet mountain air, gazed with wonder at Indian grass and delicate yellow range daisies bathed in the warm morning sunlight. Life was a precious gift.

His chest ached, but he was no longer sweating. Jeremiah's poultices had stopped the bleeding. His head spun when he moved, so he lay still, listening to the bird's melodious warbling, punctuated by the gusty breathing of the man asleep beside him.

Pain lanced into his heart. Jeremiah had always snored at night. *God, I'll miss even that!*

The deputy stirred and sat up. In the early-morning quiet, the two men studied each other.

Ben broke the silence. "I don't know if I can do what I've got to do, Jeremiah. It's like cutting off my arm."

Jeremiah rolled his stocky frame out from under the rumpled wool blanket and stood up. Dark circles under his eyes told Ben he hadn't slept much, either.

"Spit it out, Colonel."

Ben swallowed against rising nausea. "My head spins when I move. You're going to have to help me mount."

"You sure you're ready?"

"Hell, no. But I won't be able to travel at all if I don't get on a horse. Even so, I won't be able to move fast. I want you to ride on ahead."

Jeremiah's thick eyebrows rose.

"There's a telegraph office in Deer Creek," Ben continued. "Wire Fort Umpqua. Tell the commanding officer to send a detail for those rifles. Tell him…"

He paused to steady his voice. "Tell him where they're hidden, and pray to God Black Eagle doesn't find out. I wouldn't give one silver dollar for your hide if that wily old fox discovers you sent his rifles back to the fort.

"As for you…" Ben shut his eyes. Tears stung under the lids. "A soldier," he said, his voice unsteady, "would face a firing squad for what you've done."

"I know that, Colonel." Jeremiah's voice was so quiet Ben could hardly hear it.

"A gentleman," Ben continued, "would find himself left alone with a pistol on the table."

Jeremiah turned his face away, staring out across the valley spreading below.

Ben cleared his throat. "I always considered you a gentleman, Jeremiah. A friend. But you've got to pay for what you've done."

Jeremiah nodded.

"So, here it is. Since you're not going to pay the bride price you promised her father, I want you to take Walks Dancing back to Black Eagle. It's not a simple thing—you'll be lucky to get away with your scalp, especially if the chief considers her dishonored. But it's a chance you'll have to take. You earned it."

The deputy bent his head.

"If by some miracle you do survive—" Ben's words choked off "—don't come back to Wildwood Valley. I won't want to see you."

He waited until he could trust his voice again. "One more thing," he said quietly. "Say goodbye to Jessamyn when you leave. She'll want that."

Unable to speak, Jeremiah gripped Ben's hand so tightly the knuckles whitened. "Thanks, Ben."

"You're a damn fool to thank me, Jeremiah. I'm sending you on a suicide mission. Even if you have the bad luck to live through it, there's not many places that'll welcome you and an Indian wife." He raised his head to study Jeremiah's face. "Dying would be easy. It's living that's going to be hard. But, as one man to another, that's what I'm asking you to do."

"A debt of honor, like," Jeremiah said in his raspy voice.

"Help me mount," Ben ordered.

Jeremiah saddled the gelding and boosted Ben up with his broad shoulder. In heavy silence he kicked dirt over the fire pit, then mounted his own horse.

Ben looked straight into his deputy's soft brown eyes. "Now, damn you, ride out of here."

Jeremiah snapped him a military salute. "Colonel."

"And Jeremiah—" Ben nudged the gelding close to his deputy's mare.

"Yeah?"

"When you get to the bend in the trail up ahead, don't look back."

Jeremiah reached one hand to Ben's good shoulder. "Take care, Ben."

Ben covered the gentle, blunt fingers with his own.

Summoning all his strength, Ben slapped the chestnut mare's rump, and the animal jolted away. He watched the stocky man in the droopy brown hat until his vision swam. Then, more weary than he'd ever been, Ben stepped the gelding forward, toward home.

* * *

Jessamyn propped her hands on her hips and surveyed the dripping piece of machinery Gus and Zed Marsh wrestled through the front door of the news office. She pursed her lips in consternation. River water sluiced from every opening in the big iron press. Silt gritted under her fingertips when she ran them over the once-shiny black finish. How could they have done this, dumped her precious press into the tumbling waters of the Umpqua? It was a wonder the sand hadn't scoured the finish right down to the bare metal.

The instant she was alone, Jessamyn tied on her apron and got to work. Every single moving part would have to be wiped down, the toggle joints and press lever greased, the bits of dirt and river sand brushed out of each crevice. But Goliath, as her father had dubbed the heavy press, was back in place, safe and relatively sound. She should thank her lucky stars the damage wasn't irreparable.

A hot afternoon breeze kicked up dust devils in the street outside. Jessamyn slid the front window shut to keep out the flies and dust while she greased the press joints. Frieder's Mercantile had been out of lubricating grease that morning. "Shipment is again late," Otto had explained. He sold her a jar of molasses instead. To soften her exasperation at his depleted stock of goods, he'd poured an extra-large scoop of penny candies into her palm.

Jessamyn suspected it was the Frieders' new baby girl more than a late shipment that affected Otto's supplies. She complimented herself on her choice of a substitute greasing agent until the flies discovered the sticky, sweet molasses. The minute she smeared the press joints with a film of the brown goo, dozens of the winged creatures zoomed in the doorway.

Maybe it was just as well, she thought with a sigh, as she closed the door. While it was maddening to feel vulnerable to the antics of a bunch of drunken rowdies, it was unnerving to realize she could have been hurt in the fracas. If the worst of the whole business was a few flies in the news office, well, she could surely manage that. And it most certainly wasn't going to stop her from getting out the next edition! A Whittaker, Papa always said, never gave up.

Jessamyn's hand slowed to a stop. *This* Whittaker, however, was beginning to think there might be more to life than newspapers. She wondered where Ben was, whether he had sprung his trap and captured her father's killer. Unconsciously she began to hum along with the piano rendition of "Aura Lee" drifting on the hot, dry air. She failed to notice the door open behind her until two dusty boots planted themselves on the threshold.

"Jeremiah!" She flew toward him, a molasses-soaked rag in one hand. "Oh, Jeremiah! I'm so glad to see you!"

"Miss Jessamyn." The deputy removed his floppy brown hat and sniffed the air. "Smells like Shoofly Pie in here! What you been doin'?"

Jessamyn laughed. "It's the molasses. Some men broke in last night and dumped my press in the river. When Gus pulled it out this morning, it had to be greased. The mercantile didn't—"

She stopped short. Jeremiah's expression was odd. "Jeremiah? Where's Ben? Is anything wrong?"

"Yes, ma'am. Plenty. But it's gettin' righter with every passin' minute. I'm sure sorry about your press, though. I just rode in from the telegraph office over in Deer Creek. Got some...orders, you might say, from Ben. What I got to do is gonna take me away from here."

"Away?" Jessamyn stared at the solidly built man, noticing his travel-worn clothes, the scuffed, dirty boots. "For how long?"

"Can't exactly say, Miss Jessamyn. It's...well, kinda open-ended, like."

She studied the man's expressionless square face. "I hoped you would help me again with the newspaper," she said softly.

"Oh, I surely would like that, missy. Nothin' I like better'n fine, pretty words lined up in a thought. But—"

"Something's happened hasn't it? Is Ben with you?"

Jeremiah swallowed. "Ben's behind me a ways. He should be here by evening." The stocky man rocked sideways from foot to foot, his soft brown eyes thoughtful.

"He's hurt, Miss Jessamyn. He took a bullet in his chest, and he's gonna be all right, but he's ridin' slow and careful."

Jessamyn's hand went to her throat. "You left him on the trail?" She stared at him, aghast. "Wounded?"

"Had to. He gave me orders. Had to do something important for him over in Deer Creek, and now I got to—"

"Who shot him?" Jessamyn said, struggling to keep her voice steady. "The same man who shot my father?"

The deputy opened his mouth, closed it, opened it again. "Yeah, missy. The same. Jack Larsen. Railroad man. But don't you worry none, Miss Jessamyn. Jack's dead now. I killed him myself."

Jessamyn gasped. "Oh, Jeremiah! You saved Ben's life!"

The deputy gazed down at his boots. "I owed him that."

"*Owed* him? Why, whatever—"

"Miss Jessamyn, if you don't mind, I'm not wantin' to talk about it just now."

"Why, of course, Jeremiah. You just sit—"

"I can't stay. Me and Walks Dancing are goin'…." He swallowed. "Away. That's part of what I got to do for Ben—sort of a matter of honor. A gentleman's understanding between us."

"You're leaving Wildwood Valley? You and Walks

Dancing? But where will you go?" Frowning, Jessamyn studied the deputy's somber face.

Jeremiah coughed. "First, to her father, Black Eagle. After that... Well, there might not be no 'after that.'"

"Jeremiah, you will let me know, won't you? Send word some way that you—and Walks Dancing—are all right?"

A heavy silence fell. After a long moment, Jeremiah smiled at her, his shy grin revealing a row of crooked white teeth. "Sure. If I'm able."

Jessamyn laid the grease rag on her desk. Facing the deputy, she felt her throat tighten. "You came to say goodbye, didn't you?"

He swallowed. "I reckon so." The deputy's jaw worked, but he said nothing.

Jessamyn pulled a polished amber comb out of her hair and slipped it into Jeremiah's large hand. "Give this to Walks Dancing, will you? And this is for you." She stretched up and kissed his leathery cheek.

Jeremiah grasped her shoulders and pulled her into a clumsy hug. "Mind if I give you a little advice, missy?" he rasped.

Jessamyn shook her head, her cheek brushing his blood-stained canvas shirt.

"Might not be a bad idea to get Gus and some of the men down to the river crossing 'bout sundown. Ben's not too weak to ride good, but swimming a horse across that current... Well, that might be more'n a tired man could handle."

"Yes," she promised, steadying her voice with an effort. "I'll do that."

"One more thing 'fore I go," the deputy said in his soft, rough voice. "He's hurt more on the inside than the outside, if you take my meanin'. His trust in people—specially people close to him—well, it's been shook up pretty bad. You just give him a bit of time and some talk-back."

"Talk-back?"

Jeremiah chuckled and squeezed her shoulders. "Don't take no for an answer. He's balky as a Mexico mule, and you're about as bad, but he wants you. It's plain as pie. Don't let him forget it."

Jessamyn hugged the solid body. "I won't. I promise."

"I gotta go now, Miss Jessamyn," he whispered. "Take care of your sweet self." He planted a whiskery kiss on her forehead and turned away.

Dazed, Jessamyn stared after him as he marched through the doorway and down the boardwalk past her front window. A fly buzzed against the window glass. She made no move to close the door. Motionless, she listened to the saloon piano tinkle out another tune and thought about her life. And about Ben Kearney.

Jack Larsen had shot her father, and now Larsen was dead, too. Jeremiah was leaving Wildwood Valley, taking Walks Dancing with him. Her mind struggled to absorb the apparently unrelated bits of information. She could see now there was much more to life than surviving the changes it inevitably brought. There had to be more—caring and trust. And love.

She drew in a steadying breath of the dust-laden afternoon air and jolted to attention. There was Ben Kearney. He was wounded and would need help at the river crossing.

Jessamyn yanked off her apron, slammed the front door of the news office and raced for the livery stable.

"Gus!" Panting, she rounded the bend in the road and stumbled into the corral yard. "Gus!"

Oh, please God, let him be here! This was more important than pulling her press out of the river. This was pulling her heart's deepest desire toward a life of understanding and love. Ben was more important than a hundred printing presses.

"Gus!"

The liveryman met her at the stable door, a curry comb in his hand.

"Gus, I need—Ben needs—" She sagged against the door and gasped out the information.

The tall Norwegian nodded. Together they plunged toward the tack room for saddles and ropes.

Chapter Twenty-Two

"There he is!" a voice shouted. "Up on the rim!"

Shading her eyes from the glare of the sinking sun, Jessamyn stared up the mountainside where Zed Marsh pointed. A dark figure on horseback was silhouetted against the salmon-and-lilac-flamed sky.

His head bent, holding the horse's reins with one hand and keeping the other arm close to his body, the rider labored along the steeply descending trail. Five pairs of eyes followed his every halting move.

"Damn," Gus swore softly. "He's really hurtin'. Look how he holds himself. In all the years I've known him, I never saw Ben ride so stiff."

Carleton Kearney kneed his horse forward. "He looks saddle-drunk to me. I'm going up after him."

Jessamyn lifted her reins. "I'll go with you."

"No, you won't," Gus said quietly. "You got enough petticoats on under that skirt to sink Miz Boult's mare in the middle of the river."

"All right, let's go," Gus called. "Zed, you and Silas find some solid footing this side of the ford." The big Norwegian kicked his mount into a canter to catch up with Carleton's chestnut, already bounding toward the river shallows.

Jessamyn watched the two men skirt the bank of the tumbling Umpqua. When they reached the smoother waters of the ford, they swam their mounts across to the opposite side and started up the mountain. Straining her eyes, she watched the bent figure of Ben Kearney jolt down the trail toward the two men riding to meet him.

Slowly, far too slowly to suit her, the distance between them narrowed. She fidgeted on the mare, expecting Ben to pitch out of his saddle at any moment. The farther down he got on the sloping trail, the more clearly she could see how he swayed on the gelding's back.

She sucked in her breath. Dear Lord, don't let him fall! The effort of remounting or, worse, being carried down the mountainside would probably kill him.

Silas and Zed stepped their horses forward and Jessamyn reined her mare in behind. The animals' hooves clattered on the rock-lined riverbank, the sound like hundreds of pot lids clashing in an echoey kitchen. Jessamyn thought of Cora, her eyes wet, her wide jaw trembling at the news that Walks Dancing had gone with Jeremiah and the sheriff had been shot. The housekeeper had insisted the men bring Ben to the white frame house so she and Jessamyn could "tend him proper." It was only common sense, the widow reminded them.

Common sense, Jessamyn thought with a surge of emotion, wasn't so common. Waiting for the man who was turning her heart—and her life—upside down, she realized how much she valued the down-to-earth good sense people showed out here in the West. They seemed able to rise to any challenge. More than all the riches of the Orient, she valued Cora Boult and the four men who now worked to bring Ben safely down the mountain.

"Hurry up!" one of the men shouted ahead of her. "They've almost reached him!"

Without thinking, Jessamyn kicked her mare. Her petticoats fluttered out from under her skirt as the animal jolted forward. She hadn't taken time to change into her jeans, but instead had hastily bunched up her skirt to mount astride. Propriety be damned—it was time that mattered here. Ben's life hung in the balance.

She raced to the fording place and halted. The waters of the Umpqua shone like polished copper where the current eddied about huge, black boulders. Tipping her head up, Jessamyn saw the shadowed figure of the tall man slump forward over the saddle horn.

She cried out, covered her mouth with her hand and watched Gus and Carleton struggle up the trail to reach him. Carefully the two riders turned their horses on the narrow path. One man dismounted and reached out to catch the gelding's bridle; the other stepped his horse close and laid his arm across Ben's inert body. The three men inched their way slowly down the mountain to the river's edge as the sky overhead purpled with the setting sun.

Jessamyn fought back sobs. He was dead. He must be, otherwise he would sit upright. Tears slipped down her cheeks, bathed her chin. Choking with grief, she swept them away with the back of her hand.

He couldn't be dead, he just couldn't! Only a few nights ago he had given her a new, wondrous understanding of herself and her life. He could not leave her after that. God simply would not let him!

Rage tore through her. It wasn't fair! The glorious, frighteningly intense thing they had found with each other—it couldn't be over forever. She refused to believe it. God would not show her such beauty with a man and then let her live without him.

Silas's voice rang out. "They're coming across! Get another rope!"

Jessamyn slid out of the saddle. Shaking, she stumbled past Zed Marsh's horse and waded out into the water. She had to reach him, touch him. Even if he was dead, she had to be with him.

"Jessamyn!" Gus shouted from the middle of the river. "Go back! Go back!"

She froze, felt the current tug at her petticoats. A rope sailed out to her left, settled over the dark gelding swimming ahead of Gus's white mare. Another rope dropped over her own shoulders.

She fought on toward Ben, saw Carleton loop the rope around the tall figure slipping into the water. "Pull!" he yelled.

The rope went taut.

Carleton rode toward her, water spraying from his hair and his clothing. He grabbed her outstretched arm. "He's alive!"

Oh, thank God. *Thank God!* She turned back toward the bank, clutched the rope as it tightened around her shoulders. A hand grasped her elbow from behind, propelled her forward into Zed Marsh's bony arms. Behind her, horses splashed and clattered onto the river bank.

"Got him," Gus yelled. "But I sure hope Miz Boult's got some water boiling. The man's spent."

Her clothing drenched, Jessamyn rode at Ben's side, one hand holding on to his shoulder. Blood seeped under her fingers. Carleton rode on the opposite side, his arm steadying his brother's limp form.

Jessamyn gripped Ben's shoulder with all the strength she had left. "Don't you dare die, Ben Kearney," she sobbed. "And that's an order! I've got lots and lots to give a man—things I've been s-saving up all my life. So you just keep breathing, and you stay on this horse until we get to town. Do you hear me, Ben? And...and then—"

Her voice broke. And then what? Was he so weakened by his ordeal no doctor could save him?

"Stay alive!" she choked out. "Damn your Rebel hide, I'll n-never forgive you if you don't live through this!"

Carleton flashed her a look over Ben's still form. "You'll be lucky if you both don't die of pneumonia. You're soaking wet and shivering. Here." He tossed her a blanket, then spread another over his brother's back.

Cora, Jessamyn thought irrationally, will have a fit with this water all over her floor. As she rode, she tried to wring out the excess moisture with her free hand.

The elderly housekeeper met them at the front porch, a lantern in one hand, a bottle of what looked like whiskey in the other. Gus dismounted. Bolting up the steps three at a time, he snatched the whiskey out of her grasp and kissed her soundly on both cheeks.

"Stop your lollygagging!" Cora snapped. "Neither of us got time for any such tomfoolery. Take Ben right on into the kitchen—Doc Bartel's waitin'."

The four men locked their wrists and forearms to fashion a dead man's carry, then edged Ben's limp figure down the hallway. Jessamyn stumbled after them.

In the warm kitchen the men laid Ben out on the long wooden table. Red-haired Dr. Bartel bent over him, one ear to his bare chest. "Still beating," the physician muttered. "But for the life of me, I don't see how."

He straightened. "Clear out, all of you," he said. "You, too, Jessamyn. Gus, give her a shot of that whiskey—she looks white as Cora's bedsheets."

Too exhausted and heartsick to climb the stairs and change out of her wet garments, Jessamyn went down the front steps and squeezed her sodden skirts out on Cora's prize damask rosebush. All at once she remembered that afternoon in the kitchen when Gus and Silas, and finally Ben, had come calling.

"Don't marry *him*," Cora had instructed, watching both the liveryman and the sandy-haired rancher out the kitchen window. About Ben she had said nothing, and now Jessamyn understood why. More common sense. If Jessamyn was not smart enough to see Ben's quality for herself, she didn't deserve to be his wife.

Cold and weary as she was, she laughed out loud. But she *was* smart. And she most certainly did see!

She wanted Ben Kearney more than anything else in the world.

Cora's voice woke her out of an exhausted sleep. "Jessamyn! Come quick!"

Jessamyn scrambled out of bed and raced down the stairs in her white lawn nightdress.

Cora met her at the door of Ben's room. "He's awake! He's askin' for you."

Tears burned into Jessamyn's eyes as she hugged the older woman. She tiptoed to the bed as the door shut quietly behind her. "Ben?"

The dark lashes twitched, then lifted. Gray-blue eyes tried to focus on her face. "Jess?"

"Yes, Ben. I'm here." She laid her hand on his forearm.

He turned his palm up, moved so his fingers pressed hers. "Last night when I got to the river, were you wearing petticoats?"

"Petticoats!" Jessamyn frowned. What did her petticoats have to do with anything? He must be out of his head with fever.

"Yes, I was. But that was four nights ago. You've been here at the house for the past three days."

"Thought it was you," Ben said, his voice weakening. "All the way down that mountain I saw something white moving across the river. I told myself it was you. I kept riding toward those white ruffles—figured if you could mount a horse in petticoats, I could damn well live long enough to take a good look."

"It was me, Ben. I came with the men—Gus and Carleton and the others—to find you."

"Yes. I knew if I kept moving toward you, toward all those starched white ruffles down below me... I knew it had to be you. Nobody else wears that many petticoats."

Jessamyn started and withdrew her hand from his. "Now, how would you know that?"

Ben ignored the question. "Think I might not have made it if you'd—"

Jessamyn held her breath.

"—covered up your underclothes."

She didn't know whether to laugh or cry. What a thing to say to a lady.

"Should always wear petticoats," he murmured, his voice drowsy. "It gave me something to..."

Ben shifted his body, his breath hissing in as he moved. "Jeremiah?" he asked, his voice gravelly.

"He's gone, Ben," she said softly. "Jeremiah said he's just following your orders. Try to look beyond it."

Ben caught her hand, held it hard against his cheek. "When I get up out of this bed tomorrow, I want you to ride out from town a ways with me."

"Of course," she soothed. *Ride!* The man had no notion how seriously he'd been injured.

"Shoulder hurts," he mumbled.

In a tumbler of water, Jessamyn mixed half a teapoon of the laudanum Dr. Bartel had left, and held it to Ben's fever-cracked lips. She got three swallows down him before he drifted off to sleep.

Too keyed-up to go back to bed, Jessamyn dressed and went over to the news office. She tried to work, struggled to keep her thoughts focused on writing out her stories and setting them in type. But her mind was on Ben, not the newspaper.

Chapter Twenty-Three

With a groan of exhaustion, Jessamyn managed to lock up the last frame for her weekly *Wildwood Times* edition. It was a good issue, she acknowledged. But it was four days late. Unable to sleep after Ben had finally regained consciousness, she'd worked all night at the news office. After breakfast she'd slip into his room, just to check on him.

Just as she finished wiping the grime off her hands, the news office door swung open and the sheriff strode inside, his spurs chinging.

"Ben!" she gasped. "What in the world are you doing out of bed?"

He chuckled. "You know, that's just what Cora said." Gingerly, he leaned his tall frame against the wood door frame.

Jessamyn scooted off the high typesetter's stool. "Ben Kearney, does Cora know you're here?"

"Oh, hell, yes, Jessamyn. I heard about the bath those gentlemen gave Goliath."

"Bath?"

He gestured toward the iron printing press. "It won't happen again. I'll ride over to Scottsburg to press my point."

"Ride! You just got out of bed. You're not able to—Ben, it doesn't matter. The press doesn't mat—"

Ben held up a restraining hand. "Before I go, Cora said to give you a message."

"A message? What message?"

"She said to tell you to remember the view out the kitchen window."

"She said *what?* The kitch— Oh!" A flush of heat warmed her cheeks. "Oh, yes. I—I do remember."

His eyebrows rose. Shaking his head, he addressed a remark to the ceiling. "I never will understand a woman." A flicker of pain crossed his tanned features.

Jessamyn smiled up at him. "You don't have to understand me. You just have to..." She moved to face him. Gently, she touched his chest.

Ben sucked his breath in between his teeth.

"It still hurts, doesn't it?" Jessamyn asked quietly.

"Some. I'll get over it."

She shot him a quick look. "All of it? Whatever it was between you and Jeremiah? And...and Lorena?"

Ben hesitated, then reached out and pulled her into his arms. "All of it."

She smiled into his smoke-colored eyes, felt his arms tighten around her, his hands stroke up and down her spine.

She leaned her forehead against his shirtfront. He needed her. She had given her body, her soul, to this man, and she knew it had helped him come to terms with himself. If he could just accept her love, he could learn to see the beauty, the excitement, of life again.

"It won't be easy, will it?" she breathed. He knew what she meant—he wouldn't be standing here holding her like this if he didn't.

"Maybe. Maybe not. Either way, Jess, I want you with me."

She hesitated. "I—I want to be with you, Ben. Like we were at the cabin."

He was silent a long time. When he spoke, his voice was low and gentle. "We don't have a cabin here, honey. There's only Cora's extra bedroom and the sheriff's quarters across the street. Either way, it'll cause talk. You're a respectable lady, and I'm—"

"I—I know. But it will be worth it."

Ben groaned deep in his throat. "I can stand up, Jess. And I might be able to ride. But with this bullet hole in me, I'm not going to be able to..."

"It won't matter. I want to be with you," she insisted, her voice quiet. "It's worth everything, Ben. Trust me."

He tipped her chin up and studied her face, a thoughtful expression in his eyes. "If I thought..."

Suddenly he pulled her close. "You weren't thinking of marrying me, were you?" he said against her hair.

Jessamyn tilted her face up to his. "Oh, no," she said, her voice dreamy. "I certainly wasn't."

He kissed her, his mouth gentle at first, then moving on hers with purposeful invitation. "Good," he whispered when he released her. "I wouldn't hold much hope in that direction if I were you."

"Oh, I won't," she promised.

But she knew better. She'd known it ever since that night at the cabin. Ben Kearney had given her his body because he'd already entrusted her with his heart.

She'd waited days for him to realize it. She knew he wanted her as much as she wanted him, that he needed her, longed to spend the rest of his life with her. It was just hard for him to say out loud.

And it really didn't matter, because it was what she wanted, too. Her heart would stop beating if she couldn't be with him.

His arms went around her again. Bending his head, he

brushed her lips with his, then caught her mouth under his with sweet, hot urgency.

"In that case," he said in a hoarse whisper, "how about next Sunday?"

Jessamyn laughed softly. Lacing her fingers behind Ben's neck, she stretched up on tiptoe until her mouth again grazed his.

"I wouldn't think of it," she lied.

Epilogue

Wildwood Times,
July 24, 1868

Benning Larimore Kearney and Jessamyn Irene Whittaker were joined in matrimony July 5 in the rose garden at Miss Whittaker's home in Wildwood Valley. The bride wore her mother's wedding gown of white moiré silk, refashioned by Miss Addie Rice with insets of Belgian lace.

Joining the couple at the altar were Mrs. Cordella Boult, who served as the bride's sole attendant, and Mr. Carleton Kearney, who stood as the groom's man. Roses grown by Mr. Daniel Gustafsen were distributed to the guests by Miss Alice Kearney, niece of the groom.

Also in attendance at the ceremony were Mrs. Ella Kearney, Dr. and Mrs. Rufus Bartel, Mr. and Mrs. Otto Frieder, Miss Adelaide Rice and the Messrs. Silas Appleby, Zedediah Marsh and Amory Fitzpatrick, the new editor of the *Umpqua Ensign* in Scottsburg.

Of particular note was the guard of honor provided by Chief Black Eagle of the Klamath Indian nation and three of his braves. The bride and groom were escorted to their nuptials under a ceremonial arch of lances decorated with feathers and dried wildflowers.

Following the ceremony, wedding cake and iced lemonade were served by Mrs. Boult and the Ladies Auxiliary Circle under the direction of the Reverend Harve Lindstrom, who also performed the service.

Mr. and Mrs. Kearney are at home at 9 Boult Lane Thursdays from 2:00 to 4:00 p.m.

Wildwood Times,
March 27, 1869

Sheriff and Mrs. Benning Kearney announce the birth of a son, Thaddeus Whittaker Kearney, on March 14. Named after Mrs. Kearney's father, the late Thaddeus Whittaker, the new citizen of Wildwood Valley weighed 6 pounds, 4 ounces and strongly resembles his father.

In honor of his son's entry into the world, Mr. Kearney presented his wife with a gold heirloom locket in the shape of a heart, an ivory-handled Smith & Wesson revolver and a keg of printer's ink.

Journal of Jessamyn Whittaker Kearney
August 1874
A letter came today, in care of the *Wildwood Times.* The postmark read Stark County, Ohio. Inside I found only a faded photograph of a bearded man in a droop-brimmed hat with a rounded crown, standing with a beautiful Indian woman. The man held a printer's type stick in one hand, and he was smiling.

In front of the couple stood three lovely little girls, all with the same large, dark eyes. The tallest looked to be about six years old. On the back of the picture was written their names—Serena, Jessie and Mary

Irene. Below that, a single word was printed in capital letters: TROUBLOUS.

I showed the photograph to Ben at dinner. He stared at it for a long time, then put it down on the table and laid his hand over it. When he looked up, there were tears in his eyes.

This evening I told my husband I am expecting another child next April. If it is a boy, we will name him Jeremiah.

*　*　*　*　*

Author Note

Contrary to modern stereotypes of the helpless Victorian female on the American frontier, courageous and articulate women abounded in the Old West. Many of them rode horseback as well as any ranch hand, raised families, managed careers, spoke out on important issues of the day and worked alongside the men to settle and help civilize the frontier. Among these energetic ladies were some notable journalists.

Abigail Scott Duniway, known as the mother of equal suffrage in Oregon, published the *New Northwest* newspaper in Portland from 1871 to 1887.

Catharine Amanda Scott Coburn, Mrs. Duniway's younger sister, edited the Portland *Evening Telegram* from 1883 to 1888. After that, she spent a quarter of a century as associate editor of the *Oregonian*.

In Colorado Caroline Romney started *The Durango Record* in 1880. Mrs. Laura DeForce Gordon issued the *Daily Leader* in Stockton, California, in 1874, and in Wyoming the *Platte Valley Lyre* of Saratoga was published by sisters Gertrude M. and Laura C. Huntington.

In 1897 *The Idaho Woman* was published in Caldwell,

Idaho. The ladies of Caldwell operated the paper on behalf of suffrage and temperance.

And in Topeka, Kansas, Mrs. Carrie Nation promoted her prohibition and women's suffrage causes in the *Smasher's Mail,* which began publication in 1901.

(Preceding information from *Newspapering in the Old West* by Robert F. Karolevitz, Superior Publishing Company, Seattle, Washington, 1965.)

HARLEQUIN WOMEN KNOW ROMANCE WHEN THEY SEE IT.

And they'll see it on **ROMANCE CLASSICS**, the new 24-hour TV channel devoted to romantic movies and original programs like the special **Harlequin® Showcase of Authors & Stories.**

The **Harlequin® Showcase of Authors & Stories** introduces you to many of your favorite romance authors in a program developed exclusively for Harlequin® readers.

Watch for the **Harlequin® Showcase of Authors & Stories** series beginning in the summer of 1997.

If you're not receiving ROMANCE CLASSICS, call your local cable operator or satellite provider and ask for it today!

Escape to the network of your dreams.

Let's Celebrate!

LOVE & LAUGHTER™

invites you to
the party of the season!

Grab your popcorn and be prepared to laugh
as we celebrate with **LOVE & LAUGHTER**.

Harlequin's newest series is going Hollywood!

Let us make you laugh with three months of terrific
books, authors and romance, plus a chance to win a
FREE 15-copy video collection of the best romantic
comedies ever made.

For more details look in the back pages of any
Love & Laughter title, from July to September,
at your favorite retail outlet.

Don't forget the popcorn!

Available wherever
Harlequin books are sold.

 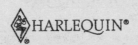 

LLCELEB

HE SAID

♥

SHE SAID

Explore the mystery of male/female communication in this extraordinary new book from two of your favorite Harlequin authors.

Jasmine Cresswell and Margaret St. George bring you the exciting story of two romantic adversaries—each from their own point of view!

DEV'S STORY. CATHY'S STORY.
As he sees it. As she sees it.
Both sides of the story!

The heat is definitely on, and these two can't stay out of the kitchen!

Don't miss **HE SAID, SHE SAID.**
Available in July wherever Harlequin books are sold.

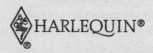

HARLEQUIN®

And the Winner Is...
You!

...when you pick up these great titles
from our new promotion at your
favorite retail outlet this June!

Diana Palmer
The Case of the Mesmerizing Boss

Betty Neels
The Convenient Wife

Annette Broadrick
Irresistible

Emma Darcy
A Wedding to Remember

Rachel Lee
Lost Warriors

Marie Ferrarella
Father Goose

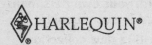 

Look us up on-line at: http://www.romance.net   ATWI397-R

New York Times Bestselling Authors

JENNIFER BLAKE
JANET DAILEY
ELIZABETH GAGE

Three *New York Times* bestselling authors bring you three very sensuous, contemporary love stories—all centered around one magical night!

It is a warm, spring night and masquerading as legendary lovers, the elite of New Orleans society have come to celebrate the twenty-fifth anniversary of the Duchaise masquerade ball. But amidst the beauty, music and revelry, some of the world's most legendary lovers are in trouble....

Come midnight at this year's Duchaise ball, passion and scandal will be...

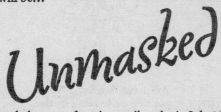

Unmasked

Revealed at your favorite retail outlet in July 1997.

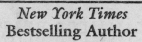